PENGUIN BOOKS

COOLIE

Mulk Raj Anand, one of the most highly regarded Indian novel-
ists writing in English, was born in Peshawar in 1905. He was
educated at the universities of Lahore, London and Cambridge,
and lived in England for many years, finally settling in a village
in Western India after the war. His main concern has always
been for 'the creatures in the lower depths of Indian society who
once were men and women: the rejected, who had no way to
articulate their anguish against the oppressors'. His novels of
humanism have been translated into several world languages.

The fiction-factions include *Untouchable* (1935), described by
Martin Seymour-Smith as 'one of the most eloquent and imagina-
tive works to deal with this difficult and emotive subject', *Coolie*
(1936), *Two Leaves and a Bud* (1937), *The Village* (1939), *Across
the Black Waters* (1940), *The Sword and the Sickle* (1942) and
the much-acclaimed *Private Life of an Indian Prince* (1953). His
autobiographical novels, *Seven Summers* (1950), *Morning Face*
(1968), which won the National Academy Award, *Confession of
a Lover* (1972) and *The Bubble* (1988), reveal the story of his
experiments with truth and the struggle of his various egos to
attain a possible higher self.

D1113407

COOLIE

Mulk Raj Anand

PENGUIN BOOKS

Penguin Books India (P) Ltd., 210 Chiranjiv Towers, 43,Nehru Place New Delhi-110019, India
Penguin Books Ltd., 27 Wrights Lane, London W8 5TZ, UK
Penguin Books USA Inc., 375 Hudson Street, New York, N.Y. 10014, USA
Penguin Books Australia Ltd., Ringwood, Victoria, Australia
Penguin Books Canada Ltd., 10 Alcorn Avenue, Suite 300, Toronto, Ontario M4V 3B2, Canada.
Penguin Books (NZ) Ltd., 182-190 Wairau Road, Auckland 10, New Zealand.

First published by Lawrence and Wishart 1936
Published in Penguin Books 1945
Published by Penguin Books India 1993
Reprinted 1997
Copyright © Mulk Raj Anand, 1936
All rights reserved

Typeset by DatIX International Limited, Bungay, Suffolk
Filmset in 9½/12pt Monophoto Times New Roman

Except in the United States of America, this book is sold subject
to the condition that it shall not, by way of trade or otherwise, be lent,
re-sold, hired out, or otherwise circulated without the publisher's
prior consent in any form of binding or cover other than that in
which it is published and without a similar condition including this
condition being imposed on the subsequent purchaser

The first edition of this novel
was dedicated to
Philip Henderson
who thought it was 'not too bad'.
I would like to add to this
new Penguin edition
the names of three other friends:

Marian Evans
who helped me with the typescript,

Eric Gill
who heard it from me and warmed to it,

and

Allen Lane
who first chose it for A Penguin.

'Munoo ohe Munooa oh Mundu!' shouted Gujri from the verandah of a squat, sequestered, little mud hut, thatched with straw, which stood upon the edge of a hill about a hundred yards away from the village in the valley. And her eagle eyes explored the track of gold dust which worked its zigzag course through rough scrub, beyond the flat roofs of the village houses, under the relentless haze of the Kangra sun. She could not see him.

'Munoo ohe Munooa oh Mundu! Where have you died? Where have you drifted, you of the evil star? Come back! Your uncle is leaving soon, and you must go to the town!' She shouted again with a shrill, hoarse voice. And her gaze travelled beyond the mango-grove to the silver line of the river Beas, and roved angrily among the greenery of the ferns and weeds and bushes that spread on either side of the stream against the purple gleam of the low hills.

'Munoo ohe Munooa!' she called again, exasperated, and raising her voice, this time, to the highest pitch to which, in her anger and hate, she could carry it: 'Where have you died? Where have you gone, you ominous orphan? Come back and begone!' The piercing soprano resounded through the valley and fell on Munoo's ears with the dreadening effect of all its bitter content.

He heard but he did not answer. He merely turned from the shade of the tree, where he sat hidden, to see her scarlet dress disappearing into the hut. He had been grazing cattle on the banks of the Beas, and had begun to play while the buffaloes and cows in his charge had entered the low waters of the marsh, where they now sat chewing the cud of little comfort that the cool of the water afforded against the torrid heat of the morning sun.

'Your aunt is calling you,' said Jay Singh, son of the village landlord, clean of face and apparel, nudging Munoo's bare body with his elbow. 'Can't you hear? Have you no manners, you savage, that you let your aunt shout herself hoarse and don't answer her?' He was Munoo's rival for leadership of Bishan and Bishambar and the other village boys. He knew that Munoo was to depart for town that day, and he wanted to hurry him out of the way as soon as possible.

'Don't go yet,' Bishan, the fat one, pleaded, 'your aunt only wants you to run an errand for her.' Then he turned banteringly to Jay Singh and said: 'You call him a savage for not going home when his aunt calls. What about you who abuse your mother for asking you to stay indoors and not go out in the heat of the noon? You won't even go to school, though your father gives you two annas a day for pocket money! We go to school. And during the holidays we graze the cattle. What are you doing here, pray, if not idling? You haven't even the courage to steal a few mangoes. Munoo collected all these, so let him suck a few before he goes home.'

'I don't steal mangoes,' said Jay Singh, 'I buy them!' And he continued righteously: 'I only said he ought to go because his aunt is so rude that she will abuse us for keeping him here. He has to go away to town with his uncle.'

'It is true you are going away to town?' asked fiery little Bishambar.

'Yes, I am going away this morning,' replied Munoo, and felt a quiver go through his belly.

'But you are only fourteen years old yet! And you are only in the fifth class at school!' cried Bishambar.

'My aunt wants me to begin earning money,' said Munoo. 'And she says she wants a son of her own. My uncle says I am grown up and must fend for myself. He has got me a job in the house of the Babu of the bank where he works in Shampur.'

'It must be nice to live in Shampur,' remarked Jay Singh, now jealous of the importance Munoo assumed in his eyes because he was going to live in town, where there were beautiful things to eat, beautiful clothes to wear and beautiful toys to play with.

Munoo smiled at this, but his smile seemed to say: 'If it wasn't my last day here, I would give you such a sock on the jaw that you would never dare to aspire to the leadership of the boys.' For though Munoo was young he had more than a vague idea of how Jay Singh's father was responsible for his impending misfortunes.

He had heard of how the landlord had seized his father's five acres of land because the interest on the mortgage covering the unpaid rent had not been forthcoming when the rains had been scanty and the harvests bad. And he knew how his father had died a slow death of bitterness and disappointment and left his mother a penniless beggar, to support a young brother-in-law and a child in arms. The sight of his mother grinding grain between the scarred surfaces of mill-stones which she gyrated round and round, round and round, by the wooden handle, now with her right hand, now with her left, day and night, had become indelibly imprinted on his mind. Also, the sight of her as she had lain dead on the ground with a horrible yet sad, set expression on her face, had sunk into his subconscious with all its weight of tragic dignity and utter resignation.

'Will you never come back?' inquired Jay Singh, more insistently.

'No, never; I never want to come back,' replied Munoo, urged by a genuine bitterness to lie, although in his heart he knew it were better to irritate Jay Singh by telling the truth. For, in spite of the fact that his aunt was always abusing him, in spite of the fact that she ordered him about, asking him to do this and to do that, in spite of the fact that she beat him more than he beat his cattle, he really did not want to go to the town.

At least, not yet.

He had dreamed, of course, of all the wonderful things which the village folk spoke about when they came back from the towns, the Lallas, the Babus, and the Sahibs from beyond the black waters; the silk clothes they wore and the delicacies they ate. He was especially interested in machines such as he had read about in the science primer of the fourth class. But he had meant to go to town when he had passed all his examinations here and was ready to learn to make machines himself.

Meanwhile, it was pleasant to sit here with his fellows, all little boys of the same age as himself, for when they had stolen enough fruit during their wanderings behind the cattle in the morning, they ate it in the humid, sweet-scented shade of the banyan tree.

Some fruit or other was always in season. Ripe yellow mangoes dropped by dozens in the spring and could be easily hidden in the grass and the hay. Purple and red jamans and long green mulberries fell in sickly profusion during the summer and could be stored on broad banana leaves. In the winter the stick-like sugar-cane aroused no suspicion in the gardener, who drowsed lazily in his siesta.

Then one could play: 'You can catch me only in the air, when I

3

am seated neither on earth nor on wood.' This involved a constant jumping on and off trees. And Munoo was a genius at climbing trees. He would hop on to the trunk like a monkey, climb the bigger branches on all fours, swing himself to the thinner offshoots as if he were dancing on a trapeze, and then, diving dangerously into space, he would jump from one tree to another.

And then there was the cool breeze which soothed the fatigue of the body and relieved the natural heat, the snow breeze that was rising even as he sat there now, stirring the acacia trees, while the cicadas rasped in the thickets, the frogs croaked in the shallows and the swamps, the birds sang, the butterflies flitted over the wild flowers and the insects buzzed over the pollen for honey.

The blood of little Munoo ran to the tune of all this lavish beauty. And he would rather have had all the machines come here than tear himself away from the sandy margins of the still back-waters where he played. But –

'Munoo ohe Munooa oh Mundu,' came his aunt's voice again.

The face of his aunt, with its hard jaw, its bright red-cornered eyes, its sharp nose and thin lips, all in a malevolent framework of dark hair, flashed across his mind.

He got up.

All the boys, even Jay Singh, rose to their feet.

He called his cattle.

The boys shouted for their cows and buffaloes, too.

The bony-hipped, thin-flanked, big-horned creatures emerged from the water and, splashing mud in the bog, dripping globules of froth, trailed wearily ahead of their little guides, mute against the abuse and beatings that were used to urge them on towards home, a little more quickly today than ever before.

II

'Walk quickly! Walk quickly! You son of a bitch!' shouted Daya Ram, the Chaprasi of the Imperial Bank of India, as he strode with big military strides, in his gold-brocaded red coat and neatly tied white turban, along the circuitous hill road constructed by the Angrezi Sarkar, of which he felt himself to be the symbol as he flourished his hand ostentatiously and angrily at his nephew Munoo.

The boy had sat down to nurse his bare feet, which were sore and weary after a ten-mile march. The sun had been shining with a searing intensity, and he was perspiring under the thick cotton tunic which had originally belonged to his uncle and looked like a cloak about him. The ochre-coloured dust, which trailed behind the reckless bullock carts around the hairpin bends, had got into his nose and irritated him. His olive face was flushed. His dark brown eyes were strained. He felt as if all the blood in his supple young body had evaporated as sweat and left him dry.

'Come quickly, or I will be late at the office!' shouted Daya Ram again. There was no question, of course, of his being either late or early at the office, as the Chaprasi was on holiday, but he wanted to impress his nephew and the rustic passers-by with the importance of the position he occupied in the service of the Angrezi Sarkar.

There were tears in Munoo's eyes as he gazed at his blistered feet and felt a quiver of self-pity go through him. 'My feet hurt me,' he sobbed in reply to his uncle's admonition.

'Come, come,' said Daya Ram irritably. And he stiffened his tall, lanky body, though he wanted to soften and be kind. 'Come,' he continued, 'I will get you a pair of shoes out of your next month's pay.'

'I can't walk,' said Munoo, hearing the screeching brakes of a cart bringing it to a halt ahead of him, where the road bent sharply round a point seven hundred feet sheer above the gorging Beas. 'That driver will give me a lift if you ask him.'

'No, no, he will want money if he lets you ride,' said Daya Ram loudly, so that the driver of the cart might hear and offer the ride free of charge. He felt much too dignified in his uniform to ask the man directly for a favour.

'Don't be too proud of your chaprasihood, and put the boy on the back here,' said the cart driver bluntly, noticing Daya Ram's manner. 'And you can get on the cart, too. You must be warm in that red woollen coat.'

'Don't you bark! I didn't talk to you,' said Daya Ram. 'Go your way, or I will have you put into prison. Don't you know that I am a government official!'

'Acha, enjoy yourself, make the poor child walk barefoot, you torturer!' retorted the driver and moved on.

'Get up, ohe you illegally begotten! You have been the bringer of disgrace to me! Get up or I will kill you!' exclaimed Daya Ram turning towards Munoo, his white teeth flashing.

Munoo sprang up, knowing that his uncle's threats of beating always led to actual blows. He wiped the tears from his eyes with the back of his hand and followed his guardian in the torrid heat, abusing him in his mind.

The curvy road inclined downwards, reaching out from the wild barren mountains to the limitless spaces of the lowlands.

After he had gone a few hundred yards, with a heart contracted by fear and a head expanded by thoughts, his feet bore the burning earth more easily. He avoided the stones by hopping about and gave occasional relief to his soles by walking a while on his toes. He was more than grateful for half a mile in a tunnel, and he grew cheerful when he saw, at the foot of the hill, a large number of tall, flat-roofed houses, crowded in irregular groups round the red stone minarets of mosques and the golden domes of temples. He forgot the inconveniences of the journey at the prospect of the journey's end.

As he descended from the hill the sun above the plateau poured its lava of light on the city, flooding it with a brilliant hue, making its heterogeneous elements stand out vivid and large. The limitless mountains were being blotted out of Munoo's mind. He felt agreeably excited about his new surroundings and everything that crowded round him.

He stared wide-eyed and open-mouthed at the marvels of different carriages, two-wheeled, box-like bamboo carts and tongas, four-wheeled phaetons and landaus, and huge, rubber-wheeled, black-bodied phat-phaties which seemed to him curious as they ran without horses on the main road. And, wonder of all wonders, he saw a black iron vehicle with two round humps like the humps of a desert camel, with hosts of little brown houses studded with glass windows behind it, rushing along furiously, puffing out a foul black smoke and shrieking hysterically. It blew a shrill whistle and made his heart leap to his throat.

'What is that animal?' he asked, rushing up to his uncle to still the thumping of his heart and to seek the confidence that knowledge brings.

'That is the injan of the rail gari,' his uncle replied, a little more kindly now that he was getting into the world where he could not pass himself of as the master he had pretended to be in the hills, but had again to be the slave of the Imperial Bank officials.

The boy looked hard at the black monster which, with a final shriek and much hoarse shouting, had now come to a standstill alongside a platform adjoining a solid hut. It released a multitudinous throng of men and women clad in milk-white cottons and silks of hues more varied than those which Munoo had ever seen in his life in the Kangra hills. 'Wonderful,' he said to himself, 'wonderful!'

'Where is the cattle which these people graze and where are the fields they plough, uncle?' he asked, turning to Daya Ram.

'They have no cattle and no fields here,' said the Chaprasi, pushing his neck back to stiff uprightness. 'It is only the rustics in the villages who graze cattle and plough the land!'

'But how do they get their food, uncle?' Munoo inquired.

'They have money,' said Daya Ram pompously. 'They have crores of rupees in my bank. They earn money by buying wheat which the peasants grow and by selling it as flour to the Angrezi Sarkar, or by buying cotton and making cloth and selling it at a profit. Some of them are Babus who work in offices, like the Babu in whose house you are going to be a servant.'

'How strange!' the child said. And he lagged behind, absorbed by the sight of huge cauldrons in the cookshops which steamed with the most spicy smells he had ever smelt. Tiers of sweets, dripping with syrup, rose from platform to ceiling in the sweetshops. Rubber balloons and little pink dolls and fluffy rabbit-like toys decorated the general stores. A stallkeeper was shouting 'Ices, cool ices,' and emptying little conic tins on to leaf cups for some customers who sat on a wooden bench before him.

Munoo felt he would have liked to taste one of those ices, but he dared not ask his uncle to buy him one. Instead he became interested in the weird tin wail of a song which issued from a box on which a black disc revolved. He smiled as the voice in the box trailed along. He retreated when it became hoarse, as if he were frightened, and then, recovering, he drew nearer.

'Come, come, or you will get lost,' his uncle called from a distance.

'What is that singing? How does a man get into a box to sing?' he asked.

7

The owner of the shop laughed and gave Munoo a contemptuous look.

'Hurry up, hurry up, you fool!' shouted Daya Ram. 'That is a phonogram. There is no man in the box, but the machine speaks.'

The boy dared not ask how the machine spoke. He tore himself away unwillingly from the wonderful spectacle, and followed. Before he had gone a few yards, however, his gaze was arrested by the curious phenomenon of little dog dolls which a man was setting into motion on the road after an ostentatious juggling with their sides.

'Tin, tin, tin tin,' a bell suddenly rang behind Munoo, and before he had time to see, a two-wheeled steel horse came towards him at a terrific speed.

'Look out, you son of a gun!' shouted the young man who sat astride it.

Munoo stepped aside and barely escaped being knocked down into the gutter.

'You illegally begotten! You will get killed! You idiot!' A tirade of abuse descended on him from his uncle, who had rushed back.

The toy-seller came and dragged Munoo safely out of harm's way, saying consolingly: 'Oh, he was only trying to make his bicycle run as fast as my dogs. But he didn't warn me that the race had begun. Don't you mind. Everything is all right. No harm done. The proper way to treat abuse is to let it come in one ear and go out the other.'

This aroused a smile on the boy's face.

'Walk quickly, you rascal! You will get killed before long if you don't look out!' his uncle shouted and struck him on the face.

Munoo began to cry. He followed, resentful and disheartened, thinking how he hated his uncle. But he saw that the fellow on the steel horse, who had been the cause of his being punished, had come to grief fifty yards ahead, having collided with a calf which strayed about among the crowds of men and women near the fruit shops at the crossroads. So he walked along reassured, forgetful still but sufficiently cautious, with one eye on his uncle ahead of him, another on the row of shops, and an occasional glance behind, to see that there was not another steel horse, or bicycle, as the juggler had called it, following.

The narrow streets, congested with rows of shops, the regular

8

pattern of whose awnings was broken, here by the sudden rift of a shadowy lane or a dark grimy gully, there by glaring patches of sunlight, seemed beautiful to him, especially when a man passed, clad in a silk tunic and dhoti and gold-embroidered shoes, or when a group of women shuffled along, swinging their elbows and flourishing their green, pink or purple silk veils. He felt as if he were walking in a dream, in a land of romance where everything was gilded and grand, so different was this world from the world of the mountains.

But, as he entered deeper into the town, and saw some people like himself who had the aspect of hill folk, as they carried weights on their backs, he felt more surprised.

He could not realize the significance of this world.

There was an eager, fluttering sense of anticipation in his heart at the sight of the grand marble building by which Daya Ram had stopped to wait for him.

'Salaam Pir Din,' Munoo heard his uncle say as he entered the high-pillared hall of the Imperial Bank.

'Salaam, salaam, you are late. The Babu Sahib is angry because there was no one to go and fetch his food at midday,' said Pir Din, coughing asthmatically, and smoothing his fiery, henna-dyed beard over the gold-braided red coat which he, too, wore. Munoo guessed this was the head peon his uncle had often spoken about.

'Is the Babu in the office, then?' asked Daya Ram, with more confidence than usual, guessing how urgent was the Babu's need for a servant and knowing he had a sure job for his nephew.

'Yes, yes, he is there,' grunted Pir Din, waving his hand. 'But the bags of money are to go to the cantonment, and it is the English-mail day, and the Lallas are coming in fast for their business. So you had better be quick.'

'Yes, Mian Sahib,' said Daya Ram, flattering his colleague with a mode of address reserved for high-class Muhammadans. Then he turned to his nephew: 'Come with me.'

The boy followed his uncle into a large cool room, past brass bars around which men crowded, eager-eyed and eager-eared, to see and hear the jingling of bright silver rupees and the rustling of clean currency notes. They entered another room. Beneath a swiftly moving pair of wings, suspended by an iron rod from the centre of the ceiling, before a huge table, on a chair much too big for him, sat a little man with an irregular, sallow face, quite vague except for a flat nose, the white spots on his cheeks, and a thin, drooping black moustache, of which each hair seemed to stand out distinct.

'I bow my forehead to you, Babuji,' Daya Ram said, joining his hands and dusting his feet as he entered.

The Babu lifted his head from the papers before him but did not reply.

'Say "I bow my forehead before you" or "Long live the Gods" to Babuji,' whispered Daya Ram audibly to Munoo.

Munoo mumbled both the courtesies, confused by the pictures aroused in his mind by his entry into a strange world of jingling coins, shuffling paper money, brass bars, tables, chairs, carpets and swiftly whirring fans. But he did not raise his head to look at the person he had addressed.

There was an awkward silence, during which a faint smile of amusement hovered on the Babu's lips before becoming a twisted smile of contempt. Munoo noticed it and looked down, half in fear, half in embarrassment.

'Maharaj,' said Daya Ram servilely as he turned to the majesty before him, 'I have brought my little nephew for your service.'

'Oh, is that he?' the Babu asked pointing to Munoo.

'Yes, janab,' Munoo heard his uncle say, and then he heard the command: 'Join your hands to the Babuji, you rustic.'

Munoo had been studying the black boots on the Babu's feet as they jutted out from under the table, and he was wondering, as he stood bent in a strained posture of humility, when he would be able to possess such a pair.

'Long live the Gods,' he suddenly broke out, joining his hands, a little too late to be seen in that reverent posture by the Babu, whose attention had been turned to a swift' succession of ringing tones which had started on a black machine on the right of the table.

'Yus sir, yus sir, fot not de junction be tehana ...' the Babu seemed to be saying to the tube into which he spoke, as he held a cap with a twisted cotton wire to his left ear. Munoo wondered whether the language that his would-be master was speaking was the angrezi speech which the village school teacher said should be learnt by all those who wanted to be come Babus. He reflected for a moment, and then he knew it was angrezi.

From wondering about the Babu's speech he fell to admiring his clothes: the high, hard, white collar which he wore; the enormous turban wound round a pyramidal Kulah of red velvet embroidered with gold thread; the khaki coat with big pockets like money bags; the wide cotton pyjamas; and the boots, the boots, the black boots. 'If only I had had black boots like that,' said Munoo to himself, 'I would have walked much quicker and my feet would not have blistered.'

'Acha!' he heard the Babu say. 'Take him to my house and put him in charge of Bibiji.'

Daya Ram bowed obsequiously over his joined hands in homage to the Babu. Then he dragged the boy away from the contemplation of the Babu's black boots, through the tidy and formal precincts of the Imperial Bank of India, up a steep circuitous road.

They went to a block of windowless houses, or hovels, squeezed one against another in an irregular pattern of uneven proportions, not without pretensions to a sort of suburban respectability, contradicted though this was by the broken bottles, rusted oiltins and leaking buckets that lay heaped here and there, with decaying vegetables and yellow paper, and piles of stones and crumbling bricks overgrown with moss.

At the farthest end of the block was the Babu's residence, a one-storied square house approached by a verandah on which a Western blackboard announced in white English letters to Eastern civilization the glory of 'Babu Nathoo Mal, Sub-Accountant, Imperial Bank, Sham Nagar.'

The sight of some buff-coloured bungalows, perched higher up on the side of the tortuous hill road, lifted Munoo to a rare world of mystery, because these buildings lay enshrouded in an atmosphere of cool, shady trees, among neatly trimmed hedges, with small palms in green barrels, beds of even grass and an abundance of many-coloured flowers. He wondered who lived there.

But his gaze was soon diverted from the heights to which it had aspired by the apparition of a man with a big red face, shadowed by a queer, khaki, basket-like head-dress, a collar like the one the Babu had worn around his thick scarlet neck, a beautiful jacket which was, however, somewhat ridiculous, as it neither covered his big round paunch nor the heavy buttocks which were shamelessly exposed by the stretch of his khaki breeches, and strange, very strange brown boots on his legs up to the knees. 'An Angrez surely,' Munoo said to himself.

'Salaam Huzoor,' he heard his uncle say, abruptly striking his right foot against the left and standing erect.

Munoo dared not look to see what the grim apparition did, but he saw the flourish of a cane and deliberately looked away downhill to the flat roofs of the houses in the town.

'He is the burra Sahib of the bank,' said Daya Ram with a mingled gesture of fear, humility and reverence, in answer to his nephew's inquiring eyes, when the man had walked down the hill beyond audible distance. Then he lunged forward and began to knock at the door of the Babu's house.

They waited in suspense for some time outside the door. Daya Ram knocked again, striking the latch against the worn-out grooves to produce a louder echo. Another little while passed. Daya Ram called: 'Bibiji, open the door.'

Then a chick lifted behind a side door and a woman appeared. She had a dark face, mobile and without any set form, except that which the tired smile on her thin lips gave it, and a sharp nose over which her brown eyes concentrated in a squint, and her forehead inclined with wrinkles. Her stern, flat-chested form was swathed in a muslin sari. He had seen none of the hill women drape it in that way, except Jay Singh's mother, the wife of the landlord, who had originally come from town and who, the village women said, was not a woman but a collection of blandishments.

Munoo waited in suspense, aware of the surprised stare in the lady's face. He was frightened with the sense of strangeness that assailed him not only from everything about the woman, but also from the polished corners of tables, chairs and pictures which showed themselves to his inquisitive eyes.

'Bibiji,' said Daya Ram with joined hands, 'I have brought my little nephew to serve you. Here he is.' Then he flashed an angry glance at Munoo and said: 'Join your hands, you pig, and say "I fall at your feet" to Bibiji.'

Munoo joined his hands, but he had hardly said 'I fall . . .' when a loud, piercing shriek came from a child somewhere in the inner chambers. Bibiji retreated and exclaimed in a hard, rattling voice: 'Oh baby, you have eaten my life! You can't rest even while I am talking business to anyone! May you die! May your liver burn! May you fade away! You of the evil star! Now, what is the matter with you? What do you want? You . . .'

And she would have continued, such a sharp, long tongue she had, and such inexhaustible resources of breath, had Daya Ram not asked: 'Will everything be all right then, Bibiji? Shall I leave him here?'

Munoo waited anxiously for her answer. He was frightened of her. Her long neck stood out before his eyes like a hen's.

'No, wait, Daya Ram,' she cried, coming back from the room in which she had disappeared to qualify her curses with a slap on the face of the child, which made it howl the more: 'Have you told the Babuji?'

'Yes, Bibiji, I took him to the office first,' said Daya Ram, 'and Babuji said I was to bring him here and to put him in your charge.'

'All right,' she said, 'but there are vegetables to fetch from the bazaar for the evening meal. Will you . . .'

At this the child in the back room, unable to draw attention by howling, began to shriek continuously, and the woman, retreating, let loose another series of curses.

Munoo felt a strange emptiness in him, a kind of embarrassment. The picture of his aunt came before him. 'But she never abused or cursed so much.'

And, in his heart, there was a lonely song, a melancholy wail, asking, not pointedly, but in a vague, uncertain rhythm, what life in this woman's house would prove.

'Will you go and tell Babuji to buy the vegetables when he leaves the office and send them by the boy?' came the voice of his mistress suddenly to Munoo's ears.

He did not attend to it for a moment. He was possessed by sadness and self-pity. He was tired after the long march through the hills. And he was hungry. He had thought that he would be able to sit down when he reached his destination, and that he would be given food according to the custom which prevails in all Indian homes of offering food to guests and visitors at whatever time of the day they arrive. Instead he was being asked to go on an errand the very minute he arrived. 'Perhaps the customs in the towns are different,' he thought, with a sinking feeling.

'All right, Bibiji,' said Daya Ram coolly. He had become too inured to the caprices of his masters to be resentful like his nephew.

13

'Come, ohe Munoo,' he said, walking along. 'You will be looked after here. You will get plenty to eat in this home. And the Babu said he would pay us three rupees a month. I will show you my room near the office. Come down there on your off-day. Don't forget to do your best for the masters. You are their servant and they are kind people.'

As Munoo listened to this, tears came rushing to his eyes. And through the tears he could see the high rocks, the great granite hills, grey in the blaze of the sun, and the silver line of the Beas, on the banks of which his herds had mooed defiance to the earth and the sky, wandering, wandering freely for miles and miles . . .

Overnight Munoo had lain huddled up in a corner of the kitchen of Babu Nathoo Ram's house. He had had a disturbed night, for he had been overtired, and sleep does not come to the weary. And he had been given a ragged, old brown blanket which was hot in spite of the big ventilator-like rents in its sparse length and breadth. His tunic had become sodden with sweat. The mosquitoes had whined in his ears all night and bitten him several times. A swarm of flies had buzzed about noisily and irritated him by settling on his face continually. Even now he could not keep his eyes closed, as he had been used to getting up early in the morning in his village.

He sighed in vain for sleep to come to him. Then he struggled to keep his eyes closed, as he felt strange in his new surroundings.

He could hear the Babu snoring loudly in another room. He did not know which room, because when he had come back with the vegetables from the market, Bibiji had called him straight into the kitchen and given him a loaf of stale pancake, after which she had asked him to peel the potatoes and help her to cook. The meal was prepared, but who ate it, and where it was eaten, Munoo did not know, as, being fatigued, he had succumbed to sleep in the corner where he lay. The only thing he remembered was the shrill voice of his mistress, which had reached his ears when he had been suffi-ciently aroused by a few digs in the ribs:

'You eater of your masters! Strange servant you are that you fall asleep before the sun sets! What is the use of a boy like you in the house if you are going to do that every day! Wake up! Wake up! You brute! Wake up and serve the Babuji his dinner! Or, at least eat your food before you sleep, if sleep to death you must!'

He looked around and scanned the various things that lay in utter confusion about him. There were plates of burnished brass with black-bottomed, bronze saucepans and tumblers of aluminium mixed with children's toys, and glass bottles, big and small, bottles of medicine like the labelled bottles which Munoo had seen in the shop of the doctor of his village. Only these were dusty, while in the doctor's shop everything was kept clean by the compounder. There were sacks of flour and lentils and huge wooden boxes and tins, containing Munoo knew not what. There were two dirty shirts and an alpaca jacket hanging from pegs in the walls, two enormous coloured pictures, the figures in which were hidden by the faded garlands of flowers that hung about them, and a large broken mirror covered with soot. Wood fuel lay heaped in one corner. And, on a line suspended from the middle of the two walls, length-wise, were heaps of old and new clothes, while several bundles of quilts and blankets hung from the ceiling. On a separate shelf, a little further up, precariously balanced on an iron tray, lay utensils of polished 'white chalk': little round cups with handles, a big pot with a beak like a pig's nose, and a jug.

Munoo did not know for what these 'white chalk' utensils were used. But something in their glossy surface fascinated him, something about them vaguely promised him a surprise more significant than the open message reflected by the burning sheen of the brass and bronze utensils, which challenged him with an injunction: 'You will have to polish us soon.'

The rest of the junk, in spite of the glamour of the pictures and gaudy mirrors, confused him. For a moment he drew back into himself, into a sort of emptiness, only slightly disturbed by the waves of light that pervaded the room. Then he wanted to get up and see what was in the other parts of the house.

His eyes lit with that impish curiosity which had always made him go out hunting for birds' eggs in the trees, the bushes and the rocks. His heart fluttered with the light easy throb with which it had beaten when he had gone stealing fruit from the gardens. He felt the lure of adventure in his bones.

With a sudden movement of his limbs he sprang to his feet and tiptoed to the door facing him. He applied an eye to the chink and saw a tiny room congested with two huge beds, several trunks and a little child's vehicle. The Babu lay on a bed with his face sunk sideways into a pillow. The angular heap which curled up under a sheet on another bed was, Munoo guessed, Bibiji.

Lest the mere act of looking on his part should arouse his master and mistress, he withdrew his gaze to peer through a half-open doorway on his right. On a clean white bed in the middle of the room lay a man, almost as white-faced as the Sahib in the basket hat whom his uncle had saluted yesterday. There was a more interesting medley of objects in this room, all neatly arranged: a vast table in one corner, majestic chairs like the thrones of which Munoo had seen pictures in his history books, photographs large and small, and calendars with dates written in black for ordinary days and red for the holidays, toys of coloured clay, among which the effigy of Ganesha, the elephant-headed god of sagacity, worldliness and wealth, ruled supreme.

Munoo's eyes roved round and explored the potencies of civilization. He would have lingered to gaze endlessly, but he saw the man (the Babuji's younger brother, he guessed, for he had heard Bibiji talk of Prem, the chota Babu) turn on his side and mutter in his sleep.

'Vay, Mundu, are you awake?'

Munoo's heart beat fast. He was breathless for a moment. He wondered whether it was the thumping of his feet as he ran which had awakened Bibiji.

'Yes, Bibiji, I am awake,' he said, adapting his hill accent to the diction of the lowlands.

'Well then, get to work,' the voice came, lazily monosyllabic. 'Rake out the ashes in the fireplace, and scrub last night's soiled utensils. You went to sleep, you dead one, so early last night that you didn't even do that! And light the fire. Then put the water on to boil in the saucepan for tea for Babuji. I will get up in a little while.'

Presently there was a sob. The little girl child, Lila, had presumably been awakened. But she was lulled to sleep again. Munoo wondered where the elder girl, Sheila, was. She was supposed to have gone to a fair with her uncle yesterday, and he had not seen her yet.

As he went kitchenwards, Munoo felt uneasy. He did not know where to begin and how to set about doing things in this house.

Besides, the first thing he had always done when he got up every morning in his village home was to run out into the fields and relieve himself, then bathe at the well, come back and eat his food before going to school or taking his flock to graze at the riverside.

Now he did not know where he should go to relieve himself. There were houses all about, and there were forbidding bungalows cresting the hill. And he could hear people walking on the road.

He did not know where the people in the towns went.

He hastened to the door leading out of the kitchen. He could not see any latrine attached to the house.

By this time he was in a panic.

He felt he could not control himself any longer.

He felt he was going to spoil his loin cloth.

He ran to the wall outside the house and sat down there.

'Where are you? Where have you died, vay Mundu?' came the voice of his mistress, as he had hardly sat down.

A sudden fear seized him that she should come and see him. But he could not check himself and get up.

'Vay, you eater of your masters! Vay, you shameless brute! You pig! You dog!' the storm burst on his head as, hearing no response to her call, she appeared at the door, saw him, and unable to bear the sight, withdrew. 'Vay, you shameless, shameless, vulgar, stupid hillboy! May the vessel of your life never float in the sea of existence! May you die! What have you done! Why didn't you ask me where to go? May you fade away! May you burn! We didn't know we were taking on an animal in our employ, an utter brute, a savage! What will the Sahibs think who pass by our doors every morning and afternoon! The Babuji has his prestige to keep up with the Sahibs. Hai! What a horrible, horrible mess he has made outside my door!'

Her voice rose from the first shock of unpleasantness, through the faint hiss of anger to the mechanical volubility of her curses and mounted to a last note of real despair. Munoo felt the blood rushing to his face. His brain seemed to be submerged in darkness. He wished he could disappear from the world somehow. For the first time in his life he felt ashamed to be seen relieving himself in the open.

Of course, now, the whole house was awake.

At first, Babu Nathoo Ram came, square-shouldered and bandy-legged, thinking with his exaggerated sense of property that a thief had attacked his house.

Then emerged the chota Babu, a handsome, well-built young man, easy-gaited and loose-mannered, saying: 'What is the matter? What is all this row about?'

Last of all, the Babu's elder daughter, Sheila, walked up, a slim child of ten, with golden hair, an ivory complexion and light brown eyes which seemed to laugh as they twinkled with mischievous gaiety at this ridiculous incident.

'This shameless rustic!' began Bibiji again, with all the vociferating intensity of which she was capable. 'He has gone and relieved himself at the doorstep of my kitchen! Heavens! Just imagine! Eater of his masters! May he die! Hai! Hai! I –'

'Why, ohe you son of a bitch!' squeaked Babu Nathoo Ram, lifting his thin, bony hand, both to quieten his wife and to threaten Munoo. 'Why did you do that?' Then, contorting his face so that his forehead was knotted into a curious twist, and dilating his lips to reveal the red gums over his badly spaced teeth, he stupidly reiterated, 'Why did you do that?'

'Because he didn't want to do it in his loincloth,' said the chota Babu, laughing and teasing. 'Then Bibiji would have had to wash those for him. As it is, the sweeper will be here soon.'

Sheila giggled and clung to her uncle's legs.

'Go away, Sheila, you shouldn't be here,' said Nathoo Ram, swallowing his anger. 'Couldn't he have gone to the lavatory? Why didn't you tell him where it was?' he said, turning to his wife.

'Ah, do you think I should let him use our lavatory!' Bibiji replied. 'Let this rustic use our lavatory! You spoil him. He will be another nuisance for me to look after! Someone had better go and call the sweeper to come and clean the mess he has made!'

'All right, all right!' said chota Babu casually. 'Don't let us frighten him, or he will make more of a mess. Now what about tea? What about tea, then, Sheila? Is your mother too angry to give us tea!'

'Can't you wait, Prem!' Bibiji exclaimed. 'Let me see to this stupid boy first –'

'Ah!' she cried in disgust at the thought of the sight, and without feeling in the least like vomiting, 'I am sick! I am sick! I am fainting!'

A rustling behind her, and she saw Munoo standing in the kitchen. She turned on him, shouting at the top of her voice: 'You eater of your masters! Where did you go?'

'I went to wash my buttocks at the pump,' Munoo replied, with a complete lack of self-consciousness.

'Go and have a bath before you come anywhere near my kitchen,' she said pushing him away with both her arms. 'Begone, out of my sight!' he heard her shout after him. 'You uncivilized brute!'

And she continued grumbling when he had long passed out of hearing distance: 'I thought there was going to be some rest for me when this servant came. Instead I have to slave exactly as in the past. What is the use of an ignorant boy like this in the house? He is more of a trouble than a help. And such a stupid fool, too, and dirty! Ah! These village folk . . .'

'Don't say anything against village folk,' mocked her brother-in-law. 'You yourself come from a village.'

'Oh please don't tease,' said Bibiji. 'We must keep up our prestige! We must keep up appearances, at least before a stranger in the house.'

'Sheila,' said Prem Chand loudly, so that his sister-in-law should hear, 'do you remember that poem about tea which you read on the posters of the Imperial Tea Company at the railway station?'

'"Hot tea cools your heart in the heat of summer" you mean, uncle?' said Sheila.

'Yes, go and say that loudly to Bibi Uttam Kaur,' he said, smiling mischievously, as he rolled about on his bed.

'Hot tea cools . . .' Sheila was going to sing.

'All right, all right!' shouted Bibiji shrilly. 'Don't eat my head! And don't mention my name in vain! I am getting tea ready! And you, you little wretch, your uncle may have become a Sahib by going to learn medicine at college. Where have you learnt to pose as a memsahib?'

Munoo was scrubbing the utensils with ashes as he sat by the slab which served both as sink and bathroom, being connected with a drain through a slimy hole in the wall where the insects buzzed and the worms crawled. The boy felt the cool odorous draught come in from the drain and dry the sweat on his face. He shifted from where he sat on his heels and turned his back to the hole. But now he faced a side door from which the smell of dung assailed his nostrils. 'That must be the lavatory,' he thought. 'Strange!'

'May I help him to scrub the utensils, mother?' asked Sheila as she stood fidgeting in the kitchen.

'Get out of the way!' screamed her mother, 'and let that good-for-nothing pig do some work for a change.'

The child went.

Bibiji took the saucepan of boiling water off the fireplace. Then she fetched the teaset, which Munoo had seen standing precariously on the shelf, and made tea in the fat pot with the beak like a pig's nose. She took care not to bring the china too near the ceremonial square which parted the sacred precincts of her cooking place from the rest of the room. She was an orthodox Hindu, and knew that her husband's and brother-in-law's Muhammadan friends had drunk tea out of the cups and saucers.

Munoo, who was interested in her every movement, observed the care she took not to taint her brass utensils by bringing them anywhere near the china. Out of the corner of his eyes, however, he saw her bring the saucepan of boiling water near the teapot and touch it in her effort to drain the saucepan and fill the teapot to the brim.

She saw him looking at her. She felt she was caught being defiled. But she was not sure. 'Do your work and don't keep staring at me while I am making the tea,' she bullied.

But, before he withdrew his gaze, he had seen what she particularly did not want him to see, that she had killed two birds with one stone, boiled eggs in the same water which she was pouring into the teapot. Even in the hills that was considered unhygienic.

She was confused. Her face was livid with anger.

To make her confusion worse, at that instant Lila, whom she had left asleep on her bed, awoke with a shriek.

'O you eater of your master, Lila! You have awakened, have you! The bane of my life! Now you will not let me rest or do anything!'

She put two pieces of double roti (English bread) in the fireplace to toast and was cutting a third.

A moment had elapsed and the child was shrieking louder.

'Oh be patient! You dead one! What has happened to you? May the witches come and devour you! What curse upon your head makes you howl all day! Even though I got you an amulet from the fakir! God! When will I get some rest! I slog, slog all day! I can't even get time to dress! Or to sit down with the neighbours for a chat! Or go to the shops! Last night I went to bed at two o'clock, washing and cleaning up! And now ... ni Sheila, ni, dead one, go and look after your little sister for a while instead of running about the house and making a noise. Go . . .'

Prem had picked up the child and, bringing her and Sheila to the sitting-room where he lay, set about to amuse them by playing the gramophone.

Munoo, who had almost finished rubbing the utensils, heard the music issuing from the sitting-room and, on the pretext of going out to wash the utensils at the pump, left the kitchen.

Bibiji had burnt the toast, as she had neglected it while shouting. She muttered curses as she set about cutting another piece of bread to toast before the fire on her skewers.

The dolorous rhythm of a love song filled the house for a minute or two.

She forgot everything in the contemplation of whether she would be able to go to the funeral of Babu Beli Ram's mother that afternoon.

Munoo had hurriedly washed the utensils and rushed into the house, not through the kitchen door, but through the verandah into the sitting-room.

'Ohe, you son of an owl,' said the chota Babu, 'have you dried your feet before entering the room?'

'No, Babuji,' replied Munoo, standing with wet feet on the carpet, the basket of utensils dripping under his arm.

'Well then, for goodness' sake please do so, on that mattress,' said the chota Babu ironically. 'That's what it is there for, if I may be privileged to tell you.'

Munoo felt encouraged. 'The chota Babu did not forbid me to come in, anyway,' he thought.

He felt emboldened. He wanted to hear the music, to see and touch the singing machine, the like of which had fascinated him in the bazaar yesterday. 'How lucky I am', he thought, 'that there is a wonder machine in the house where I have come to serve.'

He rushed back to the kitchen to dump the basket of utensils so as to have his hands free. Then he went out on the pretext of throwing the rubbish and used ashes on the road.

Unfortunately, just then the music stopped.

'What's your name? You can throw the ashes on this heap here, if you like,' said a tall boy who was filling brass pitchers at the pump, while two other younger boys sat watching.

Munoo threw the ashes on the heap which the big boy had indicated.

'Are you also a servant here, then?' he asked directly.

'Yes, I work in the house of Babu Gopal Das,' said the tall boy. 'He is bigger than your Babu. And the Babus of these two work in the court. We all come from Hoshiarpur.'

'I come from near Kangra,' said Munoo, and volunteered a whole lot of information about his uncle, about the most important men of his village, and about having been taken on a journey to Hoshiarpur by his parents when he was a little child. And, in a few seconds, they had exchanged all their confidences in the manner characteristic of the naïve, open-hearted north Indians.

A hilarious tune suddenly attracted Munoo back to the house. He ran in.

'Your paws, you monkey!' shouted the chota Babu.

Munoo fell on all fours over the mattress as if he was a real monkey and matched his good humour with his master's.

After dusting his feet and his hands he advanced, still playing the fool, and began to dance like the monkey of the village juggler whom he had seen perform every day on the crossroads on his way back from school.

'Look, Uncle! Look!' laughed Sheila. 'He is dancing like a monkey!'

'Shabash! Shabash!' said the chota Babu, joining in the sport in the role of the juggler.

Little Lila had begun to keep time by swaying her head and clapping her hands.

'I will be the bear, Uncle!' shouted Sheila.

Munoo was still rapt, dancing with awkward, silly movements, making faces, showing his teeth, rolling his eyes and shrieking like a real monkey.

'What's this noise? What's this row going on? What right has he to be in the sitting-room?' Bibiji's voice came shrill and hard, and chilled the atmosphere so that everything became still in a moment. 'What right has he to join the laughter of his superiors?'

Munoo hurried to the kitchen. But he was not crestfallen. He was beaming all over his face with the wild happiness of expressive movement native to him.

The smoke from the fireplace spread over the kitchen and hid his flushed cheeks and bright eyes from Bibiji, who still squatted on the straw mattress making toast. Otherwise, there would have been a tirade of abuse about his smiles, a little less comfortable than the disquisition upon duty with which he was greeted:

'Your place is here in the kitchen! You must not enter the sports of the chota Babu and the children. You must get on quickly with work in the house! There is no time to lose. Babuji has to go to the office at ten o'clock. Sheila has to go to school. We have employed you not to delay the work in the house, but to help to get it done. Since you are being paid a good wage, more money than you ever saw in your whole life in the village, more money, in fact, than your mother or father ever saw, it would be worth while for you to do a little work for it. And I warn you that you are never to go and settle down to relieve yourself outside my house. When the sweeper comes, ask him to show you the servants' latrine at the foot of the hill. And don't you ever touch my utensils without washing your hands. Your body is dirty and you keep touching it. Your clothes are filthy, too. I saw you wipe your hands on your shirt. And oh! I suppose you dried your body with your tunic after your bath? God! why didn't you ask me for a towel? You brute! You ought to be ashamed of yourself! Sheila, Sheila, go, my child, get a towel out of the box and give it to this savage! Do you hear, you are not to touch anything in this house without washing your hands! Now have you touched anything dirty since you had your bath?'

'No, Bibiji,' said Munoo, still dancing in his mind and listening, though not registering much of what Bibiji had said.

'All right, but you scrubbed the utensils,' she said.

'I washed my hands afterwards, Bibiji,' Munoo replied.

'Didn't you touch anything else?'

'No,' he answered.

'No? Didn't you? What about the rubbish?'

'I washed my hands at the pump after I had thrown out the rubbish.'

'Didn't you touch anything else?'

'No,' Munoo lied, exasperated and seeking to end this controversy, though he knew he had brushed his hands on the mat while he was dancing the monkey dance, and the mattress being used to dusty feet was certainly unclean.

'Well then, take the tea to the chota Babuji.'

Munoo did not know how to set about it, whether to carry the whole tray or the various things one by one. He had never handled anything like that at home. And he thought it was best to make sure.

'How shall I carry them?' he asked.

'How shall I carry them!' she burst out. 'How shall you carry them! How long shall I have to go on explaining things to you? Hai! We didn't know that Daya Ram was going to bring such a thick-headed boy as this. We –'

Munoo had pondered over the array of 'white chalk' utensils on the tray for a while, and before Bibiji had finished her new tirade, he asked impetuously: 'What are these utensils made of, Bibiji?'

'What impertinence! What cheek! To interrupt while I speak! You get on with your work! The tea is getting cold! They are made of china, of course! What else do you think they would be made of! Look, look, everyone, he has never even seen china utensils! And don't you let the tray fall and break the crockery now, or I will break your bones up for you!'

Munoo lifted the tray lightly as soon as he heard his mistress answer his question and walked away with a wonderful agility while she abused and warned and threatened with a copious flow of her hard, even chatter.

'Here we are, children!' said Prem, clapping his hands. 'Here is the tea! A bit late, but never mind!'

'The tea! The tea!' exclaimed Sheila, her blue eyes melting, her lips contracting.

'Ooon, aaan! I want the tea, too!' sobbed Lila from where she sat on a table swaying her head to the music, in a ridiculously childish manner which amused her elder sister, her uncle and her father, when that last worthy was not too embarrassed to come and play with his children.

'Put it down here, you black man!' said Prem, with mock anger in the wrong Hindustani which he sometimes affected, especially in the face of anything so European as a tea-tray or when dressed in an English suit, an imitation of the tone in which Englishmen tàlk to their native servants. 'Put it down on this table, black man, you who relieve yourself on the ground!'

'Babuji, come and have tea!' Sheila was calling her father, who still lay getting an extra wink of sleep in the bedlam of his three-roomed house.

'Why should he get up?' nagged Bibiji. 'Why should he get up? He wields an axe felling trees at the office all day!'

Babu Nathoo Ram stirred himself to alacrity. Pale, haggard and stooping, he walked into the sitting-room with a weak smile of fear on his face. He was a hen-pecked husband and wanted to avoid his wife first thing in the morning.

Munoo had placed the tray safely on a small table and retreated to the doorway. From there he stood watching the ritual which the chota Babu performed, rather self-consciously, pouring first milk from the long jug, then tea from the fat pot with the beak like a pig's nose, adding sugar in the cups that lay before him.

'Strange,' he said to himself.

What was the idea of pouring milk from one jug and tea from another? For, at home, his aunt boiled milk, tea leaves, sugar and water all in a big saucepan and poured it into brass tumblers, ready to drink. And then, what was the use of burning that funny fat bread before eating it? He had never seen English bread before in his life.

'Where is the cream? Where is the cream, you little monkey?' asked the chota Babu, eager and merry. 'Go and get Bibiji to give you some butter or cream.'

This disturbed Munoo's reverie.

'Here is the cream *and* the butter,' called Bibiji. 'Give it to them, so that they may eat and fatten while I slave. You forgot to take it.'

Munoo conveyed the cream to the sitting-room in a flash. Then he stood again, looking round, as if attracted by the warmth that the chota Babu radiated. The burra Babu eyed him, as, with a yawn and a stretching of his arms, he brought his lustreless skeleton to rest on the lotus seat like an emaciated beggar.

The chota Babu seemed to do it all so easily, biting the bread which he had smeared with butter and then taking a gulp or two of tea from the cup he held in his right hand. The burra Babu found it difficult, apparently, as he shifted about in his seat, dropped the crumbs on himself and the carpet, poured the contents of his tea cup into the saucer, blew at the steaming liquid cautiously, and sucked noisily as from time to time he wiped the bristles of his drooping moustache with his dirty, yellow tongue.

'Come, vay, you dead one! Where are you now?' shouted Bibiji, presumably aroused at overhearing Sheila asking her uncle if she could give Munoo some tea. 'Isn't there any more work to do here? Do you think that just because you have lifted a tray of tea-things and taken it over to the next room, you have earned your wages?'

Munoo withdrew to the kitchen, rather sorry for himself, as Sheila's kind offer had touched him to the quick.

'Come and scrub these utensils with the ashes, you idler! . . . Not a speck of dirt or grease must remain on that!' she roared. Then, as he applied himself to the task, she cried: 'Oh, God, leave it, leave it! You are no good! I will have to do it. I must do everything myself. Nobody does anything satisfactorily. Can't you see, you idiot, that that black must come off? Just compare the sheen of those utensils which lie polished on the rack with those you have cleaned today! You must get the same brilliance.'

Luckily for Munoo there was a call for her from the sitting-room: 'Oh, I say, the mother of my daughter,' said the burra Babu, in the archaic convention of Indian family life, 'bring another cup, for Babu Ram Lall has come, and get some hot water ready for shaving. Sheila should be bathed and got ready for school. Babu Ram Lall's daughters are almost ready to go.'

Bibiji took an extra cup and saucer from the shelf to the sitting-room, with a coyness that contradicted the high-pitched tone of her immodest voice and hardened exterior.

Munoo enjoyed a little less attention from her for a while, as, when she came back with Sheila and Lila from the sitting-room, she sent him off with the hot water which the Babus wanted, and engaged herself in bathing her daughters and dressing them.

'What an awful bitch of a woman,' he thought. He had been awaiting an excuse to go out from the kitchen to the sitting-room, for that was a much nicer world, the world where tea was being drunk by the jocular chota Babu, where the queer-looking burra Babu was, and where, he had now heard, another Babu had arrived.

He was rewarded not only with the sight of an amiable little man who was reciting Punjabi verses such as he had heard the professional clowns recite in his village, but by the far more amazing spectacle of the chota Babu soaping his cheeks and rubbing the teeth of a bright steel machine.

What was the Babu doing, he wondered. Then his mind went back to the barber's shop in his village and he understood. 'Shaving' he said, half-audibly. And he stood and stared at the process.

Of all the most marvellous, the most mysterious things he had seen since he came to town yesterday, the little machine with the teeth seemed the most marvellous, the most wonderful. In his village the barber shaved the beards of men with a long, sharp razor. This machine he had never seen. 'It cannot be very dangerous,' he thought, 'if the Babu is rubbing it on his face, so quickly, up and down, down and up.'

'What are you looking at, you owl?' said the chota Babu affectionately, noticing that the boy stood absorbed. This spectacle had aroused his curiosity, too, the first time he had seen it.

Munoo smiled, slightly embarrassed.

'Babuji,' he ventured after a while, 'does this machine cost a lot of money?'

'Why,' said the burra Babu, with an attempt at light-hearted irony, 'why, do you want to shave the hair on your head off? Have you become an orphan?'

'I am an orphan, Babuji,' said Munoo self-pityingly.

'Oh!' said the visitor humorously, 'you haven't yet risen to the height of my little finger and you want to possess a razor to shave with!'

'All right,' said the chota Babu in his naturally bantering manner, 'if you will be good enough to go and get me a towel from the other room, I shall give you, not a machine, but a blade to cut your throat with if you like.'

Munoo ran back for the towel, his heart beating in admiration and love for the chota Babu. He could feel a kinship with this light-hearted man.

When he came back he was confronted with the sight of yet another miracle which, this time, the burra Babu was performing, revolving a small handle on the side of a shining, egg-shaped machine.

He stared hard, trying to comprehend what was happening, and before he could muster enough courage to ask the dry, pale man what he was doing, his mind went back to the piece of lathe on which the barber in his village used to sharpen his long razors.

'This,' he said impetuously to the Babus, to share with them the joy of his discovery, 'this is surely a sharpening machine.'

'Vay, you eater of your masters,' came Bibiji's bark, and he knew that she had heard him talking to the Babus. 'Where have you flown to? Is there no work to do that you go wasting your time! Haven't I told you that your place is in the kitchen? Won't it sink in your brain, or do you want your bones broken, before you understand? I have all the work to do. This witch has to go to school and the Babuji is soon going to the office. I don't suppose you have even learnt to make dough in the hills where you come from. Besides, your hands are dirty. I will never let you touch any of the food in the house. I must do it all. No use depending on you. You –'

'What shall I do now, Bibiji?'

'Vay, don't eat my head,' she yelped again. 'Isn't there anything to do before you? Are you blind or what! Look at those utensils, tea-things, which want cleaning, vegetables to be peeled.'

Munoo got down to the job of cleaning the teaset.

He found that as soon as he poured water on the 'white chalk' the utensils became clean. 'That is easy,' he thought. And he hurriedly washed some cups and set them apart to dry.

'Vay, what are you doing?' she barked more sharply. 'Rub that china with the ashes exactly as we do the brass utensils, and clean them thoroughly, so that not a speck of dirt or the taint of anyone's mouth remains. We are not so debased as the Sahibs, that we should eat and drink out of our dirty utensils after merely washing them. We may have to respect them because they are our officers, but they are dirty. They bathe in tubs in the dirty water that comes off their bodies, lying there all the time, even after they have rubbed themselves with soap and washed off the dirt. The ayah of the Mem of the Bank Sahib told me that they eat the flesh of cows like the Muhammadans, and of pigs like the Sikhs.'

'I also eat the flesh of cows and pigs, you know,' said Prem teasingly, as he wandered into the kitchen to see if the slab of stone in the corner was unoccupied and he could have his bath.

'Oh, don't say that please, you make me feel sick,' appealed Bibiji. 'Really –'

Munoo sat there rubbing the utensils with ashes and washing them, quickly and with not too fastidious a care for the corners and depths of the pots. He was essentially impetuous by nature, and as yet too young to have disciplined his hands to the adequate performance of menial jobs.

At home his aunt, in spite of her dark, brooding hatred of him, had done the housework herself, untiringly, uncomplainingly and quietly. He remembered that he had often volunteered in a rush of sympathy to sweep the floor, to treat it with antiseptic cow dung and to run errands for her. The only quarrel between himself and his aunt, he realized, was that she could not have children and people shamed her for her barrenness. Otherwise, he remembered how often she had taken him in her arms and kissed him, and how often he had gone to sleep embracing her. But this woman seemed to hate him for nothing.

As he wiped the utensils with a dirty cloth, he hoped that she would stop nagging one day, that he would settle down and not feel so much of an outsider in the house. The chota Babu was nice and the children were amused by his monkey dance. The burra Babu was all right, because one could avert one's eyes from him. But Bibiji –

He checked his mind from running into a violent criticism of her, because he felt if he abused her she might somehow come to know of his thoughts and take him to task for it. He switched his mind off to the contemplation of the fine, well-cut silk clothes he had seen hanging in a corner of the sitting-room, clothes like those which the Sahib wore, whom he had seen yesterday. He felt he would like to see the chota Babu putting them on. But as he got up to go he met the chota Babu coming towards him.

'Has Your Highness finished working on the slab, and is it free for me to take a bath on?' he asked with an air of humorous subservience.

'Yes, Babuji,' Munoo answered. 'I –'

But at this Bibiji descended on him like lightning.

'Finished washing the utensils?' she snapped. 'Well, where are you going then? What do you want in the other room?'

'I –' Munoo strained to invent an excuse.

'You are going to tell me a lie,' she said, threatening to strike him with her fist. 'Go and put those utensils away. The Babus want to take their baths. Peel the vegetables and clean up here. Haven't I told you that you are not to go into the other room unless you are wanted? When they have all gone, you can clean the carpet and make the beds. I don't know whether you know how to do these things. I suppose I will have to show you. But meanwhile there is work to do here in the kitchen. All that you seem to want to do is to run round, you inquisitive little fool. You have never seen anything in your life in the hills and now your eyes are bursting at the sight of all the beautiful things in our home.'

'The flood has started,' said Prem, throwing jugfuls of water on his head. 'Look out, you fool, you will be submerged not only in the ocean of words but in the sea of water.'

Munoo suppressed a smile at the good humour of the chota Babu, but muttered a curse as he recollected Bibiji's stream of words.

She went to give Sheila some pocket-money as the child stood ready to go to school, else she might have caught him doing something wrong. He now believed she could always find something to abuse him for, some fault, the slightest detail, the way he placed a pot, the manner in which he handled the broom, or the way he held the potatoes as he peeled them.

During the brief respite his mind wandered from the chota Babu's beautiful white body, glistening with water, to the clothes that would adorn it soon, the wonderfully cut silk clothes. And suddenly, as if out of the blue, a picture of the boots, the burra Babu's black boots, came before him, with their gloss and their intricately tied laces. He wondered if the chota Babu had also boots like that.

'Sheila! ni Sheila!' a young voice disturbed his cogitation from outside.

'Yes, coming,' shrilled Sheila from the bedroom.

A young girl with a fine, wheat-coloured face, framed modestly but prettily in a pink muslin head-cloth, looked in through the kitchen door.

'Sheila's mother!' she called, and then uttered a sudden 'Oo' at the sight of Munoo.

'Why, ni, witch with long hair and crooked feet, why are you running away?' teased the chota Babu, as he went to the sitting-room.

'Kausalya, ni Kausalya,' called Bibiji after her, 'don't be afraid of this rustic, my little sister, the eater of his masters is really harmless. You don't know what he did this morning. He went and relieved himself by the wall outside there – Now Sheila is ready. Do take her and look after her, won't you, my child?'

'Isn't he funny, this servant of yours,' remarked Kausalya, looking in again. 'My Babuji told me he dances like a monkey. But come, Sheila, quick, my sisters are waiting and we will be late for school.'

Munoo felt humiliated. He did not know how to face people if they were all going to be told what he had done this morning. He realized finally his position in this world. He was to be a slave, a servant who should do the work, all the odd jobs, someone to be abused, even beaten, though as yet it had not come to that. He felt sad; lonely.

The sudden emergence of the chota Babu, immaculately dressed in a tussore jacket and smartly creased trousers, a flannel hat on his head and a pair of beautiful brown shoes on his feet, excited him.

He loved this man, admired him as his hero. He wanted to be like him.

'Where is Bibiji, oh devil without horns?' queried the chota Babu.

Munoo smiled, embarrassed, but happy.

'Here I am,' she said, coming in from the outer door. 'Now what do you want?'

'Five of those wonderful silver rupees of which my brother earns one hundred and fifty every month from the Imperial Bank of India,' Prem mocked. 'I am going to see a patient at the other end of the town. And it is good tactics to have plenty of money jingling in your pockets, because the world believes you are well off and they bring you all their diseased relatives to cure. Money, you see, attracts money.'

She relaxed her hard face to return the twinkle in his eye.

As she left the room, however, she gave a stern glance to Munoo as if to forbid him from following her course to the cash box where she hid the family wealth.

This, she felt, did not have the effect she intended. She saw him peeping towards the corner where she had retreated. She shuffled and shifted to camouflage the movement of her key in the lock of the cash box.

'You thief,' she shouted. 'Do your work and don't follow me about with your gaze.'

Munoo was disgusted with her insinuations. He went on peeling the vegetables.

Then he heard the chota Babu slam the door of the sitting-room and walk out with his elder brother.

'Go and sweep the rooms now and do the beds,' Bibiji said a

little more calmly as she came back. 'I will put the vegetables on to cook and knead the flour into dough for the chapatis.'

He lost himself in the fairyland of the sitting-room, as, squatting on his heels, he swept the carpet with the broom. His eyes caressed the mahogany varnish of the throne-like chairs. They dwelt with admiration on the various photographs. Twice or thrice he could not resist the temptation to get up and look closely at the pictures. He scrutinized everything with wonder and love, tracing the colours, the shapes and sizes of all the things, inquiring into their meanings. 'What is written in that book, I wonder?' he asked himself. 'How does the big clock work? . . . The voice in the box: I wonder how it arises?'

'Don't you wake Lila up,' Bibiji called as she heard him push a chair. 'I will come and help you to do the beds.'

She came. She had quietened a bit, though she abused him for being too quick in getting through things.

After the rooms were done she asked him to go and fill the pitchers at the pump. Later he sat down to learn to cook under her orders.

His uncle came to fetch the midday meal for Babuji and for Sheila and asked him: 'Do you like it here?'

He could have cried at that, but Bibiji was there. So he answered 'Yes, I like it very much.'

But when Daya Ram asked Bibiji's permission to take him along to show him the way to Sheila's school, so that he could go and meet her every day, he burst out weeping on the way and complained about the hard, bitter life which he had had since he arrived, specially about Bibiji's continual nagging.

'You are their servant,' said Daya Ram. 'You must not mind what they say. You must grow up and work. You have had too easy a life at home. Your mother spoiled you. Your aunt was too kind to you.'

Munoo suffered this. But, out in the open, his strong wild self came back to him with the contagion of the elements, and he could have hit his uncle.

On his return Bibiji gave him two chapatis and a spoonful of lentils and vegetables. He had to eat on his hands, being considered too low in status to be allowed to eat off the utensils. The insult stung him. He could hardly swallow his food.

But it was no use caring, he felt now.

Bibiji went out visiting some neighbours, taking Lila with her, after the midday meal.

Munoo began to scrub the utensils again. Before he had finished, the afternoon was over. He perspired with the heat and work. He felt tired and lay down.

But Sheila came back with the tall girl Kausalya, who had looked in in the morning, and two other little girls. They all began dancing in the sitting-room.

Munoo would like to have joined them. So he rushed in and began to perform the morning's monkey dance. This amused them and they let him play with them, though they had begun by pushing him away, saying: 'You are a servant, you must not play with us.'

The chota Babu came back with some other Babus and demanded tea.

Bibiji was called.

Munoo's spirits revived in the atmosphere created by the chota Babu's jollity. His mouth watered at the sight of the rasgulas, the gulab jamans and the strange English sweets which the chota Babu had brought. He gave him a portion on a plate to eat. Munoo's heart went out to him. He answered every little gesture of command with the alacrity with which the little boys in the village used to do things for him. He felt sorry when the chota Babu went away for a walk.

Bibiji began to nag again towards dusk, as if she had been accumulating her breath all the afternoon.

He was grinding spices in a stone mortar with a wooden pestle. He spilt some juice over, on account of the excessive energy which he put into the art of grinding. A storm of anger blew forth.

He did not wash his hands before he handled a saucepan. A hurricane of abuse rained down.

He sat back, tired after doing all the preliminary work for the cooking of the evening meal, and his eyes closed in sleep. A very typhoon burst over his head.

But he was too deeply drowned in the oblivion of sleep to mind being lashed by a furious tongue or being dug in the ribs.

Life in the Babu's house soon resolved itself, for Munoo, into the routine of domestic slavery.

He did not settle down to it easily. The wild bird is not easily caged.

'What am I – Munoo?' he asked himself as he lay wrapped in his blanket, early one morning. 'I am Munoo, Babu Nathoo Ram's servant,' the answer came to his mind.

'Why am I here in this house?' a further question occurred to him. 'Because my uncle brought me here to earn my living,' his mind reflected vaguely, the waves in his brain struggling to flow. 'He could probably get me the job of a chaprasi, like himself, I suppose,' a sudden tide arose and said, 'or a job in someone else's house.'

It did not occur to him to ask himself what he was apart from being a servant, and why he was a servant and Babu Nathoo Ram his master. His identity he took for granted, and the relationship between Babu Nathoo Ram, who wore black boots, and himself, Munoo, who went about barefoot, was to him like sunshine and sunset, inevitable, unquestionable.

Then with curious abruptness he thought of the sweets which the chota Babu invariably brought in the afternoon and of which he gave Munoo a small portion, if Bibiji was not looking. His mouth watered with the memory of the relish of the syrup. The angrezi sweets were more beautiful than the rasgullas and gulab jamans and pairas. But you had to be a Babu or a Sahib to eat them. You had to wear silk clothes like the chota Babu, and a basket cap of flannel. Also boots. He would prefer to have the burra Babu's black boots rather than the chota Babu's brown shoes with the buckles. The latter looked so much like the plain shoes that the southern leatherworkers sold to the peasants in the street. The chota Babu had marvellous clothes in his boxes, silk handkerchiefs and warm woollen suits. Wonderful they were! He would love to touch them. Perhaps when he was big enough to be able to wear those clothes he could ask the chota Babu to give him a shirt and coat for a gift. Had not he already given him a razor blade? He was a generous man, and kind.

He was clever, too. The way he could read the messages of people's hearts and tell what diseases they were suffering from, by means of that machine with rubber tubes, the ends of which he applied to his ears and whose mouth he rested on the chest of a person. He had other machines in velvet boxes. How he would like to handle them, Munoo thought. How he would like to be the chota Babu, a medicine man! He would not even mind being like the burra Babu, an official in the bank, whom all the townsmen saluted. But

So he was disturbed, his consciousness extending from his person to which, with curious naïveté and accidental profundity, it had traced itself, beyond the circle of the home into the town where his master was a slave to someone else.

His ego, conditioned by the laws and customs of the society in which he had been born, the society whose castes and classes and forms had been determined by the self-seeking of the few, of the powerful, sought all the prizes of wealth, power and possession exactly as his superiors sought them.

If only the shimmering waves which struggled to flow along the well-worn grooves in his brain had not ended in the confusion of froth, they might have revealed to him potentialities in his make-up hitherto unknown to him. The bottom would then have been knocked out of his hedonism and he would have discovered the fatuity of his desire to be like his superiors.

But the stories of his ancestors, the stories of his village, the stories of his province, his country, which he had read at school and excelled at remembering, had all been records of the desire for power, the desire for property and the desire for honour of a few chosen men. And, like every child in the world, like most grown-ups even, he had been blinded by the glamour of greatness, the glory and splendour of it, into forgetting that he was condemned by an iniquitous system always to remain small, abject and drab.

The biological expedient, however, which made him want to live, was forcing the multi-coloured cells in his body to reach out instinctively to the space about him, even for a breath of the foul air in his master's dingy little kitchen and for a crust of bread. He was vaguely aware of the need for love in his orphan's body. But he was as yet essentially an ineffectual 'pawn on the chessboard of destiny' such as the village priest had declared all men to be, with perverted ambitions in a world of perverted ideas, and he was to remain a slave until he should come to recognize his instincts.

These people were superior, superior to all the hill people, he thought, though were they superior to the retired Subedar of the village, and Jay Singh's father, the landlord, he wondered? What constituted their superiority, he did not know. They all wore nice clothes, had nice things. That was enough to convince him that they were marvellous, wonderful people. He did not search for causes and effects. He did not know that the superciliousness, the complacency, the assurance, the happiness they radiated was built on the strong foundation of money, that easy, privileged and secure life of theirs; that good health was nourished by the food which money bought.

And thus, thoroughly convinced of his inferiority, accepting his position as a slave, he tried to instil into his mind the notion of his brutishness that his mistress had so often nagged him about. And he promised himself again that he would be a good servant, a perfect model of a servant.

Unfortunately, however, the road to perfection is punctuated by pitfalls, and it was not long before he tripped up and brought the odium of his mistress's wrath upon himself.

It so happened that Mr W. P. England came to tea with Babu Nathoo Ram and family one afternoon.

Mr England was the chief cashier of the Sham Nagar branch of the Imperial Bank of India in whose office Babu Nathoo Ram was a sub-accountant. He was a tall Englishman with an awkward, shuffling gait accentuated by the wooden, angular shape of his feet marching always hesitantly at an angle of forty-five degrees, and with a small, lined, expressionless face, only defined by the thick glasses on his narrow, myopic eyes. He had a rather good-natured smile on his thin lips, and it was that which had led to the tea party.

Babu Nathoo Ram had seen this smile play upon Mr England's lips every morning when the Sahib said 'good morning' to him in response to his salute. There seemed little doubt that it was a kind smile which betokened the kindness of Mr England's heart, exactly as the frown on the face of Robert Horne, Esq., Manager of the Imperial Bank of India, Sham Nagar, betokened a vicious temperament. But then Mr England spoke so few words. The smile might just be a patronizing put-on affair. And it was very important to Babu Nathoo Ram's purpose to know whether it was a genuine smile or an assumed one. For he wanted a recommendation from Mr England to support his application for an increase in salary and promotion to the position of the accountant. He had aspired to this position for a long time now, but he had not been able to attain it because Babu Afzul-ul-Haq occupied it, as he had occupied it for the last twenty years.

Mr England was a new officer. The Babu wanted to get him to write a recommendation before he was influenced by all the other English officers in the club and began to hate all Indians, before the kind smile on his lips became a smile of contempt and derision, or before it became sardonic on account of the weather. So he did not wait till he got to know Mr England better, or till Mr England got to know his work a little more, but he asked him to tea.

It had taken a great deal of courage, of course, and a lot more effort for him to ask Mr England to tea.

At first he had tried several mornings to muster enough courage to say something beyond the usual 'Good morning, Sir.' There seemed to be nothing to make the basis for an exchange of words, not even a file or letter, because they met on arrival at the office before the mail was opened. And, later in the day, there was much too much to say about files for an informal exchange of ideas. Babu Nathoo Ram began to contemplate Mr England's ever-ready smile with a certain exasperation. And he believed more than ever that these Englishmen were very slippery and confounding because they were so reticent, just gaping at you without talking and without letting you talk.

Then someone (it was a barrister friend of Nathoo Ram's) told him that, from his experience in England, he had found that the only way of starting a conversation with an Englishman was by talking to him about the weather.

'Good morning, Sir,' said Babu Nathoo Ram, respectfully every morning, without daring to use the new knowledge.

'Good morning,' mumbled England, always smiling his nice smile, but rather self-conscious, because he saw that the Babu was older than he by at least twenty years, and his reverence seemed rather out of place. Besides, the Babu was a rich man. He had forty thousand rupees' worth of shares in the Allahabad Bank and was surely a trusted ally of the government which owned most of the banks. He certainly was highly thought of and honoured by the English directors of most of the banks. But why did he not live up to his status? Horne was right, he reflected, when he said that these Indians were embarrassingly obsequious. He did not ask, however, why they were obsequious.

Nathoo Ram walked sheepishly behind Mr England in the hall one day, and the Sahib was rather ill at ease as he stepped angularly along in the cool shade cast by the drawn blinds on the windows.

'Fine morning, Sir! Beautiful day!' announced Nathoo Ram suddenly.

Mr England shuffled his feet, hesitated and turned round as if a thunderbolt had struck him. His face was suddenly pale with peevishness. Then he controlled himself and, smiling a sardonic smile, said: 'Yes, of course, very fine! Very beautiful!'

The Babu did not understand the sarcasm implicit in the Sahib's response. He was mightily pleased with himself that he had broken the ice, although he could not muster the courage to say anything more and ask him to tea.

That he did after sitting in the office for whole days, waiting in suspense for the right moment to come. It came when England, seeking to relieve the tension and to put Nathoo Ram at ease, approached the Babu's table one day before going off to lunch.

'How are you, Nathoo Ram?' he asked.

'Fine morning, Sir,' said Nathoo Ram, suddenly looking up from the ledger and springing to attention as he balanced his pen, Babu-like, across his ear.

'Yes, a bit too fine for my taste,' replied England.

'Yes, Sir,' said Nathoo Ram, wondering what to say.

There was an awkward pause in which England looked at the Babu and the Babu looked at England.

'Well, I am going off to lunch,' said the Sahib, 'though I can't eat much in this heat.'

'Sir,' said the Babu, jumping at his chance, 'you must eat Indian food. It's very tasty.' He couldn't utter the words fast enough.

'The Khansamah at the club cooks curry sometimes,' returned England. 'I don't like it much, it is too hot.'

'Sir, my wife cooks very good curries. You must come and taste one of our dishes,' ventured Nathoo Ram, tumbling over his words.

'No, I don't like curries,' said England. 'Thank you very much all the same.' And smiling his charming smile, he made to go. He had realized that he was becoming too familiar with the native, a thing his friends at the club had warned him about.

'Will you come to see my house one day, Sir?' called Nathoo Ram eagerly and with beating heart. 'My wife would be honoured if you would condescend to favour us with the presence of your company at tea, Sir. Mr brother, Sir –'

England had almost moved his head in negation, but he ducked it to drown his confusion.

'Yes, Sir, yes, Sir, today.'

'No,' said England. 'No, perhaps some day.'

After that Nathoo Ram had positively pestered England with his invitations to tea. Every time he met him, morning, noon, afternoon, he requested the favour of Mr England's gracious and benign condescension at tea.

At last England agreed to come, one day, a week hence.

For a week preparations for this party went on in the Babu's household and Munoo had more than his share of the excitement. The carpets were lifted and dusted, and though all the paraphernalia of the Babu's household, pictures, bottles, books, utensils, and children's toys and clothes, lay in their original confusion, a rag was passed over everything to make it neat and respectable.

The news of a Sahib's projected visit to the Babu Nathoo Ram's house had spread all round the town, and in the neighbouring houses, dirty sackcloth curtains were hung up to guard female decorum from the intrusion of foreign eyes.

As Mr England walked up, stupidly dressed for the occasion in a warm, navy blue suit, with Nathoo Ram on one side and Prem Chand, the Babu's doctor brother, on the other, and with Daya Ram, the chaprasi, in full regalia following behind, he felt hot and bothered.

Between mopping his brow with a large silk handkerchief and blushing at the Babu's reiterated gratitude and flattery, England wondered what Nathoo Ram's house was going to be like. Would it be like his father's home in Brixton, a semi-detached house on the Hay Mill estate, which they had furnished on the hire-purchase system with the help of Mr Drage and where he had occupied the maid's room when he was a clerk in the Midland Bank, before he came here and suddenly became a chief cashier? Or would it be like the house of 'Abdul Kerim, the Hindoo', in that Hollywood film called *The Swami's Curse*, with fountains in the hall, around which danced the various wives of the Babu in clinging draperies and glittering ornaments?

The outlook of the flat-roofed hovels jutting into each other on the uprise to which the Babu pointed was rather disconcerting.

'Sahib! Sahib!' a cry went up, and there was a noise of several people rushing behind sackcloth curtains.

'The Muhammadans keep strict purdah, Sir,' informed Babu Nathoo Ram. 'And it is the women of the household of Babu Afzul-ul-Haq, running to hide themselves.' 'Fate is favourable,' the Babu thought, for he had been able to have a dig at his Musalman adversary.

Mr England smiled in a troubled manner as he looked aside.

'Look out!' Dr Prem Chand called. 'Your head!'

Mr England just missed hitting his forehead against the narrow doorway which led beyond the small verandah into the Babu's sitting-room. The pink of his face heightened to purple.

There was hardly any room to stand or to walk in the low-ceilinged, six foot by ten room, especially as both Nathoo Ram and Daya Ram had rushed to get a chair ready for the Sahib to sit upon.

Mr England stood looking round at the junk. He felt as tall as Nelson's column in this crowded atmosphere.

He could not see much, but as he sank into a throne-like chair, he faced the clay image of the elephant god, Ganesha, garlanded with a chain of faded flowers. He thought it a sinister image, something horrible, one of the heathen idols which he had been taught to hate in the Weslyan chapel he had attended with his mother.

'The god of wisdom, worldliness and wealth, Sir,' said Babu Nathoo Ram, defining his words rather pompously, as he knew his illiterate wife was overhearing him talk English to a Sahib, on an equal footing, for once in his life.

'Interesting,' mumbled Mr England.

'I hope to go to England for higher studies, Mr England,' said Dr Prem Chand, more at ease because he was an independent practitioner of medicine and not the Sahib's subordinate like his elder brother.

'Yes, really!' remarked England, brightening at the suggestion of 'home', as all Englishmen in India learn to do.

'I suppose you have a big residence there,' asked Prem Chand, 'and perhaps you could give me some advice about my courses of study.'

'Yes,' said England in reply, blushing to realize that though he had to pose as a big top to these natives, he had no home to speak of, the semi-detached house in Brixton being not yet paid for, and he remembered that he had never been to a university and knew nothing about 'courses of study', except those of Pitman's typewriting and shorthand school in Southampton Row, which he had attended for a season before going to the Midland Bank. He felt he should make a clean breast of it all, as he was really extremely honest. But his compatriots at the club had always exhorted him to show himself off as the son of King George himself if need be. A guilty conscience added its weight of misery to his embarrassment.

'This is a family photograph taken on the occasion of my marriage, Sir,' said Nathoo Ram, lifting a huge, heavily framed picture off its peg and clumsily dropping two others, so that Munoo, who stood in the doorway, staring at the rare sight of the pink man, rushed in to save them.

Mr England looked up with a face not devoid of curiosity.

The Babu brought the picture along and, half apprehensive of the liberties he was taking, planted it on the Sahib's knees. Mr England held it at the sides and strained his eyes almost on to the glass to scrutinize it.

Munoo was drawn by the instinctive desire for contact, which knows no barriers between high and low, to come and stand almost at the Sahib's elbow and join in the contemplation of the picture.

'Go away, you fool,' whispered the Babu, and nudged the boy with his sharp, bony elbow.

Mr England, who was almost settling down, was disturbed. He did not know who Munoo was, but he might be the Babu's son. If so, it was cruel for Nathoo Ram to drive him away like that, though he was glad that the dirtily clad urchin had not come sniffing up to him, for he might be carrying some disease of the skin. All these natives, Horne said, were disease-ridden. And from the number of lepers in the street he seemed to be right.

'The servant boy,' said Nathoo Ram confidently to the Sahib in a contemptuous tone, to justify his rudeness to Munoo.

The Sahib assented by twisting his lips and screwing his eyes into an expression of disgust.

'This is my wife, Sir,' said Nathoo Ram, pointing to a form loaded with clothes and jewellery, which sat in the middle of the group, dangling its legs in a chair and with its face entirely covered by a double veil. Mr England looked eagerly to scan the face in the picture and, not being able to see it, blamed his myopic eyes, as he pretended to appreciate the charm of the Babu's wife by saying: 'Nice, very nice.'

But lifting his hand he saw that it was covered with dust, which lay thickly on the back of the frame, and that his trousers were ruined. He frowned.

'My wife does not observe purdah, but she is very shy,' said the Babu apologetically. 'So she will not come in as is the custom with the women of your country.' In the same breath he switched on again to the picture: 'This is my humble self as the bridegroom, when I was young.'

Mr England saw the form of a heavily turbaned, feebler incarnation of Nathoo Ram, with rings in his ears, garlands round his neck and white English-Indian clothes, as he stood stiffly, caressing the arm of his bride's chair with the left hand and showing a European watch to the world with the right.

Mr England's eyes scanned the wizened forms of dark men in the background of the picture. They then rested on two boys, who lay, reclining their heads against each other and on their elbows, in the manner of the odd members of cricket teams in Victorian photographs.

'Ain – ain – wain – ain – ain – ai – an,' a throaty wail wound its way out of the trumpet of the gramophone which Dr Prem Chand had set in motion.

Munoo rushed up to the door, really to hear the voice from the box sing, but making an excuse of the message that tea was ready. Sheila, who had just returned from school, came in too.

'This is our Indian music, Sir,' said Nathoo Ram proudly; 'a ghazal, sung by Miss Janki Bai of Allahabad. My elder daughter,' he added, pointing to Sheila. Then turning to her he said: 'Come and meet the Sahib.'

The child was shy and stood obstinately in the doorway, smiling awkwardly.

Mr England's confusion knew no bounds. He was perspiring profusely. The noise and commotion created by the 'ain – ain – wai – ain' were unbearable. His ears were used at the best to the exotic zigzag of Charleston or Rumba or his native tunes 'Love is Like a Cigarette', 'Rose Marie, I Love You' and 'I Want to be Happy, But I Can't be Happy Till I Make You Happy Too.' And he felt the children staring at him.

He wished it would all be over soon. He regretted that he had let himself in for it at all.

'Go and get the tea,' said Nathoo Ram to Munoo.

'Yes, Babuji,' said Munoo as he ran back, excited and happy.

He nearly knocked into his uncle Daya Ram, who was coming towards the sitting-room bearing heaps of syrupy Indian sweets and hot maize flour dumplings which Bibiji had been frying in a deep pan of olive oil the whole afternoon.

Bibiji saw Munoo rushing and would have abused him, but she was on her best behaviour today. Only, she gave him a furious look as she pushed some dishes of English pastries from outside the four lines of her kitchen, commanding him to take them to the sitting-room.

Munoo was in high spirits, far too exalted by the pleasure of the Sahib's company in his master's house to be dampened by Bibiji's frowns. He took the dishes over, his mouth watering at the sight of the sweets.

He placed the pastries on the huge writing-table which had been converted for use as a dinner-table. He waited to look at the Sahib. A scowl on the Babu's face sent him back to the kitchen to fetch the tea-tray.

Meanwhile Babu Nathoo Ram had begun to offer food to the Sahib. The Babu took up two dishes in his hands and brought them up to Mr England's nose.

'Sir, this is our famous sweetmeat, gulab jaman by name,' he said, 'and this is called by the name of rasgula. Made from fresh cream, Sir. The aroma of the otto of roses has been cast over them. They were specially made to my order by the confectioner.'

The perfume of the rasgulas and gulab jamans as well as the sight of them made Mr England positively sick. He recoiled from the attack of the syrupy stuff on his senses with a murmur of 'No, thank you.'

'Oh, yes Sir, yes Sir,' urged Babu Nathoo Ram.

If Mr England had been offered a plate and a fork, or a spoon, he might have taken one of the sweets. But he was supposed to pick them up with his hand. That was impossible to the Englishman, who had never picked up even a chicken bone in his fingers to do full justice to it.

'Some pakoras, then,' said the Babu. 'They are a speciality of my wife. Come, Daya Ram.'

43

The peon brought up the dish of the maize flour dumplings. The sharp smell of the oily dark-brown stuff was enough to turn Mr England's liver. He looked at it as if it were poison and said, 'No, no thank you really, I had a late luncheon.'

'Well, if you don't care for Indian sweets, Sir,' said Nathoo Ram in a hurt voice, 'then please eat English-made pastry that I specially ordered from Stiffles. You must, Sir.'

The pastries, too, were thickly coated with sugar and looked forbidding.

'No, thanks, really. I can't eat in this hot weather,' said England, trying to give a plausible excuse.

Now Nathoo Ram was disappointed. If the Sahib did not eat and did not become indebted to him, how could he ever get the recommendation he needed?

'Sir, Sir,' he protested, thrusting the food again under England's nose. 'Do please eat something, just a little bit of a thing.'

'No, thank you very much, Nathoo Ram. Really,' said England, 'I will take a cup of tea and then I must go. I am a very busy man, you know.'

'Sir,' said Nathoo Ram, his under-lip quivering with emotion. 'I had hoped that you would partake of the simple hospitality that I, your humble servant, can extend to you. But you will have tea, tea . . . Tea, oh! Munoo, bring the tea!'

Munoo was hurrying in with the tea-tray. When he heard his master's call he scurried. The tea-tray fell from his hands. All the china lay scattered on the kitchen floor.

Mr England heard the crash and guessed that a disaster had taken place.

Babu Nathoo Ram's heart sank. He had spent five rupees of his well-earned money on the tea party. And it had all gone to waste.

Dr Prem Chand walked deliberately out into the kitchen and cowed Bibiji into a forced restraint, poured the remains of tea and milk into a cup and brought it on a neat saucer, saying coolly with a facetious smile: 'Our servant, Munoo, Mr England, knows that a Japanese teaset only costs one rupee twelve annas. So he does not care how many cups and saucers he breaks.'

Mr England was sweating with the heat. He became pale with embarrassment and fury. His small mouth contracted. He took the cup of tea and sipped it. It was hot, it almost scalded his lips and his tongue.

'I must go now,' he said, and rose from his eminent position on the throne-like chair.

'We are disappointed, Sir,' said Nathoo Ram, apologizing and humble. 'But I and my wife hope you will come again.' And he followed the Sahib sheepishly, as England veered round suddenly and shuffled out on his awkward feet.

'Look out! Your head!' said Dr Prem Chand, warning the Sahib in time before he was again likely to hit the low doorway. 'Good afternoon.'

Mr England smiled, then assumed a stern expression and walked out silently, followed by Babu Nathoo Ram and Daya Ram, past groups of inquisitive men and children.

The tea party had been a fiasco.

Dr Prem Chand fell to. He was going to enjoy the sweets. But his sister-in-law was shouting at Munoo.

'Vay, may you die, may you be broken, may you fade away, you blind one! Do you know what you have done? May the flesh of your dead body rot in hell! With what evil star did you come to this house, that you do everything wrong? That china cost us almost as much money as you earn in a month.'

'That Englishman has no taste,' said Prem Chand, coming in, 'he did not eat a thing.'

'It is all the fault of this eater of his masters,' she cried, pointing to Munoo. 'May he die!'

'How is he responsible for that monkey-faced man's bad taste?' asked Prem Chand. 'And how is he to blame for all this junk in your house which apparently annoyed the Sahib?'

'Don't you encourage this dead one, Prem!' said Bibiji. 'Our house used to be like the houses of the Sahib-logs until this brute came from the hills and spoilt it all. That lovely set of china he has broken, the uncivilized brute!'

'Well now, you get a pair of sun-glasses gratis for every four annas' worth of Japanese goods that you buy in the bazaar,' mocked Prem, 'so we will all have eye-glasses, even you, Bibiji!'

Munoo did not know whether to laugh or to cry. A shock of apprehension had passed through him when he dropped the china, and seized his soul in a knot of fear. He stood dumb. The mockery of the chota Babu stirred the warmth on the surface of his blood. He awakened from his torpor and smiled.

Bibiji sprang from her seat near the kitchen and gave him a sharp, clean slap on the cheek. 'You spoiler of our salt!' she raved. 'You have brought bad luck to our house! You beast! And I have tried hard to correct you –'

'Oh, leave him alone,' said Prem. 'It is not his fault.' And he went towards the boy.

'Don't let me hear you wail, or I will kill you, you stupid fool!' said Babu Nathoo Ram angrily as he came in with tear-filled eyes.

It was not the first time that Munoo succumbed to sleep, stifling his sobs and his cries.

For days he went about work as if he were in a dream. He casually performed his duties, but his heart was not in the job. He wanted to get away from it, and he looked forward to his afternoons off.

On the afternoon of the day which happened to be his half-holiday that week, Bibiji saw him sulking about at work in the morning, and she determined not to let him go. She knew that he went to his uncle during his time off, and she did not want him to report to Daya Ram that he was being ill-treated.

But to Munoo's wish to escape from this atmosphere charged with sharp abuse, unending complaints and incessant bullying was added, that morning, a yearning for the home dishes, the lentils and rice, that his uncle cooked, and of which he gave Munoo a portion on the days on which the boy visited him.

This made him refuse to eat the turnip curry which Bibiji offered him from the remainders on her husband's plate, and announce that he was going to see his uncle.

'Look! The world is darkening with shame!' Bibiji cried to her husband. 'Look! Did you hear? He doesn't like the food he gets here! Heavens! And he wants to go away without scrubbing the utensils or washing up, to eat with his uncle! Now, I will have to slave all day! Gracious! What is the use of such a servant?'

'Why ohe?' said Babuji, twisting his face into an angry contortion. 'Why don't you eat what is given you? Are you the son of a Nabob, that you turn your nose up at turnips? Go now, go and eat rice and dal with your uncle!'

Munoo sneaked away at the barest mention of the word go.

As he descended the hill, memories of the unpleasantnesses he had suffered in that house, the humiliations he had endured, assailed him. He made a brave effort to check his tears, but something inside his belly seemed to send up quivers of self-pity to his face, where they gathered into a cloud of heat which suddenly burst through his eyes.

As he turned the corner of the bank and entered into the passageway leading to his uncle's room in the servants' quarters, he wiped his face with the edge of his tunic and blew his nose by catching it between the thumb and forefinger of his right hand.

Daya Ram lay snoring on the neat bedstead in his small, dark hole, hardly six foot by six, bare except for an earthen oven, some brass utensils and a tin trunk.

Munoo tiptoed in, bent over his uncle's shins, and, catching hold of the big toe of his right foot, shook it to wake him.

'Who is it? What do you want?' snarled Daya Ram, opening his eyes.

'Is there any food left, uncle?' Munoo said.

'What time is this to come to me for food, you illegally begotten?' hissed Daya Ram like a snake, showing his pink tongue. 'Don't you get any food at the house of the Babu?'

'Will you give me some money then, so that I can go and get some food at the cookshop in the bazaar?'

He never had any money himself, because the Babu handed his pay of three rupees to his uncle every month.

'You son of a bitch!' Daya Ram sat up and shouted. 'How can I get you the clothes you want, and shoes, if you spend all the pay money which I am keeping for you?'

'But you haven't got me any clothes,' protested Munoo. 'I am wearing the ragged tunic which Bibiji gave me, and you haven't bought me any shoes.'

'You impertinent little rogue!' raved Daya Ram as he sprang up and collared Munoo. 'So you dare to ask me for accounts, eh, you son of a swine! This is the reward I get for keeping you so long, and for finding you a job! Money! Money, money you want all the time!'

And he shook the boy roughly and struck him blow after blow in the ribs.

'Oh, don't beat me, please don't beat me, uncle,' cried Munoo. 'I only want food.'

'Where were you eating the dung at meal-time then?' shouted

47

Daya Ram. 'Why didn't you come here earlier if you wanted food? And don't they give you any food there?'

'Bibiji kept me working,' the boy sobbed. 'She wouldn't have allowed me to come at all. You don't know how she beats me. You wouldn't beat me if you knew. They had turnips today, and I don't like turnips. I like rice and dal!'

'You liar! You complainer, you swine!' shouted Daya Ram: 'You complain all the time,' fisting the boy against the wall.

'Oh mother! Oh my mother!' Munoo wailed.

The pitiful cries did not seem to have any effect on Daya Ram, however. He had been hardened into cruelty by his love of money, by the fear of poverty and by the sense of inferiority that his job as a peon in the bank gave him. His eyes were bloodshot, his skin taut. He seemed prepared for murder as he gnashed his teeth. He looked hard at the boy. He bawled: 'Tell me the truth, tell me where you have been vagabondizing?'

Munoo had not the heart to speak. He stood weeping.

'Where were you? Answer me!' shouted Daya Ram, coming nearer.

'I was at home,' Munoo sobbed.

'You lie! You cur! You are a rogue!' hissed Daya Ram. 'Don't I know you? Rather than do their work properly you laze about! I will kill you if I find you complaining about them again. You broke their china the other day and showed them up in such a bad light to the Sahib!'

Rushing at the boy, he kicked him again. Then he went on: 'Mischievous and self-willed and obstinate, you imagine yourself hard-working! You have ruined the Babu's prestige before the Sahib! Brought a complaint from the Babu on my head! I was considered a good servant here in the bank till you came. I've had to work hard for my living, and I've built up a reputation here by pleasing my masters. And here you come complaining about the treatment you get at the house of our noble Babuji. You go and stick it, if you value your life, or I will kill you! Leave off that reading habit of yours and lazing, you swine! And now get back and ask Bibiji to give you some food. I have neither sympathy nor food for you!'

And he picked up the boy and threw him out.

*

Munoo came back to walk the path of perfection in the Babu's home.

He turned quickly away from the bank into the street, and then threaded his way aimlessly through the gullies, hiding his swollen, tear-washed face. He could not think for some time.

'Hateful, hateful uncle!' he muttered through his breath. 'Son of a bitch! I hate you!'

And he ground his teeth in fury, as if to put some power into the thoughts of revolt that possessed him.

'I shall go away!' he said to himself. 'I shall just disappear from this place, away from that woman and Daya Ram! Then they will look for me, and have a drum beaten all over the town by the town crier to find me, and I shall not be found. That will serve them right. But I haven't any money. I have nothing. How shall I get food if I go away? And they might catch me and bring me back here again. Then they will beat me more cruelly.'

The sparrows in the gutter of the weavers' lane twittered accusingly at him.

His mind was a blank to all the noise of the gullies: the chatter of women gossiping at their doorsteps, the droning of their spinning wheels, the shrieking of the children as they played blind man's buff in the shade.

He had a queer taste at the root of his tongue, a dissatisfaction, a sickness, a sense of betrayal and the ravenous pang of hunger, all at the same time. He made a wry face as if he were swallowing some unpleasant physic and sped homewards. He walked unconsciously, accepting everything about him.

Bibiji was not at home. So he helped himself to some food and lay down to rest, trying to sleep off his misery. Thoughts raced through his head, wild thoughts, thoughts of revenge soaring up to the pitch of cruelty that had been displayed by his uncle. 'I will flay him alive,' he said to himself, 'I will tear him to bits while he is asleep. I will murder him.' But the cool earth seemed to sponge his brain and suck up his strength, till he fell asleep. Then he was like a corpse, incapable of anything, unruffled on the surface even though his soul bubbled inside him.

In a few days, however, he had recovered his old insouciance, his vigour, his zest for life, his fire – the fire that tingled in the cells of his body at all the sights and sounds about him.

'How is Your Holiness?' he mockingly addressed Varma, the Brahmin servant of the sub-judge, who monopolized the use of the communal pump because he was older than all the other servant boys in the neighbourhood.

He was feeling in a great good humour that afternoon because he had not been abused much by Bibiji during the morning.

'Don't bark, you dirty hill man,' said Varma, with a frown on his coarse, bestial face, as he swaggered beneath the cloak of his saintliness and strength. 'How does your mistress treat you now? Does she still abuse you, or does she give you the teats of her beautiful hard breasts to suck for the milk of human kindness?'

'Shut up,' said Munoo, blushing and suddenly indignant. 'Are you not ashamed of yourself talking like that? I never say anything to you about your mistress!' And he felt furious to think that he had cut a joke with Varma.

'Why do you flare up so now?' said Varma. 'That shows she has given you her favours and endeared herself to you! I see! That is why she abuses you such a lot and you bear her abuse! What is she like under her dhoti? Like this?' And he made a vulgar sign with his fingers.

'Oh, shut up!' cried Munoo. 'And get away. I want to fill my pitcher with water. You have been usurping the pump for hours.'

'Oh, look at this hill man,' said Varma to Lehnu, another servant of the neighbourhood about as old as himself and a thin-lipped, sharp-nosed Brahmin, who had come down in life like his friend. 'He objects to my praise of his mistress' breasts and her —. And she ill-treats him all day. Don't you think he is in love with her?'

'Let me get my water,' said Munoo, and came up to the pump.

'Give him one, Varma,' said Lehnu. 'He seems to be very proud of his strength. I know where he gets his power. He steals money from his mistress's allowances for shopping. I saw him eating sweets in the shop of Bhagu the other day.'

'That is a lie,' said Munoo, outraged by the aspersions that they were casting on him. 'Let me get the water and go.'

'And now you are in a hurry suddenly,' said Lehnu. 'After calling me a liar. Give him one, Varma.'

Varma pushed Munoo aside as he was looking towards Lehnu, impotent with rage. The boy slipped on the green grease that had mixed with the moss on the sides of the enclosure in which the pump stood. He recovered himself, however, immediately and came and drew himself to his full height next to Varma's naked, light-brown body. His eyes glistened with the fire of retaliation.

'Strike me now when I am looking,' he roared. 'You sly dog of a Brahmin.'

'Look at the airs he gives himself!' said Varma, slinking away and guarding the pump.

'Is this your father's pump that you reserve it and don't let anyone else use it for hours?' Munoo shouted.

'I will teach him the lesson of his life,' said Lehnu, coming forward and wresting at Munoo's arm to drag him away.

Varma kicked him from behind.

Munoo shook away from Lehnu's grasp and sprang like a tiger upon Varma. He caught hold of his enemy's body round the waist and would have flung it over the precipice into the ditch below, but at the crucial moment the spectre of the death he would be inflicting flashed across his mind, and he relaxed his hold.

Varma slipped out of Munoo's grasp and struck him a resounding slap on his face. Lehnu came and, placing his right leg across Munoo, flung him head downwards on the brick floor.

Munoo rallied back to his feet. But now Varma held a log of wood with which he had been beating clothes clean. And Lehnu towered over him menacingly.

With a ferocity to which the double danger in front of him seemed to add a wild fire, he fell upon Varma and, catching hold of him by the waist, lifted him over his shoulders. Then he carried him about twenty yards away from the pump and flung him guardedly on to the earth.

Lehnu had disappeared when he returned.

He applied the narrow mouth of his brass pitcher to the pump and heard the water fall gurgling into its drum-like belly. He had forgotten all about this furious activity, regarding it as a sort of wrestling match to which no ill will was attached. And he stood unconscious.

Varma tiptoed up behind him and struck him with the log of wood. Munoo turned round and warded off the blow by lifting his biceps over his shoulders. Varma struck again, and this time the blow fell aslant on Munoo's forehead. Munoo sought to catch hold of the log in his hands. But Varma began to wave the wood aimlessly. Each time it fell on Munoo's palm it slipped out. He made a sudden dart at Varma's neck, caught hold of the tuft of hair that ritualistically swayed on top of the Brahmin's head and tugged at it to make him relax his hold of the log. Then he wrested it out of Varma's hand and threw it away into the ditch.

He could hear his pitcher overflowing with water now. He disengaged himself from Varma and rushed towards the verandah of the house, his face covered with blood.

'Go and hide yourself in your mistress' —,' Varma was shouting behind him.

'You eater of your masters!' greeted Bibiji when she saw him rushing in through the kitchen door. 'What have you done? Whom have you been quarrelling with?'

'With no one,' Munoo said as he deposited the brass pitcher in the kitchen. He went past her to the oven. He picked up a handful of ashes and applied it to his forehead, from which the blood was spurting.

'Vay! Vay! Show me where you have been hurt!' she shouted, very moved. 'Look at all that blood trickling down your face! Is it that lecher Varma who has beaten you? Haven't I asked you not to associate with him? He talks bad things and you like listening to him! Now enjoy the fruits of your friendship with such as he!'

'It is nothing! It is nothing! It is only a small bruise!' Munoo said, capering away.

'Look at him! Look at him!' said Bibiji, going into the sitting-room, where her brother-in-law, the chota Babu, was ironing his collars. 'Look!' she cried. 'He has been quarrelling and is wounded on the head!'

'Come here, ohe Mundu!' shouted the chota Babu.

'Yes, Babuji,' answered Munoo, pale and rather dazed, but completely unconcerned about his wound.

'Come and show me your head,' said the doctor.

'It is all right, Babuji,' replied Munoo casually 'I have treated it with ashes. It will be all right.'

He was convinced that the treatment of wounds with earth or ashes which the village barber recommended was perfect.

'Come here, you fool,' shouted the doctor, laughing. 'The wound will become septic with those filthy ashes. Come and show it to me.'

Munoo submitted to the diagnosis.

The doctor found that it was a dangerous cut, reaching almost to the skull. He lit a primus stove to get some hot water ready. Then he washed the wound and dressed it.

Munoo had been exerting his imagination a little too intently over the stove which smelt of paraffin and the cloth which smelt of medicine. So he felt dizzy.

The doctor laid him to rest in his corner of the kitchen.

As the forgetfulness of sleep crept up to his eyes and the pain weighed down his eyelids, Munoo heard Bibiji shouting, not at him, this time, but at Varma and his employers:

'Eaters of their masters! They have raised their heads to the skies! They think that just because they have prestige in this world they can do anything! We may not be getting as much pay as they do, but we are as good as they are, any day! If they are big people they must be big in their own house, we are in ours . . .'

The judge's wife had come out and was abusing Bibiji: 'These low Babus are getting so uppish. Let my husband come and we will show you what it is to insult your superiors! Dogs! Pigs! They are getting so proud just because they have an uncouth boy from the hills come to be their servant!'

The words of his mistress' abuse now fell weak and distant in the troubled sleep to which Munoo had succumbed. There was only the soundless speech of a rippling breath as it travelled gently, like a heartbeat, through his dilating nostrils, and which flowed back with the answer that there was yet life in his body.

During the days of his confinement to his corner in the kitchen, Munoo got scant attention from Bibiji, but the chota Babu regularly dressed his wound in the morning while Sheila looked on silently in her curious child's way and sympathized.

Munoo had suffered acute pain when the first flush of wild heat had left his body and the bruise called up all the blood in his veins. A fever had possessed him and he wept bitterly and moaned, his moans rising to a screaming crescendo of pain.

Then he was in a delirium. Everything seemed to go dark as the sky at night, except a few bright stars of thought which glittered in the walled-in darkness. And, all the time, there was the roaring of space in his eardrums. He quivered as he lay huddled in the corner.

53

He could not feel. His body was numb to all emotion and time seemed frozen into a never-ending moment.

He had sweated profusely with some medicine that the doctor gave him. After that, in the depths of his breast, behind the emptiness, he was conscious of the flow of his sub-human emotions. Later his brain grappled with the things around him as it had done before his illness.

But as he became aware he felt as if he had emerged from centuries of forgetfulness, like a wave which comes rippling against the tide, shivering against contending waves, fading backwards, breaking, reforming and thrusting its steel-grey head onwards.

The dawn of new life was like a light which illumined the passages of his career in this home. He recalled the advice his uncle had given him when he arrived here. He felt his mind trace itself back to the insecurity he had experienced then. He felt shades of the emotions which had possessed him at odd times. His uncle had minimized the difficulties of the job and glossed things over with vague promises. How difficult he had found things. He had never been taught the first thing about housework. And his mistress had raged all the time. The flaming anger which she had burst into when he dropped the china on the day the Sahib came. The chota Babu was the only kind person in this house. How he laughed over everything!

His uncle, he faintly remembered, had come to see him recently. But he hated his uncle. He hated everyone except the chota Babu and, perhaps, Sheila. She was nice, though elusive. The way she mocked at him! 'Come, ohe monkey, come and eat your food.' That was nice and familiar. He liked her for that. He also liked to look at her. The picture of her as she came out of the bath after her mother had subjected her to forcible ablutions came before his mind: a tracing of the outline of her figure behind the poor concealment of her wet muslin dhoti, which stuck to her limbs, a silhouette of pale bronze, with a delicate light on her regular, mobile features, a light which seemed to burst into a merry laugh and to cast a halo around her sometimes active, sometimes somnolent body. He had been told in his childhood to regard every woman as a mother or sister. He called the apparition of Sheila in his mind 'sister'. But as it recurred again and again and made him want to play with her he forgot to label it 'sister'. Only he bent his head with shame every time he saw her, either really or in imagination, in the same way in which he had bent his head in early spring at the ripening fruit in someone else's garden in his village, with the faint tinge of a hungry smile on his dark lips. The half-conscious sigh of tenderness that trembled upon his lips was smothered by another thought, another desire, arising from the anticipation of the hopelessness of his love. If only he had money, if only the Babu did not give the pay which was due to him to his uncle, Daya Ram, he would have saved the money and run away to become a hawker of sweetmeats, like the boy who sat outside Sheila's school and earned a rupee a day. 'Money is everything,' his uncle had said on the day of his journey to town. 'Money is, indeed, everything,' Munoo thought. And his mind dwelt for the first time on the difference between himself, the poor boy, and his masters, the rich people, between all the poor people in his village and Jay Singh's father, the landlord.

He saw the shrivelled-up skeleton of old Gangu, the seventy-years-old grandfather of his school friend, little Bishan, who worked as a labourer on the fields of anyone who could employ him. He recalled the lean face of Bishambar's mother, who went charring in the house of the landlord. He remembered, vaguely, the hollow eyes of his own father looking down at him tenderly before he 'fell asleep for the last time'. He could, even now, feel the warmth of his mother's lap as he had lain in it while she moved the mill-stone round and round, round and round, till she had languished and expired. How empty he felt without that warmth now, as if that warmth were a necessary clothing for his body. But there were so many people, so many poor people and only one or two rich people in his village. He wondered whether all those poor people would die like his parents and leave a gap in his belly as the death of his father and mother had done. In the town, of course, there seemed many more rich people than poor people. But then, it occurred to him, there were hundreds of villages for one town, and if there were as many poor people in all the villages as there were in his, surely there were many more poor people in the world than rich.

Whether there were more rich or more poor people, however, there seemed to be only two kinds of people in the world. Caste did not matter. 'I am a Kshatriya and I am poor, and Varma, a Brahmin, is a servant boy, a menial, because he is poor. No, caste does

55

not matter. The Babus are like the Sahib-logs, and all servants look alike: there must only be two kinds of people in the world, the rich and the poor.'

The necessity of the moment put an end to this naïve wonderment. He was now lighting a fire in the oven by blowing at the smoke where the wood fuel was arranged between two bricks. And the wistful light in his eyes was dimmed by the spurts of fumes that rose from the stubborn sticks. His eyes began to smart. He screwed them up and pressed the water out of them. His brooding soul became full of a vague and sullen resentment. He could have cried. His will seemed to have been shattered by his illness.

But though his will was broken, with the gathering of strength in his body Munoo again entered the busy round of scrubbing utensils, peeling vegetables, sweeping floors, making beds, serving food and generally doing everything that the caprice of his mistress imposed on him. And, with this return to activity, his physical body exuded the continual warmth, the living vitality that reached out in a wild frenzy of movement to any and every feeling and object. He laughed, sang, danced, shouted, leaped, somersaulted, with the irrepressible impetuosity of life itself, sweeping aside the barriers that separated him from his superiors by the utter humanness of his impulses, by the sheer wantonness of his unconscious life force.

It was this natural impishness of his which, unschooled by all the rigours of moralizing and abuse to which he had been subjected, unchecked even by the physical hurt he had suffered, was always bringing him into trouble.

It brought him into immediate disgrace.

He heard Sheila and her girlfriends come into the sitting-room from school one afternoon, as he sat peeling potatoes in the kitchen. His mistress was away from home, gossiping with the wives of the Babus in the neighbourhood. He hurried through his task, thinking he would go and play with them.

As he was washing his hands he heard the voice from the box trailing out. Here was his opportunity, he thought. He could go and perform his monkey dance and amuse the children into allowing him to play with them as, of late, under Bibiji's advice, they had refused to do.

He burst into the sitting-room and falling on all fours began to caper round, frightening the girls and dispersing them, as they were in the midst of a classical ballet which they had learnt at school.

'Oh, go away,' cried Kausalya timidly.

'We don't want you to play with us,' said Sheila. 'Mother said we are not to play with you.'

She really liked him and was amused by his funny dance. She wanted him to play with her, but her mother's advice had sunk into her and set up an artificial barrier. She liked to touch him. She came towards him and catching him by the ear dragged him about.

He let her pull his ear like that.

All the little girls screamed with laughter.

Sheila pulled hard at his ear and he turned round and sprang upon her, snarling and gnashing his teeth as if he were a real monkey.

Before he knew what he had done he had bitten her on the cheek.

'Mother! Oh, Mother!' Sheila cried. Her mother did not hear.

Kausalya went and called her.

'Ni, Mother of Sheila! Ni, Mother of Sheila! Come and look what that brute of a hill boy has done to your daughter.'

Bibiji came rushing.

At the sight of her daughter caressing her cheek her face went livid with anger.

'Show me,' she cried, 'Show me your face, my child.'

The ivory flesh was blue where Munoo had bitten it.

'I was only playing, Bibiji,' said Munoo, anticipating a storm and seeking in vain to avert it.

'Vay, you eater of your masters! May you die! May the vessel of your life never float in the sea of existence!' the tornado of abuse burst. 'May you never rest in peace, neither you, nor your antecedents! That you should attack the honour of my child! Only a little child, too! You lustful young bull from the hills! How did we know we were taking on a rogue and a scoundrel! Let the Babuji come home! You ought to be handed over to the police! Look! Look at my child! Had you no shame! No respect! You spoiler of my salt! Didn't I ask you to leave my children alone and not to play with them! What is your status that you should mix with the children of your superiors! How did we know we were taking on a snake in our house, who would turn treacherous after we had fed him with milk! Let that uncle of yours, Daya Ram, come! You disobedient wretch! Didn't I tell you that my children are not your class! They are the children of a big Babu! You, you were born I don't know on what

57

rubbish heap! Think of our reputation! Our prestige! We looked after you when you broke your skull playing with the Brahmin boy! I was sorry for you! Now we will have to hand you over to the police! . . .'

'What has happened? What is the matter?' said Babu Nathoo Ram coming in with his head bent, his chest stooping, his face contorted into a mixed expression of fatigue and humility.

'What has happened? What is the matter?' cried Bibiji. 'Everything is the matter! This eater of his masters, may he die, may he burn in hell, may . . .'

'Oh, but what is the matter? What is it?' said the Babu, irritated and indignant.

'I am telling you, my heart is burning! This spoiler of our salt has bitten Sheila on the cheek! Has not the wicked age come! This boy! He is hardly yet born! And he attacks the honour of his master's child! Heavens!'

'Why, oh you illegally begotten!' screamed the Babu, twisting his eyebrows in line with the furrows on his forehead and showing his teeth up to the gums. 'What have you got to say to this?'

Munoo stood, his head bent, his face flushed, his heart throbbing. He did not answer.

'Look, people, the darkness has enveloped the world! Look! . . .' Bibiji was beginning again.

Babu Nathoo Ram advanced with a flourish of his hand to still his wife and to slap the boy.

'Why, ohe swine! Why don't you answer me?'

'Babuji, I was only playing,' Munoo said, looking up at his master furtively, nervously.

'Playing, oh you were playing!' the Babu ground the words in his mouth. 'You son of a dog!'

And he slapped Munoo on the cheek with his thin, bony hand and kicked him with the shiny black boots, the boots which had been the dream of Munoo's life . . .

'Forgive me, Babuji, forgive me!' shrilled Munoo, tottering on the floor.

'Forgive you!' said Nathoo Ram. 'Yes, I will forgive you properly, you dirty dog!'

And kicking the boy again, ferociously, he made towards the corner where a thick stick lay.

The boy's soul surged up in rebellion and hate, a hate of which he had not thought himself capable. He was startled. But he dared not revolt.

'Oh Babuji, forgive me, forgive, forgive please!' he screamed and squirmed, grovelling on the ground.

'Yes, I will forgive you!' the Babu hissed as he came sweating and struck him blow after blow.

Munoo writhed with pain and groaned.

'Oh Babuji, forgive, forgive, only forgive!' he called.

'You son of a dog!' said the Babu, raising his stick again with a hard glint in his eyes.

'Leave him now, the ungrateful wretch!' said Bibiji.

'Oh forgive, oh forgive, only forgive!' Munoo moaned in the gathering darkness.

A whipped dog hides in a corner, a whipped human seeks escape.

Munoo slipped out of the Babu's house in the twilight, immediately after the family had withdrawn into the kitchen and left him in disgrace. He ran down the hill through the avenue of kikar trees, past the bank, past the big houses whose ornamentation indicated wealth, into the large and well-frequented bazaar. The huddled confusion of big shops and small shops was illuminated into grotesque shapes by the electric lamps and oil lamps and by the jets of small cotton wicks in earthen pots. The glare of the lamps disturbed his tear-filled eyes. He sought relief in occasional peeps down intersecting lanes. But there were much more disturbing lights in the eyes of the crowds that sauntered to and fro. He avoided looking them straight in the face. So he diverted his attention to their bodies, as they tossed their arms aloft, talked loudly, moved their heads wildly and jerked about in a frenzy of extravagant gestures. He longed for silence, he longed for darkness to conceal him. He wanted to get away from this riot of human beings with their vermilion turbans, white and black caps, rustling red silks and fawn-coloured muslins which jostled against each other. He wanted to drown in some pit of oblivion where he could forget, forget the humiliating memory of the beating he had suffered. He did not want anyone to recognize him. He hurried through the streets, taking long steps and short capers, and then actually ran. The sweat poured down his body.

He emerged into a highway flanked by small booths, shadowed by ragged jute cloth awnings with big rents, and a few closed shops lost in the blackest shadows.

Beyond, a dense darkness masked an arched entry to a courtyard in which, at odd spaces, little piles of wood fuel burnt the bodies of the dead. Here all was quiet, all motionless. Munoo whispered in the terror of the silence to reassure himself.

A couple of prowling dogs rooted amid the garbage in a gutter, making him jump. The shrill whistle of an engine in the railway yard pulled at his heart.

He had reached the rear end of the railway godown.

He ran like mad by the wall of the cremation ground which bordered the yard. He scraped through the iron railings in a positive horror of being pursued either by a ghost or by one of the night watchmen. He was soaked in sweat, but he did not care.

He was now in the station compound.

He threaded his way through the network of railway lines, which seemed to carry the message of swift death under the monstrous black engines. He panted for breath.

The red and green signal lamps drew him on.

Once he stumbled over some wires and fell on his palms on the railings. He felt he would be instantaneously killed, though the nearest shunting engine was two hundred yards away and there were no trucks near.

Then, however, the distant whistle of the shunting engine made his body jump. He rushed headlong towards a long row of carriages which stood almost indistinguishable from the darkness, except where black pits of emptiness yawned squarely from their sides. He scrambled up the thick wooden planks that served as footrests. But the reflection of a moving green and red lamp in the hands of some invisible man started a panic in his soul. He fell and muttered a curse. Luckily the light walked away.

He got up and jumped into the yawning window of the door like a tiger leaping into the darkness of a cave for fear of some silent hunter.

He had fallen on his side on a hard bunk. A shooting pain went up from his ribs to his head. He felt dizzy with the ache, with the heat of the running and the stuffiness of the compartment.

He sank to the floor, nursing his side and wiping the sweat off his face with his sleeve.

He had never felt so alone, so intensely alone, as during the suspended moments of his descent into this inferno. But as he lay in the tense emptiness, opening his thick tunic and his dhoti to show his bare body to the atmosphere in a vain attempt to dry the clammy sweat, he heard a beetle whining in the distance. The atmosphere of the carriage was grim.

Then, suddenly, he heard the eager feet of hordes of men rushing, stamping into the compartment, and the heavy thud of loads of baggage falling all around him. He dragged his body to safety, deeper into the space under the bunk, and rested his face on the floor to soothe the white fumes of heat.

The noise round him became more significant. There were shouts of 'Where are you, Ala Dad Khan?' 'Oh what has happened to you, Devi Singh?' 'Lalla Churanji Lall, have you got a seat?'

Munoo's heart beat to an easier rhythm. He raised his ears to listen and felt his cheek coated with the dust. The sweat soaked his body. His veins seemed to have swelled. He felt like a mass of lead.

The train started. He could now breathe the foul air of other people's breath, if not the fresh breeze which was coming in from the fields.

Later, he breathed the pure air.

He did not know where the train was going, but he was thankful to be in the moving thing.

III

'Hoon ... hoon,' moaned Seth Prabh Dyal, as he strained to drag his bundle from under the bunk of a third-class carriage in the slow train which jerkily ran from Sham Nagar to Daulatpur.

The Seth, a broad-shouldered, tall, gaunt man from Kangra, who seemed more a soldier than a business man, was half asleep. He had sat through the night in an awkward, cramped position on the wooden boards in the packed compartment, and was getting ready to disembark long before the train was anywhere near its destination.

He blew a mouthful of heavy breath as he struggled to gather his luggage from under the bunk where he had placed it, and mopped his brow to wipe off the sweat.

'Hoon – an – haan ...' he heaved again. The bundle seemed heavy as lead, though it was soft to the touch and slippery.

'Hoooo ... haa,' he now dragged, willing more power into his limbs, and drew, half in fear, half in wonder, the sleeping body of Munoo from where it had lain all night buried amid the congestion of trunks, wooden boxes, rolled-up bedding, and bundles of all kinds, from dislocated bedsteads wound in their hemp mattresses to shapeless mounds of foodstuffs, clothing and knick-knacks bound in sheets of cotton, roughly knotted on the top.

'Ram re Ram!' the Seth exclaimed, reverently, but with a broad grin on his pale, brave face, adorned with a well-groomed black moustache.

'What occasion is there for such hilarity early in the morning!' muttered Ganpat, the Seth's young partner in business, with a dark-brown, goat-like face, hollow-cheeked and pinched, as he lay sprawled on some sacks of merchandise in a vain effort to sleep.

'La hol wallah!' shouted a Muhammadan peasant as he gazed at Munoo, who now lay curled up at Prabh Dyal's feet. 'Who could this be? The son of Elbis!'

'Wah Guru! Wah Guru!' whispered a Sikh peasant in consternation. 'Strange are the ways of the Wah Guru!'

'Is he alive or dead?' a woman strained to know as she crouched on the floor, holding the teat of her breast to give suck to the child in her arms.

Other passengers in the compartment half opened their eyes through the dawn and, dazed with wonder at so uncanny a spectacle, began to ask: 'Who is it? Where does he come from?'

Munoo could not speak. He was terror-stricken.

When Prabh Dyal fished him out he was in a nightmare, in which elephantine giants were trampling on his body and weird two-horned devils were lashing him with fury.

'Strange are the ways of God indeed!' said Prabh Dyal, more to himself than to anyone else. 'He is a very auspicious find. He seems to be from the hills.'

'You should be happy now,' said Ganpat, mocking. 'Here is a son for you, ready-made and complete. And you can forget all about the herbs that you were going to fetch for your wife – or yourself, for I suspect,' he added grimly, 'that you want medicine for yourself. It is you who are impotent, and not your wife who is barren!'

'What is your name? Where do you come from? Whose child are you?' asked Prabh Dyal in the hill man's accent that he had not forgotten, though he had left home early and lived in the city of Daulatpur, working his way up from a coolie in the streets to the proprietorship of a pickle-making and essence-brewing factory.

'I was called Munoo at Bilaspur, Mundu at Sham Nagar,' Munoo began, as if the accent of the hills had suddenly released his speech.

'My father died and then my mother died too. My uncle, Daya Ram, who is a chaprasi in the office of the Bank of Sham Nagar, got me a job as a servant in the house of a Babu. Yesterday the Babu beat me and I have run away . . .'

At this he was possessed by a mixture of fear and self-pity, and his face twisted against his will, and he began to cry. Then he was ashamed of his tears and he hid his eyes behind the rubbings of his right fist.

'He is *bithot tikkus*!' said a young Hindu student, who affected an English accent both to impress the illiterate peasants and to live up to his strange conglomeration of English and Indian clothes – a faded, spotted necktie, a velvet waistcoat, a pair of khaki shorts and a most flamboyant turban.

'We had better take him with us,' said Prabh to his partner.

'We don't know who he is,' replied Ganpat. 'He may be a rogue, a thief. But of course, we need another boy at the works to help Tulsi, Maharaj and Bonga, to run errands and do odd jobs. And, it seems, he will be glad enough to have the food, and we need not pay him.'

'Will you come with us, ohe Munoo?' asked Prabha, ignoring his partner's advice and gently stroking the boy's dark hair, which grew long on all sides and shadowed his wheat-coloured face. 'Will you come and live with us? I am from Hamirpur, near Bilaspur, so we will look after you.'

Munoo moved his head up and down to signify assent, but did not speak as he hovered on the edge of a doubt. For he had not thought about what he was going to do since he had escaped, having been too occupied by the fear of being caught and taken back.

The Seth Prabh Dyal patted the boy on his back and said: 'Come, come now, be a brave lad. Wipe your eyes. We will take care of you. Look, we are almost nearing Daulatpur!' He made room for the boy on the bunk by withdrawing his left leg and squeezing him in the space thus vacated.

He felt very tender towards the boy. He had suddenly recognized a kinship with him, the affinity his soul felt for his unborn son. Only he tried to make himself believe that it might be possible to regard this completely strange boy as a son. He tried to imagine what his parents were. 'They must have been poor,' he thought, 'but then, all hill folk are poor.' He recalled the images of his own father and mother, who had died at Hamirpur during his absence in the city of Daulatpur: his earnings as a coolie had not been enough to procure them all rice twice a day. He wished they were alive now and could enjoy the comfortable income the factory brought in. He heaved a sigh to forget the impossible. 'This boy's parents', he reflected, 'died before he became a wage-earner. He is not as guilty as I.' But the boy was like him really. He would probably feel the same about his parents. It was always like that except for a rich man's son like Ganpat, whose father was a successful broker and had given him money, even when Ganpat had disgraced the family by gambling, drinking and whoring. 'Strange', Prabha wondered, 'that a youth like Ganpat who had everything should have wasted his time, while I myself have pined for knowledge and have never had the chance of acquiring it. And this boy, I wonder whether he can read and write . . .'

'Did you go to school, ohe Munoo?' he asked gently, turning round.

'Yes, I was in the fifth class when my uncle brought me to earn my living in town.'

'He will be able to do accounts for you,' mocked Ganpat, waking from a doze.

'Yes,' Prabha said, taking up the suggestion. 'We will make him our clerk.'

'Don't puff the boy up from the very start,' remarked Ganpat with bitter malice. 'The seducer of his daughter! He won't rest his feet on earth, what with your desire to adopt him as a son and to give him the status of a Munshi. You hardly know yet who he is. He is probably a thief, the runaway scamp!'

Prabha smiled sheepishly, as if he were afraid of his partner. But he could not help being naturally paternal to the boy.

The train was speeding through the outskirts of Daulatpur. Munoo was staring out of the window. The golden domes of a temple flashed past his eyes on a background of broad-leaved banana trees. He inclined towards the window and traced the naked forms of men, some dragging water from a well and pouring it over their heads, some rubbing each other's bodies with oil, others wrestling on a pitch. But the scene passed before he had taken it in completely. He prepared himself to take in the next sight: a mosque with four minarets from which a green-turbaned, white-robed figure, whom he presumed to be a mullah, was bawling out the call to prayers. His eyes sped past the scores of flat-roofed houses and rows of stands and stalls at a crossing where, beyond a blue-uniformed signalman who waved a green flag to the train, crowds of quick-moving city folk were already busy buying and selling. Then Munoo's rudimentary stare travelled with the motor cars and lorries that moved, leaving clouds of dust behind them, along a road parallel to the railway. The smoke of a factory chimney on the back wall of which was written in huge Hindustani letters 'Soda Water Works' lured him beyond the neighbouring tanks of the 'Burma Oil Company' to the heavens, where, unlike anything he had seen before, unlike anything he had ever imagined, flew a droning bird, a queer steel bird with straight wings, leaving a streamline of smoke in its trail across the even blue sky. Retracing their course to the earth, his eyes now surveyed miles and miles of the houses of Daulatpur city and, as if overpowered by the vast magnitude of this amorphous world, they turned to see the inmost thoughts in his breast. There was only a curious flutter of excitement in his heart, like the thrill of fear and happiness which had filled him when he first laid eyes on Sham Nagar – the fear of the unknown in his bowels and the stirring of hope for a better life in the new world he was entering.

A ragged canvas cloth covered the skeleton of the high bamboo cart in which Munoo sat sandwiched between Ganpat and Prabha and four other men on the way home from the station. So he missed the bazaars of Daulatpur. All that he saw was the few shops at the entrance to Cat Killers' Lane outside which the yekka stopped, and the lane itself, a narrow, sordid little gully, chockful of rubbish which festered in the shade by the congested gutters, bordered by tall, three-storied houses.

He felt strange and awkward as he walked behind Prabha and Ganpat past the half-naked women who sat on open-fronted platforms making dishes and pots of dried leaves, which the pure Hindus use instead of utensils on ceremonial feasts and in catering food for large parties. By the look of them, these women were all from the hills: wives of coolies, they supplemented meagre incomes by a little domestic industry. He was reassured when they greeted his benefactors in the language of the hills, saying, 'Jay deva Sethji. Have you come back happy and well? Is everyone well at home?' And Prabha replied by joining his hands and saying: 'I fall at your feet.'

He entered through the huge doorway of a big house into a courtyard flanked by small, dark rooms, outside which were more hill women engaged in making leaf pots. Prabha and Ganpat were immediately surrounded by old women and young girls, who greeted them cordially and asked them what gifts they had brought from the hills.

Munoo was embarrassed when Prabha smilingly pointed him out as the only gift he had brought.

As they went up ten flights of wide steps to a huge room which looked down on the compound, Munoo faced a slight, modest woman, whose eyes lit up with a tender, gambolling light, and who, he presumed, was Prabha's wife. She was rather pale and reticent, but the wonderful eagerness with which she came up to Munoo and without asking who he was, took him in her arms and patted him on his forehead, at once put him at ease with her, and made him realize, what we always realize in one subtle moment, the living warmth that is going to endear us to a person.

'I fall at your feet, sister-in-law,' said Ganpat with a sneer of mockery.

'May you live,' answered Parbati gracefully, and continued in a bantering manner, 'Didn't you get a pretty hill woman for a wife, then?'

'No,' he replied sardonically, 'but I have brought you a ready-made son.'

'Yes,' she said, hugging Munoo, and dropped the conversation. And then she addressed her husband: 'I am just getting the meal

66

ready. Will you take your bath so that you can rest afterwards and sleep off the fatigue of the journey?'

'All right,' said Prabha, affectionate but undemonstrative, in true Indian convention. And, drawing a hemp bedstead from where it stood leaning by a wall, he flung his bundles on it and asked Munoo to sit down.

Munoo contemplated the contrast of the cool shade of the tall room and the blazing sunshine in the courtyard outside. He wiped the sweat off his face and wondered where the factory was.

His thoughts were disturbed by the tumbler of sherbet which his mistress handed him.

And then Prabha led him to a slab of stone in the corner to bathe.

The meal followed. There was rice, both plain and sweet, and dal and vegetables, tamarind pickle, all hill dishes which he had missed in the Babu's home, and a few city ones, four dumplings mixed with curds and kara parshad. It was the most sumptuous meal he had eaten since the feast on the death anniversary of his father and mother, which his aunt had given three months before he left the hills.

His stomach was full, his body cool and he had hardly laid down on the charpai when he fell asleep.

When he awoke it was afternoon.

'Go down there,' said Prabha, who sat smoking a hubble-bubble with a coconut shell bottom, 'and look at the factory. There is the entrance to it. Somebody will lift you down over the well.'

Munoo walked up to a small window in a corner of the room and looked down. He stood hesitant. It seemed so awkward and danger-ous to descend into the strange, dark, airless outhouse of the factory, which sank like a pit into the bowels of the earth, among the tall surrounding houses in the heart of the town. The window was precariously perched on the side of a well. And Munoo was afraid of falling into the well.

But he stood looking on with the naïve enthusiasm characteristic of him, excusing the unwholesome outlook of the place by recalling the good fortune he had had since he was picked up by Prabha in the train, and the hospitality he had received from him.

Under the thick shade of corrugated-iron sheets he could see the mouths of two black caverns opening out into a narrow yard. On one side were three ovens topped by huge steaming cauldrons. On another side, in a niche under stacks of wood fuel, stood a long wooden platform with a greasy iron safe, some ochre-coloured account books, a papier-mâché inkstand and a bottle of black ink. Close by the ovens and the well stood huge barrels, some containing copper flasks, others full of soaking aulas and arirs and ginger. A narrow passageway, a yard wide, led to a small door which opened into an alley of which the factory was the dead end.

There was something nauseating in the touch of the man who lifted him from the window over the well into the factory. He was a massive, shapeless man with a thick animal face, of which each feature was hard muscle. He had big sodden hands and feet, on which corns had formed and the veins stood out swollen and fat. His skin must be stricken with leprosy, Munoo thought, because it had curious white patches over the brown surface. And there was an absent air about his whole form, rudely clothed in a homespun tunic and loincloth, which proclaimed the simpleton, the idiot.

Munoo shrank away from him with a start as the man lifted him down to the platform of the well and, smiling, stared at him.

Then he heard Ganpat say: 'Get on with your work, ohe Maharaj.'

That, Munoo felt, was a hint for him to move away.

He turned towards the caverns, self-consciously.

But the suspicion in the red eyes of a short, thick boy, with a pale, clayey face, bare except for a loincloth, who stood near the mouth of the cavern facing the ovens, confused him still more. And when this boy began to push him away and, opening his mouth, made strange noises, Munoo felt very uncomfortable.

'Bonga is asking you to sit down,' said Ganpat from where he smoked the hubble-bubble on the platform in the niche. 'He is deaf and dumb.'

When Munoo was reassured and put at ease, he strayed in the direction of the caverns past the ovens. Here stood a light-coloured, good-looking boy with a muslin shirt and loincloth, his hair parted like the Babus and the Sahibs, emptying a huge cauldron full of hot water into a ditch.

'Look out, you fool!' he snapped with a sharp, sudden anger as Munoo rushed past him to the accompaniment of cries of 'Hai! Hai! He is scalded! Undone! Burnt to death?' from the ghostly forms of wrinkled old women who were busy peeling apples in the caverns.

'Sit down, you swine! Where are you straying?' shouted the goat-face. 'Tulsi is getting the flask of essence ready. He will soon be taking the essence of keora to our clients, and he will take you along to show you the shops where you are to deliver the flasks from tomorrow. Meanwhile, don't interfere with anyone's work. Don't fidget. Learn to sit still. You would have been in the hands of the police, or you would have had to walk hungry and forlorn in the city if we had not brought you here. You are not to walk round getting in other people's way.'

And he directed Munoo to a four-legged stool, thickly encrusted with dried mud, which was used for shoes and was thus considered a fit place for the workers to sit on.

Munoo looked round at the thick walls from which small bricks, worn by years of damp air, jutted out, except where patches of cow dung or dirt or mould plastered the wall, or where the spiders had woven long, delicate webs, or where the soot hung in slimy black clots and the bats clung like crystals in a cave.

His straying gaze met Ganpat's eyes. So he turned to look at the low and heavy logs of wood which stood covered with cobwebs, and the corrugated-iron sheets coated with smoke, which pressed down upon the yard like a dead weight. It seemed the wind of the heavens never visited this world, and the sun never entered it, except through the nail holes and chinks and slits in the sheets, where it crept like snails.

As he was thus engaged, a blast of steam oozed from the boiling water which Tulsi had emptied into the ditch and dimmed his eyes. His gaze retreating to himself, he suddenly felt small and insignificant in this underworld of cauldrons and barrels, long, black caverns and crumbling yet solid walls.

As he rubbed his eyes to ease them he felt that the three other workers in the yard were looking at him askance: 'Who are you? Where have you come from?'

He felt an intruder in the place. And a tense irritation possessed him.

The heat of the cauldrons alternated with a stale, smelly draught that came from the caverns, rusting the iron and mixing with the sweat on the flesh to produce a sticky dirt on which the flies buzzed insidiously.

He would have flown away out of there if he had had wings.

But just then Seth Prabh Dayal came in and the atmosphere became charged with a comfortable presence. 'Where are you, O Munoo?' asked Prabha, searching for the boy, as he strained to accustom his sun-soaked eyes to the gloom of the factory.

'There he is,' said Ganpat, pointing from the cavern with his finger. 'The brute almost got burnt, messing about near the ovens when Tulsi was emptying boiling water out of the cauldron.'

Munoo got up and came near Prabha.

'Come,' said the master, smiling. 'I will take you round to the shops and show you to the clients to whom you will be delivering goods. Also, you might like to see a few sights and come to the temple with me.'

'Yes, go and spoil him as you have spoilt every one of these servants,' remarked Ganpat icily.

Prabha smiled, took an ochre-coloured account book, and walked out.

Munoo followed eagerly behind him.

If the town of Sham Nagar, at the foot of the hills, had far exceeded in complexity anything conceived by the imagination of Munoo the hill boy from Bilaspur, the feudal city of Daulatpur was an even more staggering confusion of things. In the face of it he had only one feeling, that of holding himself together and in close connection with Prabha, so that he might not get lost.

As he emerged from Cat Killers' Lane into the Misri bazaar behind Prabha, and faced an adjacent turning into the Bazaar Jhatkian, another into the Bazaar Sabunian and another into the Bazaar Chabuksawaran, he did not know which turning he had taken, the right or the left. It was all a maze. He certainly knew he could neither go forward nor find his way back alone.

So with one eye on his master, another more eager on the shops, he capered ahead through the narrow, irregular street, past swarthy faces with gleaming eyes and white teeth, past pale faces and pale-brown faces, all mixed together and distinguished only by the varied colours and shapes of their clothes.

'Come, Seth Prabh Dayal, have you come back?' called someone, and Prabha stopped.

Munoo stopped too, sweeping his eyes across the shops that lined

the way, grottoes lighter than those inside the factory and more
visibly packed, with sweets of a hundred different kinds or iron
locks of every conceivable variety, cloth of different patterns, leather
goods, saddles, collars, straps and horn fittings, all shaded by awnings and supported by carved posts resting on the lowest storey,
raised from the street by low platforms which served both as
counters and working benches for the merchants, who squatted
upon them and combined the functions of manufacturer and sales-
man. After a momentary confusion, Munoo discovered that Prabha
stood five yards away by a shop full of bottles, oils, perfumes and
essences, the shop of a Hakim, apparently, because a crowd of all
ages and sexes thronged around it with pale faces, covered with
glittering ornaments and many-coloured silks.

'This is a new boy who will come to deliver essences,' said Prabha,
dragging Munoo up to face a pot-bellied Lalla who squatted com-
placently but alertly on the platform with a greasy cow-tailed
cushion behind him.

'Acha,' assented the Lalla.

Prabha joined his hands meekly, bowed and moved on.

Munoo followed like a dog behind his master.

He fell to reading the signboards of the various shops. Each shop
had invariably two, three and sometimes four boards. And, whether
it was on that account or because the street abounded in doctors, he
read the names of at least fifteen, written out in huge letters in both
Hindustani and English, with all their degrees and titles. Dr Hira
Lal Soni, MB, BS (Punjab), LRCP, MRCS (Eng.), DTM (Liverpool),
DOMS (Bristol). So read a signboard outside one of the shops, a
shop different from the rest in that there were tables and chairs
arranged in it. He read the names and titles aloud to himself eagerly,
wondering what they meant.

A shop where small, many-coloured bulbs burned along a magic
wire, without being fed by oil or wax, disconcerted Munoo. But he
had learnt in Sham Nagar to label everything he could not understand as English. So he did not pause to inquire, but moved on to
contemplate, with dilated eyes, a row of antique buildings of which
the second storey was supported over the shops by intricately carved
columns and painted in floral designs such as he had seen in the
picture of the *Diwan-i-khas*, the Emperor Shah Jehan's Council
Chamber, in his Urdu history book. Beyond this Munoo's eyes

71

were caught by a shop in which a group of tailors sat stitching away at garments, while one of them worked a Singer sewing machine; again, by a shop where jewellers sat studding little bright stones into brown wax; again by a cookshop; and next by a fruit shop, where oranges and melons and bananas and mangoes spread their riot of colour and perfume to feast the senses. An ascetic with an ash-smeared body and shaggy hair, naked except for a rag suspended across a brass chain round the waist to cover his fore and aft, glided by Munoo, striking a long pair of tongs and swaying his garlands of thick beads. The crowd became thicker and more varied, as baggy-trousered Muhammadans alternated with loinclothed Hindus and trousered Babus. Prabha caught hold of Munoo's finger, and pressing by the big wheels of a bullock cart which had got stuck against a phaeton, brought him into a narrow street where the effigies of the various gods were displayed behind small sanctuaries in red and black paint overflowing with the grease of oily offerings. They skirted the domed shrine or mausoleum of a Sikh saint and entered the courtyard of the vast medieval Lotus temple of Vishnu, before which was a holy tank. Prabha bought a string of marigold and jasmine flowers. Just then a drum began to beat in the courtyard below the steps. People hurried round to take a place at the tank. Munoo had never before formed part of so vast a congregation of humanity as now murmured prayers to the solar disc which seemed to set fire to the water as it reflected its last flames across the edge of the sky before going under for the night.

They moved away at last, bending their steps towards the temple lights that adorned the blue-black of the parting hour. Prabha offered the garland in the shrine to an image which stood swathed in all the magnificence that gold-embroidered clothes and silks and jewels could lend. Munoo looked dumbly at the ritual of tinkling bells and chantings of hymns and loud hysterical shouts of 'Long live the Gods.' And he followed his master sheepishly into a shady square punctuated by beds of flowers and garden bowers, where naked ascetics sat growing lean by pyres of burning wood, surrounded by devotees with offerings of food, fruit and flowers; and yellow-robed, clean-shaven mystics, with clouded eyes intent on something which people called God, but which for the life of him Munoo did not know and could not understand.

On the way home Munoo thought of the varied succession of the day's events. He felt he was in a strange world. 'The house of the master is nice,' he felt. 'I shall be comfortable there and free to wander where I like, and the factory is dirty enough not to be spoilt by sitting round. I don't know what work I shall have to do, but I shall be well looked after.' The prospect of visits to the bazaars was exciting. There were so many things to look at, strange things, stranger than those he had seen at Sham Nagar. All kinds of things. It was truly a wonder city. He remembered what he had thought of for a moment during the concluding part of the journey in the morning, that the city of Daulatpur occurred in his geography book as one of the two oldest and most important in Northern India. He recalled that it was said to have been founded by Maharaja Daulat Singh, the Rajput king who ruled here in the days when Rama, the hero of the Ramayana, ruled in Oudh. And that it had been the scene of various battles in history, having been conquered by Mahmud Ghaznawi, the idol-breaker and looter of the buried treasures of the temple of Somnath. He wondered whether Mahmud had plundered any gold or jewels from the temple he had just visited. But he remembered that Akbar, the great Moghal, had given money to the priests of this city and encouraged their religion. The Sikhs had defeated the Moghals outside the town and Ranjit Singh had given away its old houses to his beloved councillors. But the Angrezi Sarkar had conquered it before the mutiny.

The resplendent figures of all the kings of India, as they appeared in the pictures of his history book, passed before his eyes, garlanded with rows upon rows of necklaces, with plumes in their turbans and jewels on their dresses. 'This city was,' he thought, 'when my village did not exist.' He felt confused and bewildered by its mosques and temples, its old shops and new shops. He would rather have lived outside the city, where the railway station was and the English quarter, plain and simple. He wondered why the Angrezi Sarkar had not razed the old city and built shops and houses like their bungalows here, and decorated them with tables and chairs. But he was lucky to be here at all, he reflected. 'I do not know where I should have been if Prabha hadn't picked me up. I might still be in the train, hungry and lost.'

He rushed, as he had been lagging behind his master, and caught hold of his finger.

*

73

'Wake up, ohe Munoo! Wake up!' Munoo heard the distant rumble of Tulsi's voice early in the morning. Then he felt the big toe of his right foot being twisted. And again he was conscious of a clear whisper: 'Wake up, ohe Munoo! Wake up!'

His eyes opened slightly under the thick crusts of grit and he moaned in a sleepy tone.

'Wake up! Look sharp, or the young Seth will be angry!' Tulsi said.

Munoo yawned and stretched his arms. Then he rubbed his eyes with his fists and looked round. The shades of the night enveloped the white-sheeted humanity which lay spread on charpais on the flat roofs of nearby houses. But twilight was coming. The air had the tang of dawn in the hills. The horizons of the high rocks about his village came back before his eyes; also the herd of cows, walking under the sky which was dotted by swarms of birds veering out in an anguished flight towards the slopes of the mountains. He had seldom remembered home at Sham Nagar, because there he had got up comparatively late, when the sun was already up. But he did not want to remember home, he said to himself. Nor did he want to think of the Babu's house. 'They must be missing me now,' he reflected. 'I wonder what they will do. My uncle must be angry. I shall write to him and tell him I am safe and sound, but that I don't want to come back.'

'Come,' said Tulsi, rolling up a ragged carpet and a dirty shirt around a greasy pillow which made his bedding, and securing the bundle under his arm.

Munoo followed Tulsi past sleeping people, tiptoeing awkwardly. The atmosphere of the dark, dusty stairs was humid and stale, because the air had lain locked up in the house overnight. He felt moist on the brow as he groped his way downstairs.

'Let me lift you,' said Tulsi, as he descended from the window over the well into the factory.

But Munoo climbed down with the alacrity of the old days when he used to jump trees.

Tulsi went towards the niche where the wooden platform was, and, shaking two huge mounds of flesh roughly, called: 'Get up, ohe Maharaj! Get up, ohe Bonga!'

Munoo could see the elephantine idiot and the deaf-and-dumb coolie huddled against each other in sleep. He stared at them as he

74

leaned over the barrels from the platform of the well. 'They sleep here every night,' he surmised. He felt happy to be the favoured one who had been privileged to sleep on the top of the house where his master and mistress, Ganpat and Tulsi, slept. On a separate bed, too, though it was a small bed. He knew who to thank for it. He had heard Prabha and Parbati talk of adopting him as a son when he fell asleep during the meal. He liked the mistress. She had patted him on the head and given him cream to eat with his bread as an extra dish. But she was so quiet. Her pale, olive face was serene except when she smiled, and she spoke so few words. He was afraid of her, afraid and shy.

'Come and sift the ashes from the cinders, ohe Munoo,' Tulsi whispered gently but firmly as he himself picked up a bent, twisted rod and began to prod the ovens.

Munoo jumped down to the floor lightly and began to sift the ashes. 'Oooi,' he shrieked, and fell back almost immediately, for he had touched a live coal as he put his hand into the heap of ashes through the aperture under one of the ovens.

'O, fool!' cried Tulsi, to cover up his own neglect in not warning the boy. 'But come, you will soon get used to it,' he added sympathetically.

Munoo drew back, nursing his hand and pulling faces with the pain that shot through his fingers. And he sat, for a moment, with the terrified hopelessness of the confident nature receiving a setback at the very start of a new job.

'Come, come,' said Tulsi, smiling, 'you will get used to it. Only try to be careful. Get a piece of tin or something to separate the coal from the ashes. Look, there is a bit of iron there.'

The boy took up a triangular piece of rusted tin from the debris that blocked the doorway of the long cave facing the ovens and attacked the job again.

He moved the tin gingerly among the ashes, keeping as far away as possible from the heap which Tulsi had raked out. For, not only was he now a burnt child who dreaded the fire, but also he felt a curious irritation at the contact of the tin with the hard, scarred pieces of dead coal; the kind of feeling which he used to get walking on sand in his uncle's nailed slippers in the village. But when the cinders lay heaped on one side and he put his hand into the soft, grey ashes he felt a luxurious feeling: a feeling of silk which melted in the hand. He applied himself to the job. The two feelings quarrelled within him.

'So you haven't even lit the fire yet!' came Ganpat's voice, followed by the appearance of his person at the window over the well. He was naked up to the waist, and a hard, sullen knot of irritation wrinkled his goat-face.

'Hurry up, ohe Munoo,' whispered Tulsi, according to his familiar habit of passing on the orders of his master to the other labourers, a method which had ensured for him the position of a sort of foreman in the factory.

Munoo applied his hands more vigorously to the job, without looking up to the goat-face whom he had by now come to fear as he had feared the Babu's wife and his uncle. 'It is sad,' he said to himself, 'that my good luck in finding work so easily should be spoiled by the presence of a cruel man. But it is a good thing that the master is kind, and the mistress gave me cream as an extra dish to eat with my bread last night.'

'Put the cinders you have collected on the grate,' Tulsi said, disturbing his thoughts. He himself had begun to arrange pieces of chopped wood that he had fished out from the black depths of a cavern.

'Where are Maharaj and Bonga?' Ganpat asked, yawning as he still stood at the window. 'Haven't they got up yet?'

'Get up, ohe Maharaj, ohe Bonga!' called Tulsi.

There was a stirring of the chain knocker on the door opening into the gully. Tulsi was going to move towards it.

'I will see to them,' said Ganpat, suddenly springing out of the window on to the platform of the well. And he walked through the passage muttering: 'They are late coming this morning and these louts haven't awakened yet. I don't know what has been happening in the factory in our absence. Everything seems to have slackened. Of course, who can expect you bastards to have any sense of responsibility? You have been enjoying a holiday while I and Prabha were away.'

'Get up, you dogs,' he shouted, abruptly stirring the labourers on the platform.

Bonga got up, rubbing his eyes. But Maharaj lay insensible.

'Get up, you son of an elephant!' roared Ganpat, rocking Maharaj's frame.

'Yes, master,' came the voice of the workman, rumbling from the depths of sleep in the gross mass of his flesh. But he did not move.

The latch on the door rattled again.

'Oh, all right, Lachi, wait,' Ganpat shouted.

And he picked up a log of fuel wood and belaboured the body of the servant, hard, till his eyes, bloodshot with the fury into which he had worked himself up, met the slave's eyes, bloodshot with fatigue.

'Come along, you swine!' said Ganpat, panting with the exercise of his limbs. 'The sunshine has spread far and wide and you are still asleep.'

Maharaj sat up and yawned tiredly. He did not seem to have been much hurt by the beating, unless his repeated moaning yawns were an indication of his pain. He contemplated the surroundings with his idiot's eyes, now watery with tears where they had been bloody with unquenched sleep.

'We need a log of wood to awaken a log of wood,' Ganpat said. 'I will break your hard bones for you if you don't rise early every morning and get down to work.'

Another sound of knocking, heavier, since he was nearer the door, disturbed him, and the groans of the coolie whom he had beaten into awakening infuriated him. He flung the log of wood away and he was going towards the door when he met Munoo's eyes, surreptitiously glancing towards Maharaj with obvious pity in their tears.

'Get on with your work, you little swine!' shouted the goat-face. 'Don't you go sympathizing with anybody or you will get it too. You mind your business or I will break that log on your bones.'

There was more knocking.

'Wait, wait now, you old hags,' he said, opening the door.

'What are you up to, beating those boys early in the morning, when you ought to be mentioning the name of God,' said Lachi, a short, thick woman, beaming with a coquettish smile on her round, regular face and winking at Ganpat with a twinkle in her mischievous eyes, and the glitter of the red stone in the small iron ring which played on her full lips.

'Ram Ram Sethji,' said the two old women who followed Lachi. They were grey-haired, bent and dim-eyed, and long years of toil were written in the wrinkles on their faces. They lifted their black

77

skirts up to the knees to avoid soaking them in the passage and gathered their ragged aprons as they followed.

Ganpat had melted at the sight of Lachi and, averting his eyes, he went for his hubble-bubble to a corner of the niche.

'Give us a little oil in our lamps and some cotton to make wicks with, vay Tulsi,' said Lachi.

They worked in the darkness of the caverns by the inadequate pale light of little earthen saucer lamps.

'All right! All right! You settle down to work,' said Ganpat as he came to fill the *chilm* of his hubble-bubble with fire.

Tulsi had just poured some kerosene oil on the coal in the ovens and applied a match to it. And though the flames had leapt up, the coal had not yet caught fire.

Ganpat had to wait to fill his *chilm*.

Munoo felt oppressed with the presence of the slave driver near him.

'Rake up the ashes from under the other two fireplaces quickly, you son of a bitch!' said Ganpat, impatient to fill his *chilm*.

'Leave the boys alone, you faithless one!' said Lachi, 'and come and count the apples to give to the women, or you will complain that I have stolen some.'

Ganpat went into the cavern.

Tulsi disappeared into the darkness behind him with a bottle of oil and some cotton wool for the lamps.

Maharaj had gone up to the well and begun to draw buckets of water to pour on to barrels of fruit with the assiduity of a machine.

Bonga, unable to shake off the lethargy of sleep, came and began to arrange wood and coal in the two ovens which Tulsi had not attended to yet.

Munoo sat absorbed in the dying lustre of the flames which arose from the spirit-soaked coal in the oven above his head. His mind was empty and his hands sifted the cinders from the ashes without much effort.

For a while all was silent.

Then a draught bearing the mingled smell of damp earth, decayed fruit, half-baked pickles, mustard oil, strong spices and the essences of rose and keora, brushed past him to the open gateway, chilling his body under the tunic and spreading particles of ash on his long hair.

'Strange place,' he said to himself. 'I hope I shall soon be able to get used to it. These people are all from the hills, and not like the Babus, except Master Ganpat, who is a city man –'

His thoughts were dissipated by the fumes, by the clouds of fumes, that the breeze from the cavern had spread all over the factory by smothering the leaping, spiral-like flames which rose from the ovens.

Munoo felt choked by the pungent smoke that had trailed out of the aperture into his nostrils. He felt the bitter taste of it in his mouth. Later he felt it descend irritatingly down his throat. He coughed. He spat a mouthful of thick spittle. His eardrums seemed to have closed. But out of the clouds of smoke there came shrill, hoarse shouts which reverberated dully on his ears.

'Oh, where are you? Where are you all, you sons of pigs? Come out, ohe you Prabha, you lover of your mother! You, yuh!!' The voice seemed to die out in a loud asthmatic cough, or rather, to linger in the cough, because when the voice was no more, the cough continued, angry and hoarse and shrill, in unending jerks like the resounding ring of false laughter.

Munoo applied his ears. He heard another voice, the clarity of whose utterance distinguished it from the previous old man's voice as an old woman's voice: 'Eater of your masters! Eater of your masters! You dirty hill men! You scum! You filth! The smoke! The smoke! Your smoke! It has entered my house even through the closed doors and windows. Hai! Hai! May you die! May you never live! May the fire of your ovens consume you! You have ruined our houses! We have had the walls white-washed only last spring! And now they are black. Hai! Hai! Where are you?'

Munoo wondered if it were not the nagging voice of his mistress in Sham Nagar that he heard in his imagination, though it was not so hard a voice, and it was husky. He looked up to Tulsi, whom he could dimly espy in the smoke, and he was going to ask: 'Who is it?'

'Sh!' Tulsi whispered, his face paler than ever as he stood fanning the oven to raise a flame in the coal.

Munoo watched the fear in Tulsi's face as the foreman, abandoning the fan, got down to bellowing with all his breath at the fire without exciting even so much as a glimmer in the oven, but sending thicker clouds of smoke up to the tin roof.

'Where are you, hohe? Where are you, hohe Prabha and Ganpat?' shouted Rai Bahadur, Sir Todar Mal, BA, LL B, Vakil, Member of the City Municipal Committee, dressed in a black alpaca frock coat, tight white cotton pyjamas and a great big heap of a turban on his long black face. And as he spoke, he thumped his thick stick agitatedly on a platform of bricks outside his house in the gully.

'Yes, where are they? Where are they? Eaters of their masters!' shouted Lady Todar Mal, dressed in a dhoti of homespun cloth which half veiled, half revealed her dried-up, dark form.

'Why don't you come out? Why don't you come out? You sons of bitches!' roared Sir Todar Mal's well-built, proud young son, Mr Ram Nath. 'Rai Bahadur wants to talk to you. We must arrange to do something about it, or you will have to get out of here.'

Silence brooded over the factory awaiting the merest excuse to break loose, while the thick clouds of smoke rolled and unrolled themselves in the heavily charged atmosphere.

'Go away! Go away!' said Ganpat, coming into the passage. 'You may be a Rai Bahadur in your house, but you have nothing to do with us.'

'Oh no?' said the young man at the door, 'so we have nothing to do with you! Come out into the gully, you bastard, and I will show you.'

'Oh don't stoop to talk to them, my child!' said Lady Todar Mal. 'Let us go away. We gentlemanly people have no way of facing these scum of the hills.'

She would have retreated at this, especially as Sir Todar Mal was going out for a drive in the city gardens in the tonga with his son before the morning advanced. But Ganpat rushed up to the door and pushed Ram Nath away into the gully.

'Think of the impudence!' shouted Sir Todar Mal, stamping his thick stick on the floor as he struggled to keep his feet against the onrush of his falling son.

'Yes, think of the impertinence! Look at this Ganpat!' shrilled Lady Todar Mal.

But their son had leapt back to Ganpat's throat and begun fisting him according to the rules of the boxing ring he had learnt at college.

Munoo, Tulsi and Bonga rushed up to the door, frightened out of their wits.

Ganpat had fallen into the gutter. But he rallied back in a vain effort to catch his enemy by the waist and was getting it hard on his face. His nose was bleeding.

'Oh, leave him, leave him!' Sir Todar Mal shouted with a distorted face, trembling with agitation as he stood safely in the doorway of his own house.

'The licentious brute! The drunkard! The rogue! The upstart!' Lady Todar Mal vociferated, flinging her hands as if she were showering curses with them.

A crowd of women had gathered in the windows of the neighbouring houses in the gully and beyond, whispering and horror-struck.

Suddenly Prabha darted from the passageway behind Munoo, Tulsi and Bonga. Leaping headlong into the fray, he caught Ganpat by the waist and laid himself bare to Ram Nath's attack, saying, 'You can beat me, Babuji, you can do anything you like. Spare him. He is a fool!'

'Leave them, my son, leave them,' urged Lady Todar Mal. 'Ashes on their heads! They have made our life bitter! They have raised their heads to the sky. The upstarts!'

'You must not begin to fight like that, Ganpat,' remonstrated Prabha, dragging his partner into the factory. 'It is the business of our landlords to deal with them. Not ours. And now you have got beaten! Wah!'

The goat-face retreated sullenly. He pushed the boys out of his way roughly, venting his impotent wrath on his own coolies, since he had been mishandled by his adversary.

'Shanti! Shanti! You must not let anger possess you like that,' said Prabha with the simple humility natural to him.

Munoo had been thrown into the mud between two barrels, while Tulsi had grazed his knee and Bonga had fallen on the platform in the niche.

They all stole to their places and began to work. Munoo went back to the ashes. Bonga got busy rubbing soft clay on the bottom of cauldrons. Tulsi began to fill a cauldron with leaves.

Maharaj, who had been drawing water, undisturbed by the commotion, like a blind man walking on and on, still drew the water, the thick blue veins of his legs and shins bulging out like the entrails of a dead animal.

'Put some water into this cauldron, ohe Maharaj,' said Tulsi.

Maharaj poured the water into the cauldron instead of pouring it into the barrels of fruit, accordingly.

'Come, ohe Munoo, you are wanted upstairs,' said Prabha.

Munoo looked up to the master. Prabha made a sign towards his mouth to signify that there was something delicious to eat waiting for him upstairs.

If Prabha regarded the quarrel between Ganpat and Sir Todar Mal's son as something which he could settle by joining his hands in humility to his neighbour, Sir Todar Mal was not going to let it rest at that. For Sir Todar Mal had a 'reach' in high quarters.

Sir Todar Mal had been for twenty years or more a luminary of the Daulatpur Bar, and was well known for his eloquent defences of many an aggrieved man and woman. The Government of India had recognized the value of his rhetoric when they made him a Public Prosecutor in the Daulatpur courts. And, though he had long since retired from that position, his prestige with the government stood high because he had rendered great services in the war, contributing as much as twenty thousand rupees to the Viceroy's fund. For the constant loyalty he had shown to the administration in the difficult task of maintaining law and order in the land, he had been given the title of Rai Bahadur; and in recognition of his services during the war he had been created a Knight Commander of the Indian Empire; while for his civic services he had been nominated an official member of the Municipal Committee of Daulatpur: impressive enough honours to cow the citizens of Daulatpur into believing him to be a great man, though they did not understand what being a knight or a municipal commissioner meant.

Some people, on account of his strange decision during the last political riots to take refuge, with his family and most valuable possessions, in the Daulatpur fort, called him a traitor. But everyone was afraid of him, and even those who did not respect him humbly joined their hands to greet him as 'Rai Bahadur Sahib' whenever he passed by with his rickety tonga and the fleabitten horse driven by his son. He vaguely saw through their attitude of feigned flattery and would have gone away to live outside the city in one of his three bungalows if these had not brought in good rents from the Englishmen who lived in them. And Lady Todar Mal, being illiterate and not well-versed in European modes of living, would have found it rather uncongenial to reside among English people in the civil lines and would have missed the opportunities for gossip and an occasional fight with the women of the gully that the city house afforded. Several times during recent years Sir Todar and Lady Mal had contemplated exile in order to escape from the smoke of the pickle factory. But the men and women of the neighbourhood, forgetting all about Sir Todar Mal's betrayals, had 'put their humble heads on his respected feet' and 'glorying in his *izzat* with the Angrezi Sarkar' begged him not to withdraw the shadow of his protection. So Sir Todar Mal decided to stay and die, as he had lived, among his brethren. True, he had sought to make his stay in the old house more comfortable by asking the landlords of the neighbouring house, the Dutt brothers, to turn the factory wallahs out. But the Dutt brothers saw no reason why they should forego the rent of an otherwise useless outhouse. Sir Todar Mal had bullied the successive owners of the factory. Now that had ended in a brawl. The possibility of building a chimney had never occurred to him, or, for that matter, to anyone else.

He would write and complain to the Public Health Officer, Dr Edward Marjoribanks, his friend and colleague on the Municipal Committee. He wrote:

To Dr Edward Marjoribanks, Esq., MA, DPH, LRCP, MRCS and F. (Oxon).

From Rai Bahadur, Sir Todar Mal, BA, LL B, KCIE, Advocate High Court of Punjab, Retired Public Prosecutor, Daulatpur.

Honoured Sir.

The omission on my part to render you a tribute of the heart's best regard and esteem due from man to man in the shape of occasional epistles is, I have always felt, a wrong and such as I can hardly plead any cause to mitigate the enormity of. I am therefore greatly ashamed to present myself before you through the medium of this communication. Nevertheless, let me carry to you my cordial assurance that your name is indelibly impressed on the tablet of my memory as my greatest friend both inside and outside the Municipal Committee.

Now I have to request the honour of your visit to Cat Killers' Lane, which is full of smoke on account of the burning of stone coal in the pickle factory next door to my house.

I shall be greatly honoured if you do so, because shortly after dawn on the twenty-sixth ultimo, my son, who told off the proprietors of the pickle factory about creating smoke in their blast furnaces, was attacked by one Ganpat. And though Mr Ram Nath, my gallant son, turned the tip of Ganpat's nose down, he received hurt himself. His face and limbs are stiff, cold and blue and his fingers contracted into hard fists.

My services to the government are well known to you. I gave twenty thousand rupees to His Excellency the Viceroy's war fund, in recognition of which I have received the splendid title of knighthood. I hope that bearing in mind the services I have rendered to the benign Empire, you will come and rid me of the affliction of this smoke, which is a constant cause of worry, remorse and sorrow to me and mine.

With my wife's modest salaams to Mrs Marjoribanks, I am your most faithful servant and ever grateful memorialist,

Todar Mal

Unfortunately the Health Officer ignored this letter.

When Dr Marjoribanks neither answered the letter nor visited the gully, Sir Todar Mal was angry. He waited anxiously for a general meeting of the Municipal Committee which was to take place on the first of September.

On the morning of that day he rode out early, by the side of his groom, in a gig which he kept besides his tonga for use on ceremonial occasions. He went first for an airing in the city gardens and then to attend the meeting of the Municipal Committee which was to take place in the town hall.

In his eagerness not to be late he arrived an hour too early for the meeting. The heat of the September sun and the fury of the grievance which he nourished in his breast made him sweat. And he walked up and down the corridor of the town hall in a towering rage, punctuated by fits of asthma.

At last the hour of ten struck on the bronze gong of the town hall, and he entered the committee room.

He was the first member to be there.

For half an hour he was the only member to be there.

For an hour he was the only member to be there.

Then a peon came in to brush the chairs and tables.

Half an hour later the secretary arrived, Mr Hem Chand, BA (Cantab.), a young man with thin glasses, who bowed obsequiously to Sir Todar Mal, as he was in the habit of bowing obsequiously to every Municipal Commissioner, since his job was dependent on them.

'Half past eleven, Babu Hem Chand.' said Sir Todar Mal, taking out his gold watch by its heavy silver chain from the inside pocket of his frock coat, 'and no one here yet!'

'You know what these Lallas are,' said Mr Hem Chand, flicking the ash from his cigarette and settling down to write the minutes of the last meeting. 'They will never learn local self-government since they are so unpunctual.'

It was true, Sir Todar Mal knew, that most of the members of the Municipal Committee were illiterate shopkeepers who did not even know how to sign their names and had to make a mark with their thumbs whenever they signed a paper. And they did not understand a thing about the matters discussed by the council. Would they be able to understand the nature of his complaint against the Dutt brothers, the owners of the pickle factory, and, most of all, against the Health Officer, who had completely ignored his letter? He had prepared a red-hot speech to deliver to the council asking them to discharge the Health Officer. But would not the Hindustani words be a bit too difficult for these Punjabi Lallas?

'Oh, Sir Todar Mal,' said Hem Chand, suddenly. 'Dr Marjoribanks showed me your letter about the smoke from the pickle factory in your neighbourhood. He seldom finds the time to go down visiting the gullies, but he said he would like to come down with you. Of course, under Regulation 317, para. 10 of the Local Self-Government Act – '

'Mr Hem Chand,' said Sir Todar Mal, 'I want you to put a complaint against the Health Officer on the agenda for this meeting –'

'Oh, Rai Bahadur,' said Hem Chand. 'You know how impossible it is to discuss anything in the Municipal Council. Most of the members are sycophants of the government who don't know a thing about civics. Lalla Churanji Lall will get up and make an oration lasting three hours, Sheikh Iftikhar-ud-din will pour forth his venom for an hour, Sardar Kharak Singh will wag his beard – and your motion will never be put to the vote, because everyone will say something different, and no one wants to discharge an English Health Officer, as the government is only too ready to withdraw the privilege of local self-government if its interests are not kept first. Dr Marjoribanks is in the office. I will ask him to go and inspect the pickle factory with you at once. You have been a well-wisher of the government. Why make enemies with an Englishman in your old age?'

'Very good, very good,' said Sir Todar Mal, seeing the prospect of unpleasantness if he washed his dirty linen in public and of honourable settlement out of court, as it were, in the way that the secretary suggested. The vision of himself driving through the bazaars of his native city next to an Englishman flashed across his mind, with the implied prestige it would bring. For, however much the Indians resent the presence of the English in India, most of them have a servile admiration for the white official and enjoy the thrill of contact with him. 'Very good,' agreed Sir Todar Mal.

Mr Hem Chand went and called Dr Marjoribanks.

Dr Marjoribanks came, a short, fat man, about forty, baldheaded and prim, with a genial smile under his thin, fair moustache, and dressed in breeches, gaiters and a Norfolk jacket, with his polo topee in his hand.

'Good morning, Sir Todar Mal,' he greeted. 'I am sorry I didn't have time to answer your letter. But I was away playing cricket for the gymkhana at Lahore.'

'Good morning, Sahib,' said Todar Mal, bowing with a humility strangely in contrast with his own dignity.

'Come into my car,' said Marjoribanks, in a smart tone which derived its snappiness from the fact that, like all Englishmen in India, he played tennis, cricket, polo, drank whisky and tried to keep young, because he knew that that was the only way to retain the affections of his wife and to be happy. 'Brand-new Ford my wife has just brought from "home". I am sure you will like it.'

There was method in his mad rush towards the car. He did not want to go riding in Sir Todar Mal's gig, as he hated to be stared at and salaamed by all the 'niggers'.

Sir Todar Mal saw his dream of being seen driving with the Englishman in an open carriage through the bazaars of the city fall to pieces. 'Very good, Sahib,' he said, gathering as much grace as he could in his answer and stepping rather awkwardly into the car. Dr Marjoribanks came and sat beside him.

'Rai Sahib's house, huzoor?' queried Sucha Singh, the Sikh chauffeur.

'Yes,' answered Marjoribanks.

As the car sped along, Sir Todar Mal, though sorry to be hidden from the world under the hood, consoled himself with the feeling of luxury afforded by the spring seat sinking up and down beneath him.

Dr Marjoribanks had not counted on the fact that the streets were too narrow beyond the Clock Tower Square for the car to go right up to Cat Killers' Lane.

Sir Todar Mal bowed graciously to all the shopkeepers when he walked down the Mai Sewan Bazaar by the side of the Health Officer, whether they were looking at him in the company of this official or whether they were too busy to notice them at all.

Dr Marjoribanks had never got used to the idea of being followed by swarms of dirty urchins, who begged for the gift of a pice, stubbornly, brazenly. By the time he had reached Cat Killers' Lane he was scarlet with self-conscious fury. The ogling eyes of men and women who got up in their shops to stare at him made him bend his head down in wild rage.

The cow dung, straw, torn rags, broken earthen utensils, stale food and other rubbish which lay in heaps in different corners of the lane disgusted him. Sir Todar Mal was not making it easy, either: 'Sahib, the municipal sweepers don't perform their duties well,' he complained.

A housewife threw a packet of mess into the gully just then, almost on to the Health Officer's head. Dr Marjoribanks closed his mouth tight and contracted his fist.

A drain on the second storey of a house, which had no pipe attached to it, splashed the bath-water of a pious Hundu down into the narrow width of the alley. Dr Marjoribanks could have wrung his hands in despair at this India.

'That is my house and there is the factory, Sahib,' said Sir Todar Mal.

'I see!' said Marjoribanks. He did not know whether to brave it any further into the slimy, damp gully. Duty beckoned. He heard curious, low whispers behind him. He could not go back. He advanced hesitantly.

'Come out, vay Prabhia! Come out now!' Lady Todar Mal called, coming to the door of her house with her apron drawn over her face.

Dr Marjoribanks entered into the yard of the pickle factory.

'Gut noon,' greeted Munoo as he sat on the platform in the niche, naked except for the loincloth. He had learnt the English greetings for morning, noon, afternoon and night from the chota Babu at Sham Nagar and thought to put his knowledge to use.

'Good morning,' said Marjoribanks, slightly taken aback. He surveyed the yard with its muddy passageway, its beer barrels full of fruit, its cauldrons over the furnaces. He was sweating. The heat was terrible. He took out his handkerchief and wiped the beads of perspiration from the top of his bald head, taking care not to hide his eyes as he heard footsteps behind him, and he had the eerie feeling, encouraged by the penny bloods he had read at 'home' as a child, that a dark nigger with a dagger might suddenly spring from somewhere at his side and stab him to death.

But it was Prabha who saluted him with a bow as he turned round to guard himself against the shuffling behind him.

'You master here?' he said in his Englishman's bad Hindustani.

'Yes, Jenab,' said Prabha, trembling, pale and frightened.

'All right, Rai Bahadur,' said Dr Marjoribanks, turning to Sir Todar Mal. 'I will see what I can do about it. I wish there were not all these people blocking my way up there. Can't you disperse them?'

'Jao!' shouted Sir Todar Mal, awakening to the Sahib's discomfort. 'I will see you off, Sahib,' he continued, brandishing his huge stick towards the crowd of men, women and children gathered at the head of the lane.

'Good afternoon, Sahib,' shouted Munoo mischievously from the door of the pickle factory.

Marjoribanks turned back at the sudden unfamiliar voice with a frown which could not help turning into a smile at the sight of the ragged brown boy speaking English.

Prabha was in a panic. He thought that the Sahib would certainly send him to jail. He hurried into the factory and filled two jars of pickles and jams respectively. Giving them to Munoo to hold, he led the boy up to Lady Todar Mal, who was shouting as she stood in the hall of her house: 'Now, you wait and see. What a dance I will make you dance, you who have raised your heads to the sky!'

Joining his hands, Prabha bent and laid his head on Lady Todar Mal's feet, saying: 'Forgive me, mother, forgive us all our faults. Here is an offering. Deign to accept it and forgive.'

'What is he doing here now, this rogue! What does he want? I will see him ejected!' said Sir Todar Mal, coming back, feeling a new strength in his ageing limbs, the strength of that pride which showing himself off to the world as the friend of an Englishman gave him.

'Forgive them, let us forgive them,' said Lady Todar Mal. 'Don't let us be the cause of sending them to jail. Already we have a great many sins to expiate!'

'Offer the jars to Rai Bahadur, ohe Munoo,' said Prabha.

The rich man's greed made him relent.

For Prabha it was a very serious matter, because he was sure that Sir Todar Mal would land him in jail.

For Munoo it was all a joke as he sat boasting to Tulsi and Bonga and Maharaj that he had met an Englishman before and knew their language.

For the most part men realize themselves through the force of external necessity, in the varied succession of irrelevant and unconnected circumstances.

Munoo soon got used to life in this primitive factory.

It was a dark, evil life. He rose early at dawn before he had had his full sleep out, having gone to bed long after midnight. He descended to work in the factory, tired, heavy-lidded, hot and limp, as if all the strength had gone out of his body and left him a spineless ghost of his former self.

But he had learnt to be efficient. His first job was to sift the cinders from the ashes. Then he helped Tulsi to light the fires, waiting in suspense for the rich neighbours to burst out, for, though Prabha had placated them with bribes of pickles and jams and essences, there was no telling when they might forget about the gifts.

The goat-face came bullying the boys and hurrying them. But, since the quarrel with the neighbour's son, he had cooled down a great deal and even taken to visiting the temple with Prabha in the morning. As the ablutions in the sacred tank and the circumambulation round the shrine lasted till late into the morning, and as he went out canvassing for orders to the bazaars after the midday meal, and for a ride on his new Japanese bicycle in the evening, his grim shadow was absent most of the time.

Still, he might come back at any moment. And then it was difficult if he caught any of the boys lazing about. Munoo did not know what was the matter with him. Why did he always remain 'burnt-up', with a frown on his face, abuse on his tongue and his bullying fist upraised? He did not know that Ganpat was a rich man's son, born and bred in the lap of luxury, with a grievance against fate because his father had gambled away his fortune on the stock exchange and left him penniless to work for his own living; and that, though he had been taken up by Prabha and lived in comfort through his partner's kindness, he was always afraid that he had neither the skill nor the will to work, and felt himself a mere parasite. To ward off the possibility of his downfall he had cultivated a tough skin and a bullying manner which, with his ambition to amass wealth and to rise in the world, had developed into instruments of personal hate and a perverse selfishness, defeating the very ends they were employed to serve. The hate that gleamed from his bloodshot eyes made him loathsome to look at, demonish and malevolent like a would-be murderer, and people turned their faces away as he stared at them stubborn, tight-lipped and relentless.

Munoo did not laugh and talk even as much as he used to at the Babu's house. He went in continual fear of the goat-face. He was possessed by moods of extreme melancholy in the mornings, dark feelings of self-distrust and a brooding, sinking feeling which oppressed his heart and expressed itself in his nervous, agitated manner. He felt he could neither face nor talk to anyone in the mornings, least of all his master and mistress, that he would break down if they said a kind word to him or looked at him tenderly.

The only thing that relieved these fits of depression was the silent comradeship which existed between him and the other coolies.

When Ganpat was away they would all fall to singing a hill tune as they raked the fire, watched the essences brew in the cauldrons, drew pails of water from the well, or peeled the fruit in the caverns The doleful melody traced its long-drawn notes from a painful cry through the full, clear accents of a verse quickly mounting to an agonized crescendo. Then, retracing itself to a minor key, it reiterated the sympathetic flow of words along the ringing tenderness or the song to a final despair. As an alternative to the sad songs which soothed the suffering of these exiles, they sang one of the ribald and boisterous popular folk songs of the season. Munoo then regained the wild freedom of his childhood and moved to a quicker tempo, cutting jokes with all and sundry, teasing the old women in the caverns by hiding their fruit, and especially making of Maharaj and Bonga butts for good-humoured raillery.

Also, he would settle down for a while on the platform in the niche, with a cheap looking-glass and a celluloid comb which he had bought, and would start to dress his hair as he had seen the chota Babu dress it in Sham Nagar, parting it on the side. But his long, thick black hair did not easily submit to the discipline of civilization. He would then set about washing his hair with the Pears' soap which Tulsi had bought to whiten his skin, and he would steal his colleague's perfumed hair oil and literally pour it on to his head. His hair emerged a soft, wavy, glossy black and was then easily parted. But, of course, the parting must be brushed away as soon as the goat-face arrived in the factory, for one day he had beaten Tulsi for pretending to be like him when he saw the boy parting his hair. Munoo would have liked to have shaved his beard with a sharp, long razor of his master's which was used to sharpen pencils and lay near the inkstand. But there was as yet no hair on his cheeks or his chin. He wished he could grow up soon and have a beard. He wanted to be a man, to flourish in the true dignity of manhood, like the chota Babu at Sham Nagar. He was a little sad to realize that there had not been any appreciable change in his height and girth since he left the village.

He was content to think, however, that he was taking enough exercise. To carry heavy copper flasks of essence from the factory to the various retail shops on his head was a pleasant exercise, since it meant an escape from the gloom of the factory into the world of fine-clothed men and women, and of wonder shops. Unfortunately Ganpat, if he were about, kept a vigilant eye on the time spent on these errands, and woe betide the coolies if they were caught walking leisurely back, enjoying the sights of the bazaar. For then they were punished by being ordered to stay indoors for a week and draw fifty pails of water a day, and Maharaj, who did not care if he went out or not, was asked to go and deliver the flasks instead.

Thus they worked from day to day in the dark underworld, full of the intense heat of blazing furnaces and the dense malodorous smells of brewing essences, spices and treacle, of dust and ashes and mud, which became kneaded into a sticky layer on the earth of the passage with the overflow of water from the barrels of soaking fruit, and plastered the bare toes of the labourers. They ran about barefoot and naked except for loincloths, emptying the boiling water which hummed ceaselessly in the cauldrons, refilling them, joining the receptacles to tin tubes with smears of sticky clay and rags, cooling the flasks, transporting them, then coming back to wash the fruit, dole it out to the women and help them to peel it till the next flasks of essences were ready, drawing water out of the well or helping the bosses in the intricate business of making jams and pickles. They worked long hours, from dawn to past midnight, so mechanically that they never noticed the movements of their own or each other's hands. Only the sweat trickled down their bodies and irritated them into an awareness that they were engaged in a strenuous physical occupation. Or, when they went up to the house by turns to eat the rice and dal which the mistress cooked in the middle of the day, they felt tired and sleepy and did not want to come back.

When the summer turned to winter Munoo felt more at home in the factory. For the dark recesses of the subterranean cellars into which his eyes had travelled during the first months after his arrival did not seem so sinister now as they had once appeared. He began to recognize the tins and jars of pickles and jams, which lay in rows along the walls of the caverns. He no longer had the hallucination of seeing two jawless monsters with glistening white teeth, who seemed to belch a cold, foul breath, sometimes with a bellowing groan, sometimes with a hungry, steel whistle. And in the winter there was also no danger of snakes, while during the summer he himself had seen a monstrous python with a flowing beard sitting over the fuel in a deeper chamber of the grotto facing the ovens. And another day Maharaj had brought out the coiled bodies of two snakes which had apparently died quarrelling. And Prabha had discovered a reptile with a mouth at each end, dead, in a tin of jam.

Also, with the coming of winter it was not so stuffy and hot in the factory yard. And one could sit quite near the ovens watching the red flames of the fire cast a glow of warmth on one's body. Munoo sat staring at the flames leaping up from the surface of the coal very eagerly every morning. He was in love with the fire, seeing it heighten the health of his pale body and the ochre-coloured bricks on the walls, noticing it enact an eerie devil dance, and filling his soul with the warmth he needed so much under the grey shade that seemed to hang under the corrugated-iron sheets, as the gloom of a cold grey night hangs upon the earth like a leaden roof.

Towards the spring Munoo became very happy indeed. For then, early at dawn, came mangoes, green mangoes, big and unripe, like those which he had stolen from the gardens in the village. Sackfuls of them were delivered in the mornings by coolies, bigger than himself, and emptied into the caverns where Lachi and the old spinsters and widows congregated to peel them for pickling and jam-making.

Munoo's heart beat wildly at the sight of this fruit, and he waited in suspense for the goat-face to leave the factory, as, indeed, all the workers did during those days, for they were all eager to eat the fruit.

But Munoo's ravenous hunger for the mangoes was to cause him trouble. For you cannot eat a great deal of the mango, even when it is at its ripest. A large ripe one is enough for a family and of the small ripe ones five or six may be sucked. A tumbler of some cooling drink is required to offset the heat of its luscious yellow juices. Of the unripe mangoes you cannot eat even a small one without harm.

Munoo would go and pick out the ripest of the unripe mangoes, and sucking it from his left hand, he would go about leisurely working with his right hand.

But there were no ripe mangoes there, only the unripe ones being fit for pickling. Munoo's teeth ached with the sharp taste of this unripe fruit, but in his childish greed he ate more and more of it, till his eyes were sore.

The goat-face could not have had more certain proof of the fact that the boy had been stealing mangoes than his sore eyes.

As he saw him rubbing them furiously one morning, he walked up to him, forcibly wrested his hands from the reddened pupils and slapped him furiously four times.

Munoo's howls brought Prabha down from the house.

'You should have buried the unripe mangoes in straw for a few days, you fool, and eaten them when they were ripe,' said Prabha, taking him in his arms and shielding him from more blows which Ganpat threatened to deal the boy.

Munoo sobbed.

'You spoil him! You have made a thief of him!' shouted Ganpat.

'Come, I will take you to the doctor's to get some medicine put in your eyes,' Prabha said, dragging Munoo away.

'You spoil him, Prabha! You have no idea of running a business!' fumed Ganpat. 'These swine don't do any work, but laze around eating raw fruit all day. They won't work unless you goad them with the rod. Now, we will be short of a workman for several days, and this is the busiest season of the year, when we cannot afford to lose a moment, especially as I am going on tour, collecting money – '

Prabha and Munoo had moved out into the gully.

During Ganpat's absence from Daulatpur there was 'peace on earth and goodwill among men'.

Munoo was laid up with a fever and sore eyes for a few days. But this illness, unlike that which had followed his quarrel with Varma at Sham Nagar, was relieved by the tender care of his mistress. She would sit by his bed and ease the throbbing at the back of his head by pressing it with her hands with a constant, soft, firm movement. She would press his body, which was swollen and weighted with the heat in his blood. And, when the ache in his limbs was evaporating with torturing slowness in the sweat, she soothed the unbearable agony of that drawn-out languishing which his body felt after its struggle for health with kind words, such as his mother used to utter: 'May I be your sacrifice! May I die for you! May I suffer instead of you!'

The warmth of those words, the comfort of them as they insinuated their way into his soul, as the air, subtly, invisibly insinuates itself into the body, the glow of those words, like the protracted joy of sympathy ringing through space in soft music unconsciously transmitted by a rapt singer to a dimly aware audience, the magic of those words was an inheritance of this woman, through centuries of motherhood. Munoo never forgot those words, cherishing them throughout his life, cherishing them among all the irrecoverable memories of his childhood, as perhaps the most beautiful, the most painful, and the most delightful.

She would lie down by him and take him into her arms while he was tossing himself from side to side, restless and weak, and he would fall sound asleep, drugged into a stupor by the warmth that radiated from her comfortable body, intoxicated by the wonderful tenderness that was in the smell of her body.

And this was another unforgettable memory which remained ever fresh to him. A memory different from the recollection of his mother's embrace, yet like it, but with an extra element of reaching out to the unknown. A memory which stretched from the innocent joy of a child's love, learning from one woman the need to know another, a memory of love travelling from faith and trust and care, along the curves of desire, into the wild freedom of a love which is natural, which acknowledges the urges of the heart, which seeks fulfilment, like the animals, and which mocks at the subterfuges of religion and the limitations of morality.

When he recovered from his illness with the frequent doses of sherbet and Auyar Vedic powders that one of the clients of Prabha Dyal, a practitioner of indigenous systems of medicine, had prescribed, and when the passing of various slides of cool antimony by his mistress' loving hands had cured the redness of his eyes, he descended again into the inferno of the factory.

Everyone was very kind to him and he had to do only the minimum of work. He felt weak and thoughtful and still.

The goat-face took longer over the tour than was expected. But that was in a way a blessing, except that Prabha was badly in need of the money which Ganpat had gone to collect. He, however, arranged for a loan from Sir Todar Mal, who in his retirement from the role of Public Prosecutor had turned into a public persecutor, which was not very different. Prabha, who had risen from cooliedom to be the petit bourgeois proprietor of a factory, compromised with Sir Todar Mal. He gave him a note of exchange promising to pay five hundred rupees a month hence, receiving cash at a rate of 45 per cent. He had given two, three other notes of exchange for a hundred rupees each to moneylenders in the bazaar, as he had to defray bills for overhead expenses. But he knew the firm was owed about two thousand rupees and that when Ganpat came back everything would be all right.

Meanwhile, at least he had reconciled the neighbours into tolerating him, if nothing else. He knew that they were friendly because they were making money out of him. But he felt, somehow, that there was an element of goodwill in the relationship also. He sought to cement this goodwill by a further undertaking to rent a large room on the ground floor of Sir Todar Mal's house, for the purpose of housing an increased staff of women who were busy kneading rose leaves for the preparation of rose-leaf jam. More money into Sir Todar Mal's pocket meant an increasing show of patronage to the social upstart. 'Why are you getting so pale, Prabha?' Lady Todar Mal would even condescend to ask him. Prabha did not know whether she was really being kind. He joined his hands to her and apologized for nothing. For, whether there was goodwill on the side of the neighbours or not, he felt a certain reverence for them both, because they were old and rich. He wished he had nothing to do with them and that Ganpat would come back so that he could pay back the money he owed them. But Ganpat was a long time coming.

At last he came. But he brought trouble on the tip of his bad-tempered tongue. He bullied the coolies, swore at the women and was reticent with Prabha.

Munoo, who was always quick to sense people's emotions, had emerged with a capacity for more real intuitions since his illness. He had vaguely surmised the causes of Ganpat's temper long ago, from the way the goat-face looked at Prabha, at Lachi, at the workers, at the cash box and the ochre-coloured account books.

He knew on the day that Ganpat arrived that the goat-face had something on his mind. What it was he did not quite know. So he vaguely called it guilty conscience.

The goat-face caught Munoo looking at him three or four times that day. At first he stabbed him with an angry glance. The second time he scowled at him. The third time he turned his face away. The fourth time he shouted at him: 'Get on with your work, you inquisitive bastard!'

Munoo did not stare at Ganpat any more, but wondered whether it was the air and water of provincial towns that had roughened his face and made it more drawn out and ugly. He soon forgot all about Ganpat as he helped Prabha inside a cavern to fill tins with rose-leaf jam.

But Ganpat did not forget the suspicious manner in which Munoo had been looking at him. He waited for an opportunity to thrash him for his knowingness.

He soon got the opportunity.

Prabha had given Munoo a jar full of the fresh rose-leaf jam to take to Lady Todar Mal as a further bribe to cover the gap of seven days that the pro-note had been due. As Munoo ran with the jar to the gully in his eagerness to go and deliver it in a house which he liked to visit because of the marvellous angrezi furniture and pictures in it, Ganpat, who had been seated on the wooden platform in the niche puffing at his hubble-bubble, saw him. He got up to see where the boy was rushing. He went to the door. He saw Munoo hand over the jar to Lady Todar Mal, who sat gossiping with a woman in the hall of her house. He had been angry with the boy. With that anger became mixed his stored-up rage against this woman. He did not say anything, but turned back from the door with a frown on his face. He was pale with fury at the thought that Prabha should establish cordial gift-giving relations with the people whose son had beaten him and who had then brought the Health Officer to the gully. He swerved round deliberately as he heard Munoo come in. He collared the boy and shouted: 'By whose orders did you give her that jam?'

'The big Sethji asked me to go over and deliver it,' said Munoo, afraid. 'He has asked me to give her anything she wants.'

'Is that the talk, then,' Ganpat said, grinding his words between his teeth. 'And you want to be a favourite both here and with our enemies that you run so eagerly to deliver jams and essences!'

He struck Munoo a ringing slap on the right cheek.

The boy raised his left arm to protect his face.

Ganpat's second slap fell on the hard, conic bone at the corner of the joint. His hand was hurt. He was infuriated beyond control. He struck the boy in the ribs with his fist, one, two, three blows, till Munoo fell stumbling on to the mud in the passage sobbing and shrieking hoarsely.

'You go and run about in the gully, wasting your time, you son of a dog,' the goat-face shouted, to cover up his resentment against the gift-giver and gift-taker by bullying the boy. 'You go out another time and I shall break your bones.'

Prabha rushed out of the grotto and stood looking at Munoo sobbing as he lay with his face buried in the mud. His pitying glance crossed Ganpat's bloodshot eyes over the body. Then it travelled beyond the door to where Lady Todar Mal stood aghast.

She had apparently recognized in the black look on Ganpat's face the animosity which she expected, and knew the words of his outburst against Munoo were only a camouflage.

'You, eater of your masters! You mean one! That you should grudge us a jar of rose-leaf jam! And we have been so kind to you, in spite of the fact that your smoke is a nuisance to us! We should really have had you ejected! But we gave you money when you needed it! We even let you have a part of our house for those filthy women to work in! You ungrateful wretches! Don't they say truly "Whose friend is a man of the hills, he comes, he eats the rice and dal at your house and goes?"?'

'Oh, go away, go away,' said Ganpat, agitated by the storm he had created. 'It has nothing to do with you! We have a right to chastise our servants if we like.'

'You eater of your masters!' raved the woman, invoking her real fighting mettle. 'You goat-face! It is you who are the cause of all the trouble between Prabha and us. He is a gentleman. But you, you are a rogue and an upstart! Your father, the broker, was an upstart, too! Don't I know you and your family! Your father turned his wife out and lived with a Muhammadan prostitute. And you are a drunkard and a debaucher! Your father robbed other people of their money with promises to do business for them. You are robbing your partner! I can see it in your looks. You dog, you are not a fit person to be in a respectable neighbourhood where there are young daughters and newlywed brides about!'

Munoo had lowered the tone of his cries and checked his sobs as he began to hear the neighbour's wife sum Ganpat up. He got a righteous pleasure in seeing the goat-face defamed. He wished he did not have to sob, as he did not want to miss a word of what she was saying. But Prabha was speaking to her: 'Oh mother, mother, forgive us. I join my hands to you. I will fall at your feet. I will draw a hundred lines on the earth with the tip of my nose. I will do any penance you may impose on me. But please forgive him. Forgive him, for God's sake, forgive him. He did wrong. He is senseless. I shall talk to him about it! Now go and rest. You know we are your children and you are our mother. Now cool yourself! Forgive us!'

But she was not to be stopped. She leaned forward and slowly but deliberately cried: 'No, you won't have any mercy shown you this time, I forgave him the last time when he dared to quarrel with my son. I must have the keys of my ground floor. You have shown yourself in your true colours after all. Get out of my house and return our money!'

Prabha now felt the seriousness of the situation. To his natural humility was added the fear of going to the wall. He still joined his hands to the woman, but, for a moment, he tried to muster his strength against her.

'Mother, forgive us,' he said coolly. 'This man has no sense of neighbourly relationships. But you ought to have more sense. Surely you can't treat us like that . . .'

But he had not the strength to censure her.

'Don't come asking for forgiveness,' she cried. 'You are trying to shield him! Get out of my house! Give us our money back! And I will see you ejected from the shed yet.'

'Oh, forgive, mother, forgive!' Prabha wailed, abjectly now, straining for words to convey the utmost humility which he felt.

Munoo had ceased to cry and sob. His soul was full of fear, fear for his master.

The workers in the factory, too, had ceased to attend to their jobs and the women in the neighbourhood had gathered in the gully.

For a moment there was a tense silence.

Then the knowledge of other people's presence aroused the snob in Lady Todar Mal to show off a little more dramatically. She stamped her foot and shouted: 'Come out! Why do you hide yourself like women and become meek when you are challenged!'

'What is the matter? Hoooahar! What is the matter?' coughed Sir Todar Mal, coming down the stairs of his house, dressed to go out for his afternoon drive in the gardens.

'These, eaters of their masters!' cackled Lady Todar Mal, her dark face glowing at the sight of her husband and then assuming a superior air of disgust. 'They have spoiled our whole estate with their smoke, and we have been kind to them, letting them a room, lending them money, and they are so mean they resent giving us a jar of rose-leaf jam.'

'We have got enough money to buy jams in the bazaars!' said Sir Todar. 'These rogues . . . hooo ho ar har hoho.' He broke out in an asthmatic cough.

'Rai Bahadur, forgive us,' said Prabha, pushing his joined hands in front of Sir Todar Mal and making the most abject bows while Sir Todar's coughing fit lasted. 'Ganpat is senseless. I sent some jam to you as an offering. He did not know who the boy had taken it to. We get so many people coming in here to ask for gifts. He didn't know. He is quick-tempered and headstrong.'

'Oh you liar, now you are shielding him,' Lady Todar Mal shouted.

'Oh wait, let him speak,' said Sir Todar Mal, brushing his wife aside.

'But he lies, this dead one, to cover up that scoundrel, that drunkard, that frequenter of ill-famed houses,' she cried.

'You know,' said Sir Todar Mal, assuming a detached, judicious air, because he knew he would get another asthmatic fit if he shouted, 'it is a very ungrateful thing to do to resent us a little jam when I gave you money, rented you a room and withdrew my complaint against you from the Sahib.'

He mentioned the complaint last because really it had had no effect: Dr Marjoribanks had never done anything about it, having merely said one day when he met Sir Todar Mal after a committee meeting that there ought to be a chimney built on top of the factory for the expulsion of smoke, and then rushed away to play polo at the gymkhana.

'Forgive us, Rai Sahib, forgive us this once,' said Prabha, falling at Sir Todar's feet. 'It will never happen again. You are our father and mother.'

'All right, Prabha, all right,' said Sir Todar, screwing up his face not to look as proud as he felt to see a man grovelling in the dust before him. 'Don't let that swine be so foolish and mean another time.' And he moved away.

'They haven't even the shame to yield my keys, after having angered me,' Lady Todar Mal said, withdrawing and spreading her arms to address the crowd of women and children in the gully.

Prabha crawled back and picked up Munoo from the gutter.

'Throw some water on him and give him a bath, ohe Maharaj,' he said to the idiot, who was drawing pail after pail of water from the well, as usual.

'Come here, oh Munoo,' slavered Maharaj as he abruptly poured a can of water on him.

Munoo felt happy and proud in his heart that Ganpat was in

disfavour. He felt that fate had inspired everyone to take his revenge on the goat-face. He was too humiliated with weeping to look at anyone, least of all the goat-face, but after the bath he set to work more enthusiastically than ever.

'It is not nice to annoy the neighbours like this,' said Prabha to his partner in a kind manner, when things had cooled down. 'They helped us with money while you were away.'

'Oh, don't go on at me like that!' roared Ganpat. 'You are ruining the business with this gift-giving habit. They must have charged you high interest on the money they lent you!'

'But no one would give us money, Ganpat, without charging interest,' reasoned Prabha. 'You did not send any of the money which you collected. Perforce I had to borrow. As a matter of fact the pro-note has been due to be acknowledged days ago. Now tell me, how much money have you brought? Because we might settle this debt, and the two other debts I have incurred with Devi Dayal and Gansham Dass, and start clear of obligations in the summer. I forgot to ask you what you had collected.'

'About fifty rupees,' murmured the goat-face sullenly, bending his head down.

'Fifty rupees!' exclaimed Prabha. 'But we were owed seven hundred to two thousand!'

'I can't help that!' said the goat-face, cornered. 'I really collected about three hundred, but as I have not been paid my share of the profits for the last year, I have kept two hundred and fifty for myself.'

'That is different,' said Prabha. 'You gave me a shock when you mentioned fifty rupees.'

There was a tense silence between the two men as they sat on the platform.

'I didn't think you would insult me like this,' said Ganpat, in an attempt to bully his partner. But his face paled with a suggestion of guilt.

Prabha looked up at him just as the goat-face was changing the awkward expression deliberately into a contortion of self-righteousness.

Somehow, in a moment, Prabha had a sudden revulsion against Ganpat. The last look on his partner's face had broken something in him, as a word, a phrase, an act, a gesture can break the most cherished, the most stable, the most profound beliefs in men. He became conscious of his partner's selfishness. He realized what he had always ignored or forgotten, that his partner was not straight. He knew that Ganpat had something evil about him. He was through with him really, but he still felt friendly, he still felt a genuine goodwill towards him, and he was not going to let anything separate them.

'Listen,' he said in an effortless voice. 'Lend the firm two hundred rupees out of the two hundred and fifty you have kept for yourself, so that we can be rid of some of the obligations we owe to these neighbours and to Devi Dayal, both of whom are difficult people to deal with. I will go to Lahore next week and collect the five hundred we are owed there, and which you did not collect, and you shall have your money back.'

'I haven't got it,' answered the goat-face, his face going very pale. For he had been lying to his partner, having in fact realized eight hundred rupees, and having spent the best part of that money on a courtesan he knew in Lahore. 'I have spent my share of the money,' he added in a panic, 'and you won't be able to get any more in Lahore, because I did my best with the clients there and couldn't get much out of them.'

Prabha became very suspicious now. Assuming the dignity of the elder brother whom he had always fancied himself to be, he said: 'Come and tell me all the details. Let us check up the accounts and see where we can get money to meet this.'

And he called Munoo.

'Oh Munoo, come and add up the sums which Master Ganpat dictates to you.'

Munoo, who had been eavesdropping throughout the conversation as he stirred the spices in a pickle pan, began to wash his hands as a preliminary to handling the account books.

'I shall not discuss accounts before these workmen,' said Ganpat in a fury. 'And I shall not let that bastard touch the account books. You have spoiled him thoroughly!'

'That boy is an orphan,' said Prabha. 'Come, we should be kind to him for the sake of religion. We should try to train him to do accounts and things, because he is too good for coolie work. He is intelligent. And let us treat all these boys as one family. There is no harm in doing accounts before Munoo. And the others don't understand.'

'That little wretch doesn't understand either,' the goat-face sneered. 'These schoolboys don't learn to apply mathematics, they only learn to do sums. Don't let him come anywhere near me or I shall kill him.'

Prabha kept silent and made towards the account books.

Munoo stood waiting in suspense, not knowing whether to go near the platform.

There was a panic in Ganpat's soul. He knew that his little game of lying and suppressing the truth about the accounts was played out. He tried, however, to distract his partner's attention from the money question.

'Why should that bastard be treated any better than the others?'

'He is not treated any better,' said Prabha softly, and began to unfold the account books.

The hour of decision had come for Ganpat. But he still wanted to avert it.

'He raised all the trouble this afternoon,' Ganpat said, 'by giving jam to that bitch.'

'Don't fall to abusing people,' said Prabha, a little sternly. 'You know I have had to apologize to those people for your rudeness already. I sent them the jam through this boy. So it is neither their fault nor his. And I did it because I wanted to be on good terms with them, as we have not acknowledged the pro-note.'

'I don't believe in the pro-note method of raising capital,' said the goat-face, driven from one stratagem to another. 'I'd much rather borrow money without making any promises, so that if I cannot pay it back I am not committed in any way.'

'It isn't the right thing to do in business, you know, to be dishonest,' said Prabha.

'I don't care whether it is the right thing to do or not,' said the goat-face. 'If you don't give a receipt, no one can sue you for money. And don't you call me dishonest or else I shall break your bones for you.' He had made up his mind to force a quarrel on his partner.

'I didn't say you are dishonest, Ganpat,' assured Prabha. 'There is no reason to get heated. Cool down and we will talk all this over tomorrow.'

Ganpat knew that today or tomorrow he could not avert the break coming. Prabha's concessions infuriated him more than any violent reaction might have done.

'You have been insinuating that I am dishonest!' he exclaimed. 'And you believe in all that woman accused me of this afternoon. Well, I don't mind telling you that I collected eight hundred rupees and I have spent all that money save fifty. I met Amir Jan, who used to live in Daulatpur. But you need not think that I had no right to spend this money. Don't think that what I have told you gives you power over me. I shall not have any bullying from you. I am not your slave and I shall not be blackmailed.'

'Oh, but I am not blackmailing you, Ganpat,' said Prabha, pale with anger now, but torturing himself to be kind. 'It is all right. You are a young man and unmarried. Why shouldn't you have an occasional debauch? It doesn't matter about the money being spent. And I am glad you have told me. We will try and raise a loan somewhere to pay off these pro-notes and then everything will be settled.'

'You think you are going to suppress me with your meekness and humility,' cried Ganpat. 'But you will not. I can see through this saintliness and mealy-mouthedness of yours. You think you are very good, don't you?'

'Oh, don't talk like that, brother Ganpat,' said Prabha, aroused for the first time. 'It isn't fair. You know that I have never said anything to you about your private affairs, because I myself might have done those things had I been in your circumstances. You can think whatever you like about me, but I have nothing to say about your conduct. I felt angry when you lied to me about the money you collected at Moga and, you remember, I was very harsh with you. But I don't feel angry about anything like that now.'

'You are a sly devil! You are a hypocrite!' cried the goat-face.

'Please don't wrong me,' said Prabha. 'I am innocent of all you think. I am just a straightforward, blunt hill man. I have lived and worked hard throughout my life, and I don't think in town ways. I wish I were still a coolie, and not in business.'

'You innocent!' sneered Ganpat. 'You combine business with your innocence well! You are artful and sly, as artful and sly a rogue as ever wandered from the hills. You sly hill dog!'

'You can say what you like,' said Prabha in a desperate effort to lose all his pride and dignity in order to win the man back to an ordinary business connection and friendliness, though all trust between them, he knew, had been irrevocably lost. 'I am what I am, very sinful and wicked in spite of my efforts to be good.'

'I am through with you!' shouted Ganpat, suddenly rising. 'You prig! You think you are mighty good and that you will be "gooder" if you feign badness.'

'Oh, be sensible!' cried Prabha, trying to catch hold of Ganpat to make him sit down. 'Don't you see we are partners, we have everything in our joint names?'

'I shall dissolve the partnership and I shall see that you grovel in the ditch for the insults that you have heaped on me this morning. You have betrayed me. You are a dirty coolie, and a dirty coolie you will remain all your life.'

He assembled the account books and, putting them across his shoulder, went to put on his shoes to go.

'Oh, your shoe and my head,' said Prabha, taking up one of Ganpat's shoes and handing it to him, with desperate humility. 'Beat me on my head till I go bald, but don't leave me. We have been together two years and built up this business. It will be terrible for me to have to bear weights on my back as a coolie in my old age.'

'I don't care if you go to the dogs, you meek, cunning bastard,' said the goat-face. 'Give me my shoe. And go and eat dung and drink urine! Your father was a coolie and you are a coolie. I shouldn't have associated with you, you dirty swine! Go and be humble to those neighbours, worm that you are, go, you cowardly swine! I won't disgrace my prestige and go down on my knees to anyone, least of all to a low coolie like you!'

'Oh, abuse me as much as you like,' said Prabha, 'but don't go. Cool down, it will be all right! Your anger will blow over.'

'Get away, you cur!' shouted the goat-face, rushing towards the door.

Munoo, who had stood watching the tense quarrel with the fear of hell in his heart, rushed up and caught the lapel of Ganpat's tunic and pleaded: 'Oh master, don't go, don't go, this is not a good thing!'

Tulsi and Bonga and even Maharaj ran up with joined hands.

'Get out of my way, you swine!' roared Ganpat, raising his hand in an hysterical temper and dropping it on the boys like a sledge-hammer, till they slid back to the platform, some frightened, some weeping.

'Horror! Horror!' moaned Prabha, as he sat with his head in

his hand. And then, rising, he rushed to fetch Ganpat back, wailing: 'Oh come back, come back!'

'Get away, you low hill dog!' shouted Ganpat, striking him on the face with his fist and wresting his body fiercely away from his grasp. 'Go to your coolies, you dirty coolie.'

'Hai! Hai!' wailed Prabha as he fell back.

'Shut up, you demented swine, you ignoble wretch!' Ganpat shouted a last speech as he turned round with one foot outside the door and one foot in. 'Stop howling, you dog, and don't follow me. I tell you I have made up my mind. I am through with such scum as you. You are not my class. You are coolies and belong to the street and there you shall go. I spit on you.'

And he spat and shot out.

The goat-face was as good as his word. He went and opened a pickle-making, essence-brewing factory of his own. The fifty rupees he had left of the money he had collected for the old firm was enough to rent a place and buy a few necessary articles. He obtained the raw materials on credit. And he set out to establish connections with Prabha's clients, by posing as the maltreated partner of a business which was going to the dogs because of its owner's accumulation of large debts which would never be repaid.

This malicious misrepresentation of facts soon defined itself into a rumour of Prabha's impending bankruptcy. And though really Prabha was as little bankrupt, or near bankruptcy, as any of the firms which have large stocks, the goodwill of the business was lost, and creditors flocked, panic-stricken, to the doors of the factory, knocking loudly and shouting vehemently, calling on Prabha to come out and settle his debts.

'Oh come out, Prabha!' they said one after another. 'Come out and face us! Why have you retreated into your wife's womb? Come out and be a man!'

Unfortunately, Prabha had taken the departure of Ganpat very much to heart. And the fear of not being able to pay the debts at once had so upset him, that he had succumbed to a fever. His employees in the factory were too afraid to open the door. And the creditors knocked more persistently and shouted more furiously.

'Come out! Come out and face us, you upstart of a hill man! Come out, you lover of your mother!'

Prabha lay at the far end of his room and could not hear, though his wife, who sat by his bedside, heard. She got up, but, not wanting to face the crowd because of her natural and conventional modesty, looked into the factory and said to Tulsi: 'Oh Tulsi, go and tell the Lallas that your master is ill and that he will see them tomorrow.'

'Go, ohe Munoo,' said Tulsi, passing on the order as was his wont. 'Go and say that the master is ill.'

Munoo climbed up into the living-room, past Maharaj, who still drew cans of water from the well, and, going to a large window which looked out into the gully, said: 'Lallaji, Master Prabha is ill with a fever. Could you come tomorrow?'

'Ill, did you say ill?' one of the creditors, a long-faced, small man, clad in muslins, burst out. 'I know he is ill. Of course he would be ill, with so much money on his conscience. But go and bring him, or we will come and drag him out, the illegally begotten!'

'Lallaji, he is really ill,' Munoo repeated, joining his hands and assuming responsibilities. 'Be kind and go away. Tomorrow he will himself come and see you.'

'Go, go, you seducer of your daughter, go and get him,' said a merchant with an enormous turban on his head, muslins on his pot belly, and gold-worked slippers on his feet.

Munoo retreated.

Lady Todar Mal happened to be washing the floor of the kitchen on the top of her house and she did not hear anything at first, or she would have come down instantly. But as she threw her dirty water on to the gully from the terrace of her fourth storey she heard an uproar from below.

'Oh, have you no shame, no consideration, that you throw dirty water on us?' a chorus of men were shouting. 'Look, you have ruined our clothes, mother.'

'Who are you?' asked Lady Todar Mal, apologetically. 'How did I know you were there? What do you want?'

'We want this bankrupt Prabha,' one of them said.

'Hai! Hai! Ni horror! Terror! May his face be blackened,' she shouted as she rushed down the stairs. 'So he has gone bankrupt, has he?' she cried as she saw the other creditors.

'Yes, he won't come out and face us,' one of the creditors said.

'Vay, you eater of your masters!' she cried. 'Vay, may you die! May a snake bite you! Why don't you come out and face us now?

Where are you hidden? Come, give me back my husband's five hundred rupees first. Then people can have your tins of pickles. What shall we do, what shall we do for our money?'

'So he even owes you five hundred rupees,' said the long-faced small man.

'Yes, this dead one! He came being humble and played on my husband's good nature. And we let him have money in spite of the fact that the smoke of his factory has ruined our house.' And then she switched the current of her electric tongue on to Prabha's house again. 'Come, vay, open the door! Where have you absconded now? Where are you? May the vessel of your life never float in the sea of existence!'

There was no answer. Only the soft sound of someone weeping could be heard. It was Prabha's wife and Munoo, sobbing, as they embraced each other by the bed where Prabha was sleeping.

'We must go and fetch the police,' the long-faced small merchant said.

'Wait!' said Lady Todar Mal. 'My son has not become a thanedar for nothing. He is upstairs. I will call him.' And she rushed upstairs.

Prabha had been awakened by the sound of his wife's sobs.

'What is it?' he asked.

'The creditors are shouting outside,' Munoo said, with an effort. 'They want you.'

He got up at once and came to the window overlooking the gully. He was pale and his limbs shivered slightly. He joined his hands to the creditors and was going to speak to them when they burst out: 'Oh, there he is, the illegally begotten! There is the rogue! The scoundrel! Come down, you son of a dog. Come and pay us our money.'

'Oh, please forgive me, Lallaji. I will pay every one of you. I will pay every penny that I owe you, even though I may die in doing so. But please don't abuse me.'

'Come down, you son of a pig,' they shouted together. 'Come down and talk to us! Why don't you come and face us? We have been shouting for you.'

'I was ill,' Prabha said, with his hands still joined. 'And I was lying down, I didn't hear you.'

'You didn't hear us! You bastard! And we have been shouting ourselves hoarse!'

'Where is he? Where is he? Where is he now?' said Lady Todar Mal, descending with lightning speed.

'Where are you, ohe! Come down, you son of a bitch!' shouted Ram Nath, her son, as he followed her, stiff-necked and swaggering with the pride of the important position he had acquired through his father's influence. He was dressed in a khaki uniform with black belt, pistols and whistle complete.

'Oh, forgive me, thanedar Sahib!' said Prabha, trembling with fear.

'Come down, you illegally begotten, or I will skin you alive!' shouted the thanedar.

'All right, thanedarji, all right,' said Prabha. But he hesitated to decide whether he should explain to all these people how he had been let down by his partner.

'You won't come down!' shouted the thanedar. 'All right. I will go and fetch constables.'

'Forgive me, oh forgive me,' Prabha wailed. 'I am only a humble workman, a coolie. I didn't know that Ganpat would go away and leave me like this.'

'Now you know your true status,' said the pot-bellied Lalla. 'You tried to be a big Seth, didn't you?'

'Let us get him out and lock up the factory,' said the long-faced small merchant. 'We can perhaps recover our money by selling the stock.'

'I have the first right,' said Lady Todar Mal. 'I have suffered from the smoke of his stone-coal fires all these years. I will see to it that he pays my husband's debt first.'

'Come, Prabh Dyal, pay up the rent for the factory and the living-room you have occupied,' said a prim, monkey-faced man, the shining whites of his eyes exaggerating the coal black of his face as he walked up, dressed in an open-collar shirt, alpaca jacket, white cotton trousers, a christy cap on his head and black boots on his feet.

'Make way for Babu Dev Dutt,' said a woman in the crowd of men, women and urchins congregating at the mouth of the gully.

'I will pay up, Babuji,' Prabha said, extending his joined hands towards his landlord. 'I will pay you the rent even if I have to die in struggling to do so.'

'Well, your word is of no value. You are a bankrupt.'

'Wait, Babuji, you will have your money.'

Prabha darted in to get a few of his wife's trinkets to offer in lieu of rent to the landlord.

Just then a Sikh and a Muhammadan policeman, uniformed in khaki tunics and shorts, red and blue turbans, flourished their batons at the crowd to make way for the English Inspector of Police and Sir Todar Mal's son, the Sub-Inspector of Police, who were walking up with great pomp and show.

'Where is Prabha?' roared the thanedar.

'He has evaporated, the eater of his masters!' said Lady Todar Mal, hiding her breasts under her sari and self-consciously withdrawing into the hall of her house, in an attempt to reflect the modest dignity of her position as Lady Todar Mal and the mother of the thanedar to the English Inspector of Police.

'Go and drag him out, Teja Singh and Yar Muhammad!' ordered the thanedar.

The door of the factory was opening as the police constables rushed towards it, because Prabha was coming out, followed by his workmen.

'Come out, you swine! Come out, you dog!' raved the policemen as they blindly flourished their batons and collared Prabha. When they wrested Prabha from the embrace of Munoo, Tulsi and Bonga and brought him out, kicking him from behind, the creditors howled like beasts.

'Bring the dirty dog out! The dirty hill man! The scum! Push him out!'

'Take him to the police station, quickly!' said the English Inspector of police, eyeing Prabha suspiciously. 'Looks a bad character!'

'Yes, a rogue of number ten,' said the thanedar. Then he turned towards his mother and said in his own language: 'Lock up the door of the factory, till I come back.'

Next he turned to all the creditors and said: 'Come to the kotwali tomorrow, all of you; your evidence will be taken. Meanwhile go to your shops. We will deal with him!'

'Yes, jenab! Yes, thanedar Sahib!' agreed the merchants, joining hands to the mighty symbol of the Angrezi Sarkar, whom they dreaded and respected as they dreaded and respected nothing else.

Teja Singh and Yar Muhammad led Prabha away through the narrow width of the gully, past whispering, curious sightseers, all of whom seemed to be fascinated by this show of force. There were tears rolling down Prabha's cheeks as he looked back to the window where his wife stood weeping.

'Look straight, you swine, and face towards the kotwali!' roared the thanedar, who walked with his colleague and officer, the Inspector of Police, behind the constables.

Munoo, Tulsi, Bonga and Maharaj followed, Munoo sobbing, Tulsi grim and pale, Bonga staring wildly and straining to speak, Maharaj slobbering without saying a word.

As the procession passed through Cat Killers' Lane and turned into the book bazaar which led to the police station under the shadow of the clock tower, the passers-by and the shopkeepers stood to watch, some dazed, others whispering, others babbling, still others casting curses and abuse on the man whom they had once respected as Sethji.

A fair-complexioned, hawk-nosed Muhammadan sergeant was puffing at the tube of a hubble-bubble as he sat on a charpai.

'Make him confess his crime, Pande Khan,' ordered the thanedar. 'Arrested for non-payment of debt.'

The sergeant stood to attention, saluted his officers, and retreating to a room behind a verandah, brought a cane.

'Now, confess, you rogue,' he said, coming up to Prabha, where Teja Singh and Yar Muhammad still held him. 'Confess, where have you buried your money? Come, own up!'

'Huzoor,' said Prabha, joining his hands, 'I have no money buried anywhere. But I have stock. I only crave your forgiveness and I will pay up every pice that I owe to my creditors.'

'You are barking an untruth! You lie! You lover of your mother!' shouted Pande Khan. 'Confess the truth!'

And he dealt him one, two, three sharp stripes with his cane.

'I have told the truth,' wailed Prabha. 'Huzoor, I do not lie!'

'You are no angel, you son of Eblis,' shouted the sergeant, striking Prabha a blow on his face.

'It is the truth, Sarkar! It is the truth!' Prabha wailed, lifting his handcuffed hands.

'Is the thanedar Sahib lying then, you swine, and the Inspector Sahib, there?' the sergeant growled. 'Confess, you dog! Confess!' And he struck him blow after blow in a wild orgy of excitement, his face set, his lips stiff and his body towering over the poor man's frame.

111

'Oh, don't beat him, don't beat him,' cried Munoo and Tulsi. 'It is Master Ganpat who is at fault.'

The sergeant stopped to take breath.

'Strike him! Strike him like this!' shouted the Inspector of Police, striking the sergeant hard to show him how to do it. And then he turned round to the boys, who stood at his heels, as much absorbed in looking at his white skin as in watching their master being beaten up, and he roared: 'Jao!'

'Run away, you swine!' roared the thanedar after him in an accent which tore his throat. 'Run away,' he said, 'this is not a fair.' And he struck them with his birch on their naked backs and feet.

'Oh beat me, huzoor, beat me!' shrieked Prabha. 'Beat me as much as you like, but spare those boys.'

'Keep quiet, you swine!' said the sergeant, waving the cane. 'You look after your own skin and do not try to turn this into a regular fair. You have had me beaten for being mild to you. Take this, you dog!' And he lashed Prabha again, sharp, sharp, till the swish of the glistening cane was all that occupied the air.

Prabha's wails became one long howl, 'Oh my god! Oh my god! Where are you!'

Munoo, Tulsi, Bonga and Maharaj stood looking, now at their master, now at the flawless sky above them, a pain in their hearts but not a tear in their eyes. They could neither stifle nor express the hurt in their souls.

It was as if someone had died when they returned home, as if Prabha, their master, had died. The tall long room seemed to echo the soft thud, thud of their bare feet as they walked up from the courtyard in the residential part of the house. Especially Maharaj the idiot's footsteps, and Bonga's flat feet, fell heavily. And the atmosphere seemed to tremble with the anguish of their mistress' tears.

'Sit down, ohe Maharaj and Bonga,' Tulsi said with a sense of propriety that betokened his sensitiveness to the undertones of grief.

Munoo had begun to tiptoe towards the window overlooking the gully by which Prabha's wife lay huddled. But he had hardly reached the middle of the room before he stopped. Somehow the sight of that woman broken down by grief was a barrier. He had been urged by a spontaneous feeling to go to her as he used to go to his mother when he came back home from play and found her crying. But something had happened to him now, something had changed within him. He had outgrown the natural unconsciousness of his childhood and begun to recognize his emotions. He could not go near the woman.

'I will go and ask Ustad Ganpat if he will come and bail Ustad Prabha out,' said Tulsi, coming up to Munoo. Munoo lifted his downcast eyes and stared at him with a contracted face.

'Come, ohe Maharaj and Bonga,' said Tulsi, going to the door. 'Come, I will take you to eat a little fresh air.' He spoke to them as if they were small children, ignorant of the ways of the world. They got up wearily and followed him.

As Munoo stood in the room now, the half-broken, half-smothered sobs of his mistress seemed to fill the air. And his senses were blinded to everything around him.

For a moment there was a complete silence, the suspended, long-drawn-out, tense silence before a sob breaks out, overloaded with the memory of pain. One sound, one indelicate, awkward sound, Munoo felt, would be a violation.

He looked round and surveyed the things in the room. The brass utensils glistened in a corner; the floral designs of two earthen pitchers wove an intricate pattern which puzzled him; the mango designs on the cover of a quilt which hung from a line among durries and blankets, sheets and eiderdowns, obtruded on his gaze and annoyed him.

Then the sob broke, rending his heart with its reverberations.

He dragged his feet up to where his mistress lay.

'Do get up! Do get up!' he said, bending his head as he stood by her.

She sobbed hysterically now, the flow of sympathy having relieved her suffering.

He knelt down and, putting his hand on her arm, tried to raise her.

'Do get up! Do get up!' he said.

She sobbed more bitterly than ever. 'Oh, I do not know where to go, child,' she cried. 'I do not know what to do.'

Slowly she lifted her head and leant on his shoulder.

The warmth of her breath on his throat, the soft tender caress of her cheeks on his body seemed to play on his mind. He felt stiff and uncomfortable.

Then a faint tremor on her lips seemed to whisper the memory of some forgotten emotion he had felt in his sleep.

He looked at her ebony face. The black hair which strayed over her forehead, over the dark lines of her eyebrows, was unadorned today with the gold flowers which usually framed it. Her high cheekbones were flushed and made the tears in her black eyes well like pools of light. Her jaws defined her open mouth with a gentle strength that failed at the chin.

Munoo's memory went back to the days when he had been ill and she had caressed him with embraces, kissed him on the forehead and soothed him with the haunting refrains of a hill song.

He pressed her close to him. He felt her quivering. He had now thrown over the dumb burden of self-consciousness. He felt released. And, for a moment, he forgot himself in her warmth, so that only darkness, utter darkness, spread before his eyes. And his blood boiled with a love that crushed him with wild torture. The fire filled his eyes with hot tears. He broke into a passion of grief, more poignant, more heart-rending than he had ever known.

'Oh, don't cry,' he said to her, 'don't cry!'

'Don't cry, my child, you should not cry,' she said to him.

There was a soft thud, thud of footsteps, and then a continuous, heavy thud, thud, accompanied by voices in the fast-falling darkness. Munoo and his mistress still cried.

'Look, ohe Munoo, Master Prabha has come back,' came Tulsi's voice.

'Why are you weeping, both of you?' said Prabha, sinking on to the charpai near the door. 'Did you think I was dead or something?' His tone was slightly resentful. His face was pale and haggard. He lay down shivering.

'Did they leave you then, Ustadji?' asked Munoo, coming up to him impetuously.

'Yes, yes, they had nothing against me, no warrant to arrest me,' he said more to his wife than to Munoo. 'I am bankrupt, of course, and I will try to pay all my creditors at least half their money, but the police beat me for nothing – Hai – my bones ache and I feel cold. Give me a quilt or a blanket –' And he continued to murmur incomprehensibly, deliriously.

As he lay unconscious, the blue and swollen patches of his skin stared out of his tunic and dhoti, which were torn into rags, and the sores of blood on his body seemed to ooze forth a decayed smell.

Prabha's wife had rushed to the head of the bed and pressed his body as she struggled to stop her tears under cover of her head apron.

Munoo covered him with blankets, while Tulsi went to fetch a doctor who lived at the top of Cat Killers' Lane.

After the doctor had been, both Tulsi and Munoo went to the chemist in the main bazaar to fetch the medicines and ointments which he had prescribed.

They walked silently through the uneven darkness of the cloth bazaar, past a narrow lane which led on one side to the shrine of Saint Sain Das, and on the other to the Church of All Souls. There, they took a turning by the high-domed town hall, past Sher Khan's mosque to the wide main bazaar, where Indian-styled shops gave place to feeble imitations of European houses. They thought about their master's chances of living and of his possible death, and they hung their heads down as they sped along.

On the way back, however, the medicines which Sorabji, the Parsi chemist, gave them filled them with hope because of the ostentatious wrappings around them, and they relaxed.

'Where did Maharaj and Bonga go?' Munoo asked. 'They did not come back with you.'

'Master Ganpat kept them at his factory,' said Tulsi. 'He abused them and asked them to work for him. They were too afraid of him to come back.'

Munoo received the information in silence. He hated Ganpat. But he was too tired by the succession of the day's events to express his hate in any way. He stalked through the darkness as if he were heading for oblivion. But, occasionally, the curled-up body of a labourer, asleep on the pillow of his arm on the ground or the boards of a closed shop, glimmered in the light of a spark of fire in someone's hubble-bubble, and he strained to see it and to define for himself the answer to the question who it could be.

'We will also have to go and sleep in the open at the grain market tonight if we are to get jobs lifting weights tomorrow and help Master Prabha out,' Tulsi said, divining his companion's thoughts.

They did not say anything to each other.

The master fell sound asleep after he had taken the medicine. He sweated and his breathing was regular. His wife sat by his·side. She would keep a vigil, both Munoo and Tulsi knew. So they sauntered out into the night with a view to sleeping in the grain market, where the work of bearing weights was supposed to be easy to find.

They emerged from Cat Killers' Lane into the papadum bazaar, which reeks day and night of a blend of hot spices, lentils and cheese gone bad. Then they turned into the wide bamboo bazaar past Santokh Sing's Dharam-salla and entered into the salt market, where the city bulls congregate to lick the blocks of salt which the pious Hindus leave for them outside their shops. The grain market was about a hundred yards away, connected by the Hanuman Street.

They had walked blindly through the oppressive, hot night, scarcely illumined by the dim-eyed moon. They were half asleep and tired and heavy and broken, and their one thought was of rest. But the eerie noises of the Indian night, the sudden, jerky noises of consumptive throats clearing themselves of mouthfuls of spittle, as they leaned out of the windows of their chubaras, or from the flat roofs of the houses, the electric shock of crickets and grasshoppers chirping in a temple compound, the weird squeal of some unlucky cat frightened by the howling of a hungry dog, which itself had started in its sleep because a sacred bull belched like the thunder which follows lightning; this grim and tense atmosphere charged with the spirits of all the dead, who according to the Hindus come to visit their homes at night, obtruded itself on the souls of the boys. And as they sank into the ruts of the last patch of muddy road, and then pushed their feet forward, the narrow twisted opening of the grain market disclosed a more oppressive scene.

The square courtyard, flanked on all sides by low mud shops, flimsy huts and tall five-storied houses with variegated cement façades, arches, colonnades and cupolas, was crowded with rude wooden carts which pointed their shafts to the sky like so many crucifixes, crammed with snake-horned bullocks and stray rhinoceros-like bulls and skinny calves bespattered with their own dung, as they sat or stood, munching pieces of straw, snuffling their muzzles aimlessly, or masticating the grass which they had eaten some hours before, congested with the bodies of the coolies, coloured like the earth on which they lay snoring, or crouching round a communal hubble-bubble, or shifting to explore a patch clear of puddles on which to rest. The smell of stagnant drains, rotten grains, fresh cow-dung and urine, the foul savour of human and animal breath and the pungent fumes of smouldering fuel cakes, all combined to produce an odorous atmosphere in the compound, sickening until you were used to it, or till your attention was turned to keeping clear of the sprawling naked bodies, glistening with sweat, or sheeted like ghosts in a vain attempt to escape the flies and mosquitoes that hovered like an invisible plague in the darkness.

Munoo and Tulsi were already slapping their bare arms and legs where the mosquitoes had assailed them as they entered the court-yard, and they cursed furiously: 'Oh, these mosquitoes, the seducers of their daughters!'

'Who is this abusing?' came the sharp voice of a coolie from among a group.

Munoo and Tulsi were slightly taken aback, as they had not noticed that they were cursing.

'Abusing nobody, brother,' said Tulsi tactfully, 'only these mosquitoes.'

'Who are you?' another voice asked.

'Coolies,' answered Munoo, assuming a casual air because he thought Tulsi's muslins might antagonize the labourers, while his own bare body would be a recommendation.

'No room here for anyone,' muttered a coolie, his naked body shining like black ebony, while he rubbed oil to keep the mosquitoes off.

There was, indeed, no room, as the bodies here lay in a sort of row, resting their heads on the wooden beam of a doorstep, shrouded in sheets.

Munoo and Tulsi advanced cautiously through the jigsaw puzzle of fifteen or more corpses lying helter-skelter round a cart. Then they threaded their way through sacks of grain up to where they thought was a clearing.

'Who is that? If you are thieves, beware!' shouted a night-watch-man, who lay on a bedstead with his face aslant, a bamboo stick in his hand.

'Coolies,' answered Munoo.

'Go away, away from the precincts of this shop. Lalla Tota Ram does not allow any coolies to lie about near here. There is a cash box in this shop.'

'All right, Maharaj,' Tulsi said, and led the way towards the north of the square, hoping to find a patch somewhere among the hundreds of men, who shifted and turned to and fro on their sides, as they whispered, coughed or sighed in the sweltering heat that stood even, like some malevolent, obstinate clay god. The fantastic attitudes in which the coolies lay curled up here, unable to sleep and moaning 'Ram, Ram', 'Sri Krishna' or 'Hari Har', irritated Munoo. He knew they were old, or at least middle-aged men, those who remembered the name of God, and Munoo was not feeling kindly towards the Infinite after having seen the devout Prabha suffer.

So he dragged Tulsi away towards the middle of the compound, where a mound of grain sacks stood covered with a large sheet of canvas. After a stealthy prowl round the corners to see if there was not a chowkidar guarding the merchandise, he groped round for a foothold on the wall of the jute bundles. Not finding one, he crawled back to grope for something to climb up with. A pole stood some yards away, on top of which some merchant's pigeons nested. Munoo was going for it. But Tulsi held him fast.

'I will be the mare for you to climb up and then you can pull me to the top,' he said. And he bent down. Munoo swiftly jumped on to his back and, balancing himself on Tulsi's spine, scrambled up to the heap. Then he dug his feet among the sacks and, wiping the sweat off his hands, stretched his right arm down and dragged Tulsi up. It strained every muscle in his body, but there was a hot blast of wind blowing up there and he sat feeling its warm breath caress his flesh. He surveyed the scene about him, half afraid that he and Tulsi might have been seen by the night-watchman, who would order them down. But there were only corpses lying around, some on their sides, others on their backs, still others facing downwards, all contracting their limbs to occupy the smallest space, and bound up like knots of anguish whose every breath seemed to ask the elements for the gift of sleep.

'Don't you want to sleep?' asked Tulsi, who was already succumbing to the exhaustion produced by the activities of the day.

'Yes,' said Munoo, but he kept on staring at the darkness emptily, unconsciously aware of the noises around him – the sighs which came mixed with the gurgling of water in someone's hubble-bubble, the hum of conversation, the notes of a beetle and the hoarse cry of a frog. 'What are you looking at?' he asked himself. The answer came: 'Nothing.'

He lay down on his back. The surface of the sack of grain was round and comfortable. He faced the sky, a grey-blue sky with the dagger of the moon stabbing its side and shedding a few glistening drops of white-blooded stars. There was no meaning in the sky beyond that.

He closed his eyes and a picture of the congested roof of his master's house came to him: a picture of his own low bed among the lines of bedsteads. 'And now,' he said to himself, 'I am here, far away from that home, and Prabha is lying ill in the big room downstairs, and Ganpat is in a different part of the town. Maharaj and Bonga perhaps lie in the new factory sound asleep. The mistress will be thinking of us. She might be crying. Why did we come away? We should have stayed and been near the master and mistress. Supposing he should die.' The picture of Prabha lying dead was something he did not want to contemplate. He closed his eyes fast and he had scarcely done so when he was asleep.

He slept fitfully, contracting his hands into fists as if he were clutching at a last straw to save himself from drowning. His body writhed as he turned on his sides. His nose twitched as he drew large quantities of breath. He moaned once or twice, as if the curves of his soul were straightening, smoothening, from the coils caused by the impact of his horrible experiences.

When the heat of the night drifted into the cool of the dawn, the fever in Munoo's flesh abated and he nestled close to the belly of a sack as if it were the body of a warm-blooded woman. Neither the crowing of cocks in the houses of the weaver's lane beyond the courtyard, nor the twittering of myriads of sparrows, nor even the insistent cawing of crows awakened him or Tulsi, as they awakened the coolies, the bullocks, the lame dogs and the devout Hindu merchants.

But the steel spokes of the sun that came trembling with heat pierced his bare skin, and he awoke, his mouth parched, his eyelids glued, his limbs heavy and stale. He moved Tulsi's body lazily. The yellow-red sky of the morning towering over the market had blackened his form, and he felt dirty and unclean.

'Come, ohe Tulsi,' he said peevishly, rubbing his eyes.

Tulsi rose suddenly.

Munoo surveyed the scene. He did not know how to begin.

Some of the coolies were bearing sacks of grain on their backs from the two loaded bullock carts to a godown. Others sat smoking hubble-bubbles and biris, washed themselves at a pump, or still lay curled up in a miraculous sleep which looked like death in its complete negation of the hubbub about them. For life here, even before the business hours started, was a tide of seething humanity jostling in an ebb and flow of colourful cross purposes. There were Lallas going about in fine starched muslins and tussores from shop to temple and temple to shop, muttering 'Ram Ram Ram', 'Hari Hari Hari', 'Sri Sri Sri' and other incantations, one did not know whether to Mammon or to God. And there were dark, copper-coloured men, wearing next to nothing, swathed in patched-up rags, babbling, shouting, heaving, panting, or lying still, absolutely still, in complete motionlessness.

Munoo took it all for granted, as if he had been used to it throughout his life. Only the mixture of types excited him. He had seen many Hindu hill coolies together, but he had never seen so many Kashmiri Muhammadan labourers or Sikh coolies mixed up. He wondered if the Hindus did not resent the violation of their religion by mixing with the Muhammadans. He hoped they did not, for he secretly recalled how he had bought a pot full of mutton curry with swollen bread at a Muhammadan cookshop one day when he went out to run an errand, because his mouth had watered at the smell of the spicy stuff steaming away on the oven. True, he had got into the shop in order to conceal himself from the sight of any passing Hindu who might recognize him, but he had not felt there was anything strange in violating the prevailing custom, except the guilt of having tasted a dish which the Muhammadans cooked better than the Hindus. It seemed that religion did not matter, for there, there before his eyes, he could see a Rajput coolie accepting a Muhammadan hubble-bubble. If the acceptance of hookah and water were a test, surely the coolies had no religion. But he felt vaguely that they would not eat food from each other's hands. For himself, however, it did not matter. And anyway, whether it mattered or did not matter, all that he was concerned about now was to find a job. The blinding sunlight of mid-morning was coming on and they had not stirred.

'Tulsi, Tulsi,' he said, turning round in a panic. 'Let us hurry and join that crowd pressing round the shop which is opening. Come quick.'

And he jumped down and scurried towards the thronging tide of a clamorous crowd surging onwards to a wide godown which stood under a grotesquely painted four-storied house.

Tulsi followed him leisurely.

But he found it difficult to get through to the front, so wild was the rush for jobs by the taller and heftier coolies. He tried to push, to scrape through the edges, to crawl under the legs of the crowd. He sweated with activity. But he did not get anywhere near the vantage point. He stood helpless at the back, only hearing the shouts, the curses, the oaths and the prayers that arose from the throng.

'Get back, you swine! Get back!' shouted the merchant, as he stood on top of his iron safe with a bamboo pole in his hand. 'Get back, you rogues! None of you will get a job if you don't get back.'

'Oh, Lallaji! Oh, Lallaji! I am Muhammad Butt. You employed me yesterday!' a coolie said.

'Get back, you illegally begotten! Get back!'

'Oh, Lallaji! I can carry two maunds on my back easily! Please employ me!' another coolie said.

'Get back, you rogue! Get back! None of you will get a job this way!'

'Lalla, Lalla, only an anna a sack. I will take only an anna to bear the sack from here to anywhere!' a third appealed.

'Get back, you swine, or I will break your bones!'

'Oh, Lallaji! Lallaji!'

This was all that could be heard for some seconds and then the creaking of the bamboo stick falling on hard bones, and the queer angry noises at the front of the crowd, the stamping of feet as they were pressed back and the heaving of wave after wave of men as they strained to escape from the rod.

'Lalla Thakur Das's shop is opening,' someone shouted, and there was a frantic rush towards a big shop guarded by a door of iron rails.

Munoo cunningly perceived the advisability of staying where he was so that if the whole crowd fled away he would get an easy job. When Tulsi came out from the front, where he had insinuated himself and said: 'Come, ohe Munoo.' Munoo whispered: 'Stay here. All these sheep are running away. We will get jobs.'

It happened as Munoo had foreseen. But he had not foreseen all.

Only Munoo, Tulsi and five other coolies remained while the others ran towards Lalla Thakur Das's shop.

'Come, you dogs, you have made me sweat,' said the merchant, laying aside the bamboo stick. 'Come and lift the sacks in the godown and load Rahmat's bullock cart which is going to the railway station.'

FROM GOKAL CHAND, MOHAN LALL

to

RALLI BROTHERS, EXPORTERS, KARACHI

Munoo read the blue Hindustani inscription on the sacks of grain. But he was too young to know the laws of political economy, especially as they govern the export of wheat from India to England. He only rolled the word Ralli in his mouth with a taste for its melody and strangeness, as he had often rolled the words of his science primer in the old village days.

All the coolies, including Tulsi, had sat down to adjust their shoulders to the sacks which lay on a platform. And they arose, some shaking, some straining, some with ease, and began to walk away, bowed under the weight.

Munoo had waited to see how to apply himself to the job. Having seen the others, he imitated their movements from the spitting on the hands to get a grip, to the heaving. But, unfortunately, he could not lift the sack. He felt he had surely missed some miraculous movement which the other coolies had performed. So he heaved and strained and shifted and sought the hidden secret of lifting the weight. But it was all in vain.

The other coolies came back for their second load. Munoo still sat straining his muscles to lift the weight.

'Ohe, leave it, you seducer of your sister,' said a middle-aged coolie, paternally. 'You will kill yourself. You should go and lift small weights in the vegetable market.'

But Munoo was intent on earning a living for himself, for his master and his mistress.

'Come and give me a hand so that I can stand,' he said to Tulsi.

Tulsi came and lifted the sack on to his back.

Munoo arose, his legs trembling, his whole frame stretched tautly outwards to support the burden on his back. He took a step forward, two steps, three steps. Now he was under way, impelled by the mere weight of the sack to go forward in a sustained momentum. At a little ditch on the edge of the courtyard his legs crossed, but he found his balance by an effort of will. His bare, supple body was sweating with the heat of violent exercise. He radiated a fire that glistened on his pale-brown flesh. For a while he looked beautiful as he carried the burden, so finely strung his muscles seemed and so balanced their motion. Then he had to cross the square beam of the doorstep. He lifted his left foot and, before deciding whether he should jump or take a long step, lifted his right foot. His feet hit each other and he fell tottering on to the ground, completely clear of the sack of grain, but on an uprise of hard earth which stunned his head.

'Ohe, you lover of your mother,' shouted the merchant, jumping up from the platform of the shop where he had settled to do accounts in an ochre-coloured portfolio, 'Ohe, you illegally begotten, who asked you to lift that sack, you who have hardly emerged from your mother's womb? Run away, you little rascal! I didn't see you go in to lift the weights or I should have stopped you, you swine! Do you want to have me sent to jail for murder, you son of a dog? Get away, you little wretch!'

Munoo arose with a sudden jerk and, unmindful of the hurt he had received, bolted to get under cover of the sacks on which he had slept last night, so that he could go to another shop for a job later.

But the merchant was still abusing him and had drawn the attention of the other businessmen who were opening their shops and performing purification ceremonies by sprinkling holy water over their cash boxes.

They took up the cue for abuse from their brother merchant: 'Run away, you little wretch, you lover of your mother! Run away!' they shouted loudly, mechanically, without any grievance, and they worked up a scare all round the market as if Munoo were a thief or a brigand to be chased off.

Munoo made for the passage opening out of the square, as if he carried his life on the palm of his hand.

After he had run for a hundred yards or so, he slowed down. There was a throbbing in his head and streams of perspiration were running down his face. He brushed his cheeks, leaving a trail of flushed, hot blood. A cool draught was blowing through the aperture of the gully at the confluence of the two bazaars. He stopped under the shadow cast by a tall house to·feel the breeze and to recollect himself.

He thought of Tulsi carrying weights of grain. 'Lucky Tulsi, he will earn four annas today, and I shall have nothing to take home to Prabha. And it was all my idea. If I hadn't told Tulsi to wait when the coolies had been pushed back by the Lalla, he would not have got the job! I wish I had been strong enough to bear the sack of grain.' He was angry with himself and impatient. 'Oh,' he rebuked himself, 'when will I grow up and be a strong man?' Then he became conscious of the hurried glances of the passers-by. One man, who had come to the passageway leading into the market and sat down to make water by the gutter, stared at him.

'I must go,' he said to himself. 'Go home. But I can't go home without having earned any money,' the stabbing thought came.

And he stood torn for a moment, his heart beating, his head still throbbing faintly, and the heat in his body swelling in the veins of his legs. Then a sack-laden cart came by, pulled by a sleepy-eyed black buffalo, and two men who flogged the animal ruthlessly as they strained to steer the shafts of the vehicle by a thick wooden handle. Munoo had to move on, because there was hardly room for a big uncouth carriage to pass. For a while he walked emptily, hardly aware of anything. Then he suddenly stopped and asked himself where he was going. 'To the vegetable market, where the old coolie said I could lift small weights,' the answer came to him like a ray of light in the darkness. He moved on.

'Why do I suddenly die like that?' he kept asking himself the rest of the way. 'What happens to me that I can't think or see or feel sometimes, while my body goes on moving? And then, suddenly, I can recognize and hear everything. Do I die, or what? Get burnt up into a speck of ash and then evaporate into complete emptiness? How is it that I go on breathing? What is that separate thing under my skin which exists apart from the things in my head? And where do the globules of light come from, tinted on the side, which swarm before my eyes and wave, like the sunlight in Master Prabha's factory which stole through the chinks in the iron sheets in summer?'

But the problems seemed insoluble. Only the hammer of his brain struck more rapidly, and the heat of his body grew, and the minute images in the corners of his soul broke up into even more microscopic elements, till they sank into the complete emptiness from which they had emerged. Then the concrete shapes of men jostling in the street, the articles in shops and the forms of tall houses, small houses, and light cavernous gullies filled his eyes.

'Where is the vegetable market, brother?' he pulled up a coolie and asked.

The man stared at him dazed, completely taken aback. Then he said: 'Second turning on the right by the Chok Farid.'

Munoo ran away without even looking at the man or expressing his gratitude. The desire to earn money possessed him like a panic.

The vegetable market was a bazaar, rather than a square, and richer in colour and life, as business here began earlier in the day, so that the fruit and flowers might be sold before the heat of the sun tarnished their beauty. It was a riot of colour and variety, as all the multi-hued and heterogeneous greens which grow in the tropical gardens of Hindustan were there: green chillies, green cucumbers, green spinach, pale lady's-fingers, purple brinjals, red tomatoes, white turnips, grey artichokes, yellow carrots, golden melons, rose-cheeked mangoes, copper-coloured bananas, all arranged in little baskets, which sloped up from the foot of each shop to its ceiling, on both sides of the street.

And in the street were the endless streams of ill-clad servant boys, ragged men, black-skinned old widows who bargained for a commission, and rich bourgeois women in many-coloured silk shirts and tinted aprons, chaperoning their daughters or daughters-in-law, loaded with gold embroidered silks and garlands of jewels, haggling with the wild-eyed shopkeepers over the price of potatoes.

Amid the clamour of tongues, the challenge of sights and the symphony of smells, Munoo did not know which way to turn. He stared at the piles of fruit which glowed from the beds of green leaves. He nosed towards the baskets, in which the more delicate fruits were arrayed. A contingent of ripe, luscious small mangoes attracted him, and his mouth watered.

'Ohe, you seducer of your daughter!' called a shopkeeper from one side. 'Will you lift a weight for two farthings?'

'Yes, Lallaji,' shouted a chorus of five voices.

But Munoo had got hold of the basket in the shopkeeper's hand. It was as easy as that. But only for two pice.

'Oh, God! that bread should be so dear and flesh and blood so cheap!' Munoo recited the proverb as he pushed his rivals aside.

Munoo returned to the vegetable market, dawn after dawn, while Tulsi repaired to the grain market. Their total earnings were never more than eight annas a day, of which the ratio was Tulsi's six to Munoo's two. Poor enough wage! But it needed all their pluck and a bit of luck to get it.

For there were swarms of coolies about. And, urged by the fear of having to go without food, driven by the fear of hunger gnawing in their bellies, they rushed frantically at the shops, pushing, pulling, struggling to shove each other out of the way, till the merchants' staves had knocked a hill man's teeth out or bled the sores on a Kashmiri's head.. Then they would fall back, defeated, afraid for their lives and resigned to the workings of fate, which might single them out for the coveted prize of an anna job. It was not that the strongest of them were chosen and the weaker had to go to the wall. The caprice of any merchant boy decided their lot, or the shrewdness of the Lalla who could make them accept less wages for more work. Sometimes, perhaps, a subtle trick could secure a coolie a job. Certainly it was cunning which secured Munoo most of the work he got.

Knowing that there was a great deal of competition in the vegetable market, he would roam into the side streets, and, putting on an innocent expression, greet any ladies who seemed to be heading for the vegetable market: 'Mother, will you let me carry your shopping home?'

'All right, all right,' the woman would say. 'You can carry the burden if you will do it for a pice.'

'Oh, two pice, mother, two pice, please,' he insisted, pronouncing the word mother with a deliberate tenderness that he had specially cultivated for the purpose.

'All right, all right, may you die!' the woman replied.

And he would wrest the basket out of her hand, carrying it as an insignia of his established right, so that none of the other coolies should dare to approach the lady.

When the other coolies began to practise the same trick, he had perforce to think of another.

He tried to curry favour with the shopkeepers. But they were too concerned with their business, and too selfish, to appreciate his courtesies, especially as all coolies were to them a nuisance – rude, uncouth, dirty people to be rebuked, abused or beaten like the donkeys which brought the weights of vegetables to the market every morning.

He sought to trick the other coolies by spreading the rumour that the market was to be closed next day. This worked two or three times, but most of the coolies hung around the markets all day and all night, eating, drinking, sleeping and working there, and those who were gullible soon found out that Munoo was a mischievous imp, never to be trusted.

He had to fall back upon the original scheme of booking jobs with women, though he slightly varied the method of getting them now. He did not go out of the market, but while the other coolies sat admiring the beautiful young women who passed through the bazaar, he kept a look-out for the oldest, the ugliest and the most eccentric hags. The only disadvantage of this was that the old ladies bargained vociferously for hours to save a pice, spent ages superstitiously counting each half pice, and generally wanted to requite Munoo for patiently following them from shop to shop with a loaded basket half the day and for walking two miles behind them to their houses in the gullies, with a loaf of stale bread and yesterday's lentils, or haggled with him about the two pice they had promised to pay.

So all his efforts and all Tulsi's did not earn them more than eight annas a day, and this money could not feed the whole family on anything but lentils and rice.

Meanwhile, though Prabha had recovered from the fever and the bruises, he had had a relapse and lay ill with a nervous breakdown, brought about by the pain of seeing the stock in his factory auctioned away, and by the anxiety of the resolve that he had formed to pay every farthing that he owed to his creditors. He worried, too, on account of the boys, knowing from his own past experience as a coolie in the markets how hard it was to earn even a pice a day.

His condition became worse and worse, until the doctor advised him to go away to the hills if he wanted to save his life.

At last he was persuaded to go home with his wife. Tulsi was to see them off to Pathankot, to put them in a cart there and come back. Munoo was to stay in Daulatpur, as they had not enough money to buy railway tickets for all of them. But he was to join the master and mistress later on in the hills.

It was an awful parting.

Both Prabha and his wife wept bitterly.

Munoo had never seen a man of Prabha's age and size cry. That wretched face which had always smiled so gently and so good-naturedly at him and which was now hollow and dark with sickness and misery, looked ridiculous in this plight. The boy shirked coming near his master, as if he had lost all the sympathy of his nature. He looked on mechanically from a distance, asking himself in brief whispers: 'What is the matter with me? Why can't I go near him? He has been so kind to me!'

With his mistress, however, he was more affectionate. He fell into her lap as she sat in the window after everything had been packed and, bathed in her tears, felt the shy bird of his heart fluttering in a sad, silken darkness. The memory of the day when he had arrived here came back to him in vivid flashes of lightning, illuminating the gentle face of this woman, defining the evasive, tender smile with which she had made him feel at home. And then he recalled the pressure of her limbs against him when he was ill. The echo was full of a warmth similar to that which he felt now, only somehow he did not want to give himself to that warmth as he had done during his helplessness.

He withdrew from her grasp with a sudden self-consciousness and stood torn and miserable while she wept.

Tulsi came with the message that he had engaged a bamboo cart which stood waiting at the head of the lane to carry them to the station. Two coolies followed him, Tulsi's friends from the grain market, who had with a natural brotherliness offered to help with the luggage.

There was not much luggage. Only a trunk and bedding.

As Prabha arose, leaning on Tulsi and Munoo's shoulders, he surveyed the desolate room which he had inhabited in the heyday of his prosperity. Then he looked at the single trunk and the bedding being lifted by the coolies and recalled that those were the only things with which he had entered the house when he first came. And now he was going out of Daulatpur with just those two things. All the surplus goods that he had acquired during the interim were superfluous.

'It is good,' he said to himself, bending his pale face weakly, philosophically. 'It is as it should be. Man comes to this world naked and goes out of it naked and he doesn't carry his goods away with him on his chest. It is best to travel light.'

The pale afternoon sun that came in through the iron bars of the window made his home look like a mine of pure gold, giving it a sort of fairy-world enchantment. But he religiously turned his back on it and bent, weary, weak, worn-out and crushed, he walked out supported by his two protégés.

His wife followed with her apron modestly drawn over her grief and her good looks.

The neighbouring men and women had gathered in the courtyard to say farewell to the once most successful and now the most broken of all hill coolies. 'Ram Ram, brother Prabh Dyal,' they consoled in sad, sombre tones, 'Ram Ram. It will be all right. You will come back again. You come back after you have regained your health.'

'And outlived my shame, the bankrupt's shame!' Prabha added with a sneer of mockery to torture himself, so completely had he accepted all business ideals and so convinced was he of having violated the laws of society, so slavishly humble in spite of the hard knocks he had received.

And then, with tears in his eyes and a breaking voice, he waxed philosophical reciting the familiar Indian proverb: 'A wise dog should have smelt the threshold and run away.'

The cavalcade passed through Cat Killers' Lane under the amused and sympathetic gaze of men and women who had come to their doors to obtain yet another sensational topic for gossip.

The bamboo-cart driver cursed furiously when he found that his passengers were not rich Lallas but a pack of coolies. And, under the pretext of hurrying to catch the train whereas he was really anxious to pick up better fare, he flayed his horse into a dangerous canter which made the high, closed structure jolt and sway as if it were a box in a funfair roundabout. Prabha was resigned, even though his heart was in his mouth with the violent knocking and with the hard impact of the springless seats.

'Oh, go slowly, Sheikh Sahib,' said Munoo flatteringly. 'My master is ill.'

'I am not your father's servant,' said the driver, 'that I should wait about for you and miss the passengers on the Bombay mail.'

Munoo felt angry at this and wondered how a man could be so cruel to so good-natured a person as his master.

He felt sadder at the station, sadder than ever.

The train was on the platform, as it started from Daulatpur junction. But the third-class passengers were kept penned up like cattle in the iron cage of the waiting-room, barred with steel doors which were only opened five minutes before the engine gave its whistle.

As they all sat on the cement floor among hundreds of other passengers, among hundreds of bundles, among the buzzing of swarms of flies and armies of mosquitoes, they all secretly prayed to God to allow them a safe place in the train. Nothing short of a miracle would save Prahba's life in the blind rush of passengers to the platform out of this prison, Munoo divined. So he went off reconnoitring to see if there was a loophole through which they could escape to the train.

A ticket-collector with a white uniform adorned with nickel buttons was proudly walking about on the look-out for bribes. He spotted Munoo and read the anxiety in his eyes. 'Two annas,' he whispered, 'and I will let you in through a side door.'

That was half the sum of Munoo's savings for some days. He slipped it into the Babu's hand. He felt afraid that the Babu might not keep his word after accepting the bribe. But the man was quite honest except that he was poor and took bribes. He not only slipped them through a side door, but saw them safely into one of the few third-class compartments that were attached to the train.

Munoo stood sadly looking on at his master and mistress and Tulsi, who were now seated in the train. He felt miserable and alone, as if he had already been cut off from them for ever.

'You go now, Munoo,' said Prabha, dragging his wretched carcass out of the window and pressing a silver rupee into the boy's palm. 'Buy yourself some food and sleep at home for the rent is paid to the end of the month.'

'Jay deva,' said Munoo, joining his hands and overcome with gratitude and love for the man.

'May you live, child,' sighed Prabha, stroking his head.

'I fall at your feet,' Munoo said, turning his joined hands to his mistress.

'May you live, child,' she said, caressing his cheeks.

'I will come back in two days, ohe Munoo, brother,' said Tulsi.

'Acha,' said Munoo, and walked away embarrassedly.

He fondled the silver rupee in his hand and felt elated. Then he was sad to realize how kind Prabha had been to him even in his misery. 'He is surely a very religious man,' he said to himself. 'I wonder if he learnt to be kind by his devotions at the temple. I too shall go to the temple this evening. They give free food at the shrine of Bhagat Har Das. I shall save money that way and also become religious.'

His cogitations were disturbed by the furious, stamping rush of the hordes of third-class passengers who had now been released from the waiting-room and were already storming the train, because they believed that the train, being a moving thing, would move away and leave them behind if they did not run and catch it at once.

He slipped out of the railings on the side by squeezing his supple body, and came into the station yard, where the cart drivers were shouting and raving: 'To Clock Tower and Vishnu Temple', 'To Lohari Gate, Dilli Bazaar', 'To the Hira Mandi, Guru's Dharamsalla'.

'Vay, child, vay, child, will you lift this bag to Dr Sahib Singh's bungalow at the hospital for me? I will give you two annas. There is some dutiable silk in it and we will slip by the customs house if I am not riding in a carriage. It is only two hundred yards away.'

'Yes, mother,' said Munoo eagerly, and reflected. 'This is easy work; I shall come here again and lift bags for people rather than earn two pice for carrying vegetables in the market.'

Now he was alone and had nothing else to do after he had taken the bag from the railway station to the hospital in the civil lines except to eat his evening meal. He knew he could get that free at the shrine of Bhagat Har Das. According to this design and also wishing to become religious, he repaired to the temple of Vishnu, where he had only been once before, with Prabha on the day of his arrival.

He entered it this time through the portals near the lofty houses of the rich merchants of the antique bazaar. The milk-white light of a full moon made the domed roof of the tall phallic temple blossom out like a full-blown lotus, and the cornice shone from the middle of the tank.

A vast concourse of gaily dressed people were moving around it, gilded by the lamps that mocked at the silver moonshine. Munoo joined the throng and began to walk in the direction of the mausoleum of Bhagat Har Das, whose polished marble shone out, beyond the square of the tank, from a background of mouldering travertine. He wanted food more than the blessings of religion, and it was the hour when bread and lentils were distributed to the poor and holy at the kitchen of the shrine. It was this urge which had decided him not to buy flowers to offer at the temple. The vague desire to acquire holiness evaporated from his mind completely as he went along, noticing the vast shadows of the turreted and domed structure in the middle of the pond, playing with the reflection of the moon. The monumental structure inspired him with awe as if the spirit of God were torturing him with its magnificent, invisible presence. He began to walk hurriedly, his one desire being to get away from the oppressive spirit that brooded over the temple. The slow, tortoise speed of the crowd of devotees was a hindrance, but Munoo had become a past master in the art of slipping by the irregular pedestrians of the city of Daulatpur.

He passed through a tunnel leading into the yard of the shrine of Har Das. There was a stand where a devout Brahmin was distributing free water in flat brass cups, nominally free, but really to be paid for as Munoo found that all those who quenched their thirst threw a copper at the feet of the holy man, who had turned menial but had not lost the pride of his ancestral power. Munoo's throat was parched. And he lifted a cup to his mouth. But he did not throw a copper when he pushed the soiled cup away. The Brahmin scowled at him and muttered the proverb: 'May the misers fade away.'

Munoo did not mind being cursed. He had long since got used to abuse and no longer believed in its magical effect. He bolted under cover of the darkness to explore the possibilities of charity. He hoped people were not expected to pay for the free food too.

'Food from the kitchen of God!' shouted a man who held a pan by a string handle as he scurried to and fro, accompanied by an attendant with a basket.

Munoo saw young mendicants and paupers running towards him leaving the old ascetics hobbling along behind, and elbowing each other in their onrush. This surely was the dispenser of the free food. In a moment the crowd of beggars would be on the man.

He ran and spread his hands before the dispenser of food.

'Where is your plate?' the man asked.

'I haven't got one, Maharaj,' Munoo said with a tremor on his lips to convey an appeal for pity.

The attendant had, however, already thrown him two chapatis and the man with the pan had poured a huge spoonful of lentils on to the bread. They were surrounded by the pack of hungry hounds who whinnied abjectly for the food as they crowded panic-stricken round the dispenser of charity. Munoo almost dropped his food in his effort to get away from the crowd. But he scraped through by exercising a queer strength which the mere sight of food seemed to put into him.

He crossed the courtyard to the edge of a fountain playing before the summer-house of a garden. From the garden came a mixed aroma of fresh chambeli, champak and molsari flowers. He sat down and began to eat. He was absorbed in himself for a moment, relishing the taste of the lentils, crudely cooked as they were. But when the gnawing hunger in his belly was half satisfied he looked around.

The moon half veiled, half unveiled the superstructure of the summer-house, and disclosed the form of a fat yogi with shaven head, swathed in an orange-coloured robe, staring with unblinking eyes at the fountain. The yogi had assumed the sacred posture of the lotus seat, with legs crossed and hands resting like newly opened flowers on his knees. Before him crouched an old woman, dressed in a sombre grey apron and a pigeon-coloured skirt, and a young woman clad in all the finery of her bridal dress. Both seemed to be waiting for the yogi's trance to break.

Munoo got up and tiptoed towards the divine.

'And what may be your business, oh, brahmcharya, at the place where the yogi meditates on God? You should be playing with children of your age.'

'Yogiji,' answered Munoo, 'tell me why you sit here so still and without moving an eyelid.'

'Go away, go away, vay, you fool!' whispered the old woman.

'Shanti! Shanti!' the yogi said, lifting his hand with a deliberate saintliness and spiritual grace that belied the smile on his curled lips. 'He is a good portent, mother. He is the image of the child that shall be born to your daughter-in-law. God has listened to my prayers and to yours. Never turn away the messenger of God.'

'I, too, seek God, yogiji,' said Munoo impetuously. 'Teach me to seek God. I want to walk the path.'

'You are a child yet,' said the yogi. 'But come, we will make you a disciple and you may rise to be a saint if you serve your guru.'

'A teacher is what I want,' said Munoo, looking at the fruit offerings heaped up by the holy man.

'Come then, lift all the things that lie there and follow me,' the yogi said. Then he leant forward to the old woman and whispered: 'The full-moon night is propitious for the sowing of the seed. Follow this youth with your daughter-in-law at some distance from me. Come to my chubara beyond the hall of Har Das's shrine. Don't follow too close, for the world is suspicious. A respectable distance, understand, mother.'

Again he turned to Munoo and said: 'Follow me at a distance of a hundred yards and bring those ladies to the back stairs of my rooms. Keep within sight of me and don't lose your way, disciple.'

Munoo did not know what the yogi intended, but he knew that he himself was out for adventure. And the fruit he held smelt sweet and luscious. And his mouth watered at the sight of the grapes, pomegranates, copper-coloured bananas and ripe mangoes. He did exactly as the yogi had directed.

The cavalcade passed through the outskirts of the garden, still, like the leaves of the dense foliage of the hedges that made an avenue to the marble hall of the garden door.

Munoo felt he had lost sight of the yogi as he turned sharply by the shops of the flower-sellers at the gate and entered a dark gully. There he saw him beckoning from a window of the first storey of a house which looked down on the crossroads. He waited for the women, who had lagged behind, and contemplated a tobacconist and betel-leaf-seller's shop, from which a huge mirror reflected the passing pageant of life at the meeting of the four roads. He would have liked to have bought a betel leaf to chew, a luxury in which he had never indulged, and to smoke a cigarette, also to buy some snuff.

But the women came up. And Munoo led them down the gully.

The yogi had come downstairs to receive them with a hurricane lamp in his hand. He led the way up the dark narrow stairs and ushered them into what Munoo felt was a palace, with its white sheets and cow-tailed cushions, and long-tubed hubble-bubbles.

'I will go now,' said the old woman, 'and come back early at dawn, Mahantji.'

'Yes,' assented the yogi excitedly.

The woman went.

Munoo stood looking round, embarrassed.

'My life, do at least lift the apron from off your eyes and say a word to me,' said the yogi, coming towards the young woman and embracing her.

Munoo stared at the man. The scales fell from his eyes and revealed the voluptuary where he had seen the saint.

His heart beat with shame.

He slipped out of the door to go and catch the old woman to tell her what he had seen.

He innocently believed that, like him, she too would be shocked. He did not know that she was a go-between who arranged for the births of 'sons of God' to the wives of the merchant class.

Munoo slept the night on the boards of a closed shop in a street near Cat Killers' Lane, not daring to go into Prabha's home for fear of meeting a ghost or being taken for a thief. And, in the morning, he went to the yard of the railway station, thinking that he would be able to earn enough money for the day by carrying a load from the station to the civil lines, as he had done yesterday.

The morning was well advanced when he got there, and a slow train had just come in from Lahore with hundreds of passengers, rich men and women who hired phaetons and tongas, middle-class men who bargained for seats in bamboo carts with loud-mouthed drivers, and peasants who made up their minds to trudge the dusty roads to town with their belongings on their shoulders.

Munoo looked round among the excited, eager crowd, hurrying to and fro.

'May I lift your weight, Lallaji? ... May I lift your weight, Maiji?'

He tried to work out a theory in his mind, that only a miser who did not want to pay for a seat in a carriage would engage him to bear his burden, or a person who had to go somewhere near the station in the civil lines. But he knew that the hire of a seat in a cart was only an anna and came to the conclusion that even the most miserly of misers would ride, and if he did not ride he would walk and bear his own burden.

'Coolie! Coolie!' some blue-uniformed porters were shouting in the hall. Munoo saw two men put trunks and beddings on their heads and walk away.

He began to shout too: 'Coolie! Coolie!'

'Come here!' a call came from the hall.

He ran eagerly towards the corner whence the order had seemed to come, his bare feet tingling with the heat of the sand in the station yard and his face covered in sweat. He faced a police constable in khaki uniform.

'Why, oh you illegally begotten! Where is your licence?' the policeman hissed, catching hold of Munoo abruptly by the neck of his tunic.

Munoo stood dumb before the constable, his heart beating violently.

'Answer me, you swine, where is your licence?' said the constable, raising his voice from its first deliberation to a sudden hysterical pitch and waving his baton.

'Sarkar,' Munoo ventured with a fallen face, 'I . . .'

'You have no licence! You son of a pig. You were deceiving me!' roared the policeman. 'I have seen you lift bundles here for a month, you base-born!'

'No, huzoor, I have been here only once before,' Munoo ventured, afraid and making a face as if to cry, for the policeman held him hard by the wrist.

'You think I am lying then when I say I have seen you sneaking about here for well on a month,' said the policeman with mock humility.

'It must have been someone else, sir,' Munoo replied. 'Someone like me. All we coolies look alike.'

'You scum of the earth!' the policeman thundered, twisting the boy's arm. 'You swine, you trickster, I will put you in the lock-up . . .'

'Oh, no, sir, no, sir,' Munoo cried at the word 'lock-up', recalling to mind the kotwali where Prabha was beaten.

'Get out of here!' the policeman said, hitting Munoo on the bottom with his baton. 'Get away from here, you lover of your sister! Government orders: no coolies are supposed to work here without a licence!'

Munoo capered away as fast as his feet could carry him, only looking back once to see that the policeman was smoothing down his uniform and stiffening before he began to strut around again.

He began to move forward.

The currents of thought and emotion which had been washed over by the fear of the policeman slowly emerged from the mainsprings that were welling up in him in defiance of authority. 'Who is he that he should turn me out of the station yard?' he exclaimed to himself. 'The swine! He fancies himself to be a god because he is putting on a uniform. My uncle is also a servant of the Angrezi Sarkar. He is not the only one. I am not like Prabha, who let himself be beaten. I shall die rather than let him beat me. I shall live up to the name of my race . . .'

He instinctively turned round to measure the intensity of his thoughts, as if the mere act of willed defiance on his part had crushed the policeman out of existence. But he caught sight of the constable strolling towards the opening of the yard. He ran till he had entered into the Mall Road, in the civil lines, bordered on both sides with European shops.

This modern world was fearsome. Approached through spacious grounds which surrounded the bungalows of Englishmen, impressively empty in contrast to the congested world in which he lived, he felt like the outcast he was. But he liked the prim beauty of the place, its handsome villas, half hidden by hedges, half revealed through sumptuous Gothic verandahs overhung with cane chicks and tatties and pearl bead curtains, inviting the air while warding off the heat, the concrete and stone buildings, clean cut and secure, with their long show windows of glass.

His rudimentary stare explored the exquisite array of glass bowls, full of coloured water, and neatly bottled medicines and powder puffs and soaps and razors in the window of a chemist's shop. But it was beaten back by the hard, shining barrier which made the approach of his imaginary hand past its exterior impossible.

He stared fascinated at a series of enlarged photographs of beautiful Angrezi women and children and uniformed men, hung by shining brass plates outside a door. At once a wild desire surged up in his heart to see his own face in a brown picture like that of the young Sahib who stood dressed in a miniature suit with a white collar round his neck and a straw hat on his head. But the contrast of the neat way in which the Sahib was dressed and his own dirty body clothed in rags was disheartening.

137

He walked past two Indians dressed in English clothes and wondered whether one needed money or education to become a Sahib. The glimpse of a fat Lalla, the long tuft on whose head contradicted his English suit of white tussore, as he waited for customers behind the glass window of his shop, with its array of silver teasets and plates and tumblers and huge cups, answered his inquiry.

But now he walked on in sheer delight at the elegance of clear-cut building, the polished surfaces of black, blue and fawn-coloured motor cars, gigs and phaetons which passed, without raising any dust on the metal road, at a speed which created the illusion of a quicker rhythm in his own body.

'Look where you are going, you black man!' a squeaky little voice fell on his ears suddenly as he was gazing at the jars of English sweets in the windows of Messrs Jenkins' general stores. A memsahib with a pink-white face covered with brown spots, naked according to his Indian standards, for her silk dress immodestly exposed her thin arms, reedy legs and flat bosom, stood before him.

'Look where you go!' she exclaimed, stiffening and screwing up her nose with apparent distaste.

Munoo did not understand the peculiar tone of her bad Hindustani, but guessed from the manner in which she was avoiding contact with the air about him that she considered him unworthy for some reason. As, however, he had developed a strong sense of inferiority before white people, on account of his uncle and the Sham Nagar Babu's hush-hush manner of respectful attention to the Sahibs, he did not become conscious of the insult at all. Instead he felt happy to have been spoken to by the memsahib and, possessed by the desire and the hope of becoming one day worthy of walking in the same street with people like her, he rushed away to the railway bridge which divides the Sahib's world from the outskirts of the native town.

He did not want to recognize any connection between himself and the lepers who whined, 'Oh, man, give me a pice!' as they sat exposing their sores, or with the blind beggars who chanted verses as they swayed their heads up and down. He felt he belonged to a superior world because he had enjoyed the privilege of walking through a superior world. 'I have read up to the fifth class,' he said to himself to confirm his claim of superiority, 'and I have served in a Babu's house where a Sahib once paid a visit.'

The darker shades of his experience were going to crowd out the bright lights of those two peak points of glory, but he stifled them, ignoring all the memories of his life save the two acts of going to school and being in the same room with a Sahib at Sham Nagar.

The riot of noises at the carriage stand opposite the old caravanserai, however, fell on his ears and the bewildering multiplicity of sights swamped him. The sunburnt, scraggy, bearded peasants waiting for a lorry to start, with their bundles of shopping on their backs; the red-cheeked, ferocious-looking Pathans roaming about in their nattily tied turbans, gold-braided red velvet waistcoats, baggy trousers and thick slippers, selling knives and herbs; the frail Hindu confectioners crouching behind their brass trays of sweetmeats, in greasy garments; the cows and buffaloes chewing the cud; the horses snorting and neighing, were all familiar sights and sounds to him, and negligible. He did not have to make an effort to prove his eligibility among them. The real India takes everyone for granted, be he a madman looking at the sun or raving profanities, or a naked ascetic, or a frock-coated, striped-trousered European hiding his nudity in the rigid framework of 'civilized' dress. Munoo regretted that he was not an Englishman, but was soon content to be the bare-footed little coolie with a dirty tunic and loincloth and the small strip of a turban on his head.

Only the question that shaped itself in his mind was how to find work and where. He did not very much want to go back to the vegetable market, and he did not want to go home, not until Tulsi came back. At any rate, they would have to leave off sleeping there when the month was over. Then what? Tulsi was all right. 'He can earn his living at the grain market,' Munoo thought. 'I can't. What shall I do? . . .' 'Go away,' came the answer. 'Where – not back to Sham Nagar?' He recalled that he had never written to his uncle. So far as he was concerned Daya Ram was dead to him and he was dead to Daya Ram.

As he walked along head bent and absorbed, he heard the sudden beat of a drum: dhum, dhum, dhum. He looked up and saw a city crier, who had come to a standstill by the crossroads outside the Temperance Hall, with a troupe of sandwich men bearing huge coloured posters. One showed a woman in a Sahib's costume, decorated with endless medals, flourishing a whip at a pack of ferocious

lions, tigers and elephants; another displayed her as she lay supporting a colossal stone; a third pictured her pushing a carriage full of
men with her head.

'Miss Tara Bai! Miss Tara Bai!' shouted the crier, 'Miss Tara Bai!
The female giant! Owner of the most spectacular circus in the world
is beginning her last performance in the city of Daulatpur now!
Marvellous feats of strength hitherto unseen in the seven worlds!
Feats of strength and endurance and power for which she has won
trophies from all the kings and queens of Europe! Tamer of wild
beasts! Queen of artistes! Take this last opportunity to see her,
because she goes to Bombay tonight en route for England, and will
not come back this side for years. Miss Tara Bai! Miss Tara Bai!
Wonder woman of the age!' And the crier struck the drums again,
dhum, dhum, dhum, dri, dri, dhum, and walked on.

'I must go to the circus,' Munoo decided with a wild delight in
his eyes. 'And I will go to Bombay.'

He snatched a leaflet which the sandwich men were distributing
as they followed the barker. It read:

Outside Madan Lal's Theatre
By the Hall Gate
MISS TARA BAI! THE FEMALE HERCULES!
Most Magnificent! Most Spectacular Show on Earth!

There, fifty yards away, was the Hall Gate, its red bricks shining
cruelly against the glare of the sun. And there, a hundred yards
away, shadowed by the imposing architecture of Madan Lal's
theatre, was the vast circus tent.

'Bombay, Bom-Bom-Bombay,' the word seemed to strike like the
pendulum of the town hall in his brain. And, as if the reverberations
of the note had conjured up all the elements of his life in a deep
echo, the pendulum gathered up in its swing the distant memories
of all that he had heard about Bombay.

A coolie in the vegetable market, whose brother had gone to
work in Bombay, had said that one could earn anything from
fifteen to thirty rupees a month in a factory there. And that it was
truly a wonder city one should visit before one died. The coolie said
his brother had exhorted him to save money from that very moment
for the fare, and work day and night to get there. Because once you

were there, there was plenty of work. The ships sailed across the black waters, too, from Bombay, the coolie had said, and there were palm trees and coconut trees in plenty on the ambrosial isle, among which lived rich southerners and Parsis.

'It is an island, of course, it is an island.' Munoo recollected having read in his geography book that Bombay was an island on the coast of Malabar. 'Bombay, Bom-Bom-Bombay. I shall go to Bombay,' he decided.

He crossed a dirty ditch by a small garden beyond which the big top of Miss Tara Bai's circus stood. He had looked at the handbill and read that the price of the cheapest seat was eight annas. And he had decided that he was going to see the circus without paying the price of a ticket. 'I wouldn't waste the rupee Prabha gave me on useless enjoyment like this,' he said to himself, feeling the edge of his loincloth, in which the silver coin lay knotted.

His habitual recklessness had suddenly turned to unscrupulousness because his good conscience sought to defend the kindliness of his master. So he avoided the regular entrance.

A bay horse, a white mare and a snub-nosed pony stood snorting, as they grazed on a bundle of grass by a few piebald nags. Munoo detected the form of a smart man with a turned-up moustache, looking somewhat like Sorabji, the Parsi chemist, except that he wore breeches, whereas the compounder of medicines always had cotton trousers and an alpaca jacket on.

He crept under cover of a small, filthy tent and waited tensely for a while. Then he looked towards the right and sighted an elephant coming soundlessly out of the entrance of the tent, followed by a crowd of city urchins, while a black driver sat on its head with his legs hidden under the ears of the beast.

'Do you know it dances, climbs on a ladder and plays a mouth organ,' one of the urchins was saying to his friend.

Munoo ran and joined the throng of boys.

One of the leaders of the throng mistook his caper for an invasion. He lifted his strip of a turban and threw it at the elephant's trunk. Jumbo swallowed it up after a graceful salute, as if it were a piece of straw.

Munoo returned the compliment by snatching the cap off the boy's head and throwing it to the elephant.

Before he knew where he was he had been caught by the neck by the youth. He swerved, and planting his leg against his opponent, flung him, lightly into a ditch. As the young man struggled out, covered all over with slime, the urchins behind roared and screamed with laughter.

The elephant shied for a moment and the driver punched the beast with an iron handle, cursing Munoo the while. 'He started it first,' Munoo apologized. The driver jumped down and, catching Munoo by the ear, led him towards the trunk of the elephant to frighten him.

All the boys shied off screaming.

Munoo thought his last moment had come. But Jumbo only blew a heavy breath at his head and went on.

'I am not afraid,' Munoo said brazenly.

The driver smiled.

'All right,' the driver said. 'Go and call that grass-cutter who is going on the road, with the bundle of grass on his head.'

Munoo was only too willing to oblige, for he knew that if he came back with the grass-cutter he would get free access to the circus ground, where people were not admitted without a pass. He ran for the grass-cutter. He caught him at the entrance of the theatre stables and brought him back.

'I want to see the tamasha,' he said to the elephant driver, currying favour with a humble smile, when the man had brought the grass.

'Go away! Go away!' the driver said casually.

'Look,' Munoo insisted, 'I did that work for you.'

The man was walking away towards the back of the tent. Munoo followed lightly behind. 'Look, I did that work for you!' he repeated as they got well behind the tent.

'Don't pester me,' snapped the elephant driver. 'Sit down there, anywhere, and see through the hole in the canopy.'

And he walked away.

Munoo looked for a hole in the canopy. There did not seem to be one at first glance. He tried to lift it from a side.

'Don't do that,' the elephant driver's voice came sharp into his ear. 'You will bring the whole tent down. Here!'

Munoo jumped towards a rent in the canvas in which the elephant driver had dug the forefinger of his left hand.

The performance was well under way. The arena was packed in a crescent of layer upon layer of chairs.

On the near side a band played European music, while under the top of the tent a troupe of trapeze dancers had just brought off a miraculous swing, flying from one end of space to another, till their supple bodies came to a standstill and they walked out of the arena.

Munoo's heart beat wildly at the cheering which followed. Then its violent activity died down in the applause with which the audience greeted Miss Tara Bai, who came swaying, almost like the elephant, Munoo thought, who had swallowed his turban.

He could not see the details of her face through the rent in the tent, but she acted like lightning as she lay down to accept a huge stone on her stomach and rested calmly as two men beat the stone with sledge hammers, in the way in which Munoo had seen the coolies break huge boulders to make small stones for new roads. There was applause as she flung the weight off her body and stood bowing to the audience.

Munoo was spellbound.

But a noise of shuffling feet at a side entrance to the tent about twenty yards away on Munoo's left made him withdraw his eyes. It was only a white horse galloping into the arena.

He applied his eyes and saw the horse enter the ring, followed by a young man who wore what seemed to Munoo curiously tight angrezi trousers and a long cloak of silver sequins. The man might have been a rubber doll the way he leapt from the ground on to the back of the fast-moving horse, stood balanced on its back for a moment, somersaulted, then balanced himself on his head with his legs stretched in the air, and slipped off lightly over the tail of his mount, as easily as if he were walking down marble stairs.

Munoo watched enraptured, his eyes wide open, his brain in a whirl at what seemed to be a miracle.

'I should like to do that,' he said to himself, wildly excited. But then the sight of the accomplished artist jumping from a very precarious position clean on to the back of his mount and galloping away seemed an impossible feat for him to imitate. 'He will be going to Vilayat beyond the seas to where the Sahib-logs come from,' Munoo thought. 'I cannot go there, anyway. I am only a coolie. But I will go to Bombay. Probably I might earn enough there to go beyond the black waters.'

From the midst of resounding cheers a couple of clowns seemed to have been born, dressed in conic hats and loose, spotted clothes, their faces painted white, red and black. They first played with a coloured ball, balancing it on the tips of their extended noses, then aped the trapeze dancers with hesitant movements, which somehow became perfect towards the end and created in Munoo just the effect they were intended to create.

The lion cages were coming in . . .

But Munoo was disturbed by the elephant driver who was passing.

'Come, oh boy, do some work; help me to carry these buckets of water; you have seen enough of the circus now.'

It was hard for Munoo to tear himself away, but he felt that he owed the whole treat to the elephant driver and could not refuse to help. He rose limply from where he had crouched and followed the man.

'Surely an elephant drinks more than a bucketful of water,' Munoo said, shrinking from the prospect of having to carry too many buckets.

'Yes, but I am only washing his buttocks clean,' replied the driver.

Munoo lifted a bucket in each hand from the pump at a corner of the compound and carried it to where Jumbo still stood eating the grass that the driver had bought for it.

'Everyone can see that I am a coolie,' Munoo felt as he sped along. And he was slightly crestfallen at the prospect of never being able to go beyond the seas as the horse rider would. 'Perhaps I shall go to Bombay,' he said to console himself.

But the sheer strain of carrying buckets of water brought about a feeling of exhilaration in his bones. He felt light and buoyant after having done three turns at the pipe. 'I shall ask this man if he will take me to Bombay,' he said to himself, as he stood by the elephant driver, wiping the sweat off his brow.

'Can't you employ me as your assistant and take me to Bombay with you?' he asked, his voice reverberating through his body, tense and hard for a moment.

'I can't give you a job, because elephant-training is learnt through long experience and we go beyond the black waters soon,' said the driver. 'But there is no reason why you shouldn't stow yourself away somewhere in the train in which we go to Bombay. I stole rides in good trains across the whole southern peninsula when I was your age.'

'Are you talking true talk?' asked Munoo to keep up the vague promise.

'Yes,' said the driver. 'You stay here and help us to pack. I shall get you wages for the coolie work you do. And at night I shall smuggle you somewhere into the train!'

'Oh, you are a kind man,' said Munoo, his blood quickening. 'How shall I thank you?'

'Don't,' said the driver, stiffening. 'Somebody will be listening. Come, get some more grass for Jumbo.'

IV

The engine of the special circus train whistled shrilly and then began to move.

Munoo's heart throbbed with fear and with the pang of separation from Daulatpur, as he lay flat by the edge of an open truck on the thick folds of a rolled-up tent, looking up to the stars through the darkness. He recalled the grim moments of the night when he had escaped from Sham Nagar. Only he was not sweating now as much as he had sweated on that occasion. And he did not feel so guilty. He had really earned the ride by working through the whole afternoon, carrying huge, heavy steel ring tops, which came off the centre poles of the vast tent, on to the carts which brought it to the train. Nor did he feel so alone, as the elephant driver was somewhere about in a servants' compartment. But there was the same haunting, ghostly air about the whistle of the engine in the dark which had frightened him almost a year ago.

But it was of the old world, which lay in a direction different from the one to which he was going now, a world obscure and remote even from Daulatpur, a world which he felt he had long left behind.

He did not want to remember either Sham Nagar or Daulatpur. Both had treated him badly. He was going away to a new world, to the new, the wonderful world of a big city, where there were ships and motors, big buildings, marvellous gardens, and, he fancied, rich people who just threw money about to the coolies in the street.

The train was running slowly past the oil tanks of the Burma Oil Company. Munoo wished it would hurry, for though secure, he was still a little afraid that someone might come and throw him out. And then he would have to go back to the vegetable market. 'No,' he said to himself, 'I would kill myself rather than go back. I would prefer to die than to work there.' He felt, as most determined people feel when they have once conceived an idea, that the frustration of his plan would be death.

The engine was gathering speed. The previous rattling of the wheels had now become part of a uniform onward rush. The tall, five-storied houses of Daulatpur were left behind. The hot summer breeze came swishing in. The barking of the dogs was drowned in the roar of the engine.

Munoo sat up on the canvas tent and looked round. Only the deep, dark foliage of fruit trees was distinguishable against the earth and the sky. The darkness had swallowed up the house tops, the minars, the domes, the irregular walls of Daulatpur.

Lest his imagination conjure up visions of his past in the city, he lay back and sought to sleep and drown his memories in oblivion.

The train halted only once at dawn, and Munoo's slumber was slightly broken by the shouting and stamping of passengers and the rattling of trains on the adjoining platforms. 'I wonder what station it is,' he asked himself in his half sleep. But he made no effort to open his eyes. Through the voices of hawkers crying out 'Hindu sweets', 'Muhammadan bread', 'Hot tea', 'Cold water', he could hear someone shout: 'Ambala Junction, Ambala City: Change here for the Kalka line.'

The rhythmic tone of a beetle mingled with the rattling of the train. The cool breeze of the dawn soothed his brain. The world faded out . . .

He awoke at Delhi Central Station. Its tin roof gave no hint of the splendour of the capital of India, as Munoo had imagined it from his books.

Suddenly he looked out and saw men, women and children surging up to the platform, shouting and struggling as they sought to get into a compartment already crowded to overflowing. Munoo took advantage of this hubbub to jump on the offside and to relieve himself by a water-pump among the intersecting railway lines. Then he came back and lay down for a second sleep.

'Come, I will have to find room for you in a closed truck, as it will be hot here in the day. And here is some food which I have brought for you,' came the elephant driver's voice.

Munoo jumped down from the open carriage and followed his patron into a truck where hundreds of bamboo poles lay stacked.

'Here's the food,' said the driver. 'I will come and see you again at Ratlam.' And he went.

Munoo squatted on the hard, uneven seat provided by the bamboos, without thinking of the prospect of having to sit there all day.

As he began eating, the train steamed out of the station.

Between chewing morsels of delicious fried bread and carrot pickle, Munoo thought of the generosity of the elephant driver. 'Why,' he asked, 'are some men so good and others bad, some like Prabha and the elephant driver, others like Ganpat and the policeman who beat me at the railway station?' Then he gazed at the ruined fortresses, castles, shrines and mausoleums, which dug their heels into the barren earth among the gnarled roots of trees, cactus and wild shrubs, fuming with a shimmering smoke without burning under the hateful glare of the all-consuming sun. The boy thought of the legend he had heard that Delhi was founded by a dynasty of kings who owed their origin to the sun. 'Perhaps the sun, the father of the Rajput kings, who were dethroned by the Muhammadans, is taking revenge on the Musulmans by blasting their forts and mausoleums,' he said to himself naïvely.

The emergence to his view of miles and miles of the prim redbrick buildings of Sir Edwin Lutyens' New Delhi, arranged like fuel in a bonfire, confirmed the boy's vague feeling. But it seemed doubtful that the sun would burn the houses built by the Angrezi Sarkar, because he recalled the phrase taught in his history books that 'the sun never sets on the British Empire'.

The sight of two peasant boys, puny against the vast landscape, as they goaded their buffaloes behind their uncouth wooden ploughs through the open country full of dust and sand, brought him down to earth. He thought of the lives of these people, who were cultivating the desert in a vain attempt to eke out a living.

The steep rise of a cluster of hills of weathered stone and red clay barred his view of the world for a while. When the plain emerged to view, Munoo's mind had become empty, and he just gazed at the monotone of sand which stretched for miles and miles and miles, under the metallic glare of the sun, in utter barrenness, except for the withered, parched, thorny bush interspersed at occasional intervals.

A sudden squall arose, gathering dust and sand in its lap, and rolling like a ball, disappeared into a cave.

Munoo felt it was the ghost of some Rajput warrior, as a superstition prevails in India that the spirits of the dead visit the earth in the form of dust storms. But he felt secure sitting in the train as it was speeding along in defiance of the vast earth and the vaster sky, in defiance even of the merciless sun, which blasted the landscape with its malevolent fire. 'The railway is indeed a wonderful thing,' he said to himself. 'If there hadn't been engines which pulled trains I could never have escaped from Sham Nagar to Daulatpur, and I certainly should never be going to Bombay, because one could not walk all that way.'

'But,' it occurred to him suddenly to ask, 'now that I am actually going to Bombay what shall I do there? I know nobody. And how shall I find the work which brings thirty rupees a month which the coolie in the vegetable market spoke about? I would hate to be a beggar in the streets like the Bikaneris.'

The picture of himself walking about like the black men, women and children of the desert, as they whined for the gift of a pice in the streets of Daulatpur, came before his eyes with the horror of the degradation it involved. 'But I have a rupee in my loincloth,' he said to assure himself, 'and did not the coolie in the vegetable market say work was easy to get in Bombay?'

He tried to picture the streets of Bombay. Tall buildings appeared before his mind's eye, like those clean-cut, white stone buildings in the civil lines of Daulatpur. Beyond that and the conception of broad streets his mind failed to imagine anything.

The heat of the closed carriage and the rocking of the train made him fatigued and dizzy. He sought to counteract the urgings of sleep by staring out to the desert again. But the dancing shimmer of the heat waves struck a kind of awe into his brain; his eyes closed against his will, and he succumbed to forgetfulness.

The sudden jolt of his car awoke him in the afternoon to read 'Kotah Junction' written on a black board in white Hindustani and English letters. He still dozed, however, bathed in sweat and rather stiff on the bamboo poles.

'I have brought you some sweets and milk,' the elephant driver said, 'and here is a sack for you to lie on at night. I don't think you should sleep in the open truck tonight, because the Parsi Sahibs of the company walk about on the platform in the evening. My elephant doesn't need as much care as you do, but I am glad to help you, because when I was your age a man helped me to steal a ride from Calcutta to Madras. Now be careful and don't fall out.'

'Acha!' Munoo said, looking greedily at the cream cakes, the sugar plums and the earthen jar full of milk.

The train travelled again through the vast, vast surface of the desert, behind a brave, ferocious engine which whistled occasional warnings to the opposite trains passing like thunder with the speed of lightning.

There was a subtle fascination about the desert under the scorching sun. It seemed to come to life with its illusory mirages of sand and its extraordinarily sparse population of camels, tied tail to nose, nose to tail, as they threaded the wastes, behind the dour men who struggled on foot against hunger and drought. An occasional collection of tents or a ruined outhouse reminded Munoo of the caravanserais he had seen on the outskirts of Sham Nagar. And he tried to picture the rough life that the horse dealers and buffalo stealers lived. But the horizon was limitless, and the boy's eyes ached at the impact of the hot air which came trembling, as if it had been belched out of a furnace.

Towards evening the flat land gave way to sudden hills capped by forts, and to a plateau where the day's strong colours melted lovingly on groves of acacia trees and low bushes at which stray goats nibbled and camels strained their long necks. And then, beyond the empty beds of muddy rivers, little clusters of huts appeared; men who saluted the train as they leant on their staves, women who coyly covered their faces as they bore pitchers of milk on their heads, and children who stood with their eyes open in wonder, their fingers in their mouths, naked and unashamed.

Munoo thought of the days of his childhood in the hills and recalled how often he had played around the cart roads with the distended-bellied Bishan, the lean Bishambar and that superior little Jay Singh. But the purple hills of Kangra were too closed in and there was no railway there to watch. 'It was as well, in spite of the pain I have suffered,' he said to himself, 'to have come away from that world. I am now going to Bombay, and there must be wonderful things there; many more wonderful things than there were in my village at Sham Nagar or Daulatpur.'

As he cogitated, the train left behind the mounds covered with brown grass, wild flowers, low scrub, and entered a glistening green valley, bordered on the far end by a range of ochre-coloured mountains. 'The old fort of Chitore may be in those hills,' he thought, 'where Padmini fought Ala-ud-Din, the slave king of Delhi, and where the heroes of Mewar donned yellow robes and performed Johur and the women committed sati with the queen, rather than face dishonour at the hands of the conquerors. I wish I could see it, I wish I could go there. But I have no work there. I must get to Bombay – Bombay and work. I wonder when I shall get there?'

The engine screamed into Ratlam, and with the suddenness of a surprise, the day died in the darkness.

When it tore through the veil of the evening's violet air, time seemed to run fast past the telegraph poles, faster still as Munoo ate another meal which the elephant driver had brought him, and it ceased to exist at all as the clear, still night hung its low lanterns over the sand dunes and the hill tops. The sky was indigo black now, traced with a silvery sheen, and the world was full of a queer wonder, which shimmered eerily in the shadows, and wrapped itself round Munoo, like the awful stillness with which the ghosts appear out of nothing. He fell asleep cooled by whiffs of breeze, on the sack which padded the uneven surfaces of the bamboo poles.

He awoke to a rich world of palm trees and casuarina and neem and large cultivated fields, at Baroda. The special train of the Maharaja, painted white, and reflecting the gloss of a polish which shamed everything beside it, occupied Munoo's attention, and a few alpaca-coated, white-trousered men, who wore golden caps on their heads and black boots like those of the Babu at Sham Nagar. 'I could never get boots like those before,' he said to himself, 'but if I get work at Bombay the first thing I shall do will be to buy boots.'

The fertile green plains which now stretched for miles, dotted here and there with sudden steep rocks, capped by giant temples and by huge buildings with tall funnels emitting smoke, filled him with a tense nervousness. He felt he was nearing his destination and he doubted whether he would be able to find work.

As the silver line of a long water-course, which seemed to have no end, glimmered in the distance and broke up into a multitude of starry particles, his heart lightened for a moment with the joy of seeing the sea for the first time in his life. Soon the blue waterway ran at his feet, below the railway bridges, and his heart throbbed to it.

The excitement of his newly discovered joy added its weight to the feeling of fear that, momentarily suppressed, burdened his soul. He shook his body violently in an attempt to work off the silent, brooding load of terror that almost dragged him down. He rose from the crumpled sack on which he had couched and came to the window. The sea breeze fanned his face, but left a moist film of perspiration behind. He mopped himself with the edge of his dirty tunic. The particles of sand on his shirt irritated his soft, warm cheeks. He passed his hand through his hair and brought out small particles of coal dust on his palm. He felt exasperated. He sighed. He could have cried. So alone and uncertain he felt. But he sat back and resigned himself to the contemplation of the magical landscape of green fields, washed clean in the sunlight and the shimmering dews of the water from the sea.

'I shall try and look for some man from the north lands as soon as I get there. But how will I be able to find anybody in such a big city as this?'

He saw that Bombay had already begun, as he read the signboards on the walls of factories, announcing in Roman letters, as well as in the hieroglyphs of a language curious to him, difficult names like Rustamji-Jamsetji, Karimbhoy, and the letters BOMBAY. Never, throughout his long journey of two thousand miles from north to south, had he seen the outskirts of a city extend for as many miles as this colossal world he was entering.

The train rushed past groves of dates and palms, past the golden domes of temples, the long minarets of mosques, the tall spires of churches, the flowery façades of huge mansions, past mills, burning ghauts, graveyards, past stoneyards, past fish-drying sheds, past dyeing grounds over which lay miles of newly coloured silks and calicoes, past flocks of sheep and goats, herds of cows and buffaloes, past throngs of men, women and children dressed in clothes of the oddest, most varied shapes and colours.

The panic in his soul grew. The motion of his belly quickened. There was a parched taste in his mouth. His eyes glanced furtively this side and that. He fidgeted on his hard seat and, lifting his legs, felt stiff and uncomfortable. His brain whirled with excitement. His blood welled so fast that it seemed to him he was running. His face paled. His body was covered with sweat. His head was empty and dark.

Then, after flashing past station after station of the suburbs, the train whistled one last whistle, shrieked with a last tortuous pull at the brakes, and puffing, panting, sighing hoarsely, as if it were dead beat, came to a standstill by an outlying platform of the huge Victoria Station.

Munoo looked out uneasily at the empty trucks of a goods train, which stood on the offside of the platform. Should he wait for the elephant driver to come or should he run towards the godown, at whose large doors some coolies pushed bales of merchandise and through which it seemed possible to escape into the streets?

'Come, brother, you have reached the land of your heart's desire,' said the pock-marked, black elephant driver. 'This train will soon go to the Ballard Pier, where we mount the ship that is to carry us across the black waters to Vilayat. Here is some food. Come, I will show you a way by which you may get out of the station unnoticed.'

Munoo jumped down.

Now that he was face to face with the man who had been good to him, he could not even thank him. Instead, he felt embarrassed and wanted to get away from him as soon as possible. He followed him.

'The bigger a city is, the more cruel it is to the sons of Adam,' the elephant driver said, crawling under the buffers of a train. 'You have to pay even for the breath that you breathe. But you are a brave lad.'

They had reached the godown.

'Go through there as if you were an ordinary person. God be with you.'

Munoo looked up to the man. The ugly face was a mask. The boy walked on as he was told, the bottom of his heart breaking with the weight of gratitude and fear. When he looked round he had walked into a square.

Munoo emerged from the Victoria Station. Before him was Bombay; strange, hybrid, complex, cosmopolitan Bombay, in whose streets purple-faced Europeans in immaculate suits, boots and basket hats rubbed shoulders with long-nosed Parsis dressed in frock-coats, white trousers, dome-like mitres; in which eagle-eyed Muhammadans with baggy trousers, long tunics and fezes mingled with sleek Hindus clothed in muslin shirts, dhotis and black boat-like caps; in which the saris of Parsi women vied with the colourful loads of the garments on rich Hindu women and put to shame the plain white veils of purdah women and the flimsy frocks of masculine European women; in which electric motor-horns phut-phutted, victoria and tram bells tinkled tinga-linga-ling; in which was the press of many races whom Munoo vaguely knew as Arabs and Persians and Chinamen, and the babble of many tongues which he did not know at all.

He stared at this confused medley of colours and shapes and sizes, heard varied sounds, and smelt a smell different from all the perfumes, aromas and stinks he had ever smelt, the mixed smell of damp and sticky sweat, dust and heat, musk and garlic, incense and dung. He lost both the balance in his steps and the silent determination of his soul to go onwards.

He hurried towards a quiet pavement. He looked around to measure the strength of his frame against the world. The huge domes and the minarets of the General Post Office on his right, the vast domes and minarets of the railway station on his left, the great domes and minarets of the university and the law courts beyond, all vying with each other to proclaim the self-conscious heights attained by their Gothic-Mughal architecture, challenged him to decide which of them was the most splendrous, not knowing in their vanity that he was only a modest hill boy impetuously impelled by every big building to believe it to be great, and easily daunted by such grandeur into believing himself completely insignificant and small.

Oppressed and overcast, the boy walked along the square wiping streams of sweat off his face, till he sighted a bench at the foot of a marble statue of the short, stocky, broad-bottomed Victoria with a scroll in her hands and a crown on her head, on which a blue-black crow cawed defiance to the world as it danced and fluttered after relieving itself.

He sank into a corner of the bench and, withdrawing his gaze from the street, where a mixed crowd waited for the wondrous tramcar which came rolling on wheels, unpropelled by anything, he sought to collect himself and to partake of the food which the elephant driver had given him.

He opened the packet of sweets in his hand and contemplated first the yellow colour of the boondi, the chocolate of the rasgulas and the white of the cream cakes. His mouth watered. They were delicious. But there was an empty space in his belly. He ate mouthfuls, ruining the taste of the food. He could not swallow it fast enough.

When only one cream cake lay in the leaf bag in his hand he felt thirsty, and looked aside to see if there was a pump where he could go to drink water. Hardly had his gaze been diverted, when the crow which sat on Queen Victoria's head swooped down and carried the bag out of the boy's unconscious hands and threw it on the pavement.

Munoo came back to himself with a half-amused, half-chagrined smile, and cursed: 'Son of a thief!'

Just then a swarm of crows came soaring over his head and, cawing brazenly, fell on the sweets which had dropped out of the bag on to the pavement, and fluttered back to their eminent shelter on Queen Victoria's head, in her arms and around her large proportions.

Munoo got up confused and, straining not to attract anyone's notice, thought to himself: 'The son of a thief must have known that I wouldn't pick up food from the pavement, where the shoes have been, and so he waited till I wasn't looking. The cunning bastard!'

He walked down the pavement which was punctuated almost at every step by some person or another. There was here an old astrologer with the intricate caste marks of priesthood painted on his forehead, a white flowing beard and a fat body immaculately clothed in long muslin robes, telling the fortune of a Gujerati clerk; there was next a Muhammadan barber with his razors and cuticles spread before him, looking into a large dressing-table mirror as he puffed at his hubble-bubble while waiting for customers; there was further a bookseller, displaying books and magazines with the coloured pictures of beautiful European women on them and some pamphlets which proclaimed the secrets and mysteries of sex in bold Hindustani letters; there was a fruit-seller further ahead, and a sweetmeat seller and, at the edge of a footpath in a corner, a coolie lay huddled, pillowing his head on his arm, shrinking into himself as if he were afraid to occupy too much space.

Munoo's heart sank at the recognition of a labourer lying about thus precariously. 'So even here the coolies sleep in the streets!' he suddenly realized, and the memory of the words of the coolie who had said that money was strewn about the streets of Bombay sounded falsely hollow in his brain. His throat was parched and dry with thirst. His limbs sagged. Before his mind's eye arose the grim fear of the night coming and finding him alone and friendless in the streets. He tried to forget the oppressive thought. His brain became a blank and the picture faded out.

He had come to the edge of four roads, alongside which stretched avenues of tall, massive, stately edifices, eight stories high, just like those in the bazaar of the civil lines at Daulatpur, except that they seemed to continue for miles and miles.

He stood riveted to the spot for a moment, not knowing where to go and not daring to cross into the boulevards of civilization. Then he saw men walking up and down the pavements of the roads casually, among them even a few coolies with tunics much dirtier than his own. And he walked on.

He braved it and ran hurriedly past the raised arms of a black policeman, who wore a blue and yellow uniform, different from the up-country constables, bare-legged, his cap tilted nattily to one side. His heart beat wildly as he slowed down by the polished brass plates round the door lintels at the gates of a big building, on which were engraved black letters of the English alphabet. 'Cox & Co.', he read on one of them, and he felt pleased with the strange connection they seemed to establish between him and the world of Sahib-logs. He recalled, however, the rude way in which the Englishwoman in Daulatpur civil lines had spoken to him and he was again half afraid to go on. But there were plenty of Indians walking down the streets and only a few pink-faced men. So he went on. Only he felt more thirsty than ever now and, as he walked, he scanned the length of the bazaar to see if there was a charity water stall here like those in Daulatpur. The huge glass windows of furniture shops followed upon the long portals of an office, or the mysterious flight of steps of a bank, but there was no well or pump where he could get water.

At length he sighted a huge canvas lining, behind glass doors, a row of coloured soda-water bottles and, beyond the window, some people who sat on angrezi chairs by marble tables, eating and drinking and chatting. He had once drunk soda water while on an errand in the streets of Daulatpur at the shop of Bali, the ice seller. He felt he would like to drink a bottle now. But the clothes of the people who sat in the shop, as he saw from the wide-open door, were clean. They looked to be rich Babus or merchants, and he felt he was only a dirty coolie. 'But a bottle of soda water only costs an anna, and I have a rupee tied up in the end of my loincloth. I can go and buy one,' he told himself.

He almost stumbled on the doorstep, as, with heavy feet and light heart, he walked in and stood blind and uncertain in the commodious restaurant. He tried to steady himself, and felt everyone was looking at him. He sat down on a chair by an empty table that stood on his right. He felt he was floating in the air, so rapidly did his brain wheel round and round with confusion and embarrassment. He brushed his arm across his forehead to calm himself and to wipe off the sweat. He brazened himself into self-assurance and glanced at people pouring hot tea from their cups into saucers and sipping it with spattering sips. Hardly had he withdrawn his gaze from the queer people when a tall man in muslin, with his hair profusely oiled and parted in the middle, came up to him and said: 'Coolie?'

'Yes,' Munoo confessed, his heart almost missing a beat.

'Sit down on the floor, there; what do you want?' the man said insolently.

Munoo got up from the chair lamely and settled down on the cemented floor full of fear and without saying a word.

'What do you want?' the man asked again.

'A bottle of soda water,' Munoo said.

Some of the men who were spattering at tea in their saucers looked at him as if he were a leper, and the waiter winked at them a significant glance, half in mockery at the coolie who indulged in soda water and half in contempt.

Munoo felt wild with rage, but tried to still his mind by acknowledging the superiority of the clean-clothed rich people, whom he had always been told to respect. Feeling that all the men in the place were staring at him, he looked away into the street through the glass window.

'Give me the money, two annas,' the man shouted, coming almost on top of Munoo's head suddenly.

Munoo started. Then with bent head, and conscious of the stares of everyone, he loosened the knot in his loincloth and handed over the silver rupee to the waiter. The man fetched a glass of green-coloured, frothing soda water from a high stand and gave it to Munoo. Then he counted fourteen annas change on to Munoo's palm.

The sharp, cool, sweetish taste of the soda water tingled in Munoo's mouth and brought tears of acid into his eyes. He would have liked to have sipped it slowly and enjoyed the full flavour of the drink in comfort. But he was nervous and feeling extremely guilty for having intruded into the rich man's world. So he gulped the water down as fast as he could. And, placing the glass in a corner, he made to go. The aerated liquid had an instantaneous effect on his belly and he belched in spite of himself.

'Go away,' the man shouted behind him.

Munoo darted as if to save his life.

When he had reached a hundred yards or so, he looked back. The man was not following him. But he was terror-stricken. Looking furtively this side and that, fore and aft, he slunk away, cursing himself for having gone into a shop like that. He felt he had wasted his money. The man's nastiness had left such a bitter taste in his mouth. 'I was so thirsty, though,' he said to console himself, 'and now I am no more thirsty.' He belched again, and this spontaneous confirmation of his thought by his belly made him laugh.

'I should have fought hard if he had dared to turn me out or abused me,' he said to himself. 'I let him put me in my place as a coolie, but I was paying for the soda water and I am not an untouchable. I am a Hindu Kshatriya, a Rajput, a warrior.'

He felt strong and powerful at the thought of being of the warrior caste, strong and happy, his dignity coming back to him. And he walked on elated and unconscious, exercising his rudimentary stare on a huge, wonderful, coloured picture of Marlene Dietrich which stared down at him, her large eyes and long lashes seductively askance, her milk-white body naked save for a pearly bodice and a pearl loincloth. Lest the pleasure of contemplating so beautiful a vision be forbidden to a coolie, he arrested his ardent glance, looked round surreptitiously to see that no one was noticing him, and was going to move into a position from where he could command a clearer and more detailed view of the form that had now started a wild movement in his blood, when he suddenly heard the loud bellowing of raucous motor horns, the tan-tan of tramway bells, the angry yells of phaeton drivers and shouts of 'dem fool', 'black man, where are you going?' He stood dumb and still in the deathliest fear of having got into the way of the traffic. He felt as if he were dead or dying. But then a sudden impulse for life made him turn quickly on his feet. He saw that he was quite safe, but that on the other side of the pavement a scantily clad small dark man with grey hair and bowed legs, loaded with bundles, was dragging at a loaded woman, who was dragging a boy, while a frightened little girl shrieked in the middle of the road behind them.

With one of those sudden impulses that arose too often in his wild blood, he rushed into the road where the terror-stricken child stood sandwiched between the dangerous streams of traffic and, lifting her under his arm, ran across to where the helpless family fussily muttered curses and prayed to the Lord.

'Oh, may you live long, may you live, my son,' the woman 'wilked', joining her hands to Munoo and eagerly receiving her daughter into a warm embrace. Then she addressed her husband: 'What a place to bring us to!'

'Keep quiet, woman, you nearly killèd my children,' said her husband.

'You should have held them. You left me there on the road and crossed to safety yourself! Wah! Strange father you are!' she sputtered.

'Be patient, mother, be patient,' said Munoo, assuming an air of grave filial piety for a moment.

'Brother!' the old man said, patting Munoo's back and then joining his hands to him in supplication and gratitude, 'that little witch would have been killed if you had not run to save her. These machines are like devils!'

'You have so much to carry,' said Munoo. 'Where have you to go? I will help you with a load.'

'I worked at the Sirjabite [Sir George White] cotton factory six months ago, before I went to fetch my family from the village,' said the old man. 'I will go there in the morning and look for work again. Now I go into the city where there may be a corner outside a closed shop or on a pavement, where we can rest for the night. We are poor folk. Now we will be going our way, Ram Ram.' And he made to go.

'Brother,' said Munoo eagerly, 'I am a newcomer to Bombay and I want a job too. In your thought do you think it will be possible for me to get a job at the factory where you work? I am a coolie. I come from up country.'

'Ah, yes, do come, brother,' said the old man. 'If you can sleep the night with us we can all go together to the factory in the morning. And then I will present you to the big Mistri Sahib. And we can take a hut near the Meel and you can lodge with us.'

'Yes, brother, that is what I want,' said Munoo, trying to instil as much seriousness into his tone as possible.

They walked away from where the vast masses of Western big business houses and the domed splendour of great buildings cast oppressive shadows, and, passing by a playing field, entered the coloured eastern world of Girgaum.

Munoo bore the girl child on one shoulder, the boy on the other, and looked not unlike Hanuman, the monkey god, who is supposed to have carried Rama and Sita, the hero and the heroine of the Ramayana, from Ceylon to Oudh. Now that he had found company, he felt himself, and the impish enthusiasm of his being returned.

'Brother,' he said, running up to the old man who led the way, 'what is your name?'

'They call me Hari, brother; Hari Har,' said the old man, stopping to wipe the sweat which streamed down his coffee-coloured forehead over his tender eyes to his rather thick black moustache. And, resting the weight on his back by the iron cage of a young tree, he blew a mouthful of hot breath.

'How far have we to go?' asked Munoo, concerned to see that the old man was tired and that the children were dozing on his shoulders.

'We have only a little way to go through the Bhendy bazaar to Chaupatti,' replied Hari casually. And then he addressed his wife who had come to a standstill a little distance away: 'Ari, mother of Moti, sit down and rest awhile.'

The woman modestly moved her head, thickly veiled under the apron, and only shifted a small tin trunk which she held under the left arm.

'The shades of the evening are falling and the children are already asleep,' said Munoo, putting on an air of worldly wisdom. 'Let us hurry.'

'Let us mention the name of God, and go on,' said Hari. 'I know of a short cut to Chaupatti.'

They crossed into a narrow street where the houses jutted close into each other and over the pedestrians, with their fabric sunhoods, or naked, serried windows opening into rickety, carved balconies, from which the heat had licked off the paint.

It was difficult to carve a way among the throngs which leisurely strolled along in garments of colours as varied as there are cheap German dyes, in forms as tawdry as can be obtained by mixing the styles of a hundred different races.

'This', Munoo thought, 'is no different from Daulatpur or Sham Nagar, only more confusing.' And he shut his mind to the silver, the orange, the green, the gold, the blue, the flaming red colours of the trappings of the Arabs, the Hindus, the Muhammadans, the Parsis, the English and the Jews, and walked on, concentrating on himself. The kaleidoscope assumed a uniform white-coloured mass before his mind's eye.

But the riot of variety was soon illuminated by the electric bulbs which hung from every booth, stall and shop, and the vermilion, scarlet, yellow and green which shone now garishly, now dazzlingly upon Munoo's eyes. He was, however, annoyed by the strange mixture of peoples, the queer din of forty-odd lingos, and felt his northern blood quiver with self-consciousness, as he struggled along under the weight on his shoulders, on the pavement now wedged with men and women.

The wares displayed in the shops attracted him, especially the steel toys he saw on a stall and big mangoes, bigger than those which he had seen in his village, in Sham Nagar or in Daulatpur. But the shops were surrounded by rich men, who haggled loudly over the prices of goods, and Munoo had perforce to move on.

An emaciated man, the bones of whose skeleton were locked in a paralytic knot, dragged himself by the edge of the road, precariously near the wheels of passing victorias, begging with a wail, half metallic from repetition: 'O man, give me a pice!'

'Get away! Get away!' the Parsi owner of a shop cried, flourishing the big bamboo pole of an awning he had dislodged.

Further along, a grey-haired, black, blind man leant, half on the arm of his daughter, half on a stick which he held in the gnarled roots of his right hand. The girl, with clear-cut features that had once beamed with life but which now expressed nothing except abject humility, the absolute weakness of a smile and the shining, painful meekness of the eyes, joined her two hands in importunate beggary.

'Go away! Go away! Let us rest!' said a wisp-clothed Hindu, who sat killing flies in his shop, the red rubies in the gold rings of his ears reflecting a cruel glint of laughter on the woman's mask of pain.

'So, after all, there is no money to be picked up in the streets of Bombay,' Munoo reflected, 'because there are poor people here, too.' And he felt strangely heavy in his heart as he looked up to the low, deep-blue sky from which the stars stared down brightly and happily.

He hurried to get abreast of Hari, who appeared to walk very quickly and energetically for his seeming two score and ten.

'There is no air here, Hari brother,' Munoo said, 'let us run fast.'

'Where is the mother of Moti?' Hari asked suddenly. He had evidently forgotten all about her.

So had Munoo.

The old man ran back almost panic-stricken, causing anger and irritation among the crowd through whom he had to shoulder his way to search for his wife. Luckily he found her, buying bananas at a stall.

'You will get lost,' he cursed. 'This isn't the village that you can find your way back home. There is no home to go to here.'

The woman followed a little more quickly. Her heart went out to the bracelets, the culinary utensils, the ivory work and the gold and silver ornaments which lay exposed in the shops on her left, and she could not help breaking through her modesty and saying to her husband: 'I would like to come here to buy things when we are settled.'

This made Hari very angry, not with her, but with himself, and he bullied: 'Walk on! Walk on! You bitch! You have hardly a place to rest your head on for the night and you build castles in the air like Shaikh Chilli.'

Munoo had stood watching a quarrel between two phaeton drivers who, caring nothing for the right of the road, had brushed past each other so dangerously as to alarm the rich, silken-saried Parsi women pedestrians into a grave anxiety about their lives. Then the old man and his wife joined up.

They emerged from the bazaar into a residential street, with tall houses, decorated by façades of floral designs and arabesque reliefs, plastered and whitewashed in imitation of the European style. The huge posters outside a cinema at the end of the road illuminated by bulbs of coloured glass accentuated the air of civilization.

'What about sleeping here, brother?' said Munoo.

'No,' replied Hari, 'we cannot sleep near the houses of the rich. Many thefts take place here and honest folk are caught up with the dishonest loafers and thrown into prison. For us the street there, where shops close early and the boards are empty.'

Twenty weary steps and they had turned the corner.

But Hari came to a sudden halt when he should have turned to left or right.

Munoo almost dropped the sleeping children from his shoulders, as he pulled up with a start before knocking into the old coolie in his almost mad rush onwards into the broad street covered thickly by the shadows of houses over which descended the thick layers of the night.

'Have you forgotten the way, then?' Munoo asked, as he saw Hari stand fixed.

'No,' said Hari, shaking his head despondently. 'We are late. It will be difficult to find a place here. This street is full of men. We will have to wait till the shops in the bazaar that we have left behind close for the night, unless all the shelters there are taken by the coolies who work round about.'

Munoo looked back and saw Hari's wife standing still, her apron still drawn over her face, and the coloured lights of the cinema far away in the street radiating happiness. Then he looked ahead of him, exploring the avenue of the broad street by the pale light of infrequent gas lamps that illuminated it. The bodies of numberless coolies lay strewn in tattered garbs. Some were curled up into knots, others lay face downwards on folded arms, others were flat on their chests, pillowing their heads on their bundles or boxes, others crouched into corners talking, others still huddled together at the doorsteps of closed shops, or lay on the boards in a sleep which looked like death, but that it was broken by deep sighs.

'If we go further, there might be a place for us somewhere,' Munoo said, urged by the cool breeze that came like a snake swishing from the darkness of the sea on his right. And he bravely led the way.

He had hardly gone three yards when he stumbled on a heap of patched quilt that half enclosed the rotting flesh of a leper who was stretching his bandaged arm and legs as a warning to all passers-by.

Sick with disgust and pity and stung by the scorpion of fear, he capered aside only to be greeted by the hoarse moan of a sleeping beggar, who protected her little child as she lay close to it, resting her head on her elbow and looking out into the dark with a tiger's steel glance in her eyes.

Munoo came towards Hari abashed, and looked at the old man with a nervous smile on his jaws.

'Walk carefully, my son,' said Hari. 'Let us not disturb other people's rest. I will show you the way.'

Munoo made room for the old man to lead and he followed cautiously, adjusting the weight of the sleeping children. He wondered how Hari's wife could see in the dark with her head apron drawn over her eyes, and he wished he could ask her to uncover her face. If she were as old as Hari he felt he could ask her quite openly, as she could be in the position of a mother to him, who was only fourteen years of age.

He looked around with a view to seeing if he could address her. Suddenly the rapier thrust of a heart-rending shriek fell on his ears. He saw that ten yards ahead a coolie had fallen with a thud and was rolling down, kicked from behind by the caretaker of a house, who presumably wanted to close the iron door that secured his master's mansion against thieves.

There were hoarse whispers, groans and heavy, half-subdued sighs. Then a number of coolies arose from the nooks and corners where they had taken shelter for the night, apprehensive that the same fate might befall them.

The bodies which lay sprawled all over the pavements heaved to and fro, flung off their torn white sheets, surprised, and stretched their glistening black bodies in the darkness, or cast off the weariness from their sagging limbs and sat up speaking kind, soft words and incantations, as if their magic formulas would charm away all misfortunes.

Munoo shook the panic off his being as he heard Hari turn back with a reassuring message: 'Come, I see a place across the road.'

The boy followed, thinking how different seemed the bodies of the coolies here from those of the labourers in the grain market at

Daulatpur on that night after Prabha had been beaten up by the police. The hill men and the Kashmiris in the north were hard, thick, big-boned and raw, while these coolies seemed weak-kneed, spineless and thin. But then, he felt, there was really little difference between them. The up-country coolies were as afraid of the care-takers as these southerners. And he recalled the feeling of grim fear that had possessed him during the moment when he had clambered up to the top of the grain sacks, the fear of the long stave of the chowkidar.

There was, indeed, a clearing on the other side of the road by the doorsteps of a shop, a kind of gallery with a three-foot square of board, evidently used to put shoes on by the shopkeepers during the day. But why it was empty they could not make out, as they stood dubiously contemplating its advantages.

A half-naked woman who sat nursing her head in her hands, as if she were struggling to control the most excruciating pain, looked up at them and said in a voice which was smothered by her sobs: 'My husband died there last night!'

'He has attained the release,' said Hari. 'We will rest in his place.'

Munoo felt the dread of death facing him. The picture of the large, ugly, demoniac form of the god of death which he had seen in a lithograph in a shop at Daulatpur, standing guard over the souls of the wicked who strained to swim across the ocean of blood, formed itself before his eyes. The blood in his body seemed to dry up. But he felt the warmth of the child's breath on his cheek and Hari spoke: 'We are not afraid of ghosts.'

Fortunately his wife had not heard the woman's warning, as she had lagged behind, weighed down by the load she was bearing.

'Come and rest your limbs here, Lakshami,' said Hari, as she approached. And he unrolled the baggage he carried. She obeyed her lord and master.

'We will rest out on the pavement,' Hari said, putting his hand affectionately on Munoo's back. 'The children can sleep there with their mother.'

Munoo laid the boy on the unrolled bedding in the gallery. Then he came back and sat down on the pavement next to the concrete wall.

The slab of stone under him exuded the warmth which the scorching sun of the day had left in it. But he saw that there were sheeted figures sprawled all over the pavement. 'One gets habituated to it,' he thought. 'I shall soon get used to it. Only I am new here.'

As he cast his eyes along the street, this side and that, he saw why it felt strange here. The swarming houses in Daulatpur were comparatively low and the coolies huddling about them seemed like ants on a heap, while the very gigantic proportions of these colossal stone buildings which shadowed the narrow bazaars made the dark bodies of coolies seem out of place. And there was something oppressive in the low, southern sky overhead and in the dense, dark, stifling atmosphere which it enclosed. And everything seemed so still, so dead.

Munoo felt very alone.

Then he became aware of a hot blast of air which came loaded with the sickly, foetid odour of ghee, sandalwood, urine, sour milk, fish and decaying fruit. He looked in the direction from which the smell oozed. A soft breath, half moan, half sigh, was all he could hear and the movement of a corpse flinging off its blanket. He looked the other way. There was another coolie turning on his side restlessly and muttering something. He withdrew his glance. Presently he became conscious of a bare body rolling in anguish and slapping itself on the knees to the accompaniment of foul curses.

Munoo looked beyond this man, across the road, then beyond Hari, who had laid down on his left, and beyond the widow, who still sat bending her head in her hand. There were corpses and corpses all along the pavement. If the half-dead are company he was not alone. But he felt a dread steal through him, the dread of sleep, the uncanny fear of bodies in abeyance, whose souls might suddenly do anything, begin to snore, open their bloodshot eyes for a second, grunt, groan, moan, or lie still in a ghastly, absolute stillness.

Silently and quickly he extended his legs and dragged his body into the attitude of sleep, closed his eyes, and tried to assure himself that all these people were just like him, not ghosts, but men. 'They have probably all come down from the north to find work like me,' he reflected. 'I wonder if they stole rides on trains or had to pay fares. That elephant driver! He must be on the black waters now. He was kind! And Prabha! I wish they knew that I have made friends and am going to get a job tomorrow. They both said I was a brave lad. Yes, I can do things. But what could I do if all men were like Ganpat or the policeman, or the man in the food shop today. I wonder what Hari thinks. His black face always remains the same. I shall ask him to tell me his story tomorrow. His wife keeps her face covered. I would like to know what she looks like –'. A ripple of warmth passed through him at the thought. He felt feverish. 'Sleep, sleep, come sleep,' he said to himself. A queer agitation possessed him, unsettling him, exciting him, working him up into a panic, so intense that the sharp edges of his thoughts cut open his brain in their wild rush outwards. 'O, sleep! sleep!' he cried out in his soul. And he closed his eyes deliberately tight. But though his eyes were tired and his bones weary, they were too weary for sleep. His body quivered and perspired. He gasped for breath, turned on his side and saw Hari fast asleep. He tried to simulate the appearance of Hari's body, thinking that by copying the right posture on the pavement he could sleep. For a moment he rested thus, histrionically. The image of Hari's wife stood before him, veiled. He opened his eyes. It was no use. He felt he must get up and rush away, away, away, somewhere beyond the confines of the street, somewhere where there was a whiff of air to breathe. But he was afraid he would stumble on the bodies which lay along the pavement and then there would be a scene. He tossed about on his stone bed, flinging his elastic haunches from side to side till he felt his hip bones ache with the impact of hardness against hardness. Then he plunged his head on to his hands and lay face downwards. The suffocating darkness descended on him.

A cool breeze blew through the street at dawn.

It penetrated into the bodies of the coolies, lepers, beggars and paupers, through the rents and holes in the flimsy sheets that covered them.

They shivered and stirred uncomfortably, or huddled against each other, or shrank into knots, or merely turned on their sides.

Another gust.

The naked lepers moaned. The others clutched their garments closer or awakened suddenly from the intoxication of the sweet early morning's sleep, thankful to God even in their discomfort, as they murmured 'Ram, Ram, Sri, Sri.'

The breeze which came from the sea soon became a windy draught.

The names of God multiplied on the lips of the wretches, because, ritually, every spasm of cough, every mouthful of stale spittle, every blow of the nose, is in India an occasion for the invocation of the Almighty.

Those who were not awakened by the noise of an asthmatic or consumptive cough, by the sharp, thunderous spurts of spitting, or by the loud and vehement blowing of noses, or by the multifarious names of God, were awakened by the arm of the law which, baton in hand, came to clear the pavements near Chaupatti.

Munoo was one of them, Hari having got up already.

'Ram, Ram, brother,' greeted Hari. 'We should be on the way to the factory.'

'Are the children awake?' asked Munoo, with enthusiasm and alacrity. 'If not I will carry them.'

'We will rouse the affliction of God,' said Hari. 'They must learn to wake up early. They will have to go to work at the factory before sunrise every morning. Why did I go away from Bombay four months ago, if not to fetch them, so that, like the children of other men, they should begin to earn their living. Thus only can we make both ends meet.' Then he looked towards the passageway, where his wife had kept watch while the children slept all night. 'Why, Lakshami, are the children awake?'

The woman began to shake the children gently. But the little ones only moaned and stiffened.

Hari walked towards the gully menacingly.

'I will pick them up, don't disturb their sleep,' said Lakshami, leaning to protect them against her husband.

'You can't bear brats of eight and nine!' snapped Hari.

And he leapt at the little ones, picked them up by the arms and shook them. Their hands dangled limply. They only sobbed without opening their eyes and without relaxing the dead weight of sleep that made their bodies sag.

'I will bear one as I did last night, brother Hari,' said Munoo, feeling uncomfortable at what seemed likely to develop into a domestic wrangle.

Hari picked up the tin trunk, while Munoo came and lifted the boy, a firm-featured creature with an indigo shade of skin. Lakshami lifted the girl. Hari rolled the bedding. And the cavalcade moved on.

The town was coming to life in the streets. White men, brown men, chocolate men, black men, in loincloths or short trousers, were jostling along. Some opulent merchants were being carried in motor cars. Troops of schoolboys and girls in uniforms were strolling along, now leisurely and unwillingly, now eagerly. The ostentatious splendour of the jumbled styles of architecture was realizing the significance of its garish stupidity, under the flood of sunlight that spread from the heavens.

Munoo did not attend to the hubbub consciously. He was beginning to take the city of Bombay for granted, though the deep recesses of dark rooms behind the doors and windows in the heart of the houses seemed to arouse his curiosity. They seemed peopled by swarms of men and women, layer upon layer, in a sort of vertical overcrowding, literally on top of each other. They did not greet each other as they walked in and out of the buildings. 'Strange,' he reflected, 'the southerners are strange people,' not realizing why they were aloof from each other.

They walked slowly, listlessly, as if they had not quite awakened from their sleep.

Munoo hurried into a quick pace once or twice, urged by the eager impulses that ebbed and flowed in him. But his head seemed dizzy in this atmosphere, his muscles loose and unstrung.

He looked at Hari. The old man's movements were mechanical. The energy in Hari's legs seemed to have been sapped completely, as the strongest effort at quickening his pace that the old man made seemed to result merely in the flashing of his bare back legs without any conspicuous hastening.

His wife seemed hampered by the weight of her daughter, by her heavy accordion-pleated skirt and by the natural weakness of her sex.

'I wish I could relieve her of the burden of her child,' Munoo said to himself as he felt a blast of steaming, bubbling heat descend on his back with a furious impact.

The sun had arisen behind him, over the roofs of the Bombay houses, and spread on to an uprise, drying up Munoo's liver in the process, sucking up all the energy out of him and giving a parched taste to his mouth.

His veins swelled as he struggled towards the incline. He willed a kind of nervous energy into his bones and strode on quickly.

The morning mist was lifting. The surface of the uprise was broken by deep pits on the sides and little mounds topped by scattered palm trees, whose green was tinted an unearthly pallor by the glowing gold of the sun.

But distance lent enchantment to this view. For the ascent to the plateau disclosed on the left a sewerage farm, beside which thousands of hides were tanned and dried with dung by the colony of leatherworkers, who lived in a cluster of mud huts; and on the right were rows of vast grey tenements, with thousands of low straw huts at their feet, hiding the rents and the holes in their sides with ragged, jute cloth hangings – all enveloped by the clouds of smoke which spurted from the tall chimneys of countless mills.

'Not far now, only a mile,' said Hari, panting for breath and rolling his eyeballs, over which the perspiration flowed.

'But your mile in the south seems longer than our northern mile,' said Munoo, flushing light-heartedly.

'Shall we live in one of those big houses, or in a straw hut?' asked Hari's wife, swinging her hips slowly with each stride.

'Be patient, you will be lucky if we can get jobs,' said Hari, peevish and irascible with the fatigue of the journey and the fear of the impending interview with the foreman Sahib.

They walked up a roadstead of broken stones and dust, past small hovels, straw huts which spread for a hundred to two hundred yards from the rubbish heaps at their near ends to the masses of tall tenements. The high, four-storied buildings were plain enough and devoid of the city styles, but crumbling on the sides and seamed with mortar that looked a leprous white against the sooty black of the main structure of brick. And then they were in full view of their objective.

'That is the Sirjabite factory to which we are going,' said Hari, raising a finger towards a chimney taller than the rest which stood rolling out volumes of smoke across the sky eastwards into India's vast unknown.

Munoo followed the direction of Hari's finger, but his glance lost itself among the factory roofs which undulated like low hill tops to the peak points of conic chimneys.

A swarm of clamorous crows were screaming around the choking alley-ways of the straw huts, by which sat a few semi-naked men and women, praying, it seemed, after their ablutions. There was not a well or a pump near, and Munoo wondered where they had bathed. He looked deeper into space and saw, behind a small hillock, a sunken pool of murky, green water over which a thick, slimy cream had settled. The crows wheeled over the pond in great profusion, pecking at the sores of the cows and bullocks who either sat in the water or grazed on the grass by the festering marshes around the water. Munoo was fascinated by the diving antics of the little urchins who ran about. He recalled the days when he himself had bathed in the low water of the Beas in his village. He felt an irresistible impulse to strip naked and jump into the water.

'Shall we have a bath here?' he said to Hari impetuously, standing by the pool and overcoming the stink that oozed from it with his naïve enthusiasm.

'No, brother, now we are in a hurry. We can bathe here every day if we get a cottage near the pond,' said Hari.

Munoo accepted the wise suggestion more easily as he advanced a few steps and saw a huge rubbish heap piled with broken bricks and paper and broken glass, merging with all its rottenness into the slimy water.

'Only another mile,' said Hari, consoling his followers.

This mile, however, was only a bare five hundred yards from the half-finished thoroughfare on which they had walked, by a rutted pathway that ended at the shadow of a high wall, topped by pieces of broken glass which reflected the rays of the sun by day and kept the thieves off at night. But what a five hundred yards!

On the plain, cut in two by the parallel lines of a narrow-gauge railway, were scattered rusty rails, heaps of dead coal, and all the refuse which the factory emitted. Under cover of these and of the deep pits and puddles of mud into which the feet sank and stuck, at little distances, sat men relieving themselves. And on the even surfaces, fuel cakes of cow dung dried and festered with a stink that was unbearable.

Munoo's heart contracted as if some inner instinct had gathered him into a knot, so that he might remain safe against the disintegration of filth and dung outside.

The inscription 'Sir George White Cotton Mills' cut in big, broad letters, hung on the arch of a closed iron gateway.

'Halt!' shouted a tall Pathan, striking the ground with the butt end of a double-barrelled gun, as he stood, belts of cartridges slung crosswise from his shoulders to his waist over his gold-braided red velvet waistcoat, his baggy trousers rustling in the breeze under the long tunic, over the turned-up solid puthwar shoes, the loose ends of his blue silk turban tied round the embroidered Kulah, which imparted to his ferocious face a colour darker than the north Indian's.

Lakshami flew into a panic and would have aborted the child if she had been carrying one in her belly.

Munoo became aware of the authority, not of the Angrezi Sarkar, because the man was not wearing a uniform, but of the mill, especially as he could see that behind the iron gates everything seemed orderly and well organized, from the clean cut of the factory building to the even shadows it cast on the compound.

Hari seemed to know the warden of the marches.

'Salaam, Khan Sahib,' he said, exalting the dignity of the guard with a little more respect than that which is implicit in conventional flattery. 'I am Hari, the coolie who worked here four months ago and went away to fetch his family. I want to see the Chimta Sahib, foreman.'

'Acha!' said Nadir Khan contemptuously, and turned to a young Parsi errand boy, who sat, dressed English fashion, on a stool by the wooden watch box. 'Lalkaka, go and tell Chimta Sahib there is an old coolie wanting employment.'

The boy had awakened on Munoo's shoulder and the girl on Lakshami's arms had come to life too. They grovelled in the dust of the road in complete unconcern of everything.

Munoo sat on a milestone, with his face averted from the factory, looking back on the ups and downs of the dung heaps, the coal, the broken girders and the pits of filth in the wasteland that he had left behind. The impressions of the strange scenes through which he had passed, of the confusing variety of the things he had seen during the last few days, forgotten though they were in the depths of his soul, seemed to come out and people the earth around him, till he felt crushed and alone in his heart and wanted to get up and run away, run like mad across to the hills of Kangra, or to the simple main street of Sham Nagar, or even into the confused but familiar world of Daulatpur. But as he looked across the factories, there seemed something so fascinating in their bare, straightforward look that he felt at home. There was a mysterious superior life wrapped up under them, and the tall chimneys seemed to him wonders of architecture as he speculated on the forms of the machines which must lie at their hearts, working to the heat of the furnaces, mightier than the ovens he had raked for ashes in the morning in the factory at Daulatpur. Prabha should have had a structure like that built for the ejection of smoke, Munoo thought, then there would not have been any quarrels with the wife of Rai Bahadur Sir Todar Mal, and the master would not have got beaten at the orders of his son at the kotwali. But the sight of a long brick chimney in the heart of a city like Daulatpur seemed incongruous to his mind's eye. 'Old city,' he muttered to himself contemptuously. 'Bombay is not old and narrow like Daulatpur. It is nice. It is, indeed, as the coolie in the vegetable market said. It is in these mills that he must have said that high wages are paid.'

He fancied he would be able to live in one of those big houses with countless windows which they had passed.

'The Sahib is very nice,' Hari said to reassure Munoo after they had waited for about twenty minutes in silence.

Munoo's suspense was spiced by the anticipation of the exalted contact with an Englishman that he would soon enjoy. He recalled the small face of Mr England at the house of the Babu in Sham Nagar, and the glistening bald head of the Sahib who came to Cat Killers' Lane in Daulatpur. He was elated.

Lakshami looked towards her husband as if she were going to say something, because her heart too had begun to throb with the joy of being able to see one of those red-faced men whom she had always seen through her veil from afar. But she suppressed her happiness and kept quiet. She had set the children playing about with pebbles and pieces of stone on the road to divert their attention from the breakfast they might want.

'Don't throw stones about,' shouted Nadir Khan, striking the end of his rifle on the ground, when he heard the wild, free tone of the children's laughter.

They came running to hide behind their mother's skirt. Hari turned on them with a rebuke.

Lakshami pressed them into her lap.

Munoo smiled sympathetically.

At this juncture appeared Jimmie Thomas, sometime mechanic in a Lancashire mill, now for fifteen years head foreman in one of the biggest cotton mills in India, a massive man with a scarlet bulldog face and a small waxed moustache, his huge body dressed in a greasy white shirt, greasy white trousers and a greasy white polo topee, of which the leather strap hung down at the back of his thick neck.

'Salaam Huzoor Chimta Sahib,' said Hari, bending low and taking the palm of his hand to his forehead.

'Tum Harry,' said Jimmie Thomas. 'You come back?'

'Yes, Huzoor, mai bap,' said Hari, joining his hands, 'and I have brought my wife and child also to work, and a young man from the north.'

'Why did you not bring the whole of your village, you son of a dog!' said Jimmie Thomas, who had not only acquired the Indian accent, but the Indian manner and the Indian swear words.

'I will write a letter to some more people, Huzoor, if you need more workers,' said the simple Hari, innocent of the foreman's sneer.

'You stupid bullock!' said Jimmie irritably. 'There are no jobs here. Perhaps for that boy,' he continued, looking Munoo up and down, 'but I have very little room.'

'But, Huzoor,' said Hari, pushing forward his hands in abject humility, 'you are the giver of food to the poor, Sahib. You are mother and father. You can make room for us.'

'Acha, acha, thirty rupees a month altogether,' said Jimmie Thomas, raising his hands high in the air and showing the tigers, the snakes and the women he had tattooed on his bare arms, 'ten for you, ten for that boy, five for your wife, two and a half each for those children.' '

'But, Huzoor!' said Hari, touching the foreman's black boots with his hand and taking the touch of the beef hide to his forehead 'Be kind. Just think that we have to live in a room here and the food is expensive.'

'What have you done for me that I should think of that?' said the foreman, blushing purple and seeking to control his confusion by twirling his waxed moustache. 'What have you brought as a gift from your village for the memsahib that I should be kind to you? You have never given me or the memsahib a basket of fruit on Christmas Day. If the pay suits you all, take it, otherwise go away.' And he made to to go.

'Oh, Huzoor,' Hari wailed, and almost ran towards the Sahib. 'We will please you. But be kind to us. I was getting fifteen rupees a month when I was here before.'

'You think, you bloody fool,' said the foreman bluntly, 'that you can go away when you like and come back when you like and get the same pay all the time? The burra Sahib has ordered me not to take any coolies back who have once left. He doesn't want old and used men. I am doing you a favour, bahin chot!'

'Oh, Huzoor,' entreated Hari, joining his hands again, 'please be kind to us for the sake of these children.'

'Yes,' said the foreman, 'you have the pleasure of going to bed together, you damn fools, and breed like rabbits, and I should be kind to you when your child comes, you black man, you who relieve yourselves on the ground.'

'Huzoor Sahib,' interposed Munoo, 'I heard in Daulatpur that the least pay for work in a factory was thirty rupees.'

'You bark a lie!' said Jimmie Thomas. And he would have burst, but Lalkaka brought a book for him to sign.

'Let us try somewhere else,' whispered Munoo, nudging Hari by the elbow.

Hari was not so hopeful about the other factories, and he knew.

'Acha, speak, you want the job or no?' said Jimmie finally, with another twirl to the edges of his moustache. 'You will find no work elsewhere. There are hundreds of coolies in Bombay who can't find work at all. I take you because you have experience and the boy there looks smart.'

'O Huzoor,' said Hari, 'we want to work with you, but be kind and consider our lot. Rice is so dear here.'

'Acha, acha, you two can have fifteen rupees a month,' said the foreman, flourishing his hands frighteningly. 'I take pity on you this time. But you know you did not do anything for me the last time you were here ... I am kind to you folk.' He set about to do business with a sudden smile. 'And now I suppose you have no money. Well, I will advance you ten rupees at four annas in the rupee, which sum I will add to the regular monthly commission you give to me. Agreed? I will go and fetch the money.'

He went.

'I lend money on a lower interest,' said Nadir Khan. 'Two annas on a rupee.'

'Now we have agreed with the Sahib,' said Hari, his heart thumping at the thought that Nadir Khan might be angry with him.

Munoo took advantage of the Sahib's absence and Nadir Khan's momentary withdrawal into the watch cabin, to nudge Hari again and to whisper to him the absurdity of having to pay a commission to the foreman besides an exorbitant interest on the money he was borrowing.

'It is no use,' replied Hari, wearily shrugging his shoulders. 'It is the same everywhere. Paying a commission to the foreman is a question of self-preservation. He is the most important man in the factory.'

'Indeed,' thought Munoo, 'the Sahib must be an important man, but his clothes were greasy.' He did not know that the Sahib in greasy clothes was the virtual master of the factory, from the number of functions entrusted to him. He did not know that he was the employer's agent to engage workmen, the god on whose bounty the workmen depended for the security of their jobs once they had got them; that he was the man in charge, responsible for the supervision of the labourers while at work; that he was the chief mechanic who, with other mechanics, helped to keep the machines in running order; that he was the technical teacher of the workers; that he was the intermediary between the employer and the worker (it was through him that the employer signified any change he wished to communicate to the workers); that because of all this he charged every worker in the factory a price for the gift of a job, a price which went up if there were more men about than there were vacancies to fill; and that, incidentally, he ran a moneylender's business; that lastly he was a landlord who owned hundreds of straw huts in the neighbourhood and rented them out to the coolies at a profit.

It was in the capacity of landlord that he appeared when he brought the money. 'I have a hut,' he said, 'at the head of Sahib's Lane, for which the rent is five rupees a month. It is open. Go and occupy it before I let it to anyone else. I will let it to you for three rupees.'

'Huzoor, you are kind, you are my father and mother,' said Hari, touching his forehead with the palm of his hand again.

'All right, all right, go, and be here sharp to the tune of the first whistle tomorrow morning all of you,' said Jimmie Thomas, twirling his moustache again and curling his lips into a benevolence that hardened his soft, fat, padded face.

*

175

The cavalcade walked back the way it had come.

'That is the Sahib's Lane,' said Hari, as they crossed the road and entered a pit bordered by heaps of rotting garbage and pools of noisome sewers. 'And that there is, perhaps, the hut which the Sahib has rented us. Did he not say it is at the head of the lane?' He pointed to the nearest of the many straw huts, about six feet tall and five feet wide, which stood in parallel lines at the foot of the long grey tenements which stretched horizontally, a hundred yards away. The old man seemed to know every patch of ground, having lived here for a year before he went away to his village to recuperate from the strain of work and to fetch his family.

He went up to the shed at the base of the lane and, lifting the sacking which hung at the low doorway, stooped and led the party into the cavernous room.

The roof of clumsy straw mats, which drooped dangerously on the sides from the cracked beams supporting it in the middle, was not high enough for Munoo or Hari's wife to stand in, though Hari, whose back was bent, escaped hitting his head against it. The mud floor was at a level lower than the pathway outside, overgrown with grass which was nourished by the inflow of rain water. The cottage boasted not a window nor a chimney to let in the air and light and to eject the smoke. But then, had it not the advantage of a sound sackcloth curtain at its door, when most of the huts in the neighbourhood had torn and tattered jute bags, or broken cane chicks, old rags, bent tins and washing and what not, to guard them against the world?

'Let us settle down and rest,' said Hari, taking everything for granted. 'Lakshami, give us all some of the food left over from the journey.'

Munoo's dreams were shattered as he surveyed the gloom of the grave in which he stood, bending double, and as he smelt the damp, foetid smell that oozed from its sides. He had cast his eyes on the imposing tenements with the hope that he would live in one of their top storey rooms and survey the world from that supreme eminence.

He suddenly felt a sweat cover his face, and his head seemed to whirl in a frenzy of movement. Then the darkness seemed to come stealing over his eyes. He felt dizzy and faint and struggled to breathe in the suffocating atmosphere that enveloped him. He smiled and sank on to the ground to save himself from swooning.

' Lakshami, who had been distributing stale sweetbread from the trunk, rushed to his side.

The boy had sufficiently recovered from his fainting fit, the fatigue of the long train journey, the after-effects of a night in the open, and from the shock of finding himself in the industrial colony, to accompany Hari for a walk up to the bazaar of the mill land on a shopping tour.

It was about half a mile away on the main road, which left Sir George White's mill on one side and skirted past the Jamsetji Cowasji factories, a bazaar only in name. For there were a few tumble-down booths and stalls which displayed coloured rags, imitation beads and pearls, tin toys, cotton slippers, razors, knives, scent sprays, and such dazzling manufactures with which Europe has won the heart of Asia. There were, however, a few regular shops: a wine shop, owned by a fat Parsi; a betel leaf and biri shop, occupied mainly by a large mirror; a grimy cookshop ministered by a greasy Muhammadan; a cloth seller's shop, where a tailor sat wielding a Singer sewing machine; and, last, a grocer's general store, owned by a lean, white Sikh with a ginger beard, who sat dressed in a clean turban, a closed collar coat, white tight pyjama trousers and pump shoes, flourishing a hand scale in which he weighed lentils, or rice, or flour, or sugar from the tiers of baskets that rose on small wooden planks, against stone weights and weights of iron.

'Salaam Sardarji,' Hari said, the light of humility glistening tremulously in his eyes.

Munoo felt rather strange, and therefore sat down about a yard away on a brick, watching the group of coolies in waistcoat-like blouses, loincloths and turbans who formed a semi-circle two yards away from the counter of the shop, and a man with a white turban, a white coat with a tight red belt around it, who spread a sheet before him.

'Eka, eka! dua, dua!' the Sikh chanted as he weighed the rice, completely deaf to the honour that was shown him.

'When did you come back, Hari?' asked a coolie who came and stood by the wooden pillar of the shop with a fowl under each arm.

'Yesterday,' said Hari, joining his hands to greet an old comrade.

'And are the wife and children well?' the man asked.

'Yes, they have come with me,' said Hari.

'Eka, dua, eka ... don't talk and make a row!' shouted the Sikh. 'Is this my shop or a place for you to gossip? And get away, get away, give me a little air and light. You sit there with your big, hulking forms casting your evil shadows on all the foodstuff.'

The coolies became silent, and, smiling humble, sheepish smiles, looked at each other, then hung their heads down, and sat still in the fast-gathering twilight.

'Eka, dua, tria, eka, dua, tria!' the Sikh sang to remember the measure of the pulses that he was weighing out, in the silence that had ensued. 'What else does the Chimta Sahib want?' he asked, as he emptied the seventh measure of seven different foodstuffs into the corners of the sheet which the long-coated bearer of the foreman had tied into several knots by means of jute strings.

'Do double roti!' the bearer said. 'A dozen eggs and two chickens.'

'Here are the double rotis,' said the Sikh, fishing out two loaves of white bread such as Munoo knew the Sahib-logs ate. 'And here, one two, three ... here are the dozen eggs. As for the fowls ...' He switched his attention to the coolie who stood with the fowls in his hands. 'Oh, you son of an owl, Shambhu, what do you want for those two?'

Shambhu came forward, hitting one leg against another in his hurry.

'Feel this, Sardarji, feel this,' he said, handing first one, then the other cackling, fluttering cock from under his arm.

'Hum,' said the Sardar, feeling the fowl, twisting his lips into an ironical smile and winking his right eye at the bearer, all at the same time. 'This is an old cock, and the other is light as a feather. No flesh on them, all bones. How much do you want for them?'

'Sardar Sahib, you are the master, you are my father and mother,' said the coolie. 'Please give me a fair price for them. They are lusty young cocks and they have been fed on crumbs while we starved.'

'Here we are, Badr Din,' said the Sikh, handing over the fowls to the foreman's bearer, winking surreptitiously the while to ensure that nothing was said about the price at which he was selling them before the man from whom he was buying them. 'I will put it all on the Sahib's account. And here,' he continued, fishing for a handful of coloured English sweets that stood in the jar behind him, 'here is a little gift for the memsahib. You come one afternoon and we will settle the accounts.'

The bearer put the cocks under his left arm, pocketed the sweets, and walked off with a swagger characteristic of the white man's servant.

'Ohe Shambhu! Do you want money or do you want rice in exchange for the fowls?' the Sardar asked.

'Part money and part food, Sardarji,' said Shambhu, meekly.

'Acha, here is four annas in cash and I will weigh you a seer of rice,' the Sardar said, taking up the scales.

'But Sardarji,' said Shambhu, joining his hands and kneeling down in supplication, 'each of those cocks⁻is worth a rupee. My wife fed them well so that we could get enough food for a week by rearing them. I was all against selling them, but we haven't any ready money. Sardarji, be fair and deal straight.'

'And do you think I have dealt you crooked, you swine?' shouted the Sardar, his white face raging red. 'The Sahib won't pay me at all for those cocks. That is a bribe to him so that I may be allowed to trade here. I am not making any profit out of them.'

'The Sahib and you are both my masters,' said Shambhu. 'You are both rich and can afford to give gifts. I would like to make you the gift of a fowl later on. But these cocks, Sardarji, they are the only things I had in the world. I am in debt. All my pay has been confiscated for damaged cloth and for debts I owe. There is nothing for my wife and child to eat. The seer of rice won't last a day. And what can I buy in Bombay for four annas? Please be kind, I pray you, and give me a fair price.'

'Again you say I am going to give you an unfair price,' shouted the Sikh, working himself up into a show of rage and indignation. 'Unfair. You accuse me of unfairness. I, who worship the Guru Granth! You give me a bad reputation! Here is two annas over, and the rice. And now go away and don't make any more noise. I have other customers to deal with.'

'Oh, but sir!' said Shambhu, summoning all the meekness, the humility, the weakness in the hollows of his cheeks and the dim pits of his eyes. 'Please be kind, take pity on me and mine. Give me the just price for the cocks.'

'Get out of my sight, you dirty, whining dog!' the Khalsa raved, suddenly rising on his haunches and striking Shambhu with a big wooden spoon. 'Get away, you whimperer!'

Shambhu fell back, but not before he had been hit on the mouth. He wept like a child with ridiculous, hysterical sobs.

Munoo sat fixed to his seat, staring vacantly at it all, as if he were not concerned with the quarrel. His body shivered with sympathy when Shambhu was struck. But it became hard and feelingless as the man fell back.

Hari and the other coolies proceeded to help Shambhu to get up.

'Come along! Come along! Come and be a man!' the coolies were saying to disguise their sympathy for their comrade, for they were all dependent on the Sardar's bounty and dared not antagonize him.

'Here's another anna and the swine's rice!' said the Sikh. 'Take it and bear him out of my sight for Guru's sake!'

The coolies helped Shambhu to get up. He wiped the blood which trickled over his chin from the mouth, collected the money, took the conic packet of rice, joined hands to the Sardar, and wailed: 'Forgive me, Sardarji, forgive.'

And he disappeared into the darkness.

'What do you want?' the Sardar asked the other coolies.

'Nothing, Sardarji,' one of them said for the others. 'We are waiting to see if you will give us a weight which you want transported somewhere.'

'No, I have no weight to have lifted today,' he said peevishly. And he turned to Munoo. 'You, you, ohe, what do you want?'

'He is with me,' said Hari. 'He is a new employee at my mill. He wants to open an account. And perhaps you recognize me, your humble Hari. I was a coolie here last year.'

'I have raised the rate of interest on the money I lend out now, Hari,' said the Sardar.

'I have not come to borrow, Sardarji,' said Hari, 'but if you will give me two rupees' worth of rice and a rupee's worth of dal on credit, I shall be grateful. The rest of the stuff I will buy with cash.'

'The rate of interest on goods bought on credit is an anna on the rupee!' announced the Sardar.

'If that is what you will, master,' said Hari, 'I don't complain.'

'Spread your cloth, then! And tell me what are the other things you want!' said the shopkeeper, as if he were conferring a favour.

'What is the rate of flour, Sardarji?'

'Flour is a rupee a seer, rice eight annas a seer, clarified butter is five rupees a seer, best mustard oil, for cooking, a rupee a seer, dal of channa eight annas a seer, gur four annas a seer, angrezi sugar eight annas a seer,' the Sikh quoted all the prices quickly, peevishly, querulously. 'Now hurry up. I have other things to do!'

Hari prayed for ten seers of flour, fifteen seers of rice, five seers of dal, a seer of cooking oil, a seer of native sugar.

He did not reckon the money he would have to pay at the end of the month, because he could not reckon at all.

Munoo did not care how much money was spent, for the fact that he would be getting fifteen rupees a month had filled him with reckless enthusiasm.

The shrill whistle of the factory pierced the thin, cool air of the twilight.

Lakshami was already up in the hut, groping around, almost in undress, for some cold rice and dal to serve for breakfast to her family. As she crouched over the new earthen pan, scraping the last little bit of rice gruel from where it had stuck to the bottom, little beads of perspiration covered her forehead. But she did not let the discomfort of warmth irritate her in any way. Her face, the face of a young girl in spite of the fact that she had had two children, still had the bloom of youth which the open life of the village had encouraged. And whether she was still too innocent of suffering, or whether her inherited springs of energy kindled her body, there was a gambolling light in the coy black eyes that matched the rich brown of her cheeks, enhanced by the little gold point of the ring on her small nose that glistened in the semi-darkness, and there was a naïve, fearless smile on her half-parted lips, and a furtive dimple on her chin, unaware of itself and the world.

As she heard the sharp, steel song of the factory whistle she started as a deer must when it hears the lion's roar in the jungle. She felt a cold shiver of some distant fear run through her belly till she nearly laughed with the tickling agitation it had spread on the surface of her skin. And she got up to rid herself of the commotion by transferring it to her husband, like a child who goes to its parent in trouble. She caught the big toe of his right foot and shook it with as much reverence as she could put into the rude act.

'Hun, hun, ho!' bellowed Hari as he sprang up, suddenly opening his eyes.

'Time to go to work,' Lakshami said gently; 'the whistle has just gone.' And she set about waking the children by washing their eyes, full of thick crusts of grit, with a wet corner of her cotton sari.

'Awake, brother,' Hari called, stirring Munoo by the shoulder.

The boy opened his eyes slowly, moved his head sideways, yawned, stretched his arms, wriggled about on the taut muscles of his body, and sat up staring at the full vision of Lakshami's face without a veil. He had seen young girls of her age, her form, her rich, pale hue, on the banks of the Beas in the mornings. His whole being warmed with the comfort of that knowledge which a beautiful person gives one.

'May I have some water to wash my face?' he asked modestly, not addressing Lakshami, but meaning her to hear.

She looked at him, then withdrew her eyes with a wide-open smile, filled a small brass jug from the pitcher and put it near the far corner of the hut, where a slab of stone lay slanting into a hole, a drain for the water.

'No time to eat if we want to get washed at the pond before we go to work,' said Hari, seeing his wife dish out the food. 'We must get up before the first whistle from tomorrow.'

Lakshami coaxed the children to eat, in spite of her husband's orders. But the boy and girl, awakened before they had had their full sleep out, were irritable and refused to eat.

'Come along! come along!' said Hari, who was ready to go as soon as he stood up from the sheet on which he had slept. And he led the way out of the hut.

Munoo wiped his face on his tunic and followed him, feeling fresh on the cheeks, but stale in the mouth, which he had not cleaned for days.

Lakshami took time to prepare the children, herself, and the various knick-knacks, and only emerged when Hari's temper dictated sternly: 'Come out, you bitch! We will be late. Everyone is on his way already!'

She emerged, dragging the children.

As they reached the edges of the pond they dispersed to relieve themselves among the other men and women who sat answering the call of nature, little distances apart.

A second sharp, clear whistle hastened them before they had settled for very long.

They arose and finished their toilet, sprinkling first their bottoms and then their faces with palmfuls of water from under the thick crusts of scum on the surface of the pond.

The third and final whistle greeted them a few yards from the factory, as they walked with the swarm of other coolies, with uncertain footsteps through the slime and mud of the unpaved pathways, in the dew-covered fields. They were all silent, with furrows of fear fixed on their brows, with the heavy weight of thought in their bent heads. Occasionally one of the many coolies muttered a hoarse curse as he splashed the dirty water of a puddle over his bare legs, or lost his hold on the earth; or 'Ram Ram,' said a pious old coolie greeting another; or a young coolie peevishly nudged a comrade who was not agile. For the progress of this swarm was slow, very slow.

Munoo observed that the hands of the factory clock marked the hour of six.

He followed Hari past Nadir Khan, through an untidy compound littered with rubbish and congested with bales of compressed cotton behind huge motor lorries.

The factory before him consisted of blocks of buildings grouped together into a space hardly big enough to hold half of them.

The other workers did not seem to notice the cramped spaces of the factory, except perhaps Hari's wife and her children, who had put their fingers in their mouths. All the other coolies filed past as if they lived and ate and slept and had their being here, perhaps because they had got used to the look of the mill, or because they measured it against the background of the hovels in which they lived, and really liked to come away to the comparative luxury of this palatial building. Munoo preferred the outlook of a bungalow, which he later learnt to know as the house of Chimta Sahib, standing by itself in the grounds beyond the manager's office on the left, in the arena of a garden, profusely overgrown with marigolds and hollyhocks and nasturtiums.

At the door of the shed which led into the factory stood Jimmie Thomas. As each group of coolies looked up and saw him twirling the fine ends of his moustache, they would suddenly lift their hands, salaam him and simultaneously lift their feet and rush into the factory like chickens frightened by a shadow. But since the entrance to the factory was not big enough to allow of such sudden alacrity, it gave the Chimta Sahib the first of a series of opportunities to show the niggers the methods of organized behaviour in the factory.

'Son of a pig! Why do you run now? Why didn't you come earlier, that you now make up for lost time by running? Walk one after another in Indian file!' the Sahib shouted in the Englishman's Hindustani.

'Salaam, Sahib!' said Hari, wisely going up to him only after all the other workers had passed into the sheds except himself and his family.

'You new coolies,' said Jimmie Thomas, mopping the sweat off his face with a greasy handkerchief. 'Come, I will take you to your jobs.'

'Yes, Huzoor,' said Hari, and his retinue followed at these words.

The preparing-shed was on the ground floor, ten yards away from the small door which led into the factory.

The Chimta Sahib halted at its narrow entrance, through which you could only pass by lowering your head.

'Woman, children, go here. Here work. Ask matron to tell you what to do,' he said, his fluent Hindustani becoming a bit faulty. 'Matron!'

Lakshami could not understand the speech. She stood mute for a moment, the apron on her head covering her face completely.

'Chalo, chalo, be quick,' he bullied, stamping the floor with his feet, sweating and slobbering, his face suffused to a vivid pink, either with anger or with the heat in the gallery where they stood.

Mortally afraid and trembling, Hari rushed towards his wife and pushed her into the shed, quicker than she could drag the children.

'Come, come, woman, no snake is going to bite you,' said the matron, receiving her inside the door.

Munoo sensed from the Chimta Sahib's manner that it was his and Hari's turn next. So he walked carefully through the gallery up the difficult circular iron stairs, determined not to err. But, of course, he erred, on the side of caution. He minced his steps.

'Jaldi chalo!' shouted the foreman from the top where, in spite of his heavy frame, he had climbed quickly and easily. 'Am I your servant that I should wait for you all day?'

The boy hurried up the steps, afraid that one false step and he would stumble to death or break his skull on the iron staircase.

As he came past the dark wall on his left, past box-like rooms, built round heaps of machinery to which there seemed no means of access except through the door of the spinning-shed, where the

Chimta Sahib stood, he was afraid and wavered. He saw no sign of Hari. He guessed the old man knew the ins and outs of the place and had presumably gone in.

'Chalo! you swine!' roared the Sahib over the hum of machinery, and catching the boy from the back of the neck, brought him to an empty wooden stool between Hari and a thickset man of about thirty, with a handsome, round face and broken ears like those of a wrestler. 'These coolies will teach you your work,' the Chimta Sahib continued, and, much to Munoo's relief, wheeled round and left.

Munoo stared at his surroundings, hot and perspiring. The black, expressionless faces of the coolies seemed impenetrable. He lifted his eyes to the horizontal, circular, cylindrical, octagonal, diagonal shapes of the different parts of the machine. The first impact was fascinating. Then the bold gesticulation of a hundred knobs and shafts of the engine deafened him with its uproar. But the wooden columns which stood beyond him, extending from the middle of the monstrous steel plant to the low ceiling of corrugated-iron sheets, seemed to alleviate his confusion a little. Soon, however, they gave him the feeling of being shut in a cage. He looked round in an effort to quell this feeling. The strong walls, sooty with crystals of cotton flakes, seemed to beat his glance back, till he met the light stealing in through two small ventilators high in the side walls. The air grew suffocatingly hot, and a queer smell of cotton and oil came heavily up to his nostrils. The sweat covered his face and his shirt was soaking on his back. He felt alone and isolated. He felt he would go mad with the din.

'You stand here, boy,' said Hari from where he sat on his left, 'and move that handle with your right hand as I am doing. Whenever the thread breaks, join it quickly with a knot.'

That, Munoo thought, was easy. He set to work.

At first his hand seemed to move slowly, as if it were afraid.

'A little more quickly, brother,' said Hari.

Now Munoo's hand revolved the handle a bit too fast. The thread broke and he did not know how to tie the knot.

The man on his side called to him, 'Look! this is the way to tie it.' And he deliberately broke the thread and began to tie it.

Munoo imitated the movement he had been shown and got it right. He was thrilled to realize that he had learnt his job. Now he could gyrate the handle of the machine to the tempo which it dictated. It was a simple and easy job. The machine seemed to do all the work. He was only moving a handle, while the machine was gathering up the thread and weaving it into a pattern farther ahead. It was different work from any he had so far done. It was delicate and the eyes had to be kept on the thread all the time. That was a strain. But the novelty of the business interested him. And soon he felt his hand helping the machine just in time and joining broken threads up deftly. The atmosphere though, the atmosphere, the wild hum of the machine, the jig-jig-jigging of its pistons, the tick-tick-ticking of its knobs, the furious motion of the broad conveyor belts across its wheels, the clanking of chains, the heat they all generated, and the heavy, greasy odour of oil mixed with the taste of the fresh cotton thread, not offensive by itself, but sickening like bile in the mouth – from all this seemed to rise a black shadow, strangling one at the throat with its powerful invisible fingers. Munoo recalled that he had felt somewhat the same feeling in the dark sheds of the weavers in his village, and the black cavern of the oil-makers, where the bullock, blinded by leather goggles and a rag, went round and round and round, harnessed to the shaft. And this place seemed not very unlike the huge flour mill at Daulatpur, where he had borne weights of grain for the fastidious old women who liked their flour fresh.

As the morning advanced, however, the resemblance of this inferno to anything he had ever seen before began to fade away. For the June sun began to make itself felt, not only through the small ventilator in the east wall, which let in a rectangular stream of light and made the cotton dust above the machine shimmer like the colours of a kaleidoscope, but through the sheets of corrugated iron that lay darkly aslant on the roof.

By noon time Munoo felt the perspiration running down from the top of his head to his face and down his neck to his body. Being intent on his job, he could not wipe it, and he tried to get used to it, regarding it as a sort of poison which it was good for his body to cast off in liquid shape. Only it was clammy and exuded a warmth which was becoming unbearable. Besides, the streams were trickling into his eyes and falling across the lines of his body on to the drier surfaces. He was irritated, and looked round to see how the others fared in this sticky heat. The coolies about him had taken off their tunics and their bare bodies were bathed in oily smears of sweat. He felt he would take off his shirt, too. But he did not know how he could do so while his hands were engaged.

A whistle blew and the handles which the coolies wielded refused to work, though the steel wheels on the sides of the main plant continued to roar themselves hoarse.

All the coolies were getting up, draining the sweat off their faces with their hands.

Munoo got up and, walking towards the door for air, began to take off his shirt by crossing his arms and lifting the lapels over his head. The soiled, wrinkled, homespun garment came up to his head and stuck there, as he had forgotten to unbutton it in the front. He struggled to pull it off. The tunic slipped over the left arm and uncovered his eyes, but still stuck on the right arm. A great gust of hot wind that flew by the wheels of the conveyer belt blew the edge of the cloth and tore it into tatters across the wheel that gyrated at twenty miles an hour. Munoo ran for it in a kind of spontaneous despair at his loss. The wrestler coolie with the broken ears, who had sat on his right, barred his way with a strong arm and a loud curse: 'Keep your senses, you bastard; you will lose your life if you do that.'

Hari rushed up in a panic and dragged him away. As he walked out of the room Munoo felt as if the many-headed, many-armed machine god was chuckling with laughter at the grim joke it had played on him by divesting him of his shirt.

When he reached the compound he did not feel so outraged, because most of the coolies were bare-bodied anyway, and what was more, their faces were encrusted with the deep lines of their wrinkles, the ugly contortion of their furrows, the twisted outlook of the hollows in their cheeks, the pits and mountains of their jaws, while layers of fluff covered their short-cropped hair from their necks to the tips of the ritual tuft knots, their eyebrows, their eyelids and their eyelashes.

'Tiffin taime,' said Hari, looking utterly ridiculous and sounding quite funny as he whispered the English words by which the midday break was known since Jimmie Thomas came to the factory and adopted the Anglo-Indian name for what was his lunch hour, and a brief space for resting, cooling, breathing and eating for the coolies.

There was nowhere for the coolies working in the factory to

wash, except at a pump in the grounds at the back, among huge drums of oil and bales of cotton, where a hundred men crowded round to get a drink.

There was nowhere to go for a meal, not a canteen, nor a cookshop, nor even a confectioner's shop; only a man with two baskets of plain roasted gram and cheap sugar-coated stuff sat outside the factory.

But the wives of the coolies had, with peculiar female foresight, brought food for their kith and kin. And most of the coolies sat under the thin shade of palm trees, rolling great big balls of rice in their hands and swallowing them rudely, unceremoniously, as Munoo had never seen people do in the north.

'What has happened to my wife?' asked Hari, looking at the other folk feeding comfortably. And he rushed away towards the sheds to look.

Munoo lay disconsolate and sullen under the scanty shade of a hedge, anxiously expecting Hari. But the whistle blew and, after waiting till everyone had gone in, Munoo returned to work again by way of the pump, which was now hissing sharply and coolly against the torrid heat of the sun.

The stifling heat of the afternoon began to reverberate like an electric shock through his temples when he got inside. His ears sent out waves of heat on to his cheeks. His eyes began to burn with a fiery intensity. His head seemed thick and congested with a thoughtless hardness: His limbs sagged wearily. He felt languid with hunger. He felt a superstitious awe.

The Chimta Sahib had brought another coolie to sit in the place where Hari should have been.

Munoo did not know what had happened. He sat wearily, mechanically revolving the handle in his hand, with his heartstrings stretched tight in suspense.

At length Hari came rushing, panting and panic-stricken, and said that his little boy had grazed his right arm by ignorantly touching the belt of a machine in the spinning-shed.

Munoo felt hard and could not sympathize. He just looked blankly into Hari's face and remained dumb, as if now his heartstrings had contracted.

'Have you shown him to a doctor?' asked the broken-eared wrestler on his side.

'No, brother, not yet,' replied Hari, shaking and trembling. 'There is no dakdar at the mill. The Chimta Sahib has given me leave to take the boy to the hospital in town. But, of course, I will lose my job now. The Sahib is very angry that I have not put in full time on the first day of my work in the weaving-shed.' Saying this, disconsolate and broken, weary and pathetically lonely in his despair at not being able to cope with his manifold responsibilities, he made to go. Then, as if he had forgotten something, he returned and said to Munoo: 'Brother, when you come, bring the mother of my child home with you. She will not know the way on her own.'

When Hari had gone Munoo's heart went out to him. He felt he must go and bear the child on his back to the hospital, because the old man would get tired, trudging through the dust of the half-finished thoroughfares which led from the factory to town. He could see him go past the iron rails, past the stacks of timber and the rusted steel girders which lay by the upturned earth outside. He could see him walk by the pool, where cows and buffaloes would be submerged up to their necks in the murky, green water. He could see him cast a glance at their home in the straw hut with the ragged jute cloth hanging, and then get lost in the rottenness and slime on the outskirts of the town below the hide-covered plateau. Munoo did not know where the hospital was, and he could not see Hari except in the hazy desert on the edge of the town. What if the boy died on his shoulder before Hari got there? Munoo felt it would be unbearable to live with Hari and his wife if that happened, because they might connect their misfortune with their association with him. It was good that they did not know that he was an orphan, otherwise they were sure to think that he was an ominous person to have about them. 'Am I really ominous?' he asked himself. 'My father died when I was born, and then my mother, and I brought misfortune to Prabha, and, it seems, I have brought misfortune to Hari now. If I am ominous, why don't I die? My death would rid the world of an unlucky person. I would like to die. It were better to be dead. Yes, better to be dead, because this town has turned out wrong. It is so hot working here, and my aunt's mud hut in the hills was better than the damp straw hut in Sahib's Lane.'

He felt alone now that Hari was not there and he had no connection with any of the coolies. The endless, deafening roar of the machine got on his nerves. He felt torn and shattered, and hunger gnawed at his ribs like a rat, a big, slimy rat, whose very sight was sickening. The demons outside him and in him crowded round his head, diffusing his thoughts, as the collision of waves diffuses the water into froth. The tiny skiff of his soul tossed to and fro on the soft, sun-speckled edge of this foam, as if it were a small point struggling in vain to cross the river, and as if it were threatened with extinction by an unforeseen storm.

The visions of the gay bazaars with their mixed populations of superior Sahibs and rich merchants and poor men, the pictures of gigantic, wonderful houses in the town, of the tall houses in the workers' colony, the view even of the factory in which he was enclosed, cast the glamour of the strange, as yet unknown, about him. The illusion gathered force from the sound of the money the Chimta Sahib had fixed as his pay, more money than he had ever earned, from the feel of all the desirable things that he thought he would buy with it, black boots, a watch and chain, a polo topee, shorts, a tunic and all the paraphernalia of sahib-hood. But these were secret wishes, secret hopes, not to be spoiled by looking at.

'Yes, yes,' he said to himself to ensure the safety of these thoughts. And again he reached out to life, the joy of life which registered in his mind's eye the clear hieroglyphs of numerous desires. 'I want to live, I want to know, I want to work, to work this machine,' he said, 'I shall grow up and be a man, a strong man like the wrestler . . .' He looked towards the wrestler, and, as if his thoughts had been actually talking to the broken-eared coolie, he heard him say: 'My name is Ratan. I come from the Punjab. You look as if you were a hill man.'

'That is so. But I worked in the plains at Sham Nagar and Daulat-pur.'

'We be compatriots, then. What is your name?'

'Munoo,' the boy replied. And he could not help admiring the frank, open look in the man's face. And he felt he was not alone.

But exactly when he had begun to feel at home the whistle blew, and panting, fuming, hoarse and excited, the machines came to a standstill. The coolies rushed as if they were tigers who had scented flesh from afar.

Munoo entered the spinning-shed on his way out.

It was full of women with babies tied to their backs, in their laps, or wallowing in the dust on the floor, crying, screaming, sobbing, precariously perched near the claws of the machine which sifted cotton on the far side of steel planes, pistons and steam.

Munoo wondered that all the children had not grazed their arms, knocked their heads or been cut up into pieces by the parts of the machine which jutted out, without any wiring to keep them safe out of harm's way.

Lakshami was weeping when Munoo found her. He could not weep, but felt embarrassed and ill at ease as they walked away together.

By the factory clock above Nadir Khan's head eleven hours had elapsed since they had entered the factory, Munoo figured. The vertical sun had already gone down and the darkness of twilight spread like dirty linen hanging out on the Milky Way. A strange humidity had overtaken Bombay with the tense oppression of grey clouds that rolled heavy-footed across the heavens to India's farthest plains.

The afternoon of Saturday was a half-holiday, even for the coolies.

Hari had to bear his son to the hospital in town to get his arm dressed again. Lakshami wanted to look at the shops. And Munoo was eager to see the wonders of civilization. So they all walked down to the city on the afternoon of Saturday.

As the little troupe wended its way among the crowds of other coolies, who were off on a binge at the toddy shops, or for a razzle in Grant Road, a vague, sulky heat around the dusty earth which spread in a brown amber desolation filled the atmosphere, and gigantic clouds stalked the sky from south to north.

Munoo looked at the heavens, bewildered by the phenomenon. Then he looked down again, gasping for breath, staring sideways for a cool spot in the foggy haze, and thankful that he had not a clammy shirt sticking on to his skin in the torrid heat of this breathless day.

A blast of cool, sharp air struck him at the corner of the hospital. He could not see who had plunged this sudden dagger into the heart of the lull.

They had to wait in the outpatients' ward before the boy was attended to. But Hari had long since learnt to be patient. Lakshami completely effaced herself. The little girl was excited, while the boy stared blankly at the world from his father's lap. Munoo alone was conscious of the heavy atmosphere of the waiting-room, charged with the pungent smell of strange medicines, and by the superior grace of the beautiful, pink nurses who seemed to walk like electricity and talk like nightingales.

He got up from the hot corner of the last row of benches where he had taken a seat, while Hari and his family sat down on the cemented floor. There was an electric fan on top of the first row where, he thought, the air would be less stale. He walked to it and sat down on the edge of the bench.

A sick merchant in muslin who sat there moved away and pressed his weight on to the patients next to him.

A nurse, who was leisurely writing the names of the patients on a register at a small table adjacent, arose, stepped up to where Munoo had taken his seat, and, frowning so that her face was covered with lines, hissed: 'Jao.' Munoo retreated, embarrassed and blushing. He was ashamed to look at Hari and the other coolies who sat on the floor, although they were merely listless and did not care whether he was insulted or not. And he walked out of the waiting-room into the passage.

At the entrance of the outpatients' ward he could hear the sonorous gurgling of what he guessed was the Arabian sea not very far away. He ran to the end of the street, and there, past a slanting beach, he could see the agitated waves roaring onwards, prancing like angry, frothing, white horses. The violence with which they broke their knees across the beach and fell back grazed and wounded, gripped him, and he stood motionless.

Then, suddenly, a distant peal of thunder tore at the heart of the sky and scribbled vivid flashes of lightning. As the earth seemed to shake and the elements to reverberate with a weird agitation, Munoo was chilled and ran for safety back towards the hospital.

Hari's little girl greeted him with childish glee, pointing to a lone kite that soared across the sky, flapping its wings up and down, struggling against the wind which was too strong for it. But Munoo was troubled by the darkened skies from which descended sheet upon sheet of blazing light, followed with terrific suddenness by deafening roars of thunder. He dragged the child in. He met Lakshami and Hari, with the boy in his arms, coming out.

Hardly had they returned to the street, where the oil lamps burnt with a fiery heat and steam oozed out of the pans in a cookshop, when there was a hysterical growling in the sky, as if a pack of lions were at war with demoniac elephants. And then there was a mad charge of wildly neighing horses, whose steel hoofs struck fire on the cobblestones of the heaven's surface as their riders, driving the shafts of their spears into their prey, caused large drops of rain to fall like cold blood from the injured bodies of hunted beasts.

The rain fell; long, sharp, sudden, vertical, solid rain, vast and unceasing. It flooded the thirsty land with a terrific sweep of pent-up energy, so that neither man nor beast could stir.

Two hours later, when the bubbles did not explode quite so quickly on the road, Hari led his cavalcade back to the basti in pelting rain. The roads were like rivers, the plain outside the city was a lake, and the tank had overflowed and washed away the straw huts.

Drenched to the skin, soaking wet, trembling with fear at the wild noise of the rain, the sudden claps of gurgling thunder, the sharp, tearing rents of bright, white-red lightning overhead and the uncertain earth of the mill land under their feet, the family sought shelter under a grove of plantain and palm trees, which stood upon a hill surrounding the temple at the edge of the pond. Hundreds of other workers whose huts had been damaged by the monsoon were gathering in the darkness.

'Ram! Ram!' muttered Hari in long-drawn-out accents as he led the way.

Munoo followed quietly. Lakshami shivered with the vibrations of the elements. The children moaned and sobbed.

'Ohe Mundu! Ohe Mundu!' a hoarse voice suddenly fell on Munoo's ears as he bent under the weight of Hari's daughter on his back. He was occupied by memories of the flood as it used to come in his village and the delights it brought, for his mother fried sweet pancakes to celebrate the season of rains. So he was not aware of the call.

'Ohe Mundu!' the voice came again, heavy, hilarious and familiar.

'Who could it be?' Munoo wondered as he steadied his gait and looked round, exploring the dark.

'Oh, seducer of your daughter,' came the friendly voice near at hand. 'Wait, I can help you if your hut has been washed away and you want accommodation.'

Munoo recognized Ratan, the wrestler, who was his neighbour at the factory. He waited.

'Ohe, stop! wait!' came the voice, happy and guttural, and the figure of Ratan towered above him, laughing and slipping.

Hari bent beneath the weight of his son on his shoulder, Lakshami still and beautiful and poignant as she struggled to sustain her frail form, modestly assimilating the clothes which stuck to her bust and her legs like the folds of drapery round an ancient sculpture, were both too cold and miserable to wait for the voice in the dark.

'Stay, Hari brother,' shouted Munoo eagerly, turning round. 'Here is Ratan.'

But as he looked at Ratan he saw a wild light in his eyes, the deep flush of a broad grin on his cheeks, the faint smell of wine on his thick lips. And he was afraid lest the man was trifling, playing some practical joke, since the wrestler was usually very hearty and frivolous in the factory. His nervousness and trepidation increased as he saw Hari and Lakshami look back towards him and as Ratan burst out chuckling with delight at the ridiculous sight they presented, struggling to keep themselves from slipping in the mud and slush of the pathway.

'Come to our chawl,' said the wrestler, thumping Munoo on the shoulder with a bonhomie which seemed to become more dangerous. 'Come, come,' he bawled out, 'come, you seducers of your daughters, you wretches, come, I know you have nowhere to go.'

'But I am with Hari and his family!' said Munoo.

'Come, come, all of you,' roared Ratan, drunk and generous. 'You miserable beggars. I know how hard it is to fight for a wage in this cursed world and then to have nowhere to go, nowhere, nowhere but a toddy shop! Ha, ha, ha! Come, you swine! I will take care of you. Trust old Ratan! Trust the Rustum of Hindustan to guard you! Trust the mightiest wrestler in the world!' And as he thumped his chest vigorously to confirm the loud boast, he slipped and fell with a curse. 'Oh, seducer of his daughter! This rain! This rain! God has been passing water! That's what it is! He has been pissing!'

He heaved his body two or three times and arose, at length, apologizing with hiccoughs. 'Forgive me, forgive the old Ratan. He is slightly drunk, you know! But he is safe! He is quite safe! Don't be afraid! He will take you to a nice place!' And, slipping, walking, stepping up precariously, dangerously, he led the way.

Munoo waved his arm to Hari, who stood dubious and afraid.

'Come, come, come all of you!' assured Ratan, in a more normal tone. 'Trust the Rustum of Hind of help you in time of trouble!'

Munoo ran up to Hari and dragged him back. They followed the great, comic figure of the wrestler. The boy had somehow sensed Ratan's open, frank nature, where the southerners were hesitant and full of doubts and misgivings.

'Is it true? Is it true that Ratan has space for us in the room where he lives?' Hari asked, as he quickened his steps into short capers.

'Come, come, you poor wretches!' urged Ratan, with a sincerity that broke through his throat. 'Come.'

The procession slipped, slid, walked and jumped past ditches, struggled through the desolate loneliness of the dark, uneven mill land, haunted now by sharp cries, now by the wild sound of tom-toms, which kept time with the deafening swish of unceasing rain, with the flashes of lightning and the thunder in the sky.

Each one of them fell with a resounding thud in turn, and once three of them stumbled simultaneously. But they helped each other, all numb with cold and fear, except Ratan, who, though now reticent, was still warm and hearty and urged them on, till they reached the foot of the tall tenement houses three lanes away from the straw hut which they had occupied.

'Now come, you wretches, come,' said the wrestler, slapping Munoo on the back with a fresh turn of his boisterous good humour that revived the boy's spirits, though it did not warm his chill back.

'I thought my poor son would die tonight,' said Hari, almost on the verge of tears. 'But may the blessings of God be upon you both, Munoo and Ratan. You have saved his life and prevented me from dying without a son to perform my funeral rites.'

'Come, come, come upstairs,' said Ratan. 'What am I a wrestler for if I can't help you? Who would call me the Rustum of Hindustan if with a big body I had not a big heart? Come . . .'

Munoo conceived a wild admiration for Ratan. He had found a new hero. He would try to be like him.

The chawl to which Ratan took Munoo and Hari and his family was a three-storied tenement, built without any planning of the space into a courtyard, garden, road or playground, but closed in on all sides by other chawls separated from it by gullies barely a yard or two wide.

The room on the third floor, confusingly like hundreds of other rooms in the building, and approached by a narrow, winding, iron staircase, was about fifteen feet long and ten feet wide.

As Ratan led the strangers into the atmosphere of wood smoke that packed it, Munoo discerned the figures of a skeleton-like man who limped about, of a pale, slim young woman who sat huddled on her knees, and a little girl child.

The family greeted them with a tense, forbidding silence. But Munoo was becoming accustomed to the strange reticence that prevailed among the mill people, few of whom seemed anxious to know each other, though they lived and worked only a yard or two away.

The pale flame of a small, tin lamp struggled against the gloom that descended through the solitary window on the north side of the room, from the dense, dark rain-clouds that still massed the sky. But, now and then, the draught that whistled through the chinks of the window to the chinks of the door inflamed the fuel in the two brick fireplaces in the corner, and enlarged the shadows of the occupants on the south wall.

'You said you wanted to rent out half of this room, ohe Shibu,' said Ratan, as he stood at the doorway waiting for the whole troupe to come up the stairs. 'I have brought you a family with whom this boy from our parts lodged. Their straw hut in the Sahib's Lane has been washed away.'

'Acha,' said Shibu, puffing at a hubble-bubble with a coconut bottom. 'Come, come and sit down, come on our head, you are welcome,' he greeted as he saw Hari and his wife struggle in. 'And where in the north do you come from, ohe Munooa?'

'From Kangra, brother,' Munoo replied, as he put the weight of Hari's girl child off his back on the cement floor, and stood excitedly surveying the room.

'Oh, from Kangra, from Kangra; I have been to Kangra,' began the old man garrulously. 'Of course it was in the days when I was a small child. I went to the shrine where the goddess Kali appeared in the mountains . . .'

'Here is your pancake,' said Shibu's wife to stem the tide of his effusive flow.

'Oh yes, yes, father, tell us then what happened?' said his pert little daughter.

'You go to sleep, you little witch,' snapped Shibu, who wanted to discuss business before he began to entertain the newcomers. He leaned over to Ratan and whispered something in his ear.

'This room will be too hot to sleep in tomorrow,' thought Munoo as he crouched, 'but now I am cold in it. It will always be smoky, of course,' he further cogitated, 'because there is nowhere for the smoke to get out except the window. But it is better than the straw hut. The floor is solid.'

'This is a better house than your straw hut,' said Ratan, addressing Hari.

'Yes,' said Munoo before Hari had spoken. 'I wish we had come here from the very start. We would not have lost all our belongings in that hut.' He was feeling enthusiastic, as the neighbours had turned out to be northerners, and he felt he liked the garrulous old man.

'Yes, brother,' Hari answered. 'But the Chimta Sahib will be angry at our having left the hut, and will charge us rent for the whole month.'

'What was the rent you were paying there?' asked Ratan, surprised that he felt quite sober.

'Three rupees,' said Hari.

'Well, then, this is only two rupees more,' said Ratan.

'We owe ten rupees to the foreman Sahib already,' sighed Hari, 'and now we will have to borrow more money to buy food and utensils. Perhaps I can search for the old utensils in the hut tomorrow and for what is left of our belongings. God seems against us.'

'But rest assured, you have a friend in man,' said Ratan, thumping his chest boastfully and raising a sudden burst of laughter.

'You have been very kind for Munoo's sake,' said Hari. 'He saved my daughter's life the other day. Now again through him you have saved the lives of all of us. I am very grateful. I shall pay your price.'

'Leave that talk now,' said Shibu, who, once assured of the reduction in his rent because another family was going to share the room, was all generosity. 'Now, just taste the pancakes that my wife has been cooking. She has put some rice on to boil for you. Eat and lie down to rest for the night. You must be tired. We will go tomorrow when the rain has subsided and try to rescue your things from the hut.'

'This is very kind,' said Hari abjectly. 'You shouldn't give us food. You have a large family . . .'

'Come, come, brother,' said the man. 'We may be in Bombay, and poor, but we have not lost all the habits of the north yet. Here is a sackcloth. Let us spread it for you. And, if you all get together, I can spread a blanket on your legs.'

'This is needless trouble we have given you,' apologized Hari.

'No, no trouble at all,' began the old man. 'I wouldn't be my mother's son if I didn't offer hospitality to you. I have lived forty years, and I know that if you can't do a good deed by which people may remember you, you haven't lived.'

Munoo could not help congratulating himself on the fact that he had been responsible for this goodwill.

But he did not feel in the same self-congratulatory mood when, after a slumber disturbed by cold draughts, he was awakened in the morning by the inrush into his nostrils of a most foul smell.

'Where is this odour coming from?' he asked Ratan, who was already up and smoking a hookah.

'I don't know,' said Ratan casually. 'From somewhere in the gully beyond the window.'

Munoo rushed up to the window, screwing his nose and contracting his forehead. He stood on tiptoe by the little aperture and, through the dim light radiating from a sun completely hidden from view, saw that a pipe which received dirty water was choked up and overflowing into the gutter in the crowded, airless, stinking gully below.

'Ohe Ratan!' he said, 'the gully is like a river of dung.'

'Yes,' said the wrestler, perfectly nonchalantly. 'There are seven latrines downstairs for two hundred men, and there is only one sweeper to clean the night soil away. If you want to go and relieve yourself, give the sweeper man an anna and ask him to let you use the special latrine . . . But come . . . I am going there. I will show you . . .'

Munoo followed his friend down the stairs, through the corridors filled with rubbish, washing, rags, trunks, broken wicker baskets and children's toys.

As he reached the row of transverse walls, outside which a scantily clad sweeper sat smoking, he had to lift the edge of his loincloth to his nose to ward off the disgusting smell of dung and urine that oozed from the latrines.

'Mehtar, is our latrine clean?' asked Ratan, with a swagger.

'Yes, Pahlwanji,' answered the sweeper, cringing low.

'Go in then, ohe Munoo, first,' Ratan suggested, and then he turned to the sweeper and said, 'This lad is from my part of the world. Clean a latrine for him every day.'

'Yes, Pahlwanji,' mumbled the sweeper, and then led the way for Munoo.

The boy had been happy for some time at his escape from the awful necessity of having to go to a communal latrine, though the fields to which he had repaired were littered enough with dung, but he was so nauseated by the sight and smell of refuse in the gutters which passed for latrines here, that he came out within a minute of his entrance.

'Were you all right?' said Ratan as the boy emerged.

'Hun,' answered Munoo, nodding his head, as he had stuffed his nose and mouth with the lapel of his dhoti.

'There is the tap to wash yourself,' Ratan said, pointing to a pump round which a crowd of women stood with their pitchers. 'I am afraid it is the only tap for the entire block of this house. You will have to wait your turn.'

Munoo dared not cross the mud into which the water of the pump had seeped deeply for yards.

He was proceeding upstairs when he met Hari going out, he presumed to rescue the utensils from the flooded cottage.

'I will come with you,' said Munoo. 'I can have a bath at the pond.'

The next day Jimmie Thomas stood like a Colossus in the courtyard leading to the factory, twirling the needle ends of his waxed moustache, his face like the raw meat in a butcher's shop, with its vivid whisky-scarlet curdled into a purple, over which the blue lines of a frown traced their zigzag course.

Munoo saw the Chimta Sahib as he and Ratan slipped past the swarms of coolies who sped towards the factory, through the bogs of the mill land. He began to prepare himself to say 'Salaam Huzoor' to the Sahib, even though he was still a hundred yards away. Saluting the white man required a special effort on Munoo's part, he did not know why.

He soon knew, for, as he got to the iron railings of the door, he saw the Chimta Sahib gesticulating, shouting, as he kicked some coolies, struck others and ran to and fro in a towering rage.

Munoo's heart throbbed with the pang of discovering Hari among the batch of victims who, joining their hands, inclining their foreheads, bending their backs, shaking, tottering, falling, prayed for mercy with the most abject humility.

'Surka bacha! Haram zada! Why didn't you inform me before you moved out of those huts? You bahin chut!' Munoo heard the Chimta Sahib growl.

'Oh Huzoor, oh Huzoor!' That was all that he could hear the coolies say as, with piteous moans and cries, they fell back and trembled like frightened children.

'Huzoor, the roof of the hut was battered and the whole road was flooded,' Munoo heard Hari say.

His blood ran to the rhythm of that sentence, along the strength latent in its protest.

'You lie, you swine!' shouted the foreman, inclining menacingly towards him. 'I went down myself yesterday and there was no water.'

'Huzoor, there was water yesterday, and it was with difficulty that I cleared it and rescued some of the utensils.'

'Shabash! Shabash! Hari,' Munoo muttered under his breath, jumping on his feet. And he was wildly excited by the defence that old Hari was putting up, for he had not thought him capable of it.

'Then you think I am lying, do you, you swine!' raved the foreman as he advanced furiously and kicked Hari on the shins.

'Sahib, it is true, there was water in the hut,' Munoo said, standing where he was, unable to help Hari, but highly excited. 'I went down with him to get our belongings.'

'You bark an untruth! You live with him,' said the Chimta Sahib. And he lunged forward towards the boy, threateningly.

Hari's wife shrieked at this, as she stood with her children at the gate with the wives and children of the other coolies, afraid and cowed.

'That is the true talk, Sahib,' Munoo said.

The foreman raised his hands to strike the boy.

'Leave them, Sahib,' said Ratan, walking up and measuring his frame against the foreman's. He was quiet yet determined, as if his immense strength were slow to be roused. He kept a dignified balance and restraint. 'They were deluged by the rain when I found them on Saturday night,' he continued. 'The whole mill land was flooded. I myself know that the roof of the hut is broken. I have seen it. Do not dare to call me a liar, or I will teach you the lesson of your life.' This last he said raising himself to his full height, flashing his eyes, grinding his teeth and thrusting his chin forward.

The foreman saw the towering stature of the wrestler and stepped aside, saying: 'Go away, go away, get to work. Go away or I will kick you, you fool! I rented the cottage to them, not to you. It is none of your business.'

'It is my business,' roared Ratan. 'Go back to your bungla or I will break your head!'

'Ratan! Ratan!' the crowd of coolies called. 'Sahib . . .'

'You are insulting a superior,' said the foreman. 'Are you in your senses?'

'Sahib or no Sahib,' Ratan returned, 'you may be a foreman, but you have no right to beat the mill employees!'

'I shall charge the full rent for the month,' said the foreman, retreating. 'That's all! Attention! March to your jobs, all of you.'

'That you will get, anyhow,' said Ratan, 'but just you touch any of them and I will show you a bit of my mind.'

'Acha! Acha! Pahlwan Sahib!' said Nadir Khan, the Pathan warder, dragging the wrestler away and dispersing the crowd of coolies.

Ratan walked away to the weaving-shed. The coolies rushed to their jobs. They were afraid and panic-stricken.

Munoo slunk away to the workroom, making triumphant signs to Ratan as the coolies rolled the balls of their eyes.

'You look out,' a young coolie said, coming up to Ratan's seat in the shed. 'He will have his revenge on you.'

'I have seen enough like him,' said Ratan with a devil-may-care smile. 'Don't you be afraid of Reginalbite. Be confident! Trust in me! I haven't been a wrestler for nothing!'

'Ratan, brother, this is a terrible thing to have happened,' said Munoo as they settled down to their jobs.

'Don't you care,' said Ratan casually. 'I have seen enough like him. I was at the Tata steel works at Jamshedpur. There were fifty thousand workers there. And we all went on strike, because they cut our wages. Who brought the company to agree to our terms if not I?' He thumped his chest in a jocular, self-congratulatory way.

'Why did you leave Jamshedpur, then?' asked Munoo, tying a knot in the thread that had broken.

'Oh, we went on strike again as a protest against long hours, general bad treatment and bad housing conditions. And the company won over the leaders by threatening them and offering promotion. I caught hold of one of those betrayers and gave him a bit of my mind. After which I left. The strike failed because you must never start a strike immediately after you have won a strike. I didn't like the work there, anyway. It was difficult work. It was very hot.'

'I would like to go to an iron factory, though,' Munoo said eagerly. 'Do they make girders there, like those solid steel girders that lie by the railway? It must be exciting to be near the furnaces. Better than just pulling thread here and joining it when it snaps.'

'I was eighteen when I went there,' began Ratan, suddenly reminiscent. 'I had worked under artificial heat before at Daulatpur, for I am a coppersmith by birth. The heat of the furnace there was cool breath to the heat at Jamshedpur. It was a terrific, steady heat from which there was no escape. A whole acre covered with hot iron. Some smoking, some not. But always the heat waves dancing and jigging before your eyes. The glare was blinding. Night and day it was just the same. Summer and winter. If it rained, there was always a hissing noise where the water struck the hot billets. And then there were clouds of hot steam.'

'How did you get a job there?' asked Munoo, romantically pursuing the prospect of going to Jamshedpur.

'I needed the job,' replied Ratan. 'When I applied at the gate I was told to report to the foreman of the billet yard. It seemed too good to be true to me. But some kind of war was on and the company was doing big business in iron rails for the trains. The mill was busy and men were hard to find, because most of the coolies preferred to go soldiering with the prospect of certain death before them. They all want to die in glory.'

'Was the work at the factory easy?'

'What did you say, easy?' called Ratan sarcastically. 'Six to six. Seven days a week. Those were our working days, before an open furnace, where the molten steel boiled and bubbled like water in a saucepan. Above me, the chain man unhooked the smoking links from a red-hot pile of steel, just lowered by a crane. Shielding his face from the terrific heat with his left hand, as he jerked the chain loose with a crooked length of wire, he always shook his hands and shouted: "Careful, the iron is hot."

'It *was* hot, that iron. Right off the rolls of the twelve-inch mills. Red as sunset viewed through a cloud of smoke. Sometimes it took nearly half an hour to get black. And then it was more dangerous than ever. When the pile was red you knew it was hot, but when it turned black you might accidentally rest your hand against it, or put your foot on the lowest billet. You found out it didn't have to be red to burn. I put in extra hours. Sometimes, when changing from the day to the night shift, or back again, I did twenty-four hours, and once, when my relief did not turn up, I put in thirty-six hours.'

'Thirty-six hours! Didn't you want to sleep?' said Munoo naïvely. 'That is working day and night!'

'I didn't actually work all those thirty-six hours,' said Ratan. 'But I must have worked thirty-two hours. The other four I cheated the company of on the night shift. I slept. In little snatches of fifteen or twenty minutes at a time. With a plank for a bed and a brick for a pillow. Alongside the gas producer was the time-keeper's hut. But he was an opium eater. And he knew it is hard to sleep in a steel mill. There is so much noise. And things are always falling. A clumsy crane man may tip over a pile of billets and knock the shanty down. It is really safer to stay awake. But thirty-six hours is a long time to do that.'

Munoo stared at Ratan, open-eyed and admiring.

Ratan divined the youngster's eagerness and continued.

'No, don't you think of going to Jamshedpur. Stay here and work the bobbins. There, if I bumped into a protruding billet it felt as though my hip was broken. And, always, overhead were tons of steel. Being carried back and forth by the crane. A dozen billets to a load, each weighing a quarter of a ton. If they fell . . . If ever one of them fell . . . And sometimes they did fall. A chain would break once in a while, and then you ran for your life. But the chain did not have to break to make trouble. There might be a broken link in it. And it came out, spilling the load, scattering it in all directions. And running or even walking about was dangerous. It was so easy to crack an ankle against a hunk of iron. You –'

'Don't gossip! Steady at work, all of you!' the foreman shouted, hovering on the horizon.

'He will have his revenge upon us,' whispered Munoo, after he had gone.

*

203

The foreman did have his revenge. Not that day, not the next, not that week, nor the next week, not that month but a month and a half later, when the pay that was a month and a half overdue was doled out to the workers.

It was a Saturday afternoon. The malevolent sun, ascendant again after the monsoon, scorched the scantily clad bodies of the coolies in the grassless compound of the factory to a dark, copper hue, while it reddened the face of the Chimta Sahib to a still more vivid scarlet as he sat in his greasy white trousers, greasy open-collared shirt, greasy polo topee, under the shade of the office verandah, protected by Nadir Khan, the warder.

'Harry!' called Jimmie Thomas, irritated by the flies and flying bugs, which seemed to find the grease on his moustache and his clothes rather tasty.

Hari, whose ears were not quite used to the anglicized pronunciation of his name, looked absently round at Munoo and Ratan, who had begun to play chess with stones while waiting for their turn.

'Harry!' shouted Jimmie Thomas, flushed and angry, taking up a fly-killer attached to a cane and striking it a rap on his desk.

No answer. Only the coolies stared at each other, eager to produce the man, lest the wrath of the white man descend upon them.

'Harry!' he bawled out again, almost getting up in his seat.

'Hari!' Munoo nudged his friend. 'Go on, you are being called.'

Hari jumped up instantaneously and shambled forward to the pay desk, dragging his skinny, irregular, awkward legs, heaving his flat feet, which seemed weighted down to the earth through fatigue and his cares and trials.

'Hurry up! Hurry up!' said the foreman as he saw the old man coming. 'I am not your father's servant that I should wait here all day for the pleasure of handing over money to you. Your thumb!'

'Mai bap,' said Hari, saluting, pushing forward the thumb of his right hand on to the black ink which lay soaking on a pad in a tin, and then lifting it to see if it were well covered.

The foreman caught hold of his trembling hand as if he were touching a leper, and pressed it down on a register. Then he took two currency notes of five rupees each and ten silver rupees and handed it over to him, saying curtly: 'Ten rupees you owe me in cash. A rupee interest on the loan. Three rupees rent for the hut for one month. One rupee for repair of hut. Five rupees cut for damaged cloth. The remainder you receive for you, Munoo, coolie, your wife and children.'

Hari knew these phrases well from long experience: 'Loan, interest, rent, damaged cloth.' And though he resented them, he had learnt to respect them. He accepted the twenty rupees, salaamed the foreman, and withdrew.

His heart sank as he came towards Munoo. His eyes were full of tears. His face was knotted and pale, and half-told the grim tale.

'What has happened?' Munoo asked.

'Nothing, brother,' he said with choking breath. 'Five rupees deducted for damaged cloth. And after the rent on the hut and the interest and loan are paid off, we all get twenty rupees only out of the forty-five we were to be paid. Here's your portion, ten rupees.'

'No,' Munoo said. 'You keep it, Hari. I owe you that for my food and rent.'

'No, brother, why should you suffer? You take your portion,' insisted Hari.

'All right, give him five rupees for pocket expenses,' suggested Ratan to end their war of courtesy.

'Ratan,' came the foreman's call.

The wrestler arose and swaggered up to the pay desk. And he forestalled the foreman.

'No damaged cloth, Sahib,' he said. 'And no interest, because I didn't borrow money on compound interest.'

'Nineteen rupees!' said the foreman. 'One rupee cut for being late at the factory.'

'Twenty rupees!' shouted the wrestler, summoning all the power of his colossal frame into a deliberately restrained manner. 'Not a pice less.'

The foreman looked up to Ratan and blinked to meet the hard glint of the wrestler's flaming eyes. He felt uncomfortable and began to sharpen the ends of his moustache. His face went purple and pale like the back of a chameleon under the glare of the sun.

'Acha!' he said to save his dignity. 'This time you are excused. Your thumb.'

'I can write,' said Ratan sternly.

The foreman gave him a pen, laid currency notes of twenty rupees by the side of the desk, and waited eagerly for the man to be off.

Ratan took his own time about it. He slowly wrote his name in Hindustani, stood and counted the notes, and saying 'Mehrbani

Sahib', showed his back, contrary to the custom of the coolies, who bowed abjectly as they retreated.

Hari and Munoo were not to be found when he returned to where they had squatted among the crowd of coolies. He thought that they had proceeded home. He marched out of the factory.

As soon as he jumped the little ditch which separated the badly paved road from the damp field, he espied a tall Pathan with his hand on Hari's neck, while a short, stocky Muhammadan was threatening the old coolie with loud abuse and the butt end of his rifle. Munoo was nowhere in sight.

'So you thought you would give us the slip,' Ratan heard the short Pathan say, jumping towards Hari. 'You son of an ass! You heathen! You thought we would not see you under the legs of the other coolies. Pay up, pay up Nadir Khan's debt, since he is not here to exact it.'

Hari had opened the fold of his dhoti and yielded a currency note as the tall Pathan kicked him in the behind and pulled at the neck of his tunic so hard that the old coolie's teeth rattled, his eyes bulged, and his garment ripped.

'That is not all,' the Pathan said. 'The interest alone is five rupees. There is more money in your loincloth. Give it to me.'

'My wages have been cut, Khan Sahib,' said Hari, joining his hands with the note pressed between them. 'I had some money deducted·for damaged cloth. I can't pay this month. I shall pay next month.'

The short Pathan snatched the note out of his hand and the tall Pathan was about to kick Hari off, when Ratan walked up slowly, and caught hold of the Pathan by the collar.

'Leave him go, you ruffians!' he said.

'What has this to do with you, Pahlwan?' snarled the short Pathan.

'Everything, you swine!' Ratan shouted. 'He has paid you the money. What more do you want? Why do you show off your strength to an old man? Come, give me a fight, you bullies!'

'Acha! Acha! Pahlwan Sahib,' said the tall Pathan, releasing Hari from his grasp because he felt the shadow of Ratan's presence behind him, and the powerful hold of the wrestler's hand on his neck.

'Acha! Acha!' repeated the short Pathan, shaking his head a little nervously. 'The rest of the money shall be added to the capital. We shall put it in the book. Go!'

Hari broke into a short, shuffling run, his heart breaking, his eyes full of tears, and his frame hanging loose.

Ratan let the tall Pathan's neck loose.

The Pathans strode away towards some other coolies, trying to keep their heads from hanging low with humiliation.

Ratan came abreast of Hari.

So afraid was the old man of the Pathans following him, however, that he started, staggered and fell.

'Hari! Hari! Don't be afraid! It is I, Ratan,' the wrestler said, helping him up. And in complete silence they proceeded homewards.

As they came to the tenement house, through the viscid, noisome mud, they saw the chowkidar and Munoo standing by the staircase.

'He wants the rent,' Munoo said, coming towards his friends. 'I told him that Shibu would pay.'

Hari handed out three rupees from the knot of his loincloth and said: 'You pay two rupees, brother. We will settle the account later with Shibu.'

Munoo handed over the rupees.

'This is my share towards the rent,' said Ratan, handing over two rupees to the chowkidar.

Hari struggled up the staircase, his face pinched and screwed into a knot, his body lifeless and heavy, his legs shaking precariously. He sank to the floor of the room on the third floor with a sigh. Lakshami came and began to press his knees reverently.

Ratan began to smoke a biri.

Munoo, who had hitherto enjoyed the delights of smoking only surreptitiously, stretched his hands towards Ratan for a cigarette. Unfortunately, the very first puff he took made him cough. He was amused at his own discomfiture. But Ratan roared with laughter like a child.

'They have cut five rupees from our pay for damaged cloth,' Shibu said, coming in. 'This is no occasion for mirth-making.'

'They dared not cut any money for damaged cloth out of my pay,' Ratan said. 'You ought to be manly enough to stand up for yourself. Or you should come with me and join the Union. You are all so lethargic.'

'I will join the Union,' Munoo said. 'Tell me where it is.'

'Come,' he said. 'We will go and get your names enrolled. There is no time to lose.'

'All right, Lakshami,' said Hari, whose fatigue had been somewhat alleviated by his wife's attentions, 'I have enough strength now. I will go and enrol my name in the Union, too.'

'I will come, too,' said Shibu.

'All right, come,' said Ratan. 'And then I will take you for a drink at the toddy shop.'

The friendship between Munoo and Ratan grew, as friendship can only grow between two spontaneous, naïve, warm-hearted men of the Punjab. It had arisen quickly, developed fast, so that they were now calling each other 'friends since the days when they wore napkins in their cradles'.

The circumstances of their lives cemented the bond in a way which was unique, for brotherliness was the only compensation for the bitterness of life in the roaring factory and in the crowded homes in which they lived, worked and had their being.

A twelve-hour day wears one down.

And to live in a fifteen-by-ten room, cramped on the floor, amid the smoke and smell of cooking and of the food eaten, amid a chaos of pots and pans, old beds and crawling children, in the publicity of the common staircase, the common washing place, the common latrines, and amid the foul smell of sewages that filtered over the pathways, conduces to comradeship.

It was the few hours outside this hell that, more than anything else, endeared Ratan to Munoo.

He found it so hard to get up in the morning. And there was no way of getting to the factory except to walk. It took nearly an hour, as he had to complete his toilet in the fields and have a dip in the swamp. That meant crawling out of bed at about half-past four or five. By the time he had eaten a little bread left over from last night, walked to the pool, relieved himself, washed and walked to the mill, it was six. Of course, Nadir Khan, the warder, kept a record of what time every coolie came and could get your pay docked.

At night, when the six o'clock whistle blew, there was the walk home again. It was eight or nine by the time the females, tired after the day's work, could cook a meal. To get eight hours sleep it was necessary to go to bed immediately. It was not hard to go to sleep. These men did not need veronal for their insomnia. The twelve-hour day was a sedative.

But a boy like Munoo did not want to get to sleep at nine. The fields, the toddy shop, the town attracted him ever since Ratan had introduced him to them. Often it was midnight before he slept.

It was these hours spent in companionship, in the actual act of living, sentient contact with other coolies, that seemed to him the happiest. He felt he was learning to be a grown-up man. He believed he would soon be a full man. Everything he heard, said or did during these hours was important.

He always burst out with happiness on a holiday. And he joined the general exodus of coolies to the town, to see the wonderful things that were sold there, to caress them in his heart, since he could not buy them, with the warm hope that one day he would be able to possess them.

Munoo and Ratan went together on these outings on Saturdays.

The dusty road that led from the mill land to the outskirts of Bombay yielded quickly under the eager rush of coolies' feet. The smell of tanning hides, of carcasses of dead dogs and cats on rubbish heaps, the odour of decaying dung which lay in the fields and in fissures and folds, gave place to the palm-lined highways and tamarind-tree groves, hedged by rows of sweet-peas and roses. Great houses loomed up against the green parks and towered over the beds of gold mohur which grew like golden glories everywhere. The deformed, hollow-eyed, hollow-cheeked bodies of the workers began to mingle with the expensively costumed pedestrians of the town. The traffic of victorias, motor taxis and privately owned limousines increased without warning. And the habitués of mill land insinuated themselves like the oncoming twilight into the busy bazaars of Bombay city.

'I will show you a tamasha today,' said Ratan to Munoo as they sat in a toddy shop, his face suddenly lighting up with an embarrassed smile.

And, draining the last draught of Muree beer from a bottle before him, he led Munoo, under the glare of electric lights in the Abdul Rahman Street, past the gas lamps of the Bhendi Bazaar, through a dimly lit lane into Grant Road.

Munoo had had a glass of beer, and followed Ratan enthusiastically into the quaint, narrow old street whose dirt was hidden by the dark, whose unsavoury smells mixed with the perfume of the flower-stalls, and whose squalor was nicely camouflaged by the forms of the thickly painted, profusely bejewelled, gorgeously attired women who sat on low stools, padded with cushions, in the windows and balconies, over curious little shops, smiling strange smiles and winking at the swarms of men who walked along, leisurely, gaily dressed and chewing the betel leaf or betel nut, while they looked out for a bawd.

'Isn't that a lovely scene!' Ratan bent down and remarked. 'Aren't you happy to have come with me? And now tell me, which of those women do you like?'

Munoo smiled to cover his embarrassment. His heart was beating with the eager urge that Ratan's words aroused in his body. He felt warm and happy, and stared at his friend with a wonderfully innocent light in his eyes, as if he were wrapped in a wild, sensual dream.

'Come,' Ratan said, 'I know where to take you. We will go to Piari Jan.'

Munoo followed his friend, along wave upon wave of human passion that surged up and down the street, the gay, rustling, white, black, brown swarms that ebbed and flowed to the rhythm of a silent song, the song of desire which sought in music, dance, love, an escape, a death, a kind of culmination, howsoever temporary and partial, from the loneliness of the soul. The boy did not know how miserable, how brow-beaten, how utterly wretched was this humanity that crowded the street of pleasure. He was taken in by the glamour of this masquerade, and thought it to be a carnival like those fairs in the country, where people went to show off their gaudiest clothes. He had no certain aim or object himself, and thought that all these people wandered too without aim or object.

But before he knew where he was, Ratan had dragged him through a dark alley into an evil-smelling courtyard, and led him up a narrow, dark flight of steps into an open salon, brilliantly lit with tall chandeliers and decorated with paper chains and imitation flowers from the dome to the walls, where large oleographs of His Majesty King Edward VII and his grandson, the present King-Emperor, hung, side by side with lithographs of the monkey god Hanuman and large photographs of a woman, ostensibly Piari Jan, as she had appeared in the heyday of her prosperity, when she had had a salon in the best part of Grant Road, and when she had danced for all the big merchants of Bombay, and was not the broken, middle-aged, used-up creature who now sat at the window, swathed in cheap, tawdry imitation silks and draperies, and nose, ear, hand and neck ornaments.

'Ao, welcome, Pahlwanji. Where have you kept yourself hidden for so long? My eyes have gone blind looking at the way along which you were to come to grace my house,' Piari Jan said with a smile that hid the obvious insincerity of her speech.

'I have been working very hard,' said Ratan. 'Also, the foreman cut some of my pay last month.'

'I hope he hasn't cut any this month,' she said, laughing.

'No, no, don't you be afraid for your share,' said Ratan, matching her subtle question with a vague promise. And then, he twisted the embarrassing situation with mild good humour, saying: 'Look, I have brought you a handsome young gallant.'

She advanced towards Munoo and, laying her hand on his head, said: 'The Son of God himself in beauty! What a big boy! Is he your son?'

'No, he is your lover!' said Ratan. 'He is my rival.'

Munoo felt ill at ease in the face of this vision of transparent gauzes and glittering jewels. And the draughts of perfume that oozed from her body made him a bit dizzy. But he was curious to know, to feel the lure of her love. And he stood excited.

'Be seated then, Pahlwanji,' said Piari Jan. 'You are always mocking, are you not?'

'Well then, I am qualified for the job of a clown in your household,' said Ratan, keeping the conversation up in order to conceal the slight awkwardness he felt, and sinking on to the white-sheeted floor with Munoo.

'You are my honoured patron,' Piari said. 'How could I presume to ask you to join my troupe? I am your servant.' And she deftly changed the conversation to bring her customer to the point. 'Now will Your Grace have some sherbet and hear some music?'

'Han! Han!' rallied Ratan to the point, appreciating that his pleasure meant only strict business to her. 'Here is a bottle of the kind of sherbet that I think you will like,' he added, producing a bottle of port.

'It is very kind of you, Pahlwanji,' she said. 'You are generous like Hatam Tai. I will get some glasses.' And she went towards a niche where a large bed stood with that beautifully painted woodwork which is a speciality of the north Indian carpenters.

Coming back with four small bowls, she leaned over to the hall and called: 'Ni Janki, ni Gulab jan! Vay Bude Khan!'

'We are going to have some dancing, too, then?' Ratan asked. 'But you are taking a great deal of trouble. Come and sit down by me for a while.'

'May I be your sacrifice,' said Piari, coming mockingly and sitting in his lap. 'I am your servant.'

Munoo smiled nervously at this exhibition of love. He had never seen a man and woman so near to each other. His uncle had always slept in a separate bed from that of his aunt. And though Prabha's bed used to lie alongside Parbati's, he had never seen them touch each other. As for Hari and Lakshami, they seemed to belong to two different worlds. He felt a queer movement in his entrails and an affection in his chest which seemed to melt his thoughts and to intoxicate him more beautifully than the bitter liquid he had shared with Ratan.

Two lovely apparitions darted into the salon, their legs encumbered by the glittering sequins of silken trousers, their upright bodies swathed in the thin folds of flashing, starched, stiff, pink aprons, and with brave smiles on their faces which scarcely hid the pathos of their broken spirit. They stood for a moment embarrassedly looking backwards into the hall, affecting a histrionic suspense in expectation of Bude Khan, who soon appeared, a black, toothless, dim-eyed creature, clad in clean clothes which did not disguise his procurer's soul.

'Salaam! Salaam! Pahlwanji,' said the pimp. 'You have graced our salon after a very long time. We must make haste to entertain you. Now what about it, girls?' And he sat down, pressing the keys of the harmonium which he had planted before himself.

The instrument uttered a long-drawn-out, plaintive note and it seemed to produce an atmosphere in which the two dancers lost their nervousness. Piari dragged a couple of drums and began to tune them with the brisk thumps of her heavy hands. Then the harmonium released a soft note of longing and the drums reverberated like the slow thunder of a waterfall, and the two dancers began to sway their hands, which had hung loose, and to move their feet, painted red with henna, so that it seemed that they were burning with an invisible fire.

As the music rose dolefully in the air and became a sustained, palpitating rhythm, like the beating of Munoo's heart, Piari began to sing the first accents of a folk song, while the dancers advanced like the rippling of water in a pool, striking their heels together, so that the bells on their ankles tinkled in tune with the song, and the whole atmosphere was charged with the presence of a force which bound them all in a curious connection.

The insistence of Piari's voice on the amorous phrases of the song, as well as the insidious fire of the dancers, lost in a maze of movement, the undertones of the harmonium and the overtones of the tambourines, travelled through the twin hearts of Ratan and Munoo, till, when the elements of music rose to a shrill height and the dancers spun round in the most tender, affecting, weirdly disturbing circles of joy and pain, and the whole atmosphere reached a wild, hysterical pitch of emotion, Ratan undid the upper folds of his loincloth and threw a rupee on to the harmonium with a shout of 'Wah! Wah! You have made me happy, Piari, my life, my love!'

Piari moved away from the tambourines and sank felinely into Ratan's lap, saying: 'I am glad I have pleased you. But I want you to please me.'

'I am not the Rustum of Hindustan for nothing,' said Ratan. 'You wait till I get you between the legs.'

Bude Khan leered round at this, extending the corners of his dim eyes furtively. The two nautch girls, who had sunk to the floor and sat huddled against each other, arm in arm, head to head, in a kind of ecstasy, giggled at the wrestler's phrase.

Munoo's heart reached out into the space about him, straining to touch the shores of the women's bodies, like a wave, but it was beaten back before it got anywhere near them.

Piari signed to Bude Khan again and sang the first verse of a second song with a most affected shuffle of her bangles, an arched glance of her eyes, a delicate movement of her head, and cast a spell over Ratan, which the lecherous accompanist drove home by just the right accent on the harmonium.

Piari stopped to receive the gift of another rupee which prostitutes expect after the effective presentation of every verse of a song, once they have got the customer well in hand.

'A little more dancing would please my boyfriend,' said Ratan, cunningly evading the payment.

Piari signed to the dancers, laughing in the face of a look from Bude Khan which accused her of forgetting her business.

The girls arose slowly, rolling their almond eyes, which now showed the deep lines of the cosmetic around them, under the smear of their thick eyebrows and their long, black lashes.

They took up the accents of Piari's song on their fingers, and mounting the languid notes of the music, danced with a sudden, shrill brilliance, insinuating all the love, the passion, the lust of the poem with elaborate artistry, by the suggestions of their bodies, the swaying of their tapering arms, the balanced hurrying motion of snakes and vipers, the violence of panthers, the fine insinuating glides of innocent roes, the slow motion of enchantresses casting spells. The fine frenzies of their dazzling olive skins had now been transmuted from the artificiality of make-up into the transparency of mirrors which reflected the strange colour of their souls.

Ratan had bawled out approbation as the lusty chords of the song lashed his body: *'Wah, wah! shabash!'* as is the custom to do in appreciating Indian music, for the audience is supposed to be an enthusiastic part of the performance, and not a chilly embodiment of external criticism. At the end of the song he took another rupee from his dhoti and put it as a douceur on a tray.

The dancers glided away. Bude Khan shuffled out behind them.

Munoo had been spellbound during the performance. Now he was agitated. And he grew flushed and hot.

'The boy must be tired,' suggested Piari, meaningly.

'Yes. Munoo brother, you go home,' said Ratan. 'It is late. I will follow you later.'

Munoo felt that he would die with the misery of not knowing what he wanted. That he wanted something, he knew. But what, he did not know. He rose. Piari patted him on the head. The boy was weeping bitterly as he rushed out. He returned from the street of pleasure, long after midnight, through the sleepless Bombay streets, where the eternally homeless coolies squatted, slept, moaned and gossiped, outside closed shops, pale and ghastly under the glare of gas lights.

On the outskirts of the town the roads were a clear white in the uncanny darkness of the moonless night. But the deep ruts and pits of the plateau beyond them spread sinister and eerie, the more so because occasionally a firefly opened its jewel wings on a rubbish heap and, suddenly, an owl droned its heavy, ominous song of desolation from the midst of a palm grove.

The queer disturbance in Munoo's soul, after the excitement of the dance in Piari Jan's salon, seemed to become an oppressive weight on his chest. His brain reeled with the agitation of half-conscious desires that rose to his head like dim ghosts of thoughts. 'What is it I want?' he asked himself, as his body struggled along with its weight of fatigue and its burden of vague perturbation. And, as he could not get an answer to his query, he walked in a jaded indifference. Then the tread of his feet seemed to become the giant stride of some monstrous demon, who, in spite of his largeness, was uneasy and afraid of the evil spirits of the dark, which huddled together with dishevelled hair, glistening white teeth and sharp claws with long nails extended to scratch one's eyes out. He closed his eyes to escape from the vision, but he stumbled and hit his left toe against a stone. Then he ran, ran hard, and came within sight of the tenements. The witches of the night had been left behind. And there was the bright point of a lamp in a hut, glistening with a comfortable glow. He felt he was safe, though the fear of the night still lingered in his bones. He walked up the stairs as if each breath he breathed were his last.

Hari's wife was waiting for him, mending rags by the pale glimmer of an earthen saucer lamp, as she reclined against the wall, away from where everyone snored, moaned or shifted sides in the enervating heat of the asafoetidic room. She looked at him with a pained, tender light in her eyes and strained to ask: 'Where have you been so late?'

Munoo stared at her. The tears that had ebbed up to his eyes when Piari Jan put her hand on his head flowed into them again. He averted his glance from her and moved towards the part of the floor where he slept. When he looked up again, Lakshami was bending over him with a trembling, wild light in her eyes, and a warm flush on her cheeks. He shook his head and bent it low so as to escape the contact which his instincts wanted. She raised his chin with a gentle, gentle brush of her hand and, with all the pathos, all the tenderness of her mother's intuitive understanding of his need, kissed his forehead, murmuring in the faintest of whispers, like an incantation: 'We belong to suffering! We belong to suffering! My love!' And she lay down by his side and took him in her arms, pressing him to her bosom with a silent warmth which made him ache with the hurt of her physical nearness, which tortured him, harassed him, making him writhe with all the pent-up fury of his adolescent passion, till in the magic hours of the dawn it found an escape in death, in the temporary death of his body in hers.

It is difficult enough for anyone to face a Monday morning. It was like doomsday to the coolies, especially after they had lost themselves in the ecstasy of human relationships for a day and regained their souls.

But on Monday mornings they returned to work. On Monday mornings they faced death again. And, as if the monster of death were some invisible power which throttled them as soon as they set out to work, they walked to the factory in a kind of hypnotized state of paralysis, in a state of apathy and torpor which made the masks of their faces assume the sinister horror of unexpressed pain.

'Why are they sad?' Munoo wondered, because he still had a little of the stored-up vitality of his youth left in him. And he stared hard at them. Shivering, weak, bleary, with twisted, ugly faces, black, filthy, gutless, spineless, they stole along with unconscious, not-there looks; idiots, looking at the smoky heavens as they sighed or murmured 'Ram Ram' and the other names of God in greeting to each other and in thanksgiving for the gifts of the Almighty. The boy recalled how his patron Prabha in Daulatpur used to say that everything was the blessing of God, even Ganpat's ill treatment, the beating the police had given him and the fever of which he nearly died – that all suffering was the result of our having committed evil deeds. Perhaps these people also believed in Karma. Hari, indeed, had often said so, and he had hoped that one day his luck would turn, because he had done some good deeds in his life. Ratan laughed at all such wisdom, and he alone went light-heartedly through life; with a brave, handsome face, beaming with smiles, he alone went with a pride and a swagger, while the other coolies cringed with humility.

Munoo felt a superstitious awe for Ratan's fate. An overpowering sense of doom crept into his soul as he thought of him. He tried to dismiss his thoughts by repeating the Indian phrase: 'I must not think of Ratan as handsome and lucky, lest my evil eye bring bad luck to him.' But, as if his thoughts were echo-auguries, the smile on the wrestler's face faded one morning.

It was the Chimta Sahib's habit to stand by the door of the preparing-shed every morning to exact salaams and other forms of homage from the coolies. A flourish of the hand, a curse, an oath or abuse was the greeting he offered in exchange. This conduct was well suited to the preservation of peace in the mill, as even the sight of his big, beefy body cowed the coolies and put the fear of God into them, and they were then in the right frame of mind to perform their duties. Occasionally he kicked a coolie. But that was when he had got drunk early or quarrelled with Mrs Thomas, and sometimes it was when he had read in the morning paper the news of a nationalist demonstration, a terrorist outrage or an attempt at seditious communist propaganda which he, as a member of the British race of India, considered to be more a personal affront than the pursuit of an ideal of freedom on the part of the exploited. He had long since forgotten the days during which he himself had eked out a miserable existence in Lancashire.

Ratan was rather an independent-minded person. He did not bow down to salaam the foreman. He had the confidence of his own personal strength and, behind that, the strength of the Union. He knew he was a good worker and deserved full pay at the end of the month. And when his pay was not forthcoming at the time when it was due, or when he was threatened with a cut for damaged cloth or for being late, he agitated.

There was no love lost between the Chimta Sahib and Ratan.

'Salaam, Sahib!' the wrestler greeted the foreman cockily, as he strode past him.

'Come here!' called the Chimta Sahib in a sharp whisper.

'Yes, Huzoor,' said Ratan, with mock ceremony, coming back.

'You are discharged!' said the Chimta Sahib.

'But Sahib! What is my fault?'

'Jao! You are discharged!'

Ratan looked at the foreman, at first calmly, then he swayed like one struck to the heart. His full face concentrated into a knot of anguish, pride and power. Then his chin lifted a little, his teeth ground the bad taste in his mouth and the corners of his eyes were shot with gleams of fire. He stood upright, aching to express himself, to express the demon in him, the monster of pain which the actual knowledge of poverty, of the weakness of the people around him, and of their suffering, had given him. It was as if this sudden blow to his dignity had gone like a shock of electricity through him, and had illuminated his frame with the most intense sense of his own status. He raised his hand to strike. But the Chimta Sahib was moving away towards Nadir Khan, and Ratan could not violate the chivalrous law of the wrestler by hitting his adversary on the back. He shook his arms and threw off the tremendous weight of quiet power gathered in him. He loosened his muscles, bit his lower lip and felt the blood in his glittering eyes turning to water.

'They say one must never pass behind a horse or before an officer,' said Munoo consolingly. 'I will go and beg him to take you back.'

'No,' said Ratan coldly. 'I will show him a bit of my mind. Just you wait.'

And he rushed away to the office of the All India Trade Union Federation, half a mile away, believing he would be able to put his cause before Lalla Onkar Nath, the President, who came from up-country and who, he knew, would be sympathetic.

'I want to make a complaint to the President,' he said to a clerk who sat on the verandah of the bungalow which served as the office of the Trade Union Committee.

The clerk eyed him up and down and said the Sahib was busy.

Ratan pressed a nickel piece of half a rupee into the man's hand.

The clerk lifted the chick at the door of the office, went in, but returned automatically.

'The Sahib says he is very busy,' he reported. 'He orders you to write to him if you have any complaints to make. I will write the application for you for a rupee.'

Ratan felt impotent with rage. He could have wrung the man's neck, but he realized that it was not the clerk's fault, and he sat down to dictate an epistle seeking redress through the Union for the wrong he had suffered.

There was the coming and going of many men in the room where Ratan lodged that evening.

The rumour had spread that the wrestler had been discharged, and coolies came from all corners of the mill land to sympathize with him and to receive sympathy for the wrongs they too had suffered.

But they were broken, dispirited, docile and reticent, and they only stared blankly through dim brown eyes, or mumbled a conventional phrase, in a meek and holy manner: 'Never mind, brother, this is the will of God,' or 'It is sad, but in this world the wicked seem to flourish and the good always to suffer.' The misery of their lives had robbed them of all energy, till their souls seemed to have disappeared and only a bare suggestion of the memory of pain hung round their faces, like helplessness about the limbs of a sick man, tenderness about the face of a child, and weakness about the eyes of a dumb animal.

About half-past eight, however, arrived two Indian Sahibs, Sauda and Muzaffar, and an Englishman, Stanley Jackson, whom the coolies had often seen lecturing in the mill maidan.

'We hear you have been discharged, Ratan,' said Sauda.

'Yes,' said Ratan, smiling nonchalantly.

'Did the foreman give you any reason?' asked the Englishman, in broken Hindustani.

'No, Sahib,' said Ratan. 'But he has been waiting for an opportunity to do this for some time. I don't care about that so much as the insulting behaviour of Lalla Onkar Nath, the President of our Union, in refusing to see me.'

'Why didn't you come to us?' said Muzaffar. 'You have suffered because of your association with us. We have to take up your cause. Don't be down-hearted.'

'I had hoped to get a job somewhere else,' said Ratan, 'and thought that if I came to you it would be known all over the mill world and that would jeopardize my chances.'

'Why not go to the Chimta Sahib?' put in Munoo, who sat eagerly listening to the conversation and rather excited by the dramatic visit of the Red Flag Union officials to the room.

'Oh, no, there is no question of that,' said Sauda, with a flourish of his hand. 'Do not all the insults you people suffer rouse you from the apathy to which you have succumbed? Does not all the misery, all the degradation you suffer rouse you to indignation? I tell you that they have ground you down, they have fleeced and sweated you, they have tortured your lives enough!'

'That is so,' said Hari, shaking his head, as he sat bent with his curved spine.

'Look at the room you live in,' began Sauda. 'Is it big enough to house you all? And thousands of you are content to live in these tenements, and straw huts which have no paved road, no playground nor a garden. How long can you live like this? At the best six months, and then you will go home to die. And those children of yours sweat hard all day for an anna and get stunted and never grow up. When will you wake up? When will you come to your senses?'

'Don't take offence at what the Sahib is saying,' said Muzaffar, cautiously taking the sting off the vehement reproaches of Sauda.

'The Sahib loves you. He, too, has suffered from poverty. And he knows a law with which to remove poverty if you will learn it.'

'He will establish schools for your children,' said the Englishman.

'More than schools,' said Sauda. 'You want food. Your hands spin the cotton and weave the cloth on those machines. At home your hands ploughed the fields and produced the cotton. Your brethren plant grain and reap the harvest under the heat of the sun; they build the roads, work in the mines and on the plantations. The big employer Sahib takes away all that you produce, to Vilayat, and gives you a bare pittance with which you can hardly pay the rent, buy food, clothe yourself or pay your debts. You work for a while and then go away to die in the old village, and other men come to take your place. An epidemic of cholera starts and you are swept off. Now tell me, are you content to let your masters treat you like that?'

'No,' said Ratan. 'By God, no!'

'But what can we do, Sahib?' said a visiting coolie. 'You are a clever man and like a Sahib. So you can fight the other Sahibs, but who are we to protest?'

'You, you are human beings,' said Sauda, fiercely. 'Have you forgotten your notion of izzat? Would you let anyone throw away the turbans off your head?'

'No,' replied the coolie.

'But then where is your idea of izzat gone?' asked Sauda. 'Where is your sense of dignity? Where is your manhood?'

'I am a man,' boasted Ratan, striking his hand on his chest.

'That is why you have been discharged,' said Munoo, jocularly. 'You are too proud of being a wrestler!'

Everyone laughed at this and the atmosphere became less tense for a moment. Then Hari spoke, wearily, shrugging his shoulders.

'We have to work for someone; if not for the Chimta Sahib, then for someone else.'

'Yes, yes, you have to work,' said Sauda. 'Work is good, but now you sweat eleven hours a day and get bad pay. If you do what I tell you, your hours will get shorter and your pay will be increased.'

'What shall we do, Sahib?' asked Hari.

'You must walk out of the mill, all of you,' said Sauda, 'and refuse to work till your hours are shortened, your pay increased, your children given schools and till you are given new houses.'

'You go on strike,' said the Englishman, quietly.

'I shall,' said Ratan.

'You are already on strike,' Munoo teased his friend.

The other coolies remained silent. They knew that they had to slave hard, that they were being sweated and fleeced, that they were being starved to death slowly, but they thought of their immediate necessities during a strike, of the food their children would want and of their own hunger. And they were afraid, and hung their heads.

'Think over what we have said,' said Muzaffar, reasonably. 'Meanwhile, Ratan, brother, you had better come and see us tomorrow, and we will see what can be done.'

'Salaam, Sahib,' the coolies said.

'Salaam, salaam, salaam,' the three communists returned, and walked down the stairs.

Munoo was very excited and enthusiastic.

The President of the All Indian Trade Union Council was persuaded by Sauda, Muzaffar and Jackson to make representations to the Sir George White Mills on behalf of Ratan. An application was sent asking for his reinstatement and he was asked to call to see the manager personally.

The letter arrived with hundreds of other communications, concerning bales of raw cotton received in the railway godowns, orders for the dispatch of finished cloth, machinery imported from England, repairs to be undertaken, inquiries about prices and samples, and, most important of all, Sir George White's dispatches.

The manager, Mr Little, was flurried in his rush to tackle the correspondence. He did not know where to begin. He caught sight of the 'Dear Sir' on one letter, the 'Honoured Sir' on another, the 'As regards the hundred bales of cotton that were not delivered' on another, the 'Thanking you in anticipation' on still another, and he was exhausted, his gaze fluttering wildly from the difficult sprawl of the railway goods clerk in dim carbon tracing on pink paper, the crude edges of Jamsetji Jijibhoy Mills' dispatches and the immaculate sheets of Sir Reginald White's crested letter paper.

Mr Little was impatient by nature. The humid heat of Bombay, which always covered his face with sweat, had not improved his nerves. He glanced up at the electric fan over his head, he shifted his chair, he shuffled papers. His throat felt parched. He wished he could get up to pour himself out a stiff whisky. But duty called; duty, stern voice of the daughter of God, and Wordsworth suffered from the effect of the heat.

He bent down to the table, stretching for the trays into which he had roughly sorted the letters. He knew he must attend to Sir Reginald's orders first.

'Screwwallah!' he called.

A young Indian clerk came in, dressed in a white cotton English suit and a boat-like black cap, the new national headgear with which he hoped to balance up the prestige of his motherland against his predilection for European dress. His dark face was full of fear, because he had never felt quite at ease with white men ever since one had kicked him at the corner of Hornby Road for no other crime than the childish curiosity which had made him stare with wonder and admiration at the Sahib. He stood tense and still.

'For heaven's sake sit down! You give me the creeps, standing there like that!' shouted Mr Little.

'Yes, sir,' the clerk mumbled, his underlip quivering, his brown eyes full of fear and shame.

'Take this down,' ordered Mr Little in an even voice.

The clerk thought that the Sahib had recovered somewhat, and seated himself on an iron chair at the edge of the large desk. The cool draughts of air from the fan soothed the heat of his body. He lowered his eyes to the shorthand notebook to avoid staring at the Sahib and to be in readiness to take down the letter.

'Wake up!' shouted Mr Little suddenly, sending a wild wave of fear through the clerk's body, so that he drew back instinctively as if he were being hit.

'Wake up!' the Sahib repeated, modulating his tone to evenness, as he saw that he had frightened the clerk almost out of his wits. 'Begin,' he continued. '"Notice" at top, spelling – N-O-T-I-C-E.'

At this moment a fly settled on Mr Little's nose. He tried to brush it off. It came back as soon as he opened his mouth to speak.

'Lalkaka!' he shouted.

'Huzoor,' came the obedient voice, and following it, from behind the cane chick which discreetly screened the office from the gaze of the world, appeared the Parsi messenger-boy in a shirt and shorts, his profusely oiled hair parted in the middle and giving him a dignity which looked ridiculous in the child.

'Take this fly-killer and strike it on the fly when it settles anywhere in the room.'

'Yes, Huzoor,' said Lalkaka, and lifted the cane with the heart-shaped leather flap attached to it.

'Screwwallah!' said the Sahib. 'Write.'

The clerk applied pencil to paper.

'In view of the present trade depression and currency crisis,' Mr Little dictated, in a slow, deliberate manner, screwing up his eyes and puffing out his cheeks, till the words began to twist and roll like windy rhetoric, 'the Board of Directors regrets to announce that in order to keep the plant running and to curtail expenses, the mills will go on short time, immediately. There will be no work for the fourth week in every month till further notice. No wages will be paid for that week, but the management, having the welfare of the workers at heart, have sanctioned a substantial allowance. This change will take effect from May 10. (Signed) Sir Reginald White, Bart., President, Sir George White Mills.'

Mr Little was about to listen to the clerk's usual recitation of what he had taken down, when the fly settled on his forehead. He looked frowningly at Lalkaka.

Lalkaka struck the flap of the fly-killer on the Sahib's forehead, the Sahib's frown having resolved his doubt about the advisability of killing the fly.

'You damn fool! You bloody little fool!' fumed Mr Little, as he arose wildly from his chair, rubbing his forehead with his right hand and gesticulating impotently with the left. He would have kicked the boy out of the room, but the telephone bell rang the sudden, jarring refrains of its mechanical steel song: 'Terr-terr-terr-terr-terr'.

'Hello! Hello!' said Mr Little, snatching the receiver from the clerk's hand. 'Sir George White Mills!' he confirmed, his face purple with rage and scarlet where the flap of the fly-killer had struck it. 'Yes, oh yes, Sir Reginald . . . of course . . . of course! I have just dictated the notice . . . I will call Jimmie and hand it over to him . . . yes, yes . . . of course, you will . . . what time may we expect you? . . . Before lunch . . . Right, Sir Reginald . . . Good morning, Sir Reginald, good morning . . . yes . . . Not too bad you know . . . Hot . . . Stifling . . . But the orders are coming through . . . We shall expect you, then, immediately . . . Good morning.'

'Go and call the foreman Sahib, you swine,' he said, turning to Lalkaka, who stood near the door, paralysed with fright.

Lalkaka ran out, but came back.

'Huzoor, the Sahib is coming.'

'Hallo, Jimmie, good morning. The mill is going on short work from next week.'

'Goddam all the niggers!' said Jimmie. 'A peg?'

'On the sideboard! By God, I am thirsty too. Phew!'

'What's it all about?' said Jimmie, mopping his bald head, and helping himself from the whisky bottle.

'Screwwallah is typing the notice,' said Mr Little.

'Well, here's to it!' said Jimmie, handing over a tumbler half-full of neat whisky to Mr Little.

'Reggie will be here before lunch, sonny boy,' warned the manager. 'You had better keep steady.'

'Your funeral,' returned Jimmie. 'You've got to render the accounts. I don't need to keep the plant going. It goes on on its own.'

'See that the coolies get the notice only after Reggie has been,' said Mr Little. 'You know there are all kinds of fanatics among them.'

'No, I've chucked out the only fanatic,' assured Jimmie. 'A fellow who has worked at the Tatas' and was getting a bit above himself at the instigation of the Reds. Good worker, you know, but we can't have sedition going about.'

'Oh, I've received an application for his reinstatement from the All-Indian Trade Union Federation this morning. I was going to ask you about him,' said Little. 'These bloody swine are spreading discontent fast. I wonder why the government does not do something about it.'

'There are two factions in it now,' informed Jimmie, twirling his moustache. 'The old Indian Trade Union Federation started by Onkar Nath, and the Red Flag Union, recently started by a fellow called Jackson, from Manchester.'

'They should all be put up against a wall and shot, the whole bloody lot of them,' burst out Mr Little.

The sharp hoot of a car outside the office put an end to Little's vituperation. He rushed out. Jimmie put the glasses away and, lifting the chick on the floor, emerged into the verandah, steadying himself.

'Good morning, Little, good morning, Jimmie,' Sir Reginald greeted, as the liveried English chauffeur opened the door and the middle-aged baronet came out, a small, round man, with a weather-beaten face, streaked with ruptured veins.

'Has the notice been posted and explained, Jimmie?'

'No, sir, I am just going to announce it,' replied the foreman, feeling the heat of the sun on his scalp as he stood hatless in the compound.

'I should ask your wife to put on a few more clothes,' said Sir Reginald, looking towards the foreman's bungalow, where Mrs Thomas stood in a dressing-gown, excitedly watching the rare event of Sir Reginald's visit to the factory.

Jimmie flushed red and, glancing towards his bungalow, fumed with anger and then looked up to Sir Reginald apologetically.

'Well then, Little,' lisped Sir Reginald through his false teeth, as he proceeded towards the office, where Lalkaka raised the chick for the entry of the great man and the flies. 'Well, you see, the Board of Directors had serious news about a threatening crisis at home. And, in view of the Company's interests not only in this mill, but in the Calcutta Jute Mills and the Madras mines, and to guard against any loss to the shareholders, we have had to take this unfortunate decision. I am awaiting a cable from home and from Clive Street to see how we stand, but if this awful crisis, you see –'

'The auditors are checking the accounts, Sir Reginald,' interrupted Little, 'and the registers are all away. But I think we are quite safe. The last month's orders have been fairly substantial. But outside competition is pressing –'

'I am going to the Viceroy with a delegation, recommending a high tariff on foreign goods,' said Sir Reginald. 'But the government is well aware of the position. Lord Wolverhampton is a fine diplomat in the best Disraeli tradition, you know, and we have a sound man at the helm in London. Britain must go through with the Singapore arrangement and make the Indian ocean safe for our ships. But the trouble is that these Indians are getting more and more restive, and the socialists at home, you know . . . it is all very difficult what with the Quakers and Gandhists. Did you hear that the Stephenson Mills have been bought over by the Jamsetji Jijibhoy group? That makes the Indian interests in the cotton industry 75 per cent to our 25. It is a bad look-out. But', he continued, taking out his watch, 'it all depends on how . . . well, I will be late for my appointment. Send me the accounts, will you, Little, there's a good chap.' He turned and waited for the manager to lift the chick, then shuffled away, saying: 'Goodbye, goodbye,' as if a sudden fit of absentmindedness had made him oblivious of everyone around him.

The coolies were pouring into the compound from the sheds, after hearing the announcement about short work. They gesticulated behind the Chimta Sahib. They saw the long, black, polished body of the Daimler swerve round. They rushed towards it, vaguely aware that the master of the mill was being driven away after pronouncing their doom. They would have fallen at his feet with joined hands if the car had not slid away. They rushed at the Chimta Sahib and begged him with entreaties and prayers not to declare the factory on short work.

The Chimta Sahib abused and threatened to strike any 'nigger' who came near him or touched him with his dirty hands.

They prayed, they wept, they cried, they stretched their joined hands and prostrated themselves on the earth before him, for they believed somehow that he was the god, the master who could save or destroy them. Then the Chimta Sahib broke away to the safety of his bungalow. Nadir Khan dispersed the crowd.

Munoo, who knew nothing about directors and shareholders and threatening crises, believed that it was Ratan's dismissal that had been the cause of this uproar. He determined to go to the Chimta Sahib's bungalow stealthily and beg him to take Ratan back.

He darted into the godown of the factory at the back of the shed where the water pump stood. There was a vantage point at the far end of the godown whence one could jump over the fence into the garden surrounding the Chimta Sahib's bungalow.

A brisk run brought him beyond the pump, and he looked back to see that he was not being followed or observed. No. And ahead of him the coast was clear. He put his left hand on the sharp bamboo edge of the fence and jumped clean over the thorns of the rose trees that grew in the garden.

He hesitated a little on the dusty pathway that led through the garden bowers to the verandah, because no one seemed to be in sight at the bungalow and he did not know how he could approach the Chimta Sahib.

A vision of the foreman's hulking shape hovering over the verandah urged him on. His heart was thumping as he came up to the steps of the verandah and faced a memsahib, whom he presumed to be the foreman's wife.

Nellie Thomas, a dried-up small woman with streaks of grey mixed with her shock of brown hair, her sharp face bright with enthusiasm, her thin hands knitting a jumper with austere impatience, sat with her legs spreading wide on the armchair, in defiance of all Munoo's conceptions of modesty.

The boy stood afraid for a moment. Then he raised his hand to his forehead and said: 'Salaam.'

'Salaam,' she whispered. And, turning to where Jimmy stood helping himself to a peg, shrilled with alacrity: 'Oh, oh, pretty boy, you do look pretty. You are the worse off for drink and 'ere is an employee to see yer.'

Jimmie Thomas veered round where he stood and flung the bottle of whisky in his hand straight at Munoo, believing that the coolie had come to stab him with a dagger to revenge himself and the other employees for the notice of short work.

'Police! Murder!' shouted Nellie, jumping from the chair.

At this Jimmie completely lost his temper, and went with fist upraised towards his wife. But he slipped and fell with a thud beating his fist on the floor. Nellie, who had taken up a teapot from a tray, threw it at Jimmie in self-defence.

Munoo bolted.

But Mr Little, hearing the shouts of police and murder, had rushed up.

'What has happened?' asked Mr Little. 'What is the matter?'

Nellie whisked dingily but electrically from where she stood and with great presence of mind, said: 'It was like this 'ere, sir. I was sittin' knittin', and 'oo should come in but 'im, and of course he was the worse for drink. 'E says to me, 'e says, I ought to 'ave some more clothes on, damned sauce. And then 'e goes to the bottle. A boy comes in to see 'im, one of them hemployees, I think; 'e loses 'is temper and throws the bottle at 'im. 'E might have killed the poor nigger. And I hollered out Police and Murder. 'E went to fist me and slipped and fell –'

Mr Little lifted his eyebrows, and Nellie, who had paused to draw breath, continued with the next chapter of her narrative: 'I 'ave told 'im not to kick anyone when they's down, sir. The boy wasn't hurt. And I am quite willing to let bygones be bygones.'

The bland courtesy was still on Mr Little's face, but it was mingled now with the finest frown of dubiousness. He stood looking at them like a small, puzzled question mark.

'I 'it 'im in self-defence, sir,' Nellie confessed. 'Me life isn't safe with 'im. I can't bear it. I shall leave 'im.' And she began weeping with the most rueful, the most heart-rending sobs.

The coolies of the Sir George White factory crept like ghosts through the wasteland of the mills that afternoon.

They were dazed by the sudden shock of the announcement which deprived them of the only privilege left them; the privilege of work – a privilege, indeed, because it meant wages, whereas its withdrawal would mean starvation! They were willing to work. They were only too willing to haul and clean the cotton in the godowns, to tend the machines and sweep the lint along the floor, to help to turn the cotton thread into cloth. They were willing to do anything, so long as they could have their regular pay, even with a little cut for damaged cloth and for the foreman's commission and the interest of debts, so long as they could have enough to pay the landlord and to buy rice and lentils for the month. But to be told to go on short work!

They seemed to have died all of a sudden, that little spark of life, which made them move about willingly, had died, and left them a queer race of men, dried up, shrivelled, flat-footed, hollow-chested, hollow-cheeked, hollow-eyed. Their wretchedness had passed beyond the confines of suffering and left them careless, resigned.

'I went to see the Chimta Sahib about getting your job back,' said Munoo to Ratan. 'But he was very angry. He threw a bottle at me. He must be very angry with you that he has passed the order about work for all of us.'

'It isn't his anger with me, you idiot, but the big Sahib's greed that is responsible for the order,' said Ratan. 'You come with me to the meeting and you will understand. The coolies from all the factories are coming, and the trade union is going to declare a strike.'

'Oh!' Munoo exclaimed. 'Then I blamed the Chimta Sahib for nothing.'

'No, not for nothing!' shouted Ratan, wildly. 'He is a scoundrel. I will break his head, you wait and see. And I will break the head of that burra Sahib who comes in his motor car and cuts your pay!'

Hari walked, bent-backed and bandy-legged, behind them, the blind rage in his heart catching fire from Ratan's blasting tongue, but smothered by the weight of misery that oppressed him.

The other coolies followed, grim and tense like Hari, treading the earth with their big feet and occasionally shaking their heads to greet each other, and spreading out their hands in vague gestures of despair.

The sun cast angry glances at the chimneys of the mills as the huge crowd gathered in the desolate ground outside the bungalow which served as the headquarters of the All-Indian Trade Union Federation. The figures of the coolies were silhouetted against the earth as they waited for the speakers. The babble of many tongues whispering, half in fear, half in expectation, rose in waves. The loud words of an official from the middle of the throng shrilled aloft as a kite or a crow flying in a zigzag curve across the sky. A phrase like 'down with wage cuts' soared in the shimmering air and poised itself like a song-bird above the horizon, the fluctuating voice of the myriads of men becoming the one pointed symbol of their poverty and wretchedness, a pregnant cry reverberating with the pain of all these dwellers of the slums, the feeble new-born babes, the naked children with distended stomachs, the youths disfigured by smallpox and sores and hookworm, the men who were old without ever having been young, the women whose bellies were always protuberant with the weight of the unborn, the aged who hobbled about slobbering down the sides of their mouths and stinking, so that they were the butts for the jokes of their own smelly sons and sons' sons.

'Down, down with the Union Jack; up, up with the Red Flag' cries rose, and stilled the whole crowd for a moment as the electric shock of a cricket suddenly quietens the teeming vegetation of the tropical earth in the evening.

The hatred and revenge latent in the slogan stirred the chords of their beings till their faces flushed and gleams of wild, hot fire shot from their eyes and hovered on their lips.

'This is an evil age,' said a wizened old workman, fetching the words from somewhere in the depths of his chest.

'Indeed,' said a middle-aged man. 'How can we live in such times?'

'By protesting against the wage cuts,' said a youngster.

'Aye,' said the old man, 'the youths of today have no respect for anybody.'

'Grandfather,' returned the youth, 'I join my hands to you every morning, do I not? But I will not prostrate myself before the burra Sahib in the motor car. He rides in comfort and I have to walk on the dusty road under the sun. And then he declares the factory on short work.'

'Yes, he is a bad master, indeed,' agreed the middle-aged man.

'My children have no shoes. The little girl hurt her foot on a bit of glass the other day and the doctor says her foot must be cut off.'

'These Englishmen think a mere pittance can keep us, while they talk git mit, git mit with their lendis,' said the youth, half mockingly. Then he became earnest and exclaimed: 'But we are members of the Union. What is the Union going to do about it?'

The cry was taken up. 'What is the Union going to do about it?' the more enthusiastic members of the congregation shouted.

'Quiet!' said Ratan, standing up. 'Onkar Nath, President of the Union, is going to speak to us. Then Sauda Sahib, Mishta Muzaffar and Jackson Sahib of the Red Flag Union. The President, the President; come on, President!' His face flushed with the dramatic flourish with which he ended up.

'Come on, President!' Munoo shouted, taking the cue from his hero.

'Come on, President!' the cry was taken up by other members of the throng.

Lalla Onkar Nath, a prim, well-groomed man, dressed in a home-spun silk tunic and silk dhoti, came up to the dais. He was about forty, but his hair was greying prematurely, and his eyes and brow wrinkled darkly near the edges of the expensive tortoiseshell glasses. His lower lip was twisted into a sardonic contempt of everything but himself, and gave his whole sleek, clean-shaven face a curious, conceited look which adequately expressed what had happened to him since his Oxford days. He had sought glory for himself through the adoption of a socialist programme, thinking that either Gandhi or the government would buy him off in recognition of his balanced policy of compromise. But he had missed the bus. Now he had plunged into the lap of ancient and honourable Mother India and gone back on the modernity he had cultivated in England, though he said he tried to mingle the message of East and West by relating the old Indian ideas of labour and capital.

'Brothers,' he said, with a dignity that fell flat.

'What about declaring a strike, President?' said Ratan, who was not very far from the dais.

'Is he the person who wouldn't see you the other day when you were discharged?' asked Munoo, pulling at Ratan's tunic.

'Yes,' said Ratan, brushing Munoo's hand away lightly. 'Well, President, what is the talk?'

'Ratan, brother, sit down,' said Muzaffar, rising from behind the dais. 'Listen all, listen to the President.'

'Acha,' said Ratan, and sat down.

'Brothers,' began Onkar Nath again. 'In all ages labour, skilled and unskilled, organized or unorganized, has been a necessary agent for the production of wealth. In ancient India, the part played by labour in national economy and the problems arising out of the relationship between employer and employed were recognized, and one finds wisdom in the old saying: "For the labourer a discerning master is rare, as for the employer is a faithful, intelligent and truthful servant." Mr Radha Kumud Mukerji –'

'What is the Union going to do about the wage cut?' asked Ratan, whose grievance against the insult he had suffered from the President made him extremely impatient.

'Only a bad master would indulge in unreasonably overworking his men, raising their hopes without fulfilling them, withholding their wages or keeping them in arrears,' continued the President, in the academic manner of his forefathers. 'Only a bad workman would ask for wages in the course of his work, and it is only a bad master who will not pay his labourer wages due for work done.'

'Bad workman,' Ratan murmured.

'What about the strike?' someone shouted. 'What is the Union going to do about the order for short work?'

The President screwed up his sardonic lip a little more contemptuously. 'The All-India Trade Union Federation will enter into negotiations with the proper authorities,' he said.

'You did that at Jamshedpur with the Tatas last year, and nothing came of it!' shouted Ratan, pushing his head high.

'Sit down,' commanded the President. 'Don't interrupt. The Bombay mill owners are open to reason. It is no use precipitating a hopeless situation by hasty action. I stand for negotiation. There are thousands of unemployed men roaming the streets of Bombay, and we cannot go on strike without the sanction of the Indian National Congress, without the advice of the working committee.'

'Congress or no congress, we will not go on short work,' several voices broke out.

'Silence,' shouted the President. 'I have known the methods of the labour people in Vilayat. What has made the English working class strong and solid but organization? There wasn't a trade union in India till I arrived. No one had ever heard the name of such a thing. I have worked for you and I want you to take my advice and go the right way about it. The mill owners give you work. They are not your enemies. If they have declared you on short work, you must act in a sensible, organized way. The Union works in your interests. It also works for the common interest of the employer and labourer. You must have faith in the Union and the methods by which it brings about cooperation in industry between labour and capital. You must trust me and the executive committee.'

'Brothers,' shouted Sauda, suddenly ascending the platform and pushing the President aside. 'The members of the Trade Union Executive Committee are here. I am one. We will decide the question forthwith. Lalla Onkar Nath has too much faith in the mill owners. He says that the mill owners are not your enemies. You know that they are not your best friends. In fact, there is a world of difference between the mill owners, the exploiters, and you, the exploited.'

'That is right! That is the right talk!' some voices shouted.

'They are the robbers, the thieves, the brigands, the brigands who live in palatial bungalows on the Malabar Hill, on the money you earn for them with your work,' continued Sauda. 'They eat five meals a day and issue forth to take the air in large Rolls-Royces.

'You are the roofless, you are the riceless, spinners of cotton, weavers of thread, sweepers of dust and dirt; you are the workers, the labourers, the millions of unknown who crawl in and out of factories every day. You are the coolies, black men who relieve yourselves on the ground, you are the miserable devils who live twenty a room in broken straw huts and stinking tenements. Your bones have no flesh, your souls have no life, you are clothed in tattered rags. And yet, my friend Onkar Nath says that your interest and the interests of the mill owners are the same.'

'Shabash! Shabash! Sauda Sahib,' shouted Ratan.

Munoo felt his blood stirring at the passion of Sauda's speech.

'Lalla Onkar Nath', began Sauda again, 'is a very rich man. And he has never seen the wily demon of poverty drag you through the murky waters of that hell where the scorpions of hunger bite you, where the leeches suck your blood away, where the big sharks devour you. How many of you are not in the grip of the foreman of your factory? Against how many of you have not the hirelings of capitalism wreaked their vengeance? Brother Ratan there, an excellent workman, and others, have recently been discharged without any fault on their part, except that they refused to pay their foreman a commission. How many of you have not been pounced upon by the Pathan warder and moneylender outside the mill gates and even inside, on pay day? The moneylender does not want his capital back, you tell me, and is kind enough to let you pay interest. Don't you see that he records defaults so that the borrowing of a small sum leads in a few months to a permanent and heavy load of debt, till some of you have to pay him the whole of your wages, and have nothing left over for your subsistence? And when the time comes that you can't pay either the capital or the interest because you have no pay, you go home to die of misery and hunger. Oh, when will you realize, when will you learn that for centuries you have been the victims of graft and extortion!'

Munoo stared hard at Sauda and pricked up his ears to listen to every word.

'There are only two kinds of people in the world, the rich and the poor,' Sauda continued, 'and between the two there is no connection. The rich and the powerful, the magnificent and the glorious, whose opulence is built on robbery and theft and open warfare, are honoured and admired by the whole world, and by themselves. You, the poor and the humble, you, the meek and the gentle, wretches that you are, swindled out of your rights, and broken in body and soul, you are respected by no one, and you do not respect yourselves.'

Munoo felt that long ago, at Sham Nagar, he too had had similar thoughts about the rich and the poor. But he could not say them like the Sauda Sahib.

'Stand up, then, stand up for your rights, you roofless wretches, stand up for justice! Stand up, you frightened fools! Stand up and fight! Stand up and be the men that you were meant to be and don't crawl back to the factories like the worms that you are! Stand up for life, or they will crush you and destroy you altogether! Stand up and follow me! From tomorrow you go on strike and we will pay you to fight your battle with the employers! Now stand up and recite with me the charter of your demands.'

He paused for a moment. The whole throng rose to its feet, tense and excited. He continued:

'We are human beings and not soulless machines.'

The crowd recited after him.

'We want the right to work without having to pay bribes.'

'We want clean houses to live in.'

'We want schools for our children and crèches for our babies.'

'We want to be skilled workers.'

'We want to be saved from the clutches of the moneylenders.'

'We want a good wage and no mere subsistence allowed if we must go on short work.'

'We want shorter hours.'

'We want security so that the foreman cannot dismiss us suddenly.'

'We want our organizations to be recognized by law.'

The words of the charter rose across the horizon. At first they were simple, crude words, rising with difficulty like the jagged, broken sing-song of children in a classroom. Then the hoarse throats of the throng strained to reverberate the rhythm of Sauda's gong notes, till the uncouth accents mingled in passionate cries, assassinating the sun on the margin of the sky.

There was a shuffling of forms, the extended sound of black gaping mouths taking breath, even a reflection of half self-conscious, half happy smiles through the deep waters of the coolies' eyes, and for a moment one could hear the soft, moist rustle of the sea breeze stirring the blades of grass across the fields and in the marshes.

Then a screaming crescendo of pain shot into the air through the edge of the crowd. The broken accents of a voice defined the words 'kidnapped . . . kidnapped . . . Oh, my son has been kidnapped. What shall I do? This man tells me that my son has been kidnapped.'

'Kidnapped! Kidnapped!' an undercurrent of voices surged through the tense crowd. 'Kidnapped by the Pathans!' a whisper arose. 'Kidnapped! These bullying, swaggering Musulmans are kidnapping Hindu children.'

There was a pause.

'What is this?' shouted Sauda. 'What is the matter there?'

Only the moaning of a coolie could be heard, a queer, broken moaning like the howling of a she-hyena.

'Kidnapped! Kidnapped! A Hindu child has been kidnapped by the Muhammadans!' some of the coolies reported.

And then there was an undertone of fear and hate.

'Go home! Go home! It is only a base rumour spread by our enemies,' Sauda shouted. 'Don't go to work tomorrow. The Trade Union will pay you an allowance. And meet here tomorrow for a procession.'

'But a Hindu child has been kidnapped, Sahib, a Hindu child!' a voice arose again.

'Not only one, but several Hindu children have been kidnapped!' another voice declared.

'Kidnapped! Kidnapped! These circumcised Muhammadans have raised their heads to the sky! It is an insult to our religion! The sons of pigs! The illegally begotten! We will teach them a lesson!' The rumours had now become defined.

'Go away, go away, you fools!' shouted Sauda. 'We will look into the matter.'

'No, we will revenge ourselves on them! They take our money and they take our children! We will revenge ourselves on them!'

'Shut up, you fools!' shouted Ratan, jumping on to the dais. 'I will fight for you if your children have been kidnapped, but first go home and see if it is true!'

'You black lentil-eaters! You Hindus! We will teach you what it is to insult our religion!' the shouts of some Muhammadans arose from a congested corner far away from the dais, where several hands had become engaged in pulling turbans off and striking blows.

Munoo rushed up to Ratan and clung to his tunic, trembling. As he looked back he saw that the crowd was swirling in tides upon tides of faces, to and fro, in an utter panic of abandonment. He stood terrified and still, watching the rubbings of the hundreds of bodies, the pushings of the panting swarm that now pressed all around, crying loud and bitter oaths and abuses. It was sheer bedlam, only illuminated by the word 'kidnapped'. He seemed suddenly to have forgotten the invigorating air of that song of the charter and felt engulfed in an uncertain atmosphere of destruction, which the flourishing of arms, the glistening of eyes, the sharp hysteria of the voices had created. His soul swung back from the touching temper of Sauda's speech to face the pale monster of fear that the word 'kidnapped' had suddenly conjured up. In the sentient, quivering centres of his mind this conflict summoned the uncertainty of that moment when Prabha had been arrested. And the two occasions seemed similar as he saw blue uniformed policemen flourishing their batons on the outskirts of the crowd.

'Kidnapped! Kidnapped! Hai! Son of a pig! You heathen! Take this one!' the cries came.

'You go home,' said Ratan to Munoo, and, wrestling his tunic from the boy's grasp, plunged headlong into the fray.

'Oh Ratan! Ratan!' Munoo called. But his voice was lost in the pandemonium.

He stood on the dais still shouting for Ratan. Then he stared into the fast-gathering darkness to distinguish the copper-coloured faces with glistening white teeth to see if he could find Hari.

'Who are you, a Hindu or a Muhammadan?' a burly Pathan grunted, towering over him and flourishing a stave.

Munoo was dumb for a moment, livid with the fear of impending death. He wanted to shout, but his mouth opened and he could not say anything. His eyes closed and then opened. He hesitated for the briefest second, then jumped to his right and heard the Pathan's stave crash on the dais.

He tore through the crowd of rushing men, dodging his way till he was one of the many streams of coolies, hurrying away from the maidan.

'These Pathans have been kidnapping the children of the poor people for months,' Munoo heard one coolie say to another as they hurried along.

'The mill owners instigate them, and the sarkar connives at all this,' commented a third.

'Yes, yes,' another remarked. 'The Pathans have been kidnapping children and taking them away in motor cars, and the sarkar is taking no measure to stop it. How can we leave our children about?'

'But,' said a trade union official, 'the Pathans are your enemies. Two hundred Pathans were used by the mill owners to break the strike of the oil mills last year. They have been undercutting the workers who go on strike. They should be taught a lesson.'

'Let us go and demand an explanation from Sadi Khan, the moneylender in Albert Road,' said a young coolie. 'He preens himself!'

Munoo was half inclined to offer to go with this coolie, but remembered the time when he had seen Hari beaten by the Pathan moneylender. He passed by the men, who cursed or cast sporadic comment on the kidnapping.

At the head of his lane he saw an exchange of slaps and blows.

He darted towards the dusty town road, getting under cover of anything that cast a shadow in the clear, pellucid night which descended from the heavens like a woman, her apron ornamented by the stars, her deep sea-green skirt spread protectively about the cruel, hot earth.

He knew a short cut to Dhobi Tallao leading through a colony of outcastes. He turned off the road into its decline, slipping in the mud and slush of its drains, tired and forlorn. He groped through the darkness, and hoped he would be able to find somewhere to sleep.

The moonless sky was silent as Munoo entered the town, but the earth, the earth of Bombay, congested by narrow gullies and thoroughfares, rugged houses and temples, minarets and mausoleums and tall offices; Bombay, land of cruel contrasts, where the hybrid pomp of the rich mingled with the smell of sizzling grease in black frying pans; Bombay, land of luxury and lazzaroni, where all the pretences of decency ended in dirt and drudgery, in the filth of dustbins and in the germs of disease, where the lies of benevolent patrons were shown up in the sores and deformities of the poor; the earth of Bombay was, that evening, engulfed in chaos.

What had happened? Munoo did not know. He had hurried away from the disturbance outside the factories, imagining that he had left all the sounds of the mill land behind. But here was the same shouting, only more intense, because it was echoed back by the tall walls from somewhere afar.

He emerged from the gullies, in which anxious groups of men stood whispering at the doorways, into Bhendi bazaar, where wave upon wave of humanity flowed up to a square. He joined the throng, keeping a little apart from it, feeling strangely unmoved by the emotions which stirred the men, though he was curious as to the reason why they were converging. He soon knew.

A small, fat man appeared on the boards of a platform and harangued: 'Oh! Hindu brethren, awake, do not sleep if you have any regard for your mothers and sisters. Come out of your houses armed with sticks, because our benign government do not take any notice, although the wives and children of our brothers are massacred and dishonoured by Musulmans. They have, moreover, issued orders to shoot if more than five persons are collected together. We must therefore prepare ourselves for our own protection, because our benign government takes away our sticks, but does not seize their sticks and knives. What is the meaning of this? The meaning of this is that we should show our Mahratta courage to these circumcised Muhammadans! Down with Muhammadans! Down with Muhammadans! Down –'

Munoo climbed up the boards of a closed shop to get a full view of the man. He saw a heavy stave swirl in the air and fall on the hoarse voice.

There were cries of 'Hai! Hai! Killed! Murdered!'

The crowd seemed to grind its teeth for a second. A confused chatter of hard voices ensued.

Then there were cries of 'Murder the Musulmans! Take your revenge! Loot! Pillage! Burn!'

The crowd now began to struggle away, pressing towards the square, and beyond, into Abdul Rahman Street.

A young English officer in khaki, followed by ten Indian policemen, led a baton charge.

Munoo climbed down from the boards of the empty shop at the sight of the officer. He slipped in his eagerness to keep under cover of the dark. Feeling that he would be safe if he went in the direction opposite to that of the crowd, he drifted towards Sandhurst Road. His brain was seething with excitement. His temples drummed. The image of the stave swirling in the air flashed across his mind. The sudden disappearance of the man from the platform meant death. And the grim, tense silence of death cast its shadow before the boy's eyes. He murmured something to himself, in a sort of whimpering, self-pitying voice which smothered the dazed expression on his face. He walked along unconscious in a sort of delirium. 'What has happened? What happened?' he asked himself. And he looked into the street to find an answer. But the street just stared back at him, filling his mind with its tall fantastic houses leaning like hard rocks on the narrow length of the roadway, their insides gaping with the eyes of gigantic monsters through the deep shadows of balconied verandahs. He thought of the Kangra hills in whose pathways the overhanging cliffs had beaten back his mind with the same brutal answer when once he went out to search for a lost goat. There was the same eerie silence here in the deep pits of closed shops and bulging arches as in the blackest shadows of the mountains, heightened by its contrast with the echoes of thunderous noises above, away and beyond. And death stalked the earth in the illusory forms of masses of darkness, as in a nightmare, now slow, sinuous and soft, now sudden, like panting hordes rushing through time and space, convulsed, hysterical and fierce, like the hundred forms of Satan who hounded men to death.

He slowed down to reassure himself that he was not engulfed in hallucinatory visions which were frightening him into cowardice. 'I am a brave hill boy who has walked alone hundreds of times, even past graves and cremation grounds,' he said to assure himself. 'Why should I be afraid? I wonder where Ratan is now, what he is doing? And Hari? Lakshami and the children must be at home, sleeping perhaps. I don't mind being away from them here, though. Why is it that because I have walked away from the mill land I don't want to go back to it?' A shriek stabbed the heart of the darkness that spread alarmingly like the recumbent figure of a huge corpse before him. There were loud voices vowing 'Allah ho Akhar!' He started to run. Looking into a side bazaar he saw an old man with spindle legs running as fast as he could under the weight of his rags, followed by a giant Pathan. He stood tense and eager, gazing through the distance. Two long-bodied Muhammadans, who were coming from the opposite direction with staves in their hands, fell upon the old man, who now quaked with fear, like a hounded chicken, uttering: 'Ram re Ram! My life is gone!' The giant who had followed the wretch stabbed him in the back, crying: 'You heathen! You son of Eblis!' The old man shrieked, uttered a groan, and fell with a thud on the road.

Munoo turned his back on the hush that followed the tragedy and ran blindly, mistaking the breeze that came from the street towards which he was making for the hoarse whispering of Muhammadan conspirators pursuing him, their victim, with their long knives and rapiers. But as no one touched him, he ran on and on, feeling light and alert, till a very hurricane of noises engulfed his ears and his eyes met the leaping flames of a big house on fire, the flames almost licking the sky and illuminating the world in a sheer orgy of resplendent red, gold and indigo black.

'That is the house of Mulji Madharji's sweetshop, burnt down by the Pathans. Don't go, they will kill you,' said a Gujerati merchant, who stood at the doorway of his house with one hand on the door and the other on the shoulder of a friend whom he wanted to detain.

Munoo heard the remark and looked about casually to see if there was some empty space outside the barred doors of a shop, or a step at the foot of the rambling stairs of a house, where he could rest his head in comfort and safety for the night.

Hardly had he withdrawn his gaze when he heard the Muhammadan cries of 'Allah ho Akbar!' rise from under the circle of fire, followed by the noise of stamping feet rushing frantically towards him.

He bolted into a gully which led towards the opera house, but he was greeted by the howls of a woman who slapped her breasts and tore her hair as she stood by the railings of a verandah, saying: 'Where are you, my son? Oh, where are you? Where have you gone?'

Munoo dared not to go near her, for fear she should think he would assault her. He turned to see if he could go back the way he had come. No. The Pathan marauders were running riot in the street, shouting: 'Allah ho Akbar!' as they broke the doors of the houses with the butt ends of their rifles and staves and flourished daggers in their hands. He stood panic-stricken, certain that he had walked into the valley of the shadow of death. But batches of policemen came running from the direction for which he had been heading, soft-footed, Munoo knew, because they wanted to surprise the rioters. He stepped back into the hall of a shop, afraid now that one of the police might thrust a bayonet into him, and almost as certain of death as he had been a moment ago. The blue-uniformed men ran by, however, and even the woman seemed to have disappeared. He steadied himself and breathed a deep breath. Then he continued to crawl along, pressing himself to the walls, looking before and behind to make certain that he was not being noticed.

As, with hesitant steps, he reached the end of the lane, he was impelled by curiosity to look back and survey the scene he had left behind. The Pathans were towering over the policemen in a grim hand-to-hand fight. He was absorbed in the anticipation of seeing the dead fall on their backs, and he entered unconsciously into the open opera square, where two streams of rioters had met. He was plunged into the very maelstrom of passions.

Under the wild, half-smothered cries of 'Allah ho Akbar' and 'Kalī Mai ki jai! Siva ji ki jai!' the bodies of Hindus and Muhammadans struggled in murderous embraces. 'Mar! Mar! Hit and see!' a voice challenged, and was quietened by the thrust of a dagger, so that it fell instantaneously into a tottering fall and expired with a cry: 'Killed!'

'Son of an ass! Heathen!' the aggressive shouts of the conqueror tore the warm, tense air.

'This time death is certain,' Munoo said to himself, as he edged away under cover of a tram which had drawn up by the kerb edge of the square. And he felt the hard impact of large knuckles at the back of his neck and then a sudden blow on his spine. He was stretched out.

As he looked up from where he had fallen he saw a Muhammadan outlined against the tramway. He instinctively closed his eyes and loosened his body to simulate the limpness of a corpse. The Pathan kicked him with a contemptuous whisper of 'Hindu dog!' and walked away to where his companions now stood, after having killed as many Hindus as had not run away.

The square was soon deserted, because the Pathans walked away, shouting, stamping, fierce and bloody, and for a moment there was utter silence.

Then the cries of the half-dead arose with the swish of sea air that came from the Chaupatti beach, and fugitive forms nestled about as they emerged from strange unknown corners and vanished into the air.

Munoo opened his eyes to scan a triangular flower garden that stood guarded by regular railings beyond the tramway junction. He felt he would go and hide among the shrubs there. But as he strained to lift his head on his elbow he heard someone writhing in agony, while a stave seemed to strike the earth with a metallic sound. He listened to the convulsed despair of the dying man in extreme nervousness. Escape in that direction seemed impossible. He lay back and held his breath for a minute until he heard the last cry of the wretch.

He hesitated between despair and a desire to go to the man. But his body was weighted down by fear, his head bowed down, his eyes half-closed by the fatigue of waiting in the dark. And he lay resigned.

Suddenly he felt the rush of eager feet about him. 'Has my end come now?' he asked himself. But there seemed to be no answer. He lay dumb, ready for his last breath to depart. He had no time to think of the past, and the glow of desire seemed to have left his body.

But his end had not come. For two men of the Social Service League lifted him and bore him to a shelter in the verandah of a school, a hundred yards away.

Munoo had deliberately closed his eyes in order not to appear undeserving of help. Yet he was aware of everything that was happening to him. He wished he were not conscious. He wished he had really been hurt and had died or fainted. For the slow long-drawn-out torture that had spread through the furnace of his brain like an unending song of fire was unbearable. It had gone on and on and on, consuming all the elements of sensation and burning up the meagre resources of nervous energy he had left in him after months of work in the factory, until now he was merely a luminous point in the darkness staring out blankly at the various strata of this hellish night.

The volunteers of the Social Service League rested him on a mat on the school verandah, where hurricane lamps illuminated the bodies of a crowd of beggars, paupers and coolies, who had ostensibly been rescued from the streets where they ordinarily slept.

A doctor, who looked to Munoo not unlike the brother of the Sham Nagar Babu, because he wore a hat and suit, asked him where he was hurt. Munoo just moved his head negatively and lay wrapped in complete inertia. The doctor examined his body, wrote something on a paper and moved on.

A volunteer applied a cup of hot milk to his lips, and Munoo got up to drink, grateful and humble. The sweet, hot liquid rushed the blood to his face.

If only he had laid down to sleep he might have arisen soothed and balanced in the morning. But he opened his eyes to his surroundings.

The verandah was dark. There was a horrible smell of urine and dung hanging over it. And the whispers of the poor rose like thick flakes of cotton in the closed air.

Munoo tried not to breathe through the reek too deeply, but his eyes were taking in the disgusting outlook of the diseased, broken men about him, some crouching with their sleek bellies, some bending over their hollow chests, some snoring woodenly as they slept against a wall, some contemplating their wounds and sores with weak eyes that blinked not, some coughing in unending fits of jerky reiterations.

The boy was going to open his mouth to breathe a word to himself. A gust of musty damp pepper and the foul reek of excrement assailed him. He shut his mouth and only sniffed at the air. He dilated his nostrils. Again there was the dirty smell going through him. He decided to bolt from the place. It was unbearable. He would go and sleep on the sea beach. There were booths there which lay empty all night. He had seen them. He hoped nobody else had thought of the idea, and that the place would be empty.

He got up and began to walk. No one seemed to take any notice of him. The door was straight in front of him and people were coming and going. He emerged from the gate.

He realized that he would have to run three hundred yards to the Chaupatti. 'Will I be quite safe?' But he did not wait to receive the answer. He only babbled: 'Let come what may, I shall at least get away from this.' And the pictures of the men he was leaving behind shimmered in his brain against the currents of strange thoughts about himself walking barefoot on the hot sand of the road to

Sham Nagar, of his aimless wandering in the civil lines at Daulatpur and in the streets of Bombay. He was running, and the movement of his body transfigured space and time into a blank. It transformed the memory of the mutilations he had seen that evening into a prolonged moment of uncertainty, above the confusion of cries, the din of shouts and the cruel impact of brutal bands, above even the hum of innumerable waves which were billowing before his eyes to the edge of the far rocks.

He ran as if he were a rocket of fire going to be quenched in the sea. He was not conscious of his body. He shot past vast buildings across the Chaupatti bridge in a devastating whirl.

He sighted a broken wagon which was covered with a jute awning. He knew it was a coconut shop during the day. He slowed down, panting, and made for it. The marble stone of Tilak stood small and insignificant against the vast sheet of water which swished like a snake and spilled the white foam of its poison on the shores of India. He mounted into the wagon and groped around. There was plenty of space. He lay down and rested. The anarchy of the ocean drowned him in sleep.

When he awoke late in the morning, he did not know where to go, what to do, and what his soul wanted.

The coconut stall did not open till the afternoon, so no one had come to disturb him.

He sat staring at the sunshine which flooded the wagon and heard the unending roar of the sea beyond the jute-cloth curtain. The night had been cold and he had shivered at dawn. But now it was quite warm, even hot. And it was so restful, were it not that he felt this emptiness in his soul, and hunger in his belly.

He tried to console himself by feeling that he deserved this leisure after months of having to get up early at dawn. It was like the old days in the village, he felt, when he used to laze around in the afternoon and have a siesta while the cattle grazed. The wild pastures of the green sea had indeed something of the freedom of the open fields.

The mere habit of getting to the factory in the morning, however, had given him a conscience about work. And his conscience pricked him now. He felt he ought to get up and do something – anything.

But what was he to do? Where was he to go? What did he want? he asked himself again. And the answer came that he did not know.

It seemed to him that he had always felt like that when he was a derelict, and even sometimes when he was surrounded by people and busy.

During the days when he had worked, however, and come home to a meal he had seldom been lonely, even though he was tired by work and suffered inconveniences. For he talked and heard people talk, played practical jokes on people, and slept, rising to face the morning. That was life.

Now, somehow, the essential loneliness of the soul, that apartness which he had succeeded in shattering by his zest and enthusiasm for work and for entering the lives of others, by the natural love he felt for others, that loneliness mingled with the thought of worklessness, foodlessness, aimlessness, hung over his being.

He realized suddenly that he had always come to something when he began to move, to act. For instance, he had met Prabha when he ran away from Sham Nagar; the elephant driver who brought him to Bombay; Hari; and he certainly wouldn't have met Ratan if he had not come to Bombay. 'But then there have been days, months and years', he said to himself, 'when I have gone on working and wandering alone. Still, I will go back to the mills and see what is happening.'

He shook himself, stretched his arms, yawned, got up and jumped down from the wagon.

The beach was deserted except for the fishermen who were casting their nets.

He walked up to the Chaupatti bridge and saw the panorama of green, white and red houses, spread on the lower ridges of the Malabar Hill.

On the road, life seemed natural and ordinary without any trace of the happenings of last night. The motor cars sped swiftly past victorias and cycles. The boards on the shops greeted his rudimentary stare. One read 'Auto de Luxe'; another 'Bhartiya Watch Works'; another 'The American Auto Part Co.'; a fourth 'Clinical Laboratory of Dr N. J. Modi, MB, BS, MRCP (London)'; still another 'Bharat Swadeshi Stores'.

When he got to Parekh mansions, he saw some coolies, both men and women, bearing baskets of earth from a shop to a bullock cart which stood with two bullocks harnessed to its shaft. A policeman stood at the crossroads.

Munoo stopped and watched the bullocks emptily. The beasts

had curved horns and were grinding straw as they waited, patiently, without a lead, careless of the flies that sat on their rumps where the continual friction with the wood had bruised them.

The shops had not opened yet, but men passed quickly by on the pavements, umbrellas in one hand, the lower edges of their loincloths in the other, flourishing their bare, dark-brown legs. Munoo watched them go by, till it seemed to him there was nothing but legs, legs, legs everywhere.

'What has happened?' he wondered. 'Had last night's affair finished?' Certainly everything seemed orderly this morning.

'And yet', he said to himself, 'it can't be.' And he felt that all these men were cheating him with a conspiracy of silence, that they were all passing him by, deliberately suppressing the secret of the insurrection.

He ached for contact with someone, to know what was happening.

Only a crow came and settled on a window-sill before him to see if it could pick up something. Munoo looked away. For a moment his mind was empty. Then he saw the policeman superintending the crossroads talking to a rich Parsi.

Munoo moved towards them and, simulating the manner of a pauper, began to pick up the fallen leaves of trees from near the bullock cart.

'As far as the police are concerned,' said the constable to the Parsi, 'the rumour about the kidnapping was groundless. And the police tried to broadcast a notice to restore confidence. But there was violence throughout the mill areas and the town, and the whole strength of the police, including the armed police, had to be mobilized to keep the disorderly elements in check. And though so many outrages were committed, the sarkar did not call in the military. The police have won the day. The condition of the town is better this morning. The coolies in the railway workshops and the mills have gone back to work. As you see, people are walking about normally.'

Munoo was now possessed by a fit of conscientiousness. He must get back to work. The mills had opened. So there was no strike. Hari must have gone to the factory. 'I will go,' he said, and slunk away.

He had hardly gone a hundred yards when he heard two Congress volunteers engaged in a serious talk with a man in a suit, who jotted down words in a notebook which he had opened from time to time. He slowed down, shaking his right foot as if he were hurt, then settled down and poured dust on it, pretending to treat the wound on his toe.

'At 7.30 this morning,' one volunteer dictated, 'Alve and Khasle, labour leaders, took a Muhammadan contractor named Rahim to the tea shop at the corner of Suparibang Road to come to some settlement with the Pathans, when an unknown Pathan smacked Alve on the face. Within half an hour three to four thousand mill hands came down in a large body with sticks to attack the Pathan camp in retaliation for the assault on Alve. A cordon of armed policemen with a show of great favouritism protected the Pathans. The main part of the mob went back, but some of them halted at the Union office at the Domodar Thackersey Hall. The Deputy Commissioner of Police got the help of the army. Various platoons of the Warwickshire Regiment are spread over the town with machine guns, and the Home Secretary has wired to the Poona Brigade for more military aid. We have called a meeting of the Hindu and Muslim leaders here at the house of Mr Sirla –'

At this moment a limousine drew up by the pavement and the attention of the Congress men turned to the tall, burly figure, in princely clothes and astrakhan decorated with ruby red crescent moons, who emerged.

'Bande Mataram,' Munoo heard the Congress-wallah greet his majesty. He did not know who he was. But he was impressed and curious.

'What are your leaders doing?' the dignitary exclaimed. 'What are the police and the government doing? What are the newly elected members of the corporation doing? What are the leaders of the Youth Movement doing? For a whole night the Pathans have been murdered by the Hindus and the Congress has done nothing about it. If Miss Mayo came to India and wrote a chapter about children being kidnapped for sacrificial purposes, would you not deny it as a wicked libel?'

The Congress men kept quiet. The journalist with the notebook, however, thrust himself forward and asked: 'Is the situation likely to develop into an All-India Hindu–Muslim conflict, Maulana Hasrat Ali?'

'Of course it will,' replied the Maulana.

'We are going to organize the Muhammadans for the purpose of self-defence,' the Maulana's voice broke out excitedly.

'But Congress is forming a peace committee,' said one of the Congress men.

'Yes, you are always talking of peace,' said the Maulana. 'You talk of peace but mean war. Meanwhile, the Hindu hooligans of Kalbadevi have murdered three Musulmans this morning, and fifty operatives of Muhammadan mills have been assaulted. We have just been to the King Edward hospital. There are more Muhammadans wounded than Hindus.'

'Well, salaam Maulana,' said the journalist, and cleared off.

'Don't publish the interview,' the Maulana shouted after him. But the man had cycled away.

Another car rolled up.

Munoo saw another dignitary emerge and hail the Muhammadan leader and the Congress volunteers with 'Bande Mataram.' The Muhammadan seemed to take no notice of him as he walked into the palatial mansion. Pandit Madan Mohan Malabari, the new dignitary, in immaculate khaddar, followed them. The Congress volunteers began to direct the chauffeurs of the cars to move up.

The boy felt drawn towards the door of the house. He took advantage of the absence of the volunteers to go up and peer in. He could only see a long, polished flight of stairs, ascending up into the roof of the building.

'Go away! Who are you?' one of the Congress volunteers shouted as he returned to his post at the door.

Munoo started, blushed a confession of guilt, and capered on his way.

But two steps and he was riveted to the spot by the crackling noise of a long volley of shots in the direction of Bhendi Bazaar. He stared ahead; he could not see a soul. Then, suddenly, men came falling over each other, shrieking and wounded. He felt no pity for anybody, nor for himself. He could not imagine the men being mown down by machine guns. His mind was a blank.

A volley of shots followed behind him.

Munoo turned on his feet and ran up a steep alley. He could see the palm trees waving on the crest of the Malabar Hill. He made for it, drawn, as it were, by a mysterious faith in the safety of mountain tops, which seemed to be confirmed by the tranquillity of the bungalows on its edges. The sound of firing had ceased by this time, but the weird noises of the riot followed him. When he reached the end of the road he sighted an uprise. This, his instincts told him, was the slope of his objective, for there the din of the shooting seemed to have receded.

The sun was blazing and there was very little shade on the way.

Munoo sweated. He felt faint with fatigue and hunger. His body seemed no longer his own, because it lagged behind his will to go on. 'What has happened to me?' he asked himself. 'Where has my strength gone?' There was no answer and he felt stupid.

Then he thought of the men whom he had seen falling dead behind him. They must have been shot dead by the police and the soldiers. Their friends and families would mourn for them. He, too, was sorry for them. He felt he knew the pain a man must feel when he was writhing in the agony of death. At least, he thought he had tasted that pain whenever he was hurt, and the memory of a goat moaning while she was being butchered by the Muhammadans of his village on their *Id* festival came to his mind. But no occasion on which he had felt or seen death was as real as this. Before, he had always been unconscious of suffering. Now, the feeling of pain seemed to tinge everything. For the first time in his life he realized the hardness of life.

But he did not curse his destiny. Born to toil, the abundant energy of his body had so far overcome all his troubles. He had found that he was fairly happy when he had food every day. He was in love with life and thrilled to all the raptures of the senses. And he still regarded the trappings of civilization, black boots, watches, basket hats and clothes, with all the romantic admiration of the innocent child.

As he walked along he looked for one of those moving stalls which sell roasted gram and cheap sweets to the servants of Sahibs in the European quarters of Indian towns. There was no one in sight. He continued tiredly through the long avenue of the palm trees with branches flattened by the wind. On his left was the sea, on his right the bungalows of the rich, standing like inviolable fortresses on the promontories of the Malabar Hill; above him were the hanging gardens, and below, the panorama of the island and harbour of Bombay.

He stared across the drive of a square-fronted house which lay covered with close-clipped ivy, beyond to the beds of a garden guarded by a double belt of trees. There was something frightening to Munoo's humble mind in the self-conscious complacency of this building. So he withdrew his gaze and, standing right in the middle of the road, looked down to the island at his feet.

He stood dazed with the beauty of the scene. Through the dim haze of a far, far horizon could be discerned forests of masts floating in the azure waters of the sea, and sails swelling with the breeze that seemed invisible. Nearer, the shapeless mass of city buildings rested under coconuts and palms, while the fern-covered rocks bravely guarded the pearl-like bay in the shell of a transparent mist. The city, the bay, the sea, at his feet, had an unearthly beauty!

The loud honk of a car – and, before he could jump aside, he was knocked down. He rolled down the hill, urged by an instinct to avoid hurt, but the front wheels of the vehicle passed on his chest before it came to a standstill.

'Oh! what an unlucky thing to happen to us!' exclaimed Mrs Mainwaring. 'Right on the day of my arrival from "home", too. First these riots and then this accident. I hope he isn't dead! Let me see!' She applied her hand to his heart and passed it over his head with the skill of a woman who had taken a first aid diploma at the Regent Street Polytechnic. 'His pulse is all right,' she continued, 'he is only stunned.'

'Oh, Mummy, what can we do?' cried little Circe Mainwaring.

'Let us put him in the car,' said Mrs Mainwaring. 'For if someone sees him they will stone us to death. You don't know what these hooligans are! Chauffeur, put him in the car. We will take him to Simla with us. I wanted a servant.'

The chauffeur, a Muhammadan, recognized Munoo to be a Hindu, and, excited beneath his apparent reserve by strong religious sentiments, he did not care if the boy died or what happened to him. If he had met him alone, he might have killed him deliberately. As it was, he thought he had done so accidentally. He would have left him lying there, but he was afraid of the memsahib. So he lifted the heathen and deposited him in the car.

'Pick up the luggage at the Taj,' said Mrs Mainwaring, 'and let us be on the way as quickly as possible. Avoid the city and skirt round to the Colaba Road and let us be in time for supper at Baroda.'

V

Munoo revived before the motor car in which Mrs Mainwaring was travelling to Simla emerged from the outskirts of Bombay.

When the Chevrolet hooted into the rest house at Baroda at supper, he was up and doing.

And, during the leisurely, luxurious, two-day journey up to Kalka, the boy recruited his health somewhat.

But really, he was mentally and physically broken. And, as he thought of the conditions under which he had lived, of the intensity of the struggle and the futility of the waves of revolt falling upon the hard rock of privilege and possession, as he thought of Ratan and Hari and Lakshami, and the riots, he felt sad and bitter and defeated, like an old man.

To Mrs Mainwaring, however, he was not the old man he felt himself to be, otherwise she would have had no use for him and would have left him where she had found him. He was not old to Mrs Mainwaring, nor even middle-aged, nor even a brute of a young man. He was to her a young boy with a lithe, supple body, with a small, delicate face, and with a pair of sensitive poet's eyes. 'What is your age, boy?' she had asked him. 'Fifteen, Memsahib,' he had answered. And she had looked into his dark eyes for a moment with her own dark brown ones, pinched him on the arm with a playful flourish of her long, thin hands, patted him on the forehead, and, drawing her olive-ivory, Modigliani face backwards till it compressed her thin lips into a voluptuous pout, smiled at him and giggled. For a boy of fifteen was just what she wanted. And, however old Munoo felt inside him, she neither cared to know nor had the capacity to know. He was just the boy for her, just the right servant. She would be good to him, which was easy, because she was good-hearted.

Mrs Mainwaring was descended from an old Anglo-Indian family of four brothers, who had served as soldiers of fortune in the pay of the East India Company during the English wars of conquest in India. Her grandfather, the only survivor, had fought by the side of John Nicholson during the mutiny, and begot her father, William Smith, through a Musulman washerwoman. William Smith became a sergeant in the Monroe infantry, a privately owned regiment of Eurasians. On the reorganization of the Indian army by the British government in the nineties, this irregular force was disbanded and the soldier-adventurer in Sergeant Smith sought the prizes of service in a feudatory native state. Knowing that it was easy for a white man to get a higher rank, even if less pay, in the Nawab of Zalimpar's army than he would get in the British-Indian army to which he was being transferred from the Monroe infantry, he had gone and secured a direct Colonelcy in Zalimpar. Here he had married the daughter of an English engine-driver. May was the only child of the union, for the Colonel's wife left him a year after May's birth because she was expecting another child by someone else.

May was looked after in her early childhood by the wife of a Catholic missionary and then sent to the Convent of the Sacred Heart at Simla. As she grew up in the hill station among the children of English officials, who were continually talking of 'home', May developed a tremendous inferiority complex about her origin. She vaguely knew that she was English only at fourth remove, and that there was Indian blood in her from her grandmother's side, but she had to pretend to be 'pukka' in order to cope with the snobbery of the other children. She built up a fairy-tale picture of her family's estates in Western Ireland and sought to disguise her dusky hue under thick coats of powder and the camouflage of a Celtic origin. Since, however, this did not convince the smarter among the other girls of her purely white pedigree, she was miserable at school and ultimately ran away from it to Zalimpar, obsessed with the ambition of going to England to whitewash her colour if possible. Her father, of course, could not afford to send her to the Cheltenham Ladies' College where she wanted to go, and there was an awful scene between the two of them. But May's ambition to become 'pukka white', which was at the back of her desire to go to Europe, was satisfied more easily. A young German photographer, Heinrich Ulmer, who did splendid business in Zalimpar by flattering the vanity of the princes and courtiers with large, life-size portraits, fell in love with the very dusky hue which was causing her all this trouble. May persuaded herself that an alliance with a thoroughbred German was as easy a way of legitimizing her 'pukkahood' as going to Cheltenham. And, though her early training under the care of the parson's wife and her schooling in the Convent of the Sacred Heart had instilled into her mind a horror of sex, she married Heinrich Ulmer.

Unfortunately, however, the war broke out two years after May's marriage and the German was interned in a concentration camp. May already had a daughter by Heinrich Ulmer, romantically named Penelope, and a son was born to her soon after the outbreak of the war.

For a time she mourned the loss of her husband. But she had never really gone out to him in mind and body, she had never really given herself to him. For although when once he broke her physical virginity she had outdone him in her display of physical passion, she had really remained a virgin at heart, as if pulled back always by the fear of sin which had sunk deep into her subconsciousness through her early Christian training. Her warmth, her ardour, her intense capacity for desire, must have been due to the blood of her pagan Indian grandmother in her; her curious coldness of mind, the frigidity which had once made her jump into a bath of ice water in order to quell the passion in her body, was conditioned by the European-Christian doctrine of sin. The fundamental contradiction of these two opposed things in her nature resulted in perversity. She indulged in a strange, furtive, surreptitious promiscuity. She gave herself to people at the least felt impulse and, of course, invariably regretted having done so in her mind afterwards.

She exerted her female charms on the Education Minister of the Zalimpar State and got a job teaching in a children's school. To keep her job she had to please other men. And, being a pretty woman and one of the few emancipated women in a world where the female sex is veiled off from the sight of the male, she was the object of admiration of rich courtiers, high officials, eminent judges, both English and Indian. If her mind had not been reacting against the deep-rooted belief in the sin of sex, she might have had an integrity of character which would have saved her from the on-slaughts of all these men, but, vacillating between a belief she felt to be wrong and a desire which was continually insistent, she became a bitch to all the dogs that prowled round her bungalow.

Aga Raza Ali Shah, a Persian captain in the Nawab's army, who was somewhat of a poet, was caught in the mesh of her black locks. He got her to divorce Heinrich Ulmer and married her. He really loved her and would have made her happy, since he was a better lover than any she had met, more cultured than Heinrich and all the toadies and bloated idiots of the court, and a tall, handsome man with abounding energy and vigour. But now, suddenly, the ambition to regain her English nationality again began to disturb her. She played havoc with his feelings by frequenting the barracks and officers' bungalows of the English regiment in the cantonment of Zalimpar. Aga Raza Ali Shah beat her in a fit of jealousy one day and kicked her out of his bungalow.

She was not unhappy about it, because she had then been carrying on with a young subaltern of the Royal Fusiliers, a thoroughbred Englishman named Guy Mainwaring, much younger than herself and therefore easier to blackmail than an older man would have been. She told him she was expecting a child which she believed to be his. Guy Mainwaring was too 'decent' and chivalrous an Englishman not to be taken in by this.

A Muhammadan divorce is easy to obtain. She married Guy and proposed that they should spend their honeymoon at 'home' in England. Guy took six months' leave of absence and took her and her children to London. Here she presented him with a baby girl of a darker hue than Guy expected his child to be. And he had a suspicion that it looked more like Captain Raza Ali Shah than himself, a suspicion which was confirmed by May, when one day, in a hysterical fit of abject humility, she broke down and confessed to her 'guilt'. Guy Mainwaring's parents, who were supremely conscious of their true-blooded, blue-blooded, upper-middle-class Englishness, had already heard of the boy's blunder and refused to see him. Guy was lonely. He was miserable. In his utter helplessness he sought relief in May's embraces as a child in his mother's. And, having inherited with his blue blood the traditional English habit of escaping from reality, he buried his head in the sand like an ostrich and decided to forget all about life in his dedication to duty. He would muddle through this business anyhow, and never face the facts squarely with regard to May, however sensible he might be in other things.

May insisted on staying on at 'home', the heaven she had gained after all these years of waiting, when Guy's leave was up and he had to rejoin his regiment at Peshawar, on the north-western frontier of India. She made the excuse that she wanted to get a diploma in teaching at the Polytechnic and to look after the children a bit before they went to a secondary school.

Guy, the young fool, was taken in again. He was haunted by memories of the ineffable bliss he had enjoyed in May's embraces. He became a slave to her, indulging every whim, every fancy, every capricious desire that she expressed. He voluntarily made an allowance of half his pay to her and settled on her half the fortune he inherited from his mother, who had suddenly died of disappointment and chagrin at the mess he had made of his life. And he wrote her the most tender, sentimental love letters from Peshawar, where he was in a funk fighting against the Mohmand tribesmen and guarding the frontiers of the Empire of England.

May worked assiduously to regain the spiritual heritage of her race on the strength of this liberal allowance by going to cinemas, theatres, cocktail bars and night clubs. She lived in Bayswater, and being received by the retired Anglo-Indians who rotted in the boarding-houses of that district, completely out of touch with India and alienated from their own people, she fancied herself 'pukka'. When she had inured herself to the belief of her 'pukkahood' and begun to take her nationality for granted, she recognized the need to integrate herself with real culture, for these Anglo-Indians lived completely in a void, having won the whole world and lost their souls in the bargain. She secured an invitation to Bohemia through a young poet who had been flattered, by her application for his autograph at a lecture of his, into making her his mistress. She believed every rhyme to be a great poem, and every photographic portrait to be a great work of art. She slept with any verse-writer or painter who would notice her. But as she chattered incessantly about cheap Hollywood films and behaved as an utter bourgeois snob, they soon tired of her and dismissed her as a silly woman.

Guy had been writing to her dutifully, regularly, imploring her to come back to India. She had always pleaded the care of Penelope and Ralph and the baby. Then, when that excuse did not work, and realizing in a fit of thoughtfulness how good Guy had been to her, she conceded in so far as to agree that she would return to India for a year with the baby, the elder children being fixed up at a boarding-school. It was summer, however, and she said she could not bear the heat of the plains and be with him in Peshawar. So he rented a flat near Annandale at Simla for the season for her. And, while he grilled in the plains, she was now going up with Munoo and the baby to live at the capital of the government of India. Guy said he would be able to snatch a fortnight's leave and run up to the hills. But she did not care.

Munoo contemplated her with a restrained wonder, sufficiently exciting to thrill him to the marrow of his bones. No white woman, no woman even, had condescended to look at him quite like that. True, he had felt strange, inexplicable urges in his being about little Sheila at Sham Nagar, and had enjoyed sitting in the lap of Prabha's wife, and loved Lakshami, but what he felt in response to the pinching, patting and the coquettish smiles of this Memsahib was something different.

Of course, he dared not think of anything bolder in his callow, subservient soul. And he stood half afraid, on the borders of happiness, complimenting himself on the good luck he felt he had come across, and wondering if there was any significance in the Memsahib's familiar behaviour, apart from mere kindness. They had reached Kalka at the foot of the Himalayas. Mrs Mainwaring had gone to the station restaurant for breakfast. Munoo looked across at the mountains with a love for high altitudes which was in his bones, as he waited in the yard with the Muhammadan chauffeur, who was more friendly now than he had been at first.

The steep hills rose sheer before him, overgrown with an abundance of cool, green vegetation, reverberating with the delicate refrains of small waterfalls. The spring air was crisp and the sun rose almost as it used to rise over the burning, iridescent hills of Kangra, except that a few porous clouds rolled swiftly across the sky and rested like huge flakes of cotton on the peaks of these Himalayas.

The Memsahib came flustering, blustering, to assimilate her female trappings, losing her bag, finding it, dropping her pin and not finding it, trying to keep little Circe under control and exasperated because she strayed, buying fruit here, sweets there, giving instructions to Munoo to do a hundred different things on the platform, where the English soldiers on police duty whistled to her and made her uncomfortable, asserting herself by exchanging memories with the old station master whom she knew, walking past the narrow-gauge toy railway, chockful of English men, women and children, native clerks and shopkeepers and hill men with their baggage, which stood in readiness to depart, and nervously ordering the chauffeur to fill up enough oil and petrol for the fifty-mile journey ahead of them.

At last the car was on its way, skirting the hairpin bends of the wonderful cart road which seemed even to Munoo a miracle of achievement as it belted the zigzag courses of mountains and granite rocks.

He was pleased with life, especially as the Memsahib had, with her own hands, given him some apples and bananas and sweets.

And now he devoured the landscape with those restless brown eyes of his which seemed to have an insatiable zest for experience.

He was wonder-struck at the baby railway, which he had seen standing at Kalka station, ascending the gigantic heights with strange puffs such as a toddling child utters when he first learns to walk, crawling through long tunnels and circling up and up, even with the car, so slow though it seemed in its movement. He wished they had been travelling in that train, his child's heart excited by the playful interest which little Circe took in the toy thing.

The sight of stray houses on the slopes of the mountains took him back to his own home, and he had the feeling that it was only yesterday that he had left the village in the valley. A ruined fortress which capped a far distant peak encouraged the illusion because it looked like the crumbling temple of Durga near Hamirpur, and the angry nullahs that gorged their way through the fastnesses of these mountains completed the vague similarity. He saw himself in his mind's eye climbing the uphill paths and gaining steep precipices. It seemed to him that he was ploughing the terraced fields before sowing barley or wheat. He was beginning to feel in his proper element.

But the air became cooler and crisper as the car ascended higher altitudes and the deodars and cedars that grew on the flat inclines shattered the illusion. The sight of the strange modern Solon Bazaar with its gown shops and restaurants and the hotel where Mrs Mainwaring rested for tea, gave him something new to think about. He wished there had been a bazaar like that in his own village, as then he would not have wanted to go to all the big cities.

The endless lengths of the mountains, the far, far stretches of sky-high peaks covered with snow, the colossal solidity of their shapeless masses, aroused in him the feeling which he always used to have in his childhood, the urge to say what a great fool God was that when he came to relieve himself he excreted mountains and mountains and mountains, and that when he came to 'make water' he poured down vast, vast, vast sheets of rivers . . .

He did not want to make fun of God though, because he saw some coolies and hill men trudging up to Simla, borne down beneath the sacks of foodstuffs on their backs, and he thought that it was the blessing of the Almighty that he sat comfortably, being carried in a motor car. It was nice to be hurried along, past trees and houses, ponies and men, up and up to the heavenly heights above the clouds.

And when the Chevrolet sped past the stupendous castle which Mrs Mainwaring pointed out to her daughter as the Viceroy's residence, when it passed under the shadow of an amorphous world of huge offices, bungalows and huts spread on the back of a magnificent plateau, when Munoo stood securely and proudly while coolies clamoured for the right to bear the passenger's luggage, when he was driven down to Annandale in a rickshaw by coolies, he was very happy in his heart.

Munoo found that as the Memsahib's servant he had to fit into a new state of existence. His exact duties were not defined. He was just to remain at his mistress' beck and call, to do anything and everything that her ladyship desired at a particular moment. But, in spite of the miscellaneousness of his duties, his life at Bhujji House resolved itself into a kind of pattern.

He was awakened early at dawn by Ala Dad, the Khansamah, from the corner of the small, dark room in the servants' quarter, twenty yards below the bungalow, which served as the kitchen for the household and as a bedroom and living-room for the two of them. He had to light a fire in the primitive kitchen range and to put the kettle on to boil for the Memsahib's tea. Ala Dad himself sat nursing his white beard and smoking the hubble-bubble before going to the lavatory.

Munoo hurriedly made tea, showed the tray to Ala Dad to see if he had put everything in order, and bore it up to the Memsahib's bedroom.

Little Circe was already up, running round in her pyjamas, clamouring for breakfast.

Mrs Mainwaring, who had gone to bed at two or three o'clock in the morning, cursed at her daughter for disturbing her sleep, and bullied her to clean her teeth and wash her face if she wanted her chota hazri. As the child was self-willed, obstinate and disobedient and wanted to be noticed all the time, Mrs Mainwaring smacked her and sent her down to the servants' quarter for some time. She herself put on a dirty black skirt over her pyjamas and a red polo jumper over her night coat, and with Michael Arlen's *Green Hat* in her hand, sipped her cup of tea.

Munoo began to sweep the sitting-room and the verandah, happy in the contemplation of the green, rain-soaked verdure of Annandale at his feet, and intoxicated by the deep, rich smell of the pine cones and resin.

Mrs Mainwaring saw him, self-contained and absorbed, brushing the carpets, dusting the furniture, sweeping the floor, and she wondered what he was thinking, or whether he thought at all. She would have loved to have asked him to come and talk to her. But he was a mere servant. How could she think of such a thing? And yet she felt she was like Michael Arlen's Iris Storm, a much-misunderstood woman. 'Why didn't the world understand', she said, 'how a woman gives herself in love, in pity, in tenderness, in playfulness and in a hundred different moods? What right had people to judge one? Why can't I give myself to this boy?' she asked. The regular curves of his young body, its quick sudden flashes of movement, stirred the chords of her being in a strangely disturbing manner. But she, more than Iris Storm, had a pagan body and a Chislehurst mind. And she blamed the air of Simla which so conduced to thoughts of pleasure. So she arose and lazed about the bedroom, doing her long black hair, which was prematurely streaked with white, powdering and rouging her face.

Munoo, who was naturally interested in the mysteries of her toilet, stole round the bedroom arranging things, but always at some distance from the Memsahib.

Mrs Mainwaring's heart palpitated with the ache of that desire which she had sought to stifle by occupying herself at the dressing-table.

'Fetch me the scissors from the gol kamra, boy,' she ordered in a tone calculated to suppress her dim awareness of the tenderness she felt for him.

'Yes, Memsahib,' Munoo answered, and proceeded to obey her command.

When he came back with the scissors, she took them and, deliberately taking hold of his hand, which she knew to be dirty from dusting, exclaimed: 'You unclean boy, look at your hands, they are filthy. And look at your nails, they have never been cut for ages. Go and wash your hands and come back! I will file your nails for you.'

Munoo did as she asked, willingly, for he had seen her the previous night manicure her own hands with strange instruments which she kept in a velvet box.

May treated his hands with tender movements, smiled at him, and carelessly undraping her right leg before him, flourished a silken handkerchief which she had soaked in eau-de-Cologne at him. Then she looked at him with a wild flutter in her eyes, and, completing the manicure with protracted blandishments, said: 'Beautiful boy! Lovely boy! You only want a wife now!'

Munoo smiled with the quivering ripples of affection that the contact of her hands had produced in him. He felt dizzy with the intoxicating warmth that her coquettish movements had aroused in him. He hung his head down to avoid the embarrassment which he felt, and yet unable to control the fire in his blood, he fell at her feet in an orgy of tears and kisses. She pushed him away suddenly, shouting: 'What impertinence! What cheek! Go to your work! Go and get your work done! Get the breakfast ready!'

Munoo rushed away to the servants' quarter feeling very guilty, and wondered how he could face the Memsahib again. But he had to face her, because the breakfast was ready to be laid out. Only Circe made it difficult for him by asking him when he came to lay the table: 'Why are you crying? Has Mummy beaten you?'

Still, he forgot about his misery during breakfast, for this had always been a celebrated meal in Mrs Mainwaring's household, wherever that household had happened to be during the last three years. It started at eight o'clock and finished at twelve to half-past twelve. It had been adopted under doctor's orders. For Mrs Mainwaring had been ill, very ill, with a gall stone in her bladder. The surgeons in three London hospitals had advised her to have the gall stone operated upon and cut. But she was not sure whether she had a gall stone in her bladder at all. She would not have any part of her body removed, though she would not have minded having her body under the waist chopped off because, she said, she was disgusted with the use to which God put it. Anyhow, fancying herself ill and not wanting to have an operation performed, she had gone to Dr Stephenson, the food reform specialist, who declared that the pills and mixtures which the hospitals gave her were foul and that he could cure her in his own way in a day. 'Eat more fruit,' he said, like the Covent Garden posters. 'Eat apples, pears, peaches, grapes and eight shelled almonds every morning. On no account suck

259

oranges. Carry out my instructions every morning and you will become well.' She was very impressionable, and once an impulse or an idea occurred to her she was obsessed by it and made it a law. The suggestion about diet went home, because she had been over-eating for months. She took Dr Stephenson's advice and adopted apples, pears, grapes, almonds and Force, as a menu for breakfast. And, relishing the taste of the fruit, she felt she was cured, though she had really not been ill at all, and had only fancied herself as a poor, helpless, suffering little thing to get the sympathy of her friends. But the fancy was pleasant. The delights of a rich fruit breakfast were immeasurable. Especially because a fruit breakfast could not be hurried and was a convenient method of killing time. She peeled the apples and pears and even the grapes, slowly, deli-cately, with infinite care, casting the peel in saucers, in plates, on and about the table, till the table looked a sickening sight. And she sat, still in the black skirt and red jumper over the pyjama suit, a picture of sheer disintegration. By the time she had finished break-fast the bottles of brandy and gin that lay on the sideboard tempted her. And immediately after these appetizers, lunch was announced.

For Ala Dad, the Khansamah, was punctual to a minute, what-ever else he might or might not be. He pretended that it was in the Memsahib's interest for him to be 'up to taime', though the cunning old fellow knew that it was also in his own interests, because if the tiffin was not out of the way and the afternoon wore on, the Memsahib would offer to do the shopping and come to know the bazaar prices, and he would lose the commissions he received from the various merchants on the purchases. The thirty rupees' pay which 'Maining' Sahib gave him was not even sufficient to feed his wife and daughter and to keep his son at school, he thought. How could he save up for his old age, if not by earning a few rupees in commissions? And there was no harm in robbing the rich. These Sahibs had plenty of money, only the Indians were poor.

'Memsahib, what will Huzoor desire for dinner,' said Ala Dad, standing serenely by the table in his white coat and turban with a red cummerbund across his waist. 'Tum-tum [tomato] soup, Machi [fish], Stickania [steak and onions], Plumpud [plum pudding], or-right?'

'No, Ala Dad,' said Mrs Mainwaring. 'Dinner with the Stuart Memsahib downstairs, tonight. But you come and serve.'

'Orright, Memsahib,' said Ala Dad, rather crestfallen and peeved. This Memsahib knew too much. She was a kali [black] Mem, natu [native]. The real Sahibs did not know the prices in the market. If he had known that the 'Maining' Sahib had a black Mem, he thought, he certainly would not have taken this job. However, he was going to endure it as long as possible, and see how much she knew, because even the all-knowing did not know all that he knew.

'Ask the boy to get a rickshaw from the stand,' ordered Mrs Mainwaring. 'Only three coolies,' she continued, 'the boy is to be the fourth.'

'Yes, Huzoor,' said Ala Dad, bowing with a weird light in his ordinarily dim eyes.

While Mrs Mainwaring dressed, Munoo and the three other coolies he had engaged came with the rickshaw and waited on the drive.

The boy wished there was a motor engine attached to the carriage, as he was not looking forward to pushing it uphill to the Mall. But the rickshaw is the only wheeled vehicle that is allowed in Simla, except that the three great potentates of the hill, Their Excellencies the Viceroy of India, the Commander-in-Chief, and the Governor of Punjab, drive in cars or carriages drawn by horses. Apart from these, everyone, be he a Maharajah or a Member of Parliament, has to be content with a rickshaw driven by men.

It is an improvement on the jampans and dandis which used to be the only means of conveyance before the rickshaws came. For the jampan, which was not unlike a four poster bed with curtains for protection against the sun and the rain was, though comfortable enough for the rider, rather a back-aching abomination for the coolies. And the dandi, a piece of loose foot rest, was, if anything, slightly worse, because it grated the shoulders of the men away. But, as in all matters, it was ultimately the preference of the riders of jampans and dandis which led to the change. Lying flat on the back in a jampan and being carried by four men continually evoked the illusion of being carried in a hearse. And, if the ascent up the seat of the dandi was not carefully negotiated, a half somersault backward resulted, and even when the entrance was safely accomplished, the rider always appeared to himself to be occupying a rather undignified position.

The Reverend J. Fordyce, a chaplain of St Mark's Church, was much troubled by the uncomfortable thoughts of death and dignity which arose in the minds of his congregation in the Victorian age. And, being very concerned to see that the souls of his flock did not suffer from the discomforts of the body, he concentrated all his efforts to secure an adequate vehicle for the conveyance of their persons from their bungalows to the church and from the church to their bungalows. He invented the rickshaw. The people of Simla still remember his magnificent model:

> The hood of that first rickshaw
> Was square and trimmed with fringe,
> Such as dangled from the mantelpiece,
> In many a Berlin tinge.
>
> During the early eighties
> When Reverend Fordyce J.
> Invented the first rickshaw
> For Simla during May.

It was not difficult to train the coolies to run like horses, so that soon the jampans and the dandis had been ousted and the rickshaw came in. And, of course, the genius of Western man for technical achievement improved vastly on the original model in the decades following the death of Reverend J. Fordyce. The first rickshaw was iron-tyred and, it is said, used to bump and shake fearfully. On the night of a big dance or other tamasha, Simla used to be kept up by the continual rumbling roll of hundreds of rickshaws. The rubber tyre was introduced in 1898, and in 1904 the municipality made it a condition for securing a licence that a rickshaw should have rubber tyres, in view of the constant wear and tear of the road by the iron wheels. Pneumatic tyres came next. With this, and improvements in cushions and upholstery, it is now a pleasure for the rich to be driven about in rickshaws, especially as they do not disturb slumbering Simla on their return from all-night revelries. Old Gandhi refused to ride in a rickshaw as, he said, it hurt his soul to have to be borne in a carriage driven by human beings. Local opinion concurred that he was the greatest crank in history.

The usual length of the Simla rickshaw is nine feet, including the shaft, and the breadth is four feet. The weight is normally 260 to 360 lb, exclusive of the weight of the ladies and gentlemen who ride in them. The coolies curse the weight of the rickshaw in their hearts sometimes when they are driving uphill, and swear under their breath against the balance when occupied by too opulent a majesty – things, however, which the passengers never notice as they lean back while the men heave and push it from the back bar strenuously.

Munoo was in difficulties as he pushed the rickshaw on this first day. For, though Mrs Mainwaring had never heard of the rickshaw men receiving a training for their jobs, because it did not seem to her to require any, Munoo was finding it not altogether an unskilled occupation.

Mohan, a young coolie, had told him that rickshaw driving is an art which, as he himself had known from recent experience, could only be learnt from continued employment. He had said that one had to develop strong 'wind', and to learn to handle the rickshaw so as to keep it in balance, that one had to develop a sense of judgement and surefootedness, which is so necessary at turnings and steep gradients. Munoo had waved this advice aside. Now he was beginning to realize that Mohan was right.

As he puffed and panted the coolies encouraged him with 'shabash, shabash!' And when they found that the hill was too steep and was straining him, they pulled and pushed harder and took the responsibility of the rickshaw on to themselves. They were kind to him.

The rickshaw ascended past the military barracks, where the Viceroy's bodyguard lay encamped for the season, up the circuitous road to the Railway Board offices, and proceeded to the Mall. From now onwards it was less strenuous for the coolies to pull the vehicle, because the ascent up the Mall is more gradual. And once the vehicle had reached the new post office where the upper English bazaar forks away from the lower Indian bazaar, Munoo became quite excited about his job.

For, always sensitive to the straight, prim beauty of English shops, he found himself pushing the rickshaw by the varied show-rooms and windows of Whiteway Laidlaw; Lawrence and Mayo; Sahib Singh and Co., chemists; the Modern Bookshop; Jones and Jones, silversmiths and jewellers; Muhammad Gul, the Furriers; Ho Wang, the Chinese shoemaker; and other fashionable purveyors of goods suited to European tastes.

After being borne across the Mall once so that everyone should see her, Mrs Mainwaring directed the coolies to pull up by Davico's restaurant, where she had asked Mrs Stuart to tea that afternoon.

The coolies took the rickshaw away to a stand under the YWCA to wait till they were called again.

Munoo was curious to know how the angrezi-log behaved among themselves, and, from where he sat, he looked into the wonderful restaurant, where sweets were arranged in huge glass cages on one floor, and small tables and cane chairs on the other.

'Oh! Look Mummy! Our coolies are there!' cried little Circe impetuously, just as Mrs Mainwaring was being introduced into polite society.

The sight of the rude, dirtily clad, bare-legged creatures, some crouching round a hubble-bubble, some lying flat on the edge of the roadway and on the tin top of the shed, was a challenge to the complacency of the ladies and gentlemen who had tea at Davico's. But, of course, the coolies, except for a new arrival like Munoo, did not care as they rested content in any position in which they found themselves, slight, lissom, strangely still as if empty and dead.

Munoo had fever when he came back after his first day's work as a rickshaw coolie.

He had felt his legs breaking with fatigue all the way back. When he got to his room he felt listless. His limbs sagged. He stretched them, but there seemed no relief. He felt that his throat was parched. So he drank a jug of water. But his hands felt crippled and his legs seemed to sink beneath him. A complete inertia had taken possession of his bones. And the blood in his body was boiling hot.

He crouched by the fire in the kitchen and tried to ignore what he felt was only a little fatigue. His head was aching, however, and he felt like reclining on something.

He lay down on his back and curled up to receive the full glow of the fire, for he was now shivering.

Ala Dad came back from the bazaar and almost stumbled on Munoo's body in the dark. 'Who's that?' he asked. And, in answer, heard the boy's soft moaning and writhing. He knew he had fever. He ran up to acquaint the Memsahib of the catastrophe.

Mrs Mainwaring was very concerned. She was a mother and felt towards this boy now exactly as she had felt towards Ralph when he had been ill. She had him removed upstairs and put him into the bed where 'baby' slept, in spite of Munoo's protestations that he was only a servant and could not sleep upstairs. And she called a doctor, no less a person than Major Marchant, the health officer of Simla, who stayed near Annandale.

Major Marchant came, took Munoo's temperature, prescribed some aspirin, and leaving the boy with the cheering words 'you will soon be well,' hastened to satisfy his curiosity about Mrs Mainwaring. For there seemed to him something strange in this dark-hued lady who had put her servant boy to sleep in her flat.

Marchant was a young Indian Christian, and, like most converts to Christianity in India, he was originally a cobbler's son, whom an English mission had brought up and educated. During the course of his adventurous career in the hands of the padres he had always secretly enjoyed the thrill of rubbing shoulders with Englishmen. When he had gone to England and become inured to meeting the English people on a basis of equality, he had begun to regard himself as an Englishman, a belief encouraged by the faultless accent he had acquired, the young chorus girl he had married, and the complete adaptability to European conditions that he had easily cultivated. He had changed his name from Mochi [cobbler] to Marchant. He had forgotten the low-caste boy he was when he first fell into the hands of the Mission, and only recognized the successful young IMS officer he had become. The only price he had had to pay for this rise from pariahdom to the position of a dignified member of one of the Imperial services in India, was the regular allowance of half his pay which he had to send to his wife, who preferred to stay in England. As he had been very poor in his childhood, the loss of seven hundred rupees a month troubled him. He was stingy and spent little on himself, using his position as the Medical Officer of Simla to get hospitality freely. But, apart from this cancer of regrets about money which grew in his soul, and inclined him sometimes to thoughts of seeking a divorce from the chorus girl, and drove him often to the arms of other people's wives, he was very satisfied with himself. He saw that Mrs Mainwaring was almost the same colour as he, or rather the colour he would have liked to be, a dusky hue such as could be brightened into a pink by constantly rubbing a towel on the cheeks. She must be a Eurasian, he thought, and he knew that it was more easy for an Indian Christian to find an affinity with a Eurasian, than either with the 'natives' or with the thoroughbred English.

'Who is this boy, Mrs Manning?' he asked, as he came into the drawing-room.

'He is a servant I picked up at Bombay,' she replied, and continued, 'by the way, my name is Mainwaring, Mrs Mainwaring.'

'Oh, I am sorry, the Khansamah said Maina or something like that, and I guessed it might be Manning.'

'No, it is Mainwaring,' she said. 'Rather a difficult name to pronounce, isn't it?'

'Yes, but I am glad you are not a difficult person. Some of the Anglo-Indian community in Simla are the very limit, you know!'

'Yes,' said Mrs Mainwaring. But she did not want to criticize the community of which she aspired to be a member.

For that matter, Major Marchant had not wanted to institute differences between himself and the English community either, but he was trying to make conversation.

'How long have you been here, Mrs Mainwaring?' asked Marchant.

'Oh, I only came from "home" a few days ago.'

'Really,' said Marchant.

'Oh, won't you sit down and have a peg, Doctor?' suggested Mrs Mainwaring, divining the gleam of admiration in the major's eyes.

'Thank you,' said Marchant, sitting down eagerly. 'Do tell me how was everything at "home"?'

And they talked of 'home' till it was time for Mrs Mainwaring to go to dinner with the Stuarts downstairs. They had so much more to say to each other than could be said in a quarter of an hour. So Mrs Mainwaring asked the major to tea the next day on the pretext of telling him about her illness, and Major Marchant was, of course, only too eager to promise to come.

Meanwhile, Munoo lay happy to be privileged to sleep in the bungalow, though his temples palpitated with the fever.

But the glow of that happiness soon evaporated as the soft tremor of fatigue came creeping up his legs, as the blood ran up and down in his body and turned into a clammy sweat, as he tossed about the bed uncomfortably, sighed and remembered his mother.

Mrs Mainwaring came back from dinner and rubbed eau-de-Cologne on his face and pressed his head. She even massaged his body. She was very kind to him.

When Munoo had sweated out his fever and recovered, he had to revert back to his position as a servant boy and rickshaw coolie again. He did so quite willingly, since however kind the Memsahib had been to him, the deep-rooted feeling of inferiority to the superior people who lived in bungalows and wore angrezi clothes, which was ingrained in him, had never been lifted.

He went on from day to day without a break, attending on Mrs Mainwaring as she entered the gay round of pleasurable existence in Simla.

Apart from sweeping and dusting the bungalow and running errands for the Memsahib and the Khansamah, he drove the rickshaw as a fourth coolie when his mistress went shopping, or took the air each day.

For Mrs Mainwaring had found that India was a veritable paradise for the white woman. She had not spent her time trying to bleach her colour in England in vain.

She found that she had plenty of time to waste. For India was the one place in the world where servants still were servants, and one could laze through the morning and sleep through the afternoon, happy in the assurance that the cook and the 'boy' will look after breakfast, lunch, tea and dinner.

India was the one place in the world where one could come in to dress and leave the discarded garments in a heap on the floor, to be collected and folded away by the servants, whose mending needle stitched up every rent unbidden, and who picked up the ladders in one's stockings with uncanny skill!

One could engage a pony for a morning trot at Annandale for less than a shilling a day.

One could hire a rickshaw for fourpence an hour.

Eggs here were sixpence a dozen.

The laundry washed beautifully at a farthing a piece.

One could get the latest Paris models in millinery and frocks at the big shops.

There were magnificent hotels, dance halls, night clubs, and cinemas which received the latest Hollywood releases even before London.

And one could belong to two or three clubs and drink endless cocktails at other people's expense, and smoke cigarettes by the dozen, for there was no tobacco tax and a tin of Players only cost a rupee.

Why, here were all the luxuries and amenities of the West at the knockdown prices of the East, so that even Golders Green and Ealing lived like Mayfair and Piccadilly.

No wonder that all those retired Empire-builders in Bayswater and Knightsbridge looked disgruntled at 'home' and shook their heads at the shortcomings of poor old England, and sighed for the fleshpots of India!

True, Mrs Mainwaring could not enjoy all these amenities of pleasurable existence. For she was being made conscious of her 'Celtic twilight' again, having been refused admission to the Union Jack Club. The tongue of gossip, too, seemed busy about her. But though she became conscious of a vague perturbation in her soul and trod warily in consequence, she went out nevertheless, anxious to snatch at any pleasures that might come her way before Anglo-Indian society made up its mind either to shut her out completely or to accept her. And, really, all was gay and adorable.

Meanwhile, Munoo had also become inured to this life, and even enjoyed it.

It was nice, for instance, to be pushing the rickshaw along the Mall with his mistress sitting dressed up in beautiful clothes telling little Circe the names of the various celebrities in the motley crowd of gorgeously clad Englishmen and Indians who were being borne in their own rickshaws. 'Major-General Sir Claud Harrington', she would say in answer to Circe's impetuous question. 'Sir Jiji Bhoy Ismail, President of the Chamber of Commerce', 'Sir Charles Reed, Home Member', 'Lady Raffi, wife of Sir M. Raffi of the Viceroy's Council', 'Pandit Dwaraka Prashad, Congress Leader', 'The Maharanee of Landi!' But Circe was too young to understand. Only Munoo remembered.

And he was quite happy when the Memsahib ordered the rickshaw to slow down by the shops, for, as she feasted her eyes on the rich silks hanging in the Benares silk shop, the wonderful necklaces in the Curio shop, the silver cutlery in Messrs Perkins, he too contemplated the wonderful array of things displayed in the windows.

The other coolies seemed apathetic and he was rather irritated by their lack of interest in this, to him, exalting atmosphere of European grandeur. He even criticized them as uncouth rustics in his mind and, recalling that he could read and write and could have become a Babu or a Sahib if he had not been an orphan, felt superior. And when his mistress ordered the head coolie to stop outside Sahib Singh and Co., greeted the handsome black-bearded Sikh, who wore a wonderful English suit and a neatly tied pink turban, with a smile, and talked git-mit, git-mit in angrezi to him, he felt envious. He would have liked to have been like him, almost an Englishman. Indeed, he would have been more of an Englishman, because, being clean shaven as a Hindu, he need not have worn a turban and a beard to mar the beauty of the English dress. His mistress would certainly have liked him much more if there was any meaning in the kindness she had shown him at Kalka when she pinched him and again when he had been laid up with fever. But it was no use thinking such nice thoughts when he was only a servant boy, a coolie, he told himself. The Sardar was probably a rich man, a high-class man, perhaps a BA pass or fail, and the Memsahib was a Memsahib though she was not quite of the same colour as the other Memsahibs.

'Boy, come and take these things,' came his mistress' call. And he rushed forward eagerly to receive the goods from the chemist, glad to be in contact with the beautiful bottles, gladder still that his Memsahib trusted him to handle all the fragile things and not the other coolies.

And then he proudly and willingly pushed the rickshaw along, even encouraging the other coolies to start the sport of racing past rival rickshaws on the Jakhu round, in his reckless enthusiasm. And out of sheer light-heartedness he would goad his companions to sing a hill song; for, somehow, that seemed to infuse a lightness into his limbs and lift him to an ecstasy of pleasure.

But when he came back from the drive through the gay scene in the evening he felt rather sad and alone. His back seemed stiff, so that he could neither sit nor stand. And what was very strange to him, sometimes when he spat now, his spittle was red.

He did not bother about this and got busy helping Ala Dad to serve dinner. For, of late, Mrs Mainwaring had begun to entertain Major Marchant to dinner almost every day.

And then he had a hectic week when Mainwaring Sahib himself came on short leave from the north-western frontier.

Munoo liked the Sahib because he looked so young to his mind, which vague reaction arose from the fact that Captain Mainwaring was a beautiful, fair-haired, blue-eyed young man, with a modest, easy manner and an ever-ready smile on his face. All Munoo's experiences of Englishmen had so far been rather unfortunate, and he thought of them as frightening ghosts who always had a scowl on their faces. He had, of course, seen some of them smile, and even laugh, in the upper bazaar, but their smiles seemed imperceptible and were in any case only for their own kind; he had never yet received one, because as a servant and coolie he was merely supposed to be below notice. That, he thought in the light of his ingrained inferiority, was perhaps as it should be. But Mainwaring Sahib was nice. Why were not all Sahibs like him? Surely they would not lose anything if they gave their servants smiles, because Mainwaring Sahib did not lose anything by giving him a smile. Would not he do anything for this Sahib? And it was not only because Mainwaring Sahib had ordered Ala Dad to give him half of one of the three pitcher-sized melons he had brought from Peshawar; it was because of the kindliness he reflected. Munoo would have liked to have raced the rickshaw round Jakhu if he would ride in it, but he never rode, only walking by the side of the carriage as the Memsahib sat in it. Still, he had tried to show his gratitude to the Sahib by putting his heart and soul into the work at the bungalow. But he could not do enough, for the Sahib only stayed a week. Munoo wondered if he had been able to show his appreciation of the Sahib's kindness, or whether the Sahib had recognized how he had been straining to serve him, because the Sahib's face had become small and pathetically still during the last three days of his visit. When, however, the Sahib gave him a five-rupee note as bakshish at the railway station before he went, Munoo knew that the Sahib had liked him.

Major Marchant seemed mean and despicable to the boy after his experience of the Mainwaring Sahib, because he came to dinner with the Memsahib every day and did not even bring her a dali of fruit, far from giving anything to Ala Dad or to him. This Sahib was all for himself. Munoo began to resent him, especially as he ordered him away from the gol kamra if ever the boy was playing with the Miss Sahib. Then he had encouraged the Memsahib to send the Miss Sahib away to a boarding school. What was more, the Major Sahib was always encouraging the Memsahib to make the servants do difficult things, like asking Munoo to come running behind the ponies on the Jakhu round, so that Munoo could hold the reins of the animals while he and the Memsahib went down to see the waterfalls in the ravines. And now he had made her order the rickshaw to go to Mashobra on Sunday. There was consolation in the fact that the boy wanted to see Mashobra himself. But it was ten miles away and he would have to be the fourth coolie if he were not the fifth.

When the Sunday came, however, Munoo was excited into an enthusiasm by the preparations for the outing in the fresh early morning. And as the Memsahib hired four men for the rickshaw and put him on as a reserve, he felt light and easy as if he were going away for a holiday.

Indeed, the variety of scenes that unfolded itself as the rickshaw wheeled along pleased him. They went past Christ Church through the Lakkar Bazaar where the craftsmen specialize in Himalayan sticks and wooden toys, past Snowdon, the Commander-in-Chief's residence, past the orphanage school, through Sanjauli Bazaar, where the silversmiths make nose rings which kiss the lips of the hill women and the Babus of the army headquarters run secret societies to destroy the Angrezi Sarkar, through the long, dark tunnel where the bells threaded in blue-bead necklaces and carved head-stalls of the mules set up echoes of a strange, haunting music, past the residence of the Nawab of Malerkotla, past the waterworks and through the abundant leafage of thick pine forests which shadow the curvy road to Naldera, the Viceroy's golf course, and to the hot-water springs of the Bhujji State on the banks of the Sutlej, and beyond to Tibet.

The crisp mountain air seemed like delicious cold water to Munoo's warm body as he jogged lightly along with the other coolies, and the moist young sap in the trees smelt good.

As the Major Sahib wanted to trot on his high horse and the rickshaw had to run fast beyond the toll bar, Munoo found himself panting more than the other coolies when they got to Mashobra. But the Memsahib was too busy talking to the Major Sahib to alight from the carriage even when they got to their destination. And Munoo had to be in attendance on the Sahib and Memsahib at tiffin.

As the coolies were given leave to go and rest at the rickshaw-stand till they were wanted, Munoo's heart sank. But he went through it all with a grim effort not to look morose and unwilling, for he felt that after all he was the Memsahib's personal servant, and in a way superior to the other coolies.

This feeling was confirmed when he was given a whole leg of chicken and double roti, and other remains of the tiffin.

He partook of the food by the side of a water-pump and then proceeded to the rickshaw-stand to wait for the Sahib and Memsahib.

His arrival was greeted with a sneer of mockery.

'Your Memsahib is no Memsahib,' said one of the coolies. 'No other Mem or Sahib in Simla would leave a card on her.'

'I have nothing to do with that,' said Munoo. 'But you are only saying that about her because she did not alight from the rickshaw all the way up to Mashobra!'

'No, we are saying it for your good,' said the head coolie. 'You should leave her service. You have to attend on her and also drive the rickshaw.'

Munoo kept silent.

'Why can't he become a rickshaw coolie?' one of the men asked. 'Then he won't have to attend on her.'

'Because he is dying of consumption,' said Mohan. 'Look at his pale cheeks and sunken eyes!'

'Show me your pulse, ohe Munoo,' said another coolie, laughing.

'I'll have none of your jokes,' said Munoo. 'Give me a cigarette.'

He coughed all that night and kept Ala Dad Khan awake.

'It is one of those biris I smoked at Mashobra,' he apologized when the old man complained.

The next day, however, while he was cleaning his teeth and gargling to clear his throat, he saw himself spitting out streaks of blood. He hurriedly threw a handful of ashes on the puddle to conceal it both from Ala Dad and himself. But much as he tried to forget himself in his work, he felt rather frightened and depressed by the cloud that the shock of this first haemorrhage had raised in his imagination. 'Am I really dying,' he asked himself, 'as Mohan said?' He did not know what consumption was, but this congestion of his chest that he had been feeling for days and the blood that had oozed from his throat might be the disease. 'It certainly is,' his mind seemed to confirm in one breath. 'It is not, it is merely my throat which is sore with tonsils,' his will seemed to say in contradiction. For, though during the last three years he had sometimes wished he were dead, now that the question mark of death arose before his mind's eye with its message of the complete cessation of his breath, he did not want to die.

To resolve his doubts and to ease his soul he thought of writing to Ratan to ask his advice. He was feeling lonely and he wanted to do something desperate. Writing to his old friend whom he had given up for dead seemed to him at this moment the most reckless thing to do. For if Ratan was dead he himself would not mind dying, and if he were alive the wrestler would certainly try to help him.

Luckily the Memsahib, who was very excited that morning – the Khansamah said because she was making preparations to go to the *Lat Sahib's natch* [Viceroy's ball] – sent Munoo to deliver messages to her tailors, to Ho Wang the Chinese shoemaker, and to Major Marchant. On his way up to the Mall, he stopped at the little post office opposite the Railway Board office and wrote a card to Ratan, briefly describing how he had come to Simla in the service of a Memsahib, how he was unhappy because he was alone, and how he would like Ratan to come up to the hills, or, if that were not possible, how he would like to go back to Bombay.

Major Marchant sent Munoo chasing after Mr Das, an Indian official in the Foreign and Political Department, with a letter.

When the boy got to the Foreign and Political department, three miles away from the Health Office, he was told that Mr Das had gone home to Tara Devi for tiffin.

Munoo tramped another two miles and succeeded in catching the Sahib just as he was in the middle of his lunch.

'What is it?' his wife asked. 'This sarkar doesn't even let us eat our food in comfort!'

'Oh, it is not the sarkar,' the Babu said, 'it is all these sycophants. I have had twelve private requests from people this morning to help them to get tickets for the Viceroy's ball. This is the thirteenth, from Major Marchant, the health officer, asking for two tickets for himself and the Eurasian woman he is carrying on with. He attended our child when it was ill, so I suppose I will have to oblige him whoever else I may or may not oblige. All right, boy. Give my salaams to the Sahib.'

Munoo came back through the monsoon clouds that were gathering on the higher ridges of the Simla hills. As he was about a hundred yards away from the bungalow looking down on the heavenly pastures of Annandale, there were mutterings of thunder and the sky overhead was black and lurid. As soon as he stepped on to the verandah of the bungalow the trailing clouds poured down their contents.

For hours the rain continued, with intermittent peals of thunder which were echoed by the tall mountains and flashes of lightning that lit the mist on the dense vegetation with an unearthly splendour.

Then a light breeze swept the clouds away towards the plains where the water of the flooded Sutlej shone like a silver sea.

This weather continued, with intervals of a few hours, for three days. And during the dark days Munoo brooded on the physical fatigue he was beginning to feel, except when the Memsahib sent him with another urgent message to the tailor or the shoemaker.

One evening he went to the bastis of the rickshaw men to seek consolation of Mohan. These were a collection of wood huts, below the lower bazaar on the way to the cart road. A dirty, scum-covered ditch ran by them, apparently carrying the filth of the markets to the khud.

Munoo could not discover in which particular hut Mohan lived, because several coolies crowded round hubble-bubbles in each of them, in a darkness only illuminated by the fuming cotton wicks of earthen saucer lamps. He felt strangely awkward among the men, because, though mostly hill men from the Simla hill states and Kangra, they were all so diverse.

In one hut, a crowd of coolies were singing hill songs to the tune of a dholki, and he felt drawn towards it. But, on reaching it, he found that it was choking with smoke from a hearth fire over which a coolie was frying sweet pancakes. Thick clouds of fumes hung over the heads of the coolies like long snakes and pythons suspended from the ceiling, because there was no ventilator. The gas got into Monoo's lungs, as, lured by the music, he stayed for a while, and it was only when it stung his windpipe sharply that he walked out coughing and clutching his throat.

At last he found Mohan, seated to a meal in a little porch in the verandah of a hut, away from twelve other men who ate, sat, or lay asleep on the floor.

'Welcome, welcome,' cried two of them, who knew him.

Mohan silently brought Munoo a jute rag to sit on.

The old-timers looked at him. Munoo felt that they were criticizing him for being very 'green'.

'Why is everyone having sweet pancakes today?' he asked Mohan.

'Have you forgotten all your festivals, just because you are a Mem's servant?' said a coolie, before Mohan could answer. 'We are celebrating the rains.'

'Don't you take any notice of them,' said Mohan. 'They have come here season after season, and they don't know any of their festivals either, and yet they preen themselves on their experience.

274

But they are fools. They rush up here long before the season starts, just because they want to be in time to get the rickshaws which are good to look at. They are illiterate and uncouth, and they have become sterile, driving rickshaws up hill and down dale, till now there is nothing left for them but to mock at others.'

'All right, learned one, you need not lose your temper at a joke,' said the coolie who had spoken. 'And will you knock me up before sunrise tomorrow, as I have to go to Sanjauli?'

'Good,' said Mohan, and proceeded to light a biri.

'And don't forget about that loan for me from the Chaudhri for my marriage,' the coolie said, cockily.

'That I will forget,' said Mohan. 'You will become a slave to the pockmarked, fat usurer. And what is the use of your marrying, if, after marriage, you want to come here year by year? Your heart is weak now, and you might fall dead any moment.'

'And, as you said,' put in another coolie, 'he has no guts left, so what does he want a wife for?'

The company laughed.

'What shall I do, then?' the man continued.

'Go back to your land, man,' said Mohan. 'That is my advice to you. Go and work on your land.'

'My land is mortgaged already,' said the coolie.

'Then come with me, and we shall kill the landlord one day, and get you your land,' said Mohan. 'It is my object to make you people realize that if you work, you should have a share in the things that you produce with the sweat of your brow.'

'Oh, you can keep your wild notions for those others,' said the coolie. 'I want to live here, work, smoke the hookah, play cards now and then, and never be too tired to pick up another fare if it comes my way.'

'Yes, you fool,' burst out Mohan. 'You will let them kill you. You are all ignorant slaves. How can I drill any sense into your heads?'

'All right then, we will begin our lesson tomorrow,' said the coolie jocularly, and, wrapping himself in his blanket from head to foot, he affected sleep.

'I will come back in a moment,' said Mohan to Munoo, and disappeared into the road.

Munoo suddenly felt disconnected from the world of this hut. It was as if a light had suddenly been extinguished, such was the silent sympathy that flowed from Mohan to him. The coolie who had turned in to sleep, cheekily lifted his head, and said: 'Tell me, ustad Mohan –' But on looking round, he saw that Mohan was not there.

'Oh, he has gone, then,' he said. 'He is a very strange fellow. I can't make him out. If he has been to Vilayat and is such a learned man, why does he drive rickshaws and live among us?'

'He comes from a high-class family,' said an old coolie, coughing over his hookah. 'He had an easy life in his childhood and youth. And now he is doing a sort of penance for his sins. He felt very alone, he told me, isolated, and could not mix with people. And he wants to learn to be a man among men.'

'Really,' said Munoo, 'how extraordinary!'

'Mysterious!' said the coolie who was lying down.

'He is,' said the old coolie, 'but he would be in prison if he were not. The sarkar has spies about to catch anyone who goes about doing the work he does. Hasn't he talked to you yet about it?'

'No,' whispered the other coolie, rather surprised and afraid.

'Well, he will talk to you one day –'

At this, Mohan came back with a little packet in his hand.

'Here, ohe Munoo,' he said, 'here is some fruit for you to eat. We can't entertain you on anything very much in this place. There is nothing worth while in the shops, either. Sweets are poisonous. You must eat plenty of fruit and drink half a seer of milk every day. You are looking very thin! And now, you must go! The rain has just stopped. Go to bed early!'

Munoo said 'Jay deva' to all the coolies and hurried away, afraid of Mohan, and grateful. He had been absorbed in the talk of the two coolies. His mind had gone back from the sinister atmosphere which the old coolie's information had built up to the evening in the chawl at Bombay, after Ratan had been discharged and the three Sahibs had come to talk to the coolies. Was Mohan one of those Sahibs? he wondered. And he walked home wrapped in the glow of warmth that he had felt in Mohan's company.

On Friday, the day of the dance, he caught the contagion of his mistress's enthusiasm and virtually floated through the sunshine that had succeeded the monsoon, smelling the damp deodars in the thin air and listening to the sound of waterfalls on the slopes of the mountains.

And when at length his mistress walked out after a protracted toilet to take her seat in the rickshaw to meet Major Marchant for dinner at the Hotel Cecil before going on to the dance, he felt very happy and proud, especially as in her naïve enthusiasm she had asked him whether she looked beautiful and had pinched his cheeks and giggled when he said: 'Yes, Memsahib, wonderful!'

He exerted himself with renewed vigour to push the rickshaw and waited impatiently with the other coolies during the dinner, drying his clothes, which were wet with perspiration and stuck to his body.

The run from the Hotel Cecil to the Viceroy's residence was not long enough, he felt, so eager was he to enjoy the glow of the Memsahib's company as he ran past the twinkling lights on the hillside.

And he worked himself up to an extraordinarily high pitch of excitement as he sat with the hundreds of other coolies watching the fair and fortunate of Simla come in their rickshaws and walk into the long throne rooms, whose portals stood open, reflecting the dazzle of huge chandeliers on to the lawns of the Viceregal Lodge.

The Memsahibs all wore thin, silken dresses which almost swept the earth at their heels, and furs and wraps which scarcely hid their necks and shoulders either against the cold or the rude stares of the rickshaw coolies.

The Sahibs seemed to Munoo on the other hand over-dressed in their long black coats, and wax collars, and shirts and long rows of medals. And some of them were dressed in curious clothes which he did not know how they had put on, so fast did the silken knee breeches seem to stick to their legs, and so high and stiff were the collars of their short, gold-embroidered jackets.

Occasionally Indian Maharajahs were driven up in all the resplendence of their bejewelled ceremonial robes, and Munoo envied their small sons who were going into the dance hall with them, dressed up in the most perfect uchkins and white tight trousers.

The arrival of a few padres created some amusement among the coolies, as they had never imagined that these long-robed priests with huge beards would want to go to the dance. The band struck up 'God Save the King' while the guests were yet entering.

'Grand shows these dances,' said a coolie.

'Yes,' said another, 'it costs them a lot of money. It cost my Sahib two thousand rupees to buy his scarlet cape and velvet sable and satin breeches.'

'My Memsahib has paid three hundred rupees for her frock,' said Munoo, eagerly and with pride.

'And all the trouble of procuring a ticket,' added Mohan sardonically.

'You don't seem to like this show,' said the first coolie.

'I should think not, from what I have seen of them,' replied Mohan. 'It is strange how these people can think that it is amusing to spend all the money they do, to come and meet people they really do not want to meet. For they have a caste system more rigid than ours. Any angrezi woman whose husband earns twelve hundred rupees a month will not leave cards at the house of a woman whose husband earns five hundred. And the woman whose husband earns five hundred looks down upon the woman whose husband earns three hundred. There is no love in the rich. They don't really want to mix with each other. This is a ceremonial observed to show the pomp and glory of the sarkar by the tunda lat [limp Lord] who governs us. The women perspire in their tight frocks and their underclothes get wet. And the men are uncomfortable in their trousers as they flirt with other people's wives. And then they say how smart it all was as they drink tea at Davico's while you starve . . .'

'How can you say all this?' asked the first coolie. 'What do you know of the Sahib-log's life?'

'How can I say all this?' answered Mohan. 'What do I know of the Sahib-log's life? I knew a bearer to the wife of a colonel of the army headquarters who lived on Jakhu hill. She was a fair-haired, pretty little woman of about twenty-five, while the colonel was turned fifty-five. She had married him for his position and money, it seemed, because Ghulam, this servant, saw several times that when the colonel touched her she shrank back from him. He was a solid, middle-aged man with a huge, formless face, kind enough but somehow repulsive to her.

'Well, she was unhappy with him and she would begin to drink wine as soon as he went to the office in the morning. And then she would come and watch Ghulam at work in the drawing-room; just watch him and make him feel uncomfortable, because she only had a dressing-gown on over her naked body. She would ask him embarrassing questions about whether he was married and how he liked women and what not.

'He told her that he loved a girl in his village whose parents had prevented him from marrying her, but that he hoped one day to go back and find her and live with her.

'One day she came into the gol kamra very drunk and, catching hold of Ghulam suddenly, said: "I am better than that woman you loved in your village. Look, I am a white woman and the wife of a colonel. I loved a poet once and he loved me, but I did not marry him because he had very little money. Now I am sorry. But I want you."

'"I don't care whether you are a colonel's wife or who you are, Memsahib," Ghulam said. "I am sorry for you, but I don't love you." And he threw her away.

'He was afraid that she would trump up a false charge against him and have him imprisoned if he was not kind to her. But he didn't care. He ran from the place. She followed him, crying: "Oh, don't go away, don't go away from me. Oh, come back."

'He felt sorry for her, really sorry, because he liked her and would have liked to have had her. He hated the colonel for making the poor girl's life miserable. But he ran away.

'Since then Ghulam has never been bluffed by the pomp and show of these people to believe that they are happy. And I have from my own experience of Europe found that the rich only want thrills and pleasure.'

'It is strange, their dancing,' said the first coolie, now impressed by Mohan's story to question his admiration for the Sahibs and the Rajahs. 'What is the meaning of pushing a woman about here and there so stiffly?'

'It is all a kind of graceful love game,' said Mohan, 'but it has now become mere play and the love is not thought of, except that it warms up the cold natures of these people and they can go kissing and tittering in the corners and prepare to get married or to go to bed together. You don't need to dance about to go to bed with women, you roughs. You are superior to all these colonels and generals and maharajahs. But still you go on driving their rickshaws.'

'You do that too, don't you?' a coolie said.

'Yes, because I shouldn't get an opportunity to talk to people like you.'

'Look! they are walking about in couples in the garden,' said Munoo.

'Yes,' said Mohan. 'Don't explore the garden too eagerly or you will see something you won't like.'

'It is nothing to me, what she does,' said Munoo naïvely. 'I am

279

only her servant.' And he looked across the valley to the lights of Solon twinkling in the clear night. Then he sat listening to the strange zigzag music of the Viceroy's orchestra. It jangled on his nerves a bit. He was tired, and yawned. Mohan spread his cotton wrap round him, saying: 'You look ill, you ought to be asleep.'

'No, no,' Munoo protested. 'I am all right.' And then the saliva in his throat choked him and he coughed a harsh, continuous cough which seemed to distress him, till he spat out mouthfuls of blood.

'You fool! You fool!' cursed Mohan. 'I told you at Mashobra you were ill. Surely this is not the first time you have spat blood.'

Munoo waved his head to signify 'No.'

'Then why didn't you tell your Mem that you could not draw the rickshaw? Have you told her that you were spitting blood?'

Munoo kept still.

Mohan's voice of concern had roused the coolies who sat around from their apathy and they crowded round the boy.

The sepoy who stood on guard at the gates of the Viceregal Lodge thought he scented trouble. He walked up exactly as if he were on his beat, left-right, left-right, and, without relaxing his pose, asked in a stern voice: 'Who goes there?'

'A boy taken ill, Sarkar,' one of the coolies informed him.

'Take him away before the Aidi cong [aide-de-camp] Sahib comes on the scene,' he ordered.

Mohan hurriedly put Munoo across his shoulders and, saying to his colleagues: 'It is downhill coming back to the bungla, you won't need us,' he bore the boy home.

Mrs Mainwaring was quite concerned when she came out of the dance hall with Major Marchant and learnt that the boy had to be taken home because he spat blood. Her efforts at social climbing had not been very successful, because she had been herded aside with the Indian crowd and only one English cavalry officer had danced with her. She had thought of bringing the major home and forgetting all about the ball over a bottle of brandy and the supper which she had ordered. But now she felt wretched.

And, when the major examined Munoo and pronounced very unfavourably on his condition, she cried.

According to the orders of the Health Officer, Munoo was removed the next day to a segregated three-roomed hut on the slopes of

Chotta Simla, where there were two other coolies suffering from consumption. Mohan came to look after him.

He was enjoined absolute quiet and, after a brief spell of coughing and another haemorrhage, he felt well. The only trouble was that he could not walk or stand up or exert himself in the least. So he lay on the verandah of the hut, on a low bedstead, covered by a thick quilt, all day.

Mrs Mainwaring came down to see him with gifts of fruit and flowers during the first few days and even nursed him with a complacent hypocrisy, buoying up the dejected spirit of the boy with sentiments like, 'You will get well. You have no disease. You are just run down.' She was really being kind, as to a point she did suffer qualms of conscience about having ill used the 'poor dear' But she was not allowed to be kind and good.

The major forbade her from going down to the hut on pain of having to segregate her too if she persisted in her intercourse with the servant. And she had to efface herself completely and suffer in silence.

Munoo had borne a resentment against her during the later stages of her friendship with Major Marchant. And when he had begun to bleed and the knowledge of death confronted him he had hated her for a while. But now that he was actually sick in bed, vaguely torn between the fear of dying and the hope of living, something happened to him. He felt docile and good and kind towards her and everyone else. It was as if the nerves of his body in their gradual weakening had begun to accept the humiliation which in the pride of their functioning they had never acknowledged.

He looked strangely tender now, his face sunken and pale, his eyes bulging out of their deep, dark sockets, weakly exploring the hollows of the hills, his body feeling the sand run through the hourglass of time. When a haemorrhage occurred he looked terribly frightened. But when the sun shone and his breathing was a little better, he became intent and absorbed in himself.

He wanted to get well. And when he not only enjoyed regular breathing, but had no cough, he wanted to get a little better. And he made plans in his head. Ratan had written to him to come to Bombay to a small job in the pay of the Trade Union organizing the fight against the Pathan moneylenders, the foremen and the factory wallahs. Munoo felt he would go. And, since the spell of warm weather lasted and the flies and the mosquitoes were not too troublesome, he began to feel stronger every day and looked forward to testing his powers for the journey to Bombay by a long walk.

Another attack of haemorrhage, however, and there seemed no prospect of getting out of bed. And he was tortured by doubts and fears. Any slightest cough after this made him feel hopeless. And now he struggled not to get worse.

The trouble continued, though somewhat abated. An hour of sunshine seemed a blessing.

The doctor's look on his weekly visit was not reassuring, however. He could feel it behind the mask of authority that Major Marchant wore on his face. Nothing seemed to exist, therefore, outside himself, apart from the memories of his wanderings. Mohan was a consolation because he came and sat on his bed and pressed his head in the evening. But it rained and the clouds hovered menacingly over the adjacent hills.

Then the depression lifted.

And he lay watching the tiers of blue sage and barley on the slopes of the valley before him. He felt the drift of the wind and watched the unfolding of snapshots of his memories, disconnected and strange, as in a dream.

The soft bletherings of the afternoon air would develop into a storm. The congestion on his chest seemed to become acute.

The trouble was again eased, however. A few whole days of good health. 'After all, I am not going to die,' he would say to himself.

A downpour, and he began to doubt if he would ever get well. He felt exhausted and lay weary and apathetic, looking at Mohan frank-eyed and helpless, clinging to him as if the mere touch of his friend's body would give him life.

'All right, Munoo brother, you are a brave lad,' Mohan assured him.

Munoo clutched at Mohan's hand and felt the warm blood in his veins like a tide reach out to distances to which it had never gone before.

But in the early hours of one unreal, white night he passed away – the tide of his life having reached back to the deeps.

Regent Square, WC1
May–September, 1935